Death's Shadow & WOLF ISLAND

Other titles by

DARREN SHAN

THE SAGA OF DARREN SHAN

1. Cirque Du Freak*
2. The Vampire's Assistant*
3. Tunnels of Blood*
4. Vampire Mountain
5. Trials of Death
6. The Vampire Prince
7. Hunters of the Dusk
8. Allies of the Night
9. Killers of the Dawn
10. The Lake of Souls
11. Lord of the Shadows
12. Sons of Destiny

THE DEMONATA

1. Lord Loss*
2. Demon Thief*
3. Slawter*
4. Bec*
5. Blood Beast*
6. Demon Apocalypse*
7. Death's Shadow
8. Wolf Island
9. Dark Calling
10. Hell's Heroes

THE SAGA OF LARTEN CREPSLEY

1. Birth of a Killer
2. Ocean of Blood

THE THIN EXECUTIONER (one-off novel)

*Also available on audio

Death's Shadow first published in hardback in Great Britain by
HarperCollins *Children's Books* 2008
Wolf Island first published in hardback in Great Britain by
HarperCollins *Children's Books* 2008
Published together in this two-in-one edition in 2011
HarperCollins *Children's Books* is a division of HarperCollins*Publishers* Ltd,
77-85 Fulham Palace Road, Hammersmith, London W6 8JB

The HarperCollins website address is
www.harpercollins.co.uk

Darren Shan presides over the demon universe at
www.darrenshan.com

1

ISBN: 978-0-00-743650-7

Printed and bound in England by
Clays Ltd, St Ives plc

MIX
Paper from
responsible sources
FSC
www.fsc.org
FSC® C007454

FSC is a non-profit international organisation established to promote the
responsible management of the world's forests. Products carrying the FSC
label are independently certified to assure consumers that they come
from forests that are managed to meet the social, economic and
ecological needs of present and future generations.

Find out more about HarperCollins and the environment at
www.harpercollins.co.uk/green

DARREN SHAN
THE DEMONATA VOL. 7 & 8

Death's Shadow
& WOLF ISLAND

HarperCollins *Children's Books*

CONTENTS

- *Death's Shadow p. 9*

- *Wolf Island p. 245*

Death's Shadow

For:

Bas — my full-time shadow

OBE (Order of the Bloody Entrails) to:

court jester Sean Kenny — resting in fits of giggles!

Reaped grimly by:

Stella Paskins

Embalmed by:

Christopher Little & Co

PART ONE
A WHOLE NEW WORLD

snapshots of beranabus i

Brigitta was sixteen years old and about to get married. She had been promised to a prince since birth. He was handsome and kind, and she was looking forward to the wedding. She had dreams of bearing many fine warrior sons, becoming queen of a mighty empire and living a long and happy life.

But the prince angered a powerful priestess. For revenge, she summoned a demon on the day of the wedding. The beast killed many of the guests and kidnapped Brigitta. She suffered terribly, but the demon didn't kill her. Instead, several months later he sent her back to the prince — pregnant.

Brigitta was in shock, but the prince cared only about the shame this would bring upon his family. He called in a favour of King Minos and sent Brigitta to Crete on his fleet's fastest ship. Her mouth was bound and her face covered, so nobody could identify her.

At the island she was led into the infamous Labyrinth, where her face and mouth were freed under cover of darkness. She was left to roam the twisting pathways of the maze until the Minotaur found and killed her.

Like hundreds of other doomed victims, Brigitta tried to find a way out of the Labyrinth, but her quest was hopeless. She could hear the harsh breathing of the Minotaur echoing through the tunnels, and the scraping of his hooves along the dusty floor. She knew he was following her, watching, waiting, savouring her anguish and fear.

Brigitta was in the final stage of her pregnancy. She hoped the Minotaur would kill her before the baby was born, to spare the child a ghastly death. But she could not delay the birth forever. Eventually she had to lie down and, in the blood-stained dirt of the maze, delivered a squealing boy. There was no light, so she could not check if he was deformed. He felt like a normal baby, but she would never know for sure.

As she cradled her son to her breast, the Minotaur moved in for the kill. He did not mask his footsteps. The beast hoped she would run. He liked it when his prey ran. But Brigitta only sat there, hugging her baby and crying. Just before the monster reached her, she leant over the infant and whispered, "Your name is Beranabus."

Then the Minotaur was upon her, and the corridors echoed with human screams and bullish howls of vicious delight.

When he had sated his inhuman appetite, the Minotaur turned his attention to the baby. The child had been silent since the beast had separated him from his mother. The monster sat on Brigitta's severed head and picked up the baby, studying him with a vicious smile.

The Minotaur shook Beranabus wildly, to make him cry. But instead the baby did something entirely unexpected — he giggled. Although he looked like a human child, he was a creature of two universes. He had the mind and curiosity of one much older.

The Minotaur growled and held the boy up by his foot. He clamped his jaws around Beranabus's head and squeezed softly.

Again the baby laughed, then reached out with a trembling hand. The Minotaur thought the baby meant to slap him away. But Beranabus was only fascinated. He explored the beast's fangs and nose, patting and stroking them as if playing with a doll.

The Minotaur released the child's head and hoisted him up for a better look. The baby scratched the beast's scalp and horns. The Minotaur chuckled throatily, then winced as Beranabus tugged his hair. He reached sharply for the baby's hands. But although he wrapped his large, hairy fingers around the boy's pudgy wrist, the Minotaur didn't rip the fingers off or even bite them. There was something unusual about this baby which the Minotaur had never experienced before.

Beranabus wasn't afraid.

Everybody else had been terrified of the beast. His mother, the midwife, the people of his village. Even the godly Heracles shook with fright when he came to capture the Minotaur. Nobody saw the great hero's fear, but the Minotaur smelt it and as always it drove him mad with hunger and lust. During his long years of captivity in the Labyrinth, King Minos had sent many prisoners his way. Some were resigned and went to their deaths with a smile on their lips, praying for redemption. But they'd all trembled when the Minotaur breathed on the back of their neck and ran his claws along the soft skin of their stomach.

But this baby was calm and confident. The Minotaur was a bloodthirsty, savage beast, but even at that young age Beranabus had a special way with animals.

Beranabus gurgled hungrily and tugged the Minotaur's mane

again. Slowly the beast rose and smiled — it was the first tender, unhating smile of his life. He considered the problem of feeding the baby. He clawed through Brigitta's remains, but she was no use for milk as he had ripped her body apart. There was plenty of water in the Labyrinth, but the baby needed something more nourishing.

With another warm smile, the Minotaur stooped, held the boy in one hand, cupped the other and collected a fistful of blood from one of the pools around his feet. With a gurgle of his own, he held his hand to the baby's mouth. Beranabus resisted for a moment, but despite his human form, he was of demonic stock. And so, with only the slightest reluctance, he opened his lips and let the Minotaur feed him, growing strong on the cooling blood of his butchered mother.

The next few years were the happiest of the Minotaur's miserable, slaughter-filled life. The baby was his sole companion, the only person he ever loved or who loved him back. He carried Beranabus high on his shoulders as he stalked the young men and women sent to him by King Minos. Some heard Beranabus laugh or coo as they fled and wondered where the sound came from. But they never wondered for long.

Beranabus didn't see anything wrong in what they did. He knew nothing but this world of darkness and butchery. The people they killed meant nothing to him. They were creatures to chase, animals to feed on.

When Theseus finally came to the Labyrinth and, through

trickery, felled the mighty Minotaur, Beranabus wept. Vain, proud Theseus was severing the Minotaur's head, to take as a trophy, when he heard the child's sobs. Startled, he followed the sounds to their source and examined Beranabus by the light of a torch he had smuggled into the maze.

Beranabus didn't look unnatural. Theseus thought the boy was six or seven years old and assumed he was one of Minos's unfortunate victims. He tried to lead the child out of the Labyrinth. "Don't cry," he muttered awkwardly. "The beast is dead. You're free now."

Beranabus glared at Theseus and his eyes blazed with a yellow, fiery light. Theseus quickly backed away. He hadn't been afraid of the Minotaur, arrogantly sure of his success. But this child unnerved him. The boy was an unexpected find and Theseus wasn't sure what to make of him.

"Come with me now or I'll leave you," he snapped.

Beranabus only snarled in reply and crawled across to the dead Minotaur. Theseus watched with disbelief as the boy spread himself over the monster's lifeless body and wept into the thick hairs of his bloodied, ruptured chest. He stood uncertainly by the pair for a while and thought about hacking at the Minotaur's neck again, to claim his prize. But then he caught another glimpse of the boy's yellow eyes. It was ridiculous, but he had a notion the child might prove more of a threat than the Minotaur.

"Stay here then," Theseus pouted, turning his back on the boy, deciding to leave the Minotaur's head intact. If people questioned him afterwards, he would say the beast fought valiantly, so he'd decided to leave him whole as a mark of respect.

Following a trail of thread to safety, Theseus wound his way out of the Labyrinth to take his place among the legendary heroes of that time, alongside the likes of Heracles, Jason and Achilles. He left the orphaned boy alone in the darkness, weeping over the corpse of the slain, demonic beast. He assumed the child would die in the shadows of the maze, unnoticed by the world. Life was cheap and Theseus didn't think the boy would be any great loss.

The slayer of the Minotaur was a shallow, shortsighted man who cared only about his own reputation. He could never have guessed that Beranabus would outlive and outfight every legendary warrior of that golden age, and eventually prove himself to be the greatest hero of them all.

DEAD GIRLS TELL TALES

→It's strange being alive again. This world is huge, complicated, terrifying. So many people and machines. You can travel anywhere and communicate in ways I never even dreamt of when I first lived. How are you supposed to find a place for yourself in a world this convoluted and uncaring?

Life was much simpler sixteen hundred years ago. Most people never travelled more than a few kilometres from the spot where they were born. Men sometimes went off to fight in distant countries, and came back with tales of strangely dressed folk who spoke different languages and believed in frightful gods. But girls and women rarely saw such sights, unless they were kidnapped by rival warriors and carted off.

It was a peaceful time when I was born. No great wars. Food was plentiful. Laws were respected by most clans. We built huts, made our own clothes, farmed the land, herded tame animals, hunted the wild. We married young, bore lots of children, worshipped our gods and died happily if we lived to be forty.

Then demons invaded. They attacked without mercy and dug up the remains of our dead, creating new beasts out of the rotting flesh and bones, turning our own ancestors against us. We fought as best we could, but for each one we killed, five more appeared. They terrorised villages across the land. It was only a matter of time before we would all suffer horrible, painful deaths.

In our darkest hour, an unlikely saviour appeared. A gruff druid led a small band of our warriors on a mission to send the demons back to their foul universe. I went with them, and so did a simple boy known only as Bran.

We drove back the demons, but one of them – Lord Loss, a red-skinned demon master with eight arms and no heart – imprisoned me in a cave beneath the earth. I was shut off from the world of light. In the darkness, he sent his familiars to torture and kill me. The pain was unbearable and death, when it came, was a relief.

At least it *should* have been. But for some unknown reason, when my body perished, my soul remained trapped in the cave. There was to be no escape for me, even in death.

I was held captive for many long, depressing centuries. Mine was a world of darkness and absolute desolation. Lacking a body, I couldn't even sleep. I was conscious for every minute of every long day and night.

I couldn't see or learn anything of the human world,

but I was at the focal point of what had once been a tunnel between the Demonata's universe and ours. By focusing hard, I could trace the shattered strands of the tunnel back to their source, and from there magically peer into the demons' den.

Not a lot happened in that part of the universe, but demons occasionally drifted by or stopped to test the tunnel in the hope that they might be able to rekindle it. I worried that one of them might succeed, so I kept a close watch.

After sixteen hundred years my worries proved well-founded. For the first time I sensed movement in the human world. A boy of great power had come to live in the area close to the cave. I could feel him being manipulated. He was led to the cave and tricked into trying to reopen the tunnel. I tried to warn the boy, to stop him. But he couldn't understand me. The tunnel was reactivated and demons flooded through in their thousands.

That should have been the end, but the boy returned when all seemed lost. He came with another teenager and an elderly magician — *Bran*! My old friend had survived and grown more powerful than any of us could have imagined.

As strong as Bran and the boys were, it wasn't enough. Hundreds of demons stood between them and the cave. They tried to break through, but failed. It looked like everything was finished.

Then something remarkable happened. A magical force connected me with the boys. It united the three of us and we became the Kah-Gash, an ancient weapon of incredible power. Without knowing what we were doing, we took the universes back through time, to the night when the tunnel was opened. Bran and the boys seized this fresh opportunity and put a stop to the onslaught, denying the demon hordes access to our world.

During the battle an innocent bystander – a boy called Bill-E Spleen – was killed. I felt myself drawn to the dead boy. As my spirit seeped into his corpse, I found myself capable of restoring the body's functions. I set the heart beating and it pumped blood through the veins and arteries. The brain sparked at my urging. Lungs rose and fell. Bill-E drew breath... and so did I. My first free breath after sixteen hundred years of imprisonment. No words can describe the deliciousness of that.

As Bran and the others stared at me, amazed and afraid, I set about altering the body I'd taken over, reshaping it, giving it my face, my build, my sex. Within hours it was a boy's body no longer, but a girl's, with breath, a heartbeat, bones, guts, flesh, blood, a face. I was *alive*!

That's when my problems really began.

LONELY NEW WORLD

→What amazes me most about this modern world is that people aren't more amazed. I first lived in a time of magic, with priestesses and druids who could perform wondrous feats. But we had nothing like aeroplanes, computers, televisions, cars. We were servants of the natural world, ignorant of the ways of the universe and the origins of our planet. We didn't even know the Earth was round!

Today's people have mastered the land and seas, and even made inroads into the heavens — they can *fly*! There are things they can't control, like earthquakes and floods, but for the most part they've torn down trees, carved the planet up with roads and made it theirs. They've hurt the Earth, and they don't seem as happy as people in my time were, but they've achieved the incredible.

I've been here more than six months, yet I still find a dozen things each day that make my jaw drop. Like a pencil. How do they put lead inside wood? And paper

— nobody thinks twice about it, but in my previous life, if you wanted to record a message, you had to hammer notches out of a chunk of rock.

It's a terrifying world and I shouldn't be able to cope with it. I came back to life as a small, scared, lonely girl. If I'd stepped out of the cave knowing nothing of what lay beyond, I'd have fainted with shock and gone on fainting every time I recovered and looked around.

But when I took over Bill-E Spleen's body, his memories became mine. It took me a few weeks to process everything, but I soon knew all that he did. That helped me make sense of this new world and deal with it. Without access to Bill-E's memories I wouldn't have known how to use a knife and fork, knot a pair of laces, open a door or do any of the simple, everyday tasks that everyone else takes for granted.

But as helpful as that's been, it's also proved to be one of my biggest problems. Because I live with Bill-E's uncle, Dervish Grady, and I made the mistake of telling him about Bill-E's memories. As a result, he sees me as some kind of a medium, offering him unlimited access to his dead nephew's feelings and thoughts.

→"Tell me about Billy's first day at school."

We're in Dervish's study on the top floor of the house. The mansion is a three-storey monster, full of round, stained-glass windows, wooden floorboards and bare stone walls. (Except in this study, which is lined with leather panels.) All of the people from my village could have lived in comfort here. When I first saw it, I thought it was a communal building.

"His first day at school?" I chew my lower lip, as though I have to think hard to retrieve the memories. Dervish watches me intently, hands crossed on the desk in front of him, eyes hard. I don't enjoy these sessions. He brings me up here three or four times a day and asks me about Bill-E, the things he experienced, the thoughts he had, the way he saw the world.

"He wasn't nervous," I begin. "He thought it was a big adventure. He loved putting on his uniform and packing his books and lunch. He kept checking the kitchen clock, even though he couldn't tell the time."

Dervish smiles. He always grins when I tell him an amusing little detail about his dead nephew. But he's not smiling at me — he's smiling to himself, as if sharing a joke with the absent Bill-E Spleen.

I tell Dervish more, talking him through the young boy's impressions of his teacher and classmates. I find this boring as well as uncomfortable. It's like having to read chapters from the same story, over and over. My attention wanders and my eyes dart round Dervish's study, the books of magic on the shelves, the weapons on the walls. I want to flick through the pages of those books and test some of the axes and swords. But there's never time for that.

Maybe Dervish doesn't see me. Perhaps to him I'm not a real person, just a mouthpiece for Bill-E. I doubt that he can imagine me doing anything other than talk about the boy I replaced. There's nothing malicious in it. I just don't think it's crossed his mind to regard me as an independent human being.

Eventually, two hours later, Dervish dismisses me. He's had enough for now. He waves me away, not bothering to even say goodnight. I leave him staring at his crossed hands, thoughts distant, a sad wreck of a man, more lost in the past than I ever was when captive in the cave.

→I love walking, exploring the countryside between the house and Carcery Vale. I like it in the forest. The land was covered in trees when I first lived. I almost feel like I'm in my original time when I leave the roads and paths of the modern world and stroll through woodland. Sometimes I'll pluck a leaf and set it on my tongue, to taste nature. I try to trick myself into believing the new world doesn't exist, that the natural balance has been restored.

Of course that's fantasy and the sensation never lasts long. These trees have been carefully planted and the undergrowth is nowhere near as dense as it was back then. There are still rabbits and foxes, but they're scarce.

No wolves or bears. The smell of the modern world is thick in the air, a nasty, acidic stench. But if I use my imagination, I can believe for a second or two that I'm in the forest near my rath.

Sometimes, in the night, I truly forget about the present. In my dreams I'm still Bec MacConn, learning the ways of magic from my teacher, Banba. I wake up in a cold sweat, heart racing, crouched close to the wall, wondering where I am, why there's a hole in the wall and what the clear, hard material stretched across it is. I feel trapped, as if I'm back in the cave. I swipe my fists at imagined phantoms of this new, scary world.

The confusion always passes swiftly. After a minute or two I remember where and when I am. My fists unclench and my heart settles down. I find it hard to sleep again on such nights, and lie awake in the dark, often curled up on the floor in a corner, remembering those I knew, all long dead and decayed. I feel lost and alone on such nights, and tears often fall and soak my cheeks as I tremble and miserably hug myself.

But it's day now and I feel more relaxed. I move through the forest, humming a tune the world hasn't heard in more than a millennium, pretending that I'm back in my own time. I come to a bush of red berries. I'm reaching for a berry to examine it when I spot a car and realise I'm close to a road. I still feel uneasy around cars, even after six months. I haven't been in one yet, although I've been on Dervish's motorbike a couple of times, when he took me to a nearby town to get clothes.

Cars frighten me. They look vicious. Growling, screeching, fast-moving assassins. I know they're not living, thinking creatures, but I can't help myself. Whenever I see a car, I expect it to race after me, chase me through the trees and mow me down.

I wait for the noise of the engine to fade, then edge over to the road. I've explored all the area around Dervish's home and can pinpoint my position within half a minute, no matter where I am. One look at the road, the trees by its side and the bend to my left, and I know I'm a five-minute walk from Carcery Vale, the nearest village.

I haven't been to the Vale often. The people there make me nervous. I keep quiet and don't interact with them. I feel out of place, afraid I'll say something to give myself away. I'm not truly part of this world and I can't shake the feeling that our neighbours will eventually unearth my secret.

My first week here was mad. We'd just saved the world from a demon invasion, but there was no time to take pride in our achievement. Beranabus – as Bran now calls himself – left the day after our showdown with Lord Loss. We'd glimpsed the demon master's superior in the cave — a huge, mysterious, shadowy, powerful beast. Lord Loss said our hours were numbered, that we'd only delayed the day of reckoning.

Beranabus was overwhelmed by my reappearance. I was the only person he'd ever cared about, and my return brought happiness back into his life. But the ancient magician is practical above all else. He wanted to stay and spend his last few years by my side. But there were demons to fight and a world to save. There was no time for selfish pleasure.

He took his assistant, Kernel Fleck, and Grubbs Grady – another of Dervish's nephews – with him. Grubbs is very powerful, but he hates fighting demons. He'd spent his life hiding from his responsibilities, but Bill-E's death seemed to settle him on his path. As reluctant as he was to leave Dervish, as scared as he was to face the Demonata, he went anyway.

Beranabus should have taken me too. When Grubbs, Kernel and I unite, we become the Kah-Gash. We have the power to destroy a whole universe. Beranabus should have kept us together, to experiment and use us.

He left me behind for two reasons. The first was personal. I'd suffered sixteen hundred years of imprisonment and he didn't want to thrust me into the demon's universe to fight immediately. He felt I deserved a few years of peace and wished to spare me the awfulness of my destiny as long as he could.

But he was scared as well, and that was the main

reason. Beranabus had been searching for the Kah-Gash most of his life, hoping to destroy the Demonata with it. But he'd never been sure if he was chasing a mythical Holy Grail or an actual weapon. When he saw it in action, doubt crept in.

Was he right to put the pieces together? What if we fell into the hands of the Demonata and they used us to annihilate the human world? Or maybe the Kah-Gash would work against us by itself. We hadn't intentionally taken the universes back in time. The Kah-Gash did that, having manipulated Grubbs into helping the demons open the tunnel in the first place. It had a mind and unknowable will of its own. Perhaps it had saved us by accident.

Wary of the weapon, Beranabus split us up. He should have left Grubbs behind to comfort Dervish, and he would have if not for his love of me. Dervish went into a rage when he woke to be told Grubbs had slipped away in the middle of the night. Grubbs and Bill-E were his nephews, but they'd been like sons. Now he'd lost them both. He cursed Beranabus, the demons… and me. He blamed me for Bill-E's death, accused me of conspiring against the boy, tricking him so that I could take over his body.

It was the first day of my new life. Everything was confusion and uncertainty. I was awestruck, afraid, not sure what to say or how to act, delighted to be alive, but terrified. Unsure of myself, I let Dervish curse and scream. I didn't flinch when he jabbed a finger at me or lifted me off the ground and shook me hard, only prayed to the gods that he wouldn't kill me.

In the end he stormed off. He ignored me for days, and would have ignored me for longer – maybe forever – if not for Meera Flame, one of his oldest friends. In the middle of his depression, he rang her to tell her about his loss. Meera came to him immediately. After doing what she could to console Dervish, she asked if I needed anything, if I wanted to talk about what I'd been through.

Meera was wary of me. Like Dervish, she wondered if I'd led Bill-E to his death, so that I could take control of his body. Through floods of tears I convinced her of my innocence. When she realised I was just a lonely girl, as scared of this new world as I was of demons, her heart warmed to me and we were able to talk openly. I told her about my life, my centuries in the cave, the force which compelled me to take Bill-E's body.

"I didn't want to bring the corpse back to life and change it," I sobbed. "It just happened. It was lying there, good for nothing else, and I had the power to make it mine. In those first few minutes, I wasn't thinking about living again. I could see that Lord Loss was going to kill the others. I just wanted to help them."

Meera believed me and managed to convince

Dervish of the truth. She also dealt with the difficulties of Bill-E's disappearance and my sudden existence. She got Dervish to pretend Bill-E had gone to live with relatives. Through her contacts, Meera faked the necessary paperwork and arranged for officials in high positions to throw their weight behind the lie if anyone (such as Bill-E's teachers) made enquiries.

Those same contacts forged a birth certificate and passport for me. I became an illegitimate niece of Dervish's, whose mother had recently passed away. In the absence of any other living relative, I'd been sent to Carcery Vale.

It was too coincidental to pass close scrutiny. A boy's grandparents are brutally slaughtered… the boy takes off without saying a word to anyone… his best friend also disappears… and a girl nobody has ever heard of moves in with the man who was like a father to both boys. The people of Carcery Vale aren't stupid. I'm sure they knew something was wrong.

But Meera and her allies covered their tracks artfully. Police were assured by their colleagues in other districts that Bill-E was safe and the girl's story was on the level. In the face of such carefully contrived evidence, our neighbours could do nothing except watch suspiciously and wait for the next bizarre Grady family twist.

FIRST CONTACT

→From the spot on the road in the forest, I make the five minute walk to Carcery Vale, but keep to the edge of the village, circling the houses and shops. I look on enviously at the ordinary people leading their ordinary lives.

Dervish is supposed to be tutoring me at home while I recover from the loss of my mother. Meera has supplied us with school books and equipment. Of course, Dervish hasn't once sat down to help me with schoolwork, but I've been doing it by myself. I complete the necessary exercises so that Meera can show them to the relevant authorities and keep them happy.

I enjoy the homework. I never did anything like this before. I learnt how to do practical things in my rath, like cook, wash and sharpen weapons. I memorised lots of stories and Banba taught me magic. But I never studied books — they didn't exist then. I knew nothing about global history, geography, science, mathematics.

It's fascinating. I know a lot already, courtesy of Bill-E's memories, but I'm discovering much more. Like most people, Bill-E didn't retain all that he learnt, so I only have access to the bits he remembered. But my own memory is perfect. I have total recall of anything I see, hear or read. By devouring the books Meera gives me, and watching scores of television documentaries and the news, I've pieced together many of the facts of this brave new world. Ironically I probably know more about it than most of the children who are natives of this time.

I'd love to go to school and learn from real teachers. I study as best I can at home, do my homework, watch educational programmes and surf the Internet. But that's no substitute for being taught by another person. There's so much more I could do with my brain, so many things I could uncover about the world, if I only had someone to instruct me.

But I'm not ready to mix with other people yet. What would I say? How would I mingle and pass as one of their own? I'd have to guard my tongue, always afraid I'd say something that gave away my past. I have nothing in common with these folk. I know much about their ways, from Bill-E and what I've read about them and seen on television. But in my time girls married when they were fourteen. Warriors fought naked. Slavery was a fact of life. There was nothing odd about eating the heart of a defeated enemy. We worshipped many gods and believed they directly influenced our day-to-day lives.

As I brood about the gulf between me and these people, someone coughs behind me. I'm instantly on my guard — in my experience, if somebody sneaks up on you, they're almost certainly an enemy. Whirling, my lips move fast, working on a spell. There's virtually no magic in the air, so my powers are limited, but I can still work the odd spell or two. I won't be taken easily.

It's a girl. A couple of years older than me. We're dressed in similar clothes, but she wears hers more naturally. I haven't fully got the hang of shoes and laces, soft shirts and buttons. Her hair looks much neater than mine and she wears make-up.

"Hi," the girl says.

"Hello," I reply softly, putting a name to her face and letting the spell die on my lips. She's Reni Gossel, the sister of a boy Bill-E hated. Grubbs liked this girl. Bill-E did too, although he never said, because he didn't believe he could compete with his older, bigger, more confident friend.

"I'm Reni," she says.

"Yes." I think for a moment. "I'm Rebecca Kinga." That's the fake name Meera provided me with. "Bec for short."

Reni nods and comes closer, studying me. There's a hostile shade to her eyes which unnerves me. This girl has no reason to dislike me — we don't know each other — but I think she does anyway.

"You're Dervish Grady's niece," Reni says, circling me

the way I was circling the village a few minutes before.

"That's right," I mutter, not turning, staring straight ahead, shivering slightly. This girl can't hurt me, but I'm afraid she might see through me.

"Grubbs never said anything about you."

"He didn't know. It was a secret."

"A Grady with a secret." She smiles crookedly. "Nothing new in that."

"What do you mean?" I frown.

"Dervish has always been full of secrets. Grubbs too. We were close but I'm sure there were things he wasn't telling me, about his parents, his sister, Dervish." She stops in front of me. "Did you meet Grubbs?"

"Just once," I answer honestly.

"Strange how he moved out just as you moved in."

I shrug. "He was upset. When Bill-E's grandparents were killed, he wanted to get away from here. It reminded him of when his parents were murdered."

"Maybe," Reni sniffs. "But who did he go to?"

"His aunt."

Reni shakes her head. "Grubbs didn't like his aunt. Or any of his other relatives. He told me about them. Dervish was the only one he loved. Bill-E loved Dervish too. Yet both of them have gone without warning and neither has bothered to pay him a visit in all the months since. Like I said — *strange*."

Her eyes are hot with mistrust and anger. For reasons

she maybe doesn't even know, she blames me for the disappearance of Grubbs and Bill-E. And to a certain extent she's right.

I say nothing, figuring silence is better than a lie. After a minute of quiet, Reni asks softly, "Do you have a number for Grubbs?"

"No, but I could probably ask Der—"

"Don't bother," she interrupts. "I asked already, when I couldn't get through on his mobile. He said Grubbs didn't want to talk to anyone. He told me to email, and I did, but it wasn't Grubbs who answered. I'm no fool. I could tell it was Dervish pretending to be his nephew."

I'm not sure how to respond.

"This has something to do with what happened to Loch," she whispers, and her expression changes, becoming more haunted. "You know who Loch was?"

"Your brother," I croak.

She nods. "Some people might say it wasn't coincidence that the pair who were with him the day he died have gone missing. Or that the grandparents of one were butchered. Or that the uncle of another has spent the last six months looking like a man who's lost everything – every*one* – dear to him."

"What do you want?" I ask stiffly.

"I want to know what happened," she snarls and grabs both my arms, squeezing tightly. "Loch's death was awful, but I believed it was an accident, so I dealt with it. Now I have horrible, terrible doubts. There's more going on than anyone knows. Dervish is hiding the truth and I think you know what it is."

"I don't know anything," I gasp, as images and memories come flying through my head. I want to make her let go, but I can't. I'm learning far more about her than I care to know, unwillingly stripping her of her secrets. "I came here after they went away. I know nothing about them."

"I don't believe you," Reni says, glaring at me with outright hatred. "You know. You must. You're part of it. If you had nothing to hide, why stay locked away or skulk around like a thief when you come out?"

"Please… you're hurting me… let me go… I don't want to…"

"What?" Reni snaps, shaking me. "You don't want to *what*?"

"Learn any more!" I cry.

She frowns. I'm weeping, not because I'm afraid or sad, but because *she* is. I know why she's doing this, why she feels so awful, why she's desperate to uncover the truth.

"You can't change it," I moan. "You can't bring him back. He's dead."

"Who?" Reni hisses. "Grubbs? Bill-E?"

"Loch," I wheeze, and her hands loosen. "You mustn't blame yourself. It had nothing to do with you. He wasn't distracted or angry. That wasn't why he—"

"What are you talking about?" Reni shouts, clutching me hard again.

"You had a fight with him the day he died." She releases me, eyes widening, and the images stop. But I can't let it end there. I have to push on, to try and help her. "You fought about what you were going to watch on television. It was a silly, stupid argument. I'm sure Loch had forgotten it by the time he left. It had nothing to do with his death, I'm certain it didn't."

Reni is trembling. Her lower lip quivers. "How do you know that?" she moans. "I never told anybody *that*."

"It was an accident," I mumble. "It wasn't your fault, so you shouldn't—"

"*How do you know that?*" Reni screams.

I shrug. This hasn't gone like I wanted it to. I hoped to ease her pain, but instead I've terrified her.

Reni starts to say something, then closes her mouth and backs off, crying, staring at me as if I'm something hideous and foul. It's how people in my time stared at a priestess or druid if they thought that person was an agent of evil. She backs into a tree, jumps with fright, then turns and flees.

I watch until she vanishes behind the houses of Carcery Vale, then slowly return through the forest for another lonely night with the aloof and morbid Dervish.

SPONGE

→Beranabus is only half human. His father was a demon who ravaged his mother against her will. In later life, Beranabus tracked the monster down and slaughtered him. He took the beast's head as a trophy. Held it close to his chest that night and wept for hours, stroking his dead father's face, hating and mourning him in equal measures.

Meera loved Dervish when they were younger. She wanted to marry him and have children. She dreamt of teaching their kids to be Disciples, the entire family battling evil together and saving the world. But she knew he would never father a baby. He was afraid any child of his might catch the curse of the Gradys and turn into a werewolf. So she never confessed her love or told anybody.

Reni saw her mother steal a purse from a shop. It was the most shocking thing she experienced until Loch died. She spent many restless nights wondering what else her mother might have stolen, worrying about what would happen if she was caught. She wanted to discuss it with someone, but it wasn't something she could talk about, so she kept it to herself.

I know these things because I've touched those people and absorbed their inner thoughts. I'm a human sponge — I soak up memories.

I became aware of my gift not long after I returned to life. I spent hours with Beranabus that night, hugging and holding him. Memories seeped into me thick and fast, but it was a time of great confusion and I wasn't able to separate his memories from Bill-E's until later.

It took me a few days to make sense of what happened. I had all these images of the distant past swirling around inside my head — starting with his wretched birth in the Labyrinth — and I wasn't sure where they'd come from. When I worked it out, I thought it was a temporary side-effect of my miraculous return to life. Or maybe Beranabus had fed his memories to me, to help me cope with the new world.

I didn't touch anybody else until Meera hugged me, in an attempt to comfort me when she found me crying. As soon as we touched, I began absorbing. When I realised what was happening, I broke contact. I felt like a thief, stealing her innermost secrets. The flow of images stopped as soon as I let go.

I learnt less about Meera than Beranabus, since we were in contact for only a handful of seconds. The flow of information was fast, but not instantaneous. I took many of her big secrets and recent memories, but little of her younger life.

I hadn't touched anyone since then. I don't like this power. It's intrusive and sneaky, and I can't control it. I don't seem to do any harm. I think the person retains their memories, but I can't be certain. Maybe, if I held on for a long time, I'd drain all their thoughts and they'd end up a mindless zombie.

I wish I could experiment and find out more about my unwelcome gift, but I can't without the risk of damaging those I touch. If I was in the Demonata's universe, I could test it on demons — although I'm not entirely sure I want to get inside a demon's head!

Nobody knows about it. I'd tell Beranabus if he was here, but he isn't. I could search for him – I learnt what he knew about opening windows when we touched, and I'm sure I could open one myself – but I don't want to disturb him. He's on an important mission and this would distract him. If I'm lucky, the unwelcome gift will fade with time. If not, what of it? I live in seclusion and almost never touch people. I'm sure Reni Gossel won't come back for another face-to-face. What harm can a secluded hermit do to anyone?

→I'm in Dervish's study, telling him about Bill-E's problems at school. Bill-E was a shy boy. He found it hard to make friends or fit in. Dervish wants to get to the root of his nephew's difficulties. There's no point — he can't do anything to fix them now — but he's persistent.

"Was it his eye?" Dervish asks. "Billy had a lazy left eye. He often asked me to correct it with magic. If I had, would he have been more confident?"

I shrug.

"Come *on*," Dervish presses angrily. "You know. Don't pretend you don't."

For a moment I feel like telling him to stop pestering me. I want to scream at him to stop obsessing about a dead boy and let me start living a life of my own. It's not fair that I'm forced to spend my days and nights playing these sick games.

But Dervish scares me. He's not big, but he's strong, I can see that in his pale blue eyes. He might hurt me if I crossed him. I'm not sure how far he'd go to keep learning about his nephew. Bill-E loved him unconditionally, so he saw only good things in this balding, bearded man. But Dervish has a tougher side which Bill-E never saw. I'm afraid he might punish me if I annoy him. So I let my anger pass, bow my head in shame and mutter softly in response to his accusation.

"I don't know, because Bill-E didn't know. It was lots of things, all jumbled up. The death of his mum, his eye, just feeling different. There was no simple reason. If there had been, he could have dealt with it."

Dervish studies me silently, face creased. Finally he nods, accepting my answer. He doesn't apologise for snapping at me — he doesn't see any need to.

"Was he happier when Grubbs came?" Dervish asks, leaning back in his chair. We've talked about this before. We've covered most of Bill-E's life. The only part we've never touched on is the night of his death. Dervish never asks about that.

"Yes," I say, raising my head and flashing a short smile across the table. I know Dervish likes hearing about Bill-E's lighter moments, his friendship with Grubbs, hunting for buried treasure, life with his mum before she died. "Grubbs was his best friend ever, even though they didn't know each other for long."

"Did he suspect they were brothers?"

"No. He sometimes wished they were, but he never had any idea who his true father was. He thought it was you."

Dervish flinches. I knew, even as I was saying it, that I shouldn't. He feels guilty about not telling Bill-E the truth. He doesn't like to imagine he was the cause of any unhappiness in his nephew's short life.

"That's enough for now," Dervish mutters, turning away from me, switching on his computer.

I stand up and edge around the desk. My gaze settles on Dervish's narrow back. I feel an almost irresistible urge to put a hand between his shoulder blades. Partly I want to touch him just to make contact, to say, "I'm real. I have feelings. *See* me." But mostly I want to absorb his memories and secrets, learn what makes him tick. If I knew more about him, maybe I needn't be so afraid. I might find some way to break through the barriers he's erected and make him see me as a person, not just a direct line to his dead nephew.

But that would be wrong. I'd be stealing. I already feel bad for unintentionally taking from Beranabus, Meera and Reni. I won't do it on purpose, not even to make life easier for myself. So I slide out wordlessly, leaving Dervish hunched over the computer, his secrets intact, the coldness between us preserved.

FRIEND INDEED

→Meera Flame roars to a halt in our driveway, turning up out of the blue, the way she normally does. I'm watching television when she arrives. I know it's her by the sound of her motorbike, which is much louder than Dervish's, but I wait for her to knock before going to let her in. I don't want to appear overly desperate for company.

"Hey girl, looking good," Meera laughs, giving me a quick hug before I can duck. She breaks away quickly, spotting Dervish on the stairs. I don't take much from her, but what I do soak up is new, memories I hadn't absorbed before. It seems like every time I touch a person, I steal something fresh. That's useful to know.

"How have you two been?" Meera shouts, taking the stairs three at a time. She grabs Dervish hard, halfway up the giant staircase which forms the backbone of the house, and hugs him as if he was a teddy bear.

"We've been fine," Dervish replies, smiling warmly. He never smiles at me that way, but why should he? I'm an interpreter, not a friend.

"Sorry I haven't been by more. Busy, busy. It must be spring in Monsterland — demons are bursting out all over. Or trying to."

"I heard," Dervish says. "Shark has been in touch. It sounds bad."

Meera shrugs. "Demons trying to invade are nothing new."

"But in such numbers..."

She shrugs again, but this time jerks her head in my direction. Dervish frowns. Then it clicks — "Not in front of the girl. You might frighten her." I see a small, unconscious sneer flicker across his lips. He doesn't think of me as a girl, certainly not one who can be frightened by anything as mundane as talk of demons. But he respects Meera's wishes.

"Come on up," he says. "We can discuss business in my study."

"To hell with business," Meera laughs, pushing him away. "I'm here to let my hair down. I thought it was time me and Bec had a girls' night in. I bought some lipstick, mascara, a few other bits and pieces I thought might suit you," she says to me. "We can test them out later, discover what matches your eyes and gorgeous red hair. Unless you don't want to?"

"No," I grin. "That would be coolio."

Dervish winces – that was one of Bill-E's favourite words – but I don't care. For the first time in months I have something to look forward to. I experience a feeling

I haven't known for ages and it takes me a while to realise what it is — happiness.

→We eat dinner together, which is a rarity. I normally dine alone. Eating is one of the few pleasures I've been able to relish since my return. I love the tastes of the new world. I never imagined anything as delicious as fish and chips, pizza, sweet and sour chicken. The strange flavours baffled and repulsed me to begin with, but now I look forward to my meals as I never did before.

After dinner Meera banishes Dervish to his study and the two of us shut ourselves in my bedroom. Sitting on the edge of my huge four-poster bed, Meera teaches me the basic tricks of applying make-up. It's harder than I imagined, requiring a subtle wrist and deft flicks of the fingers. We try different shades of lipstick, blusher, eyeliner and mascara. It all looks strange and out of place to me, but Meera likes the various effects.

"Didn't people wear make-up in your day?" she asks, working on my eyelashes for the fourth time.

"Nothing like this. The warriors were the most intricately decorated. Many had tattoos, and some used to colour their hair with blood and dung."

"Charming," Meera says drily and we laugh. She runs a hand through my hair and tuts. It's longer and wirier than it's ever been. "We must do something with this. And pierce your ears."

"I'd like that," I smile. "I couldn't grow my hair long or be pierced before."

"Why not?" Meera asks.

"I was a priestess's apprentice," I explain. "Priestesses couldn't marry, so we weren't meant to make ourselves attractive."

"I bet that was a man's idea!" Meera snorts.

"Actually it was practical. Our magic worked best if we were unsullied."

"You mean you lost your powers if you made out with a guy?" Meera asks sceptically.

"Yes."

"Rubbish," she snorts. "I've made out plenty and it hasn't done me any harm."

"It's true," I insist. "Things were different. Magic was in the air, all around us. It wasn't like when a window opens now. We were more powerful than modern mages, but we had to live a certain way to tap into the magic. Love of any kind was a weakening distraction."

"Hmm," Meera says dubiously, brushing my hair from left to right. I'm soaking up memories each time she touches me, but contact is brief so I'm not taking too much. I try not to absorb anything at all, to block her memories, but I can't.

"You sound like Billy sometimes," Meera says casually. "You said 'coolio' earlier, and 'weakening distraction' was the sort of thing he'd say too."

"There's a lot of him in me," I admit. "Bill-E spoke much faster than I did, and he used odd words sometimes. I find myself mimicking him. It isn't intentional.

"I have his handwriting too," I confess, lowering my voice to a whisper. "I never wrote before. I wouldn't have been able to without Bill-E's memories to show me how. When I write, I do it the way he did, exactly the same style."

"I wonder if you have the same fingerprints?" Meera says.

"No," I frown, studying the tips of my fingers, recalling the whorls from before. "This is my flesh. I moulded it into my own shape. On the outside there's nothing of Bill-E left. But in here..." I tap the side of my head.

"That must be weird for Dervish," Meera chuckles. I go very quiet. She applies new lipstick in silence, then says, "Dervish never talks about you. I haven't been able to phone often, but whenever I call, I ask how you're doing. He's always vague. Says you're fine, no problems."

I grunt sarcastically.

"I don't know about your time," Meera says slowly, "but in today's world, girls love to share. Boys don't so much — they bottle things up inside, hide their pain even from their best friends. But girls know that a problem shared is a problem halved."

"Bill-E hated that cliché," I tell her. "He thought if that was true, all you had to do was tell your problem to dozens of people. Each time you told it, the problem would be halved, until eventually it would be of no real importance."

"That definitely sounds like Billy," Meera laughs, then looks at me seriously. "If I can help, I will, but first I need to know what's troubling you."

I chew my newly painted lower lip, wondering how much — if anything — I should tell her. She's Dervish's friend, loyal and once in love with him. Maybe she can only see his side of things and will turn against me if I...

No. She's not like that. Meera's criticised Dervish before when she thought he was in the wrong. She believes in being honest with everyone. I've no guarantee that she'll side with me, but from what I've absorbed, I believe she'll give me a fair hearing.

"He's only interested in Bill-E," I whisper, then fill her in on all that's happened since I stepped out of the cave, only holding back the information about my gift, since that has no bearing on what's been going on with Dervish.

She listens silently, her brows slowly creasing into an angry frown. "The idiot," she growls when I finish. "I guess anyone in his position would want to know what was going on inside Billy's head, but he's taken this way too far. Who does he think he is, treating you like dirt?"

She stands up, fire in her eyes, and strides towards the door. My heart leaps with excitement — she's going to confront Dervish and subject him to a tongue-lashing.

Brilliant! But then she slows, stops, thinks a moment and turns.

"No," she says quietly. "I can't say anything to him about this. *You* have to."

"Me?" I cry, disappointment almost bringing tears to my eyes.

"I can take you away from here," Meera says, returning to my side. "Dervish is no kin to you, so you don't have to stay with him."

"Actually," I correct her, "we are distantly related."

She waves that away. "Like I said, I can take you from him, but I don't think you'd be any happier. If you run away now, you'll always be running. You need to talk to Dervish, make him see you're not Billy's ghost, but a real child with real needs. I wouldn't treat a dog the way Dervish has treated you."

"He doesn't do it on purpose," I mutter, surprised to find myself sticking up for him. "He's sad and lonely."

"So are you!" Meera exclaims. "If I was in your place, I'd have set him straight long ago. But you're just a girl. You were afraid to hurt his feelings... maybe afraid of what he might do if he lost his temper?"

I nod softly, amazed that she can read me so easily.

"I've known Dervish a long time," Meera says. "He's not as shallow as he must seem. You've caught him at a bad time, the worst of his life. He's lost Billy... Grubbs... that horrible Swan cow didn't help matters." Dervish had been in love with Lord Loss's assistant, Juni Swan. He thought she was a wonderful, kind-hearted woman. When he learnt the truth in the cave, he killed her.

"Any other time, Dervish would have welcomed you warmly," Meera continues. "But he's mixed up and you've become part of all that's wrong with his life.

"That has to change," she says sternly. "He can't carry on like a spoilt child. If he can't see sense himself, we have to make him. *You* have to. Because you're the one who lives with him. I could shake him up, but he'd feel guilty and shameful, and that might makes things worse. You need to sort this out yourself." She smiles encouragingly and nods at the door.

"What… now?" I stammer.

"No time like the present," she grins.

"I don't know what to say," I protest.

"You'll think of something," she assures me.

"But what if you're wrong? What if he doesn't want to hear from me? What if he only wants access to Bill-E?"

"He can't have it," Meera says softly. "Billy's dead. Dervish has manipulated you to hide from that, but he can't any more. It's not healthy. Now quit stalling, get up there and put him in his place. And remember," she grins, "he's only a man. They're the inferior half of the species. He'll be putty in your hands."

WAKING THE DEAD

→I trudge up the stairs to the third floor, nervous and hesitant. I don't want to do this. I can't think of anything to say. I wish I'd kept my mouth shut.

Except Meera's right. This *is* unacceptable. I've been silent too long. The old Bec wouldn't have tolerated such disrespectful treatment. I remember when I addressed the men of my village and insisted they let me go with Goll and the others on their mission to find out where Bran came from. Conn – our king – was against it, but I stood firm. If I can stare down a king and tell him what I think, I can certainly face Dervish.

The door to his study is open. I enter, rapping on the heavy wood as I go in. The room is protected from strangers by spells. Dervish never taught me the spells, but I found them easy to break. I don't have the power I experienced when I first came back to life – the cave was filled with energy which I could tap into – but I'm much more advanced than any present day mage.

Dervish is reading a book about werewolves.

Someone in our family bred with demons many generations ago. As a result, lots of our children transform into savage, mindless beasts who must be executed or caged for life. Various family members have searched for a cure over the centuries. Dervish is the latest, but he's had no more luck than the others.

It's possible I might turn one day, but I think I'll be able to fight it. Grubbs got the better of his wolfen genes. He's part of the Kah-Gash, and the magic of the weapon gave him the power to reject the change. I suspect I have that same power.

Dervish looks up and squints. "Is that what passes for fashion now?"

I touch my face automatically. "Does it look awful?"

"No." He forces a thin smile. "I was only teasing. You look good." It's the first compliment he's ever paid me. The small act of kindness gives me confidence. I walk around the room, studying the books on the shelves and weapons on the wall. I take down a small sword and swing it experimentally.

"Careful," Dervish says. "That's real."

I whirl the sword over my head and chop down an imaginary opponent. I wasn't supposed to practise with swords, but I did when nobody was watching. Satisfied that I haven't lost my touch, I return the sword to its holder.

"Where's Meera?" Dervish asks.

"Downstairs. She went to get something to eat."

"I'll join her. I'm feeling peckish." He stands up and heads for the door.

"No," I stop him. "We have to talk."

"Later," he scowls, waving me away.

I whip the sword off the wall again, take careful aim, then send it flying across the room. It tears through the leather panel on this side of the door and slams it shut. Dervish leaps away, giving a yelp of astonishment. He looks back at me, shocked.

"We. Have. To. Talk."

"Since you put it so politely…" He returns to his chair, eyeing me warily. He glances at the sword buried in the door. Its hilt is still quivering. "Were you sure you wouldn't hit me when you threw that?"

"No," I admit.

"What if you'd struck me?"

I grin tightly. "I'm a healer. I could probably have patched you up."

Dervish strokes his beard, eyes narrow. "What do you want to talk about?"

I stroll to the chair where I usually sit and drag it around to the side of the desk, so I'm closer to Dervish. I hunch forward in the chair, maintaining eye contact. The words come by themselves.

"You never ask about Bill-E's last day or his final thoughts."

Dervish stiffens. "I don't think we need to discuss that."

"Why don't you want to know?" I press.

"Did Meera put you up to this?" he says angrily. "She has no right. It's none of her business."

"No," I agree. "It's *our* business. And it's time we dealt with it."

"What do you mean?"

"You want all of Bill-E, his life from start to finish, wrapped up neatly like a birthday present. I can't give you that unless I tell you about the end, what he felt in the cave, how he reacted to the news that Grubbs was his brother, that you'd lied to him all those years, that you allowed him to be killed."

"I didn't allow anything!" Dervish shouts. "Grubbs did what he had to. There was no other way. If there had been, do you think I would have let him… do that… to Billy?" He's shaking.

"You're right," I say softly. "It *was* necessary. Bill-E knew that too. He didn't understand everything about the tunnel and the Demonata, but he saw your pain. He knew you still loved him, that you had no choice. He died without bitterness."

Tears well up in Dervish's eyes. His hands are trembling as he nervously tugs at his beard. "He must have hated me," Dervish moans. "I betrayed him. I didn't tell him when his father died. He believed *I* was his dad. I should have—"

"He was disappointed," I interrupt. "He wanted you to be his father because he loved you so much. But that disappointment didn't change his love for you. In fact, in the middle of the madness, when he thought Lord Loss was going to slaughter you both, that love grew stronger than ever. He even found time to joke about it, but he couldn't tell you because he was gagged."

"*Joke?*" Dervish echoes, tears trickling down his cheeks.

"When Lord Loss told him you were only his uncle, he wanted to say, 'Damn! I guess this means Grubbs gets half of your money now!'"

Dervish laughs and sobs at the same time.

"He was afraid," I continue, recalling Bill-E's memories. "But he didn't resent you or Grubbs. He knew you lied because you didn't want to hurt him. He wished you'd been truthful, but he didn't hold your deception against you."

"What about at the very end?" Dervish croaks. His fingers are balled up into fists. "Did he know what Grubbs planned? Did he guess we were going to… *kill him?*" The final two words emerge as a choked whisper.

"Yes," I say sadly. "Bill-E was no fool. He saw it in your eyes."

"Did he hate us?" Dervish cries.

"No. He blamed Lord Loss and bad luck, not you and Grubbs. In fact…"

"Go on," Dervish says when I pause.

"He was pleased you were there. He was glad he was with the two people he loved most. He didn't want to die a lonely death. He thought there was nothing worse than being alone."

I'm crying as well now. I want to stop. I don't want to hurt Dervish any more. But I have to say it. I have to make him see.

"I don't want to be alone either," I weep. "I hate it, Dervish. Loneliness is horrible. I had sixteen hundred years alone in the cave. I thought I'd suffer forever, no escape, no company, not even the release of death to look forward to.

"When I finally walked free, I thought I'd never be alone again. But I have been and it's awful, maybe even worse than in the cave. At least there I didn't have any hope. But now that I'm so close to people… yet alone anyway… nobody to talk to or share my feelings with…"

"What do you mean?" Dervish says gruffly. "You have me. We talk together every day."

"No," I sniff. "You talk to Bill-E. You look straight through me. I don't think you even know I'm there most of the time — you just hear Bill-E's voice. You only care about a dead boy. You might as well be one of the dead yourself for all the interest you pay to the living… to *me*."

I'm crying hard, wiping tears from my face with both hands. Dervish is doing the same, looking at me and really seeing me – *me*, not a shadow of his dead nephew – for the first time.

"I didn't know," he groans. "I just missed Billy so much. I… I've been stupid and hurtful." He manages a weak, shivering grin. I smile back shakily. He thinks for a moment. Then, looking as awkward as a boy on a first date, he holds out his arms. I don't want to steal memories from him, but I need to be hugged, more than I ever needed a hug before. So I stretch my own arms out in response, my heart hammering with hope and joy.

Before we can embrace, the door to the study crashes open. A wild-eyed Meera bursts into the room. She slips but grabs the handle and keeps her footing. "We're under attack!" she screams.

Dervish and I stare at her.

"We're surrounded!" she yells.

Dervish's face clouds over. "Demons?" he growls, stepping out of his seat, fingers bunching into fists.

"No," Meera gasps. A howl fills the corridor behind her. "*Werewolves!*"

FIGHT

→There's a moment of total, frozen disbelief. Then Dervish grabs a sword from the wall and pushes past Meera. I follow close behind. I try to pull the sword I'd thrown earlier out of the door but it's stuck tight. While Meera hurries to get a weapon of her own, I step into the corridor after Dervish, working on a spell, not sure if it will work — there's so little magic in the air to draw on.

I hear panting. It comes from the far end of the corridor. Something growls and something else yaps angrily in reply. No sight of them yet.

Meera steps out behind us, swinging a mace. She's stuck a knife in her belt. No trace of the gentle woman who was applying make-up only minutes ago. She's all warrior now.

"How many?" Dervish asks without looking back.

"At least three. They entered through the kitchen. I'd been snacking. I was just leaving, so I was able to jam the door and stall them. If they'd burst in when I was at the table…" She shakes her head, angry and scared.

The first of the creatures sticks its head around the corner. It's recognisably human, but twisted out of normal shape. It has unnatural yellow eyes. Dark hair sprouts from its face and its teeth have lengthened into fangs. They look too large for its mouth — it must have great difficulty eating.

It skulks into the corridor, growling. Long, sharp fingernails. More muscular than any human. Hunched over. Covered in stiff hair. Naked. A male. Another two creatures appear behind the first, a male and female. The second male is larger than the first, but follows his lead. His left eye is a gooey, scarred mess. Maybe that's why he's not the dominant one.

As the once-human beasts advance, I step ahead of Dervish and Meera. I try draining magic from the air, but there's virtually nothing to tap into. In my own time, these creatures would have been simple to deal with. Here, it's going to be difficult.

The lead werewolf snaps at the female. With a howl, she leaps. I unleash the spell as she jumps. It's a choking spell. If it doesn't work, I won't know much about it — she'll be on me in a second and I'm defenceless.

The werewolf lands about a metre ahead of me, but instead of pouncing and finishing me off, she rolls aside, whining, the cords of her throat thickening, cutting off her supply of air. Score one for Bec!

The weaker male attacks on all fours. No time for a choking spell. I bark a few quick words and the creature's fingers grab at each other. He roars with surprise and tries ripping them apart. I mutter the spell again, holding them in place. It's more of a trick than a real spell. It will immobilise the werewolf for less than a minute, then he'll break free and I'll have to think of something else.

But there's the dominant male to deal with first. He's more cunning than the others and makes his move while I'm dealing with the one-eyed beast. He barrels across the floor, howling dreadfully.

Before I can react, Dervish and Meera cut ahead of me. Meera lashes out at the werewolf with her mace, swinging the spiked ball expertly, landing a blow to the beast's right shoulder. Dervish jabs at him with the sword, piercing the creature's stomach.

Neither blow is fatal but the werewolf screams with pain and surprise, and falls back a few steps. He roars at the others, summoning them. The female's throat has cleared — she's back on her feet, and although her cheeks are puffed out, she looks ready for business. Morrigan's milk! In the old days that spell would have been the end of her. Curse this modern world of weak magic.

"We can't get past," Dervish says calmly. "Back up. They were human once. If we're lucky, the protective spells of the study will halt them."

"And if they don't?" Meera asks.

"Fight like a demon," he chuckles bleakly.

We shuffle back through the open door of the study. As soon as we're in, I dart to the nearest wall and grab an axe — the swords here are mostly too big for me.

One of the werewolves howls. The female leaps into the study, fangs flashing, ready to tear us to pieces. But as soon as she crosses the threshold she screeches, clasps her hands to the sides of her head, doubles over and vomits. She looks up hatefully and reaches for Meera, then screams and vomits again. She rolls out. The males roar at her but she roars back more forcefully than either of them.

"It worked," Dervish notes dully.

The stronger male approaches the doorway. He sniffs at the jamb suspiciously and leans through. His nostrils flare and the pupils of his eyes widen. He leaps back before he gets sick. Dervish strides forward and slams the door shut.

"What are they doing here?" Meera pants. "Where did they come from?"

"No time for questions," Dervish murmurs, stroking his beard with the tip of his sword. "There are probably others with them, demons or mages. They might break the spells and free the way for the werewolves."

The creatures are scratching at the door, their howls muted by the wood.

"The window," Dervish says. "There are handholds down the wall. We can get out that way."

"*Handholds?*" Meera asks dubiously.

"Call me paranoid," Dervish says, "but I always like to have an escape route." He crosses to the window and jerks hard on the strings of the blinds, yanking them all the way up. As he leans forward to unlatch the window, I get a sudden sense of danger.

"Down!" I scream.

Dervish doesn't pause, which is the only thing that saves him. Because as he throws himself flat in response to my cry, the glass above his head shatters from the gunfire of several rifles.

Meera curses and ducks low. The bullets strike the wall and shelves, ripping up many of Dervish's rare books, knocking weapons from their holders. A few ricochet into his computer and laptop, which explode in showers of sparks.

I'm lying face down, shivering. This is my first experience of modern warfare. I find the guns more repulsive than demons. I can accept the evil ways of otherworldly beasts who know nothing except chaos and destruction. But to think that humans created such violent, vicious weapons…

"What's going on?" Meera screams as the gunfire stops. "Who's out there?"

"They didn't introduce themselves," Dervish quips.

He's sitting with his back to the wall, beneath the shattered glass of the window. He has the look of a man studying a difficult crossword puzzle.

"We're trapped," I snap. Meera and Dervish look at me. Meera's afraid, Dervish curious. "Do we fight the werewolves or the people with guns?"

"The werewolves would appear to be the preferable option," Dervish says. "We can't fight the crew outside — we'd be shot to ribbons in no time. But whoever set this up will have thought of that. I doubt we'll have a clear run if we get past the werewolves — which is a pretty sizeable *if*." He gets to his knees and grins. "How about we fight neither of them?"

"What are you talking about?" Meera growls.

"A paranoid person has one escape route, easy to spot if your foe has a keen eye. But a *real* paranoia freak always has a second, less obvious way out."

There are two desks in the study, Dervish's main workstation and a second, smaller table for the spillover. He crawls to that, wincing when he cuts his hands and knees on shards of glass. He reaches it and stands, having checked to make sure no snipers can see him. "Help me with this," he grunts.

Meera and I aren't sure what his plan is, but we both shuffle to his side and push as he directs. The desk slides away more smoothly than I would have thought, given the thick carpet which covers the floor. Dervish stoops, grabs a chunk of the carpet and tugs hard. A square patch rips loose. Beneath lies a trapdoor with a round handle. Dervish takes hold and pulls. A crawlway beneath the floor is revealed.

"Where does it lead?" Meera asks.

"There are a couple of exits," Dervish explains. "It runs to the rear of the house. There's a window. We can drop to the ground if nobody's outside. If that way's blocked, a panel opens on to one of the corridors beneath us, so we can sneak through the house."

"If we survive, remind me to give you a giant, slobbery kiss," Meera says.

"It's a deal," he grins and slides his legs into the hole.

FLIGHT

→I don't like the crawlway. The cramped space and lack of light remind me of the cave. I feel my insides tighten. But I bite down hard on my fear and scuttle after Dervish, Meera bringing up the rear. As reluctant as I am to enter, I'll take a dark, tight space over gunfire and werewolves any day.

Dervish reaches the window at the end of the tunnel. It's semi-circular, with thick stained glass. He can see out, but it would be hard for anybody outside to see in. He observes in silence. Ten seconds pass. Twenty. Thirty. I can still hear the howls of the werewolves and splintering wood. The door can't hold much longer. They might not be able to enter the protected study, but when they realise we're not there, they'll come hunting for us. What's Dervish waiting for?

Finally he sighs and turns — there's just enough space. I start to ask a question, but he puts a finger to his lips and shakes his head. I nod bitterly. There must be people with guns outside, or more werewolves. Either way, we can't go via the window. We'll have to try sneaking through the house.

We backtrack past the study, then follow the crawlway round to the right. A short distance later, Dervish removes a panel and slips through the hole in the ceiling beneath us. He helps me down, grabbing my legs and easing me to the floor. Some of his memories flow into me – mostly about Bill-E – but the contact is brief.

We're in a short corridor on the second floor of the house, close to the hall of portraits, which is filled with paintings and photographs of dead family members, most of whom turned into werewolves. Soft growling sounds coming from that direction. Dervish listens for a moment, looks around uneasily, then starts towards the hall. Meera and I dutifully follow.

The hall is a mess of shattered frames, ripped paintings and photos. In the middle of it all squats a werewolf. He's roughly tearing a large portrait to shreds, stuffing bits of canvas into his mouth, chewing and spitting the pieces out. He's urinated over some of the paintings, either marking his territory or showing undue disdain for the Grady clan.

The werewolf doesn't spot us until we're almost upon him. Then Dervish steps on a piece of frame hidden beneath scraps of paper. It snaps and the werewolf's head shoots up. His growl deepens and his lips split into a vicious sneer. Using his powerful legs, he leaps at us, howling as he attacks. He slams into Dervish and drives him to the floor.

No time to use my axe. I yelp and grab the werewolf's jaw, trying to keep his teeth from closing on Dervish's unprotected throat. Jumbled, fragmented memories shoot from the werewolf's fevered brain into mine. What I learn disturbs me, but I don't dwell on it — I have more urgent matters to deal with. The werewolf's teeth are only a couple of centimetres from Dervish's jugular vein.

I prepare a spell to force shut the werewolf's mouth, but Meera's faster than me. She takes quick aim, then brains the werewolf with her mace. The werewolf's head snaps to the left. His eyelids flicker. Then he slumps over Dervish and it's simple enough to slide him off.

Dervish is furious when he rises. "I should have seen that one coming a mile away," he snarls, wiping blood from his left arm where the werewolf gouged him.

"You're getting old and slow," Meera taunts him. "What now?"

"The cellar," Dervish says.

"We're going to cage ourselves in and get drunk?" she frowns.

"It connects with the secret cellar," Dervish says impatiently. "That's a place of magic. We can seal the doors and keep our assailants out. Unless they–"

He's interrupted by howls from the floor above. The three werewolves have either broken through the door or heard the howl of the one we knocked out. They're coming. We leap over the unconscious animal and flee for the staircase.

→Racing down the stairs, the werewolves no more than a handful of seconds behind. If there are more on the ground floor, or snipers with a clear view, we'll be easy targets.

But luck is with us. We hit the ground without encountering any enemies. The howls and screams of the werewolves pollute the air. It sounds like they're poised to drag us down at any moment, but we can't risk looking back to check.

Dervish hits the light switches as he passes, turning them off, to hide us from the snipers. He hurries to the cellar door, barges through, waits for Meera and me to streak past, then slams it shut and locks it. A werewolf batters into it less than two seconds later. This door isn't as sturdy as the one in the study. It won't delay them long.

We spill down the steps to the cellar, automatic lights flickering on as we hit the bottom. This is where Dervish stores his priceless wine collection. Rack after rack of vintage bottles. Behind one of the racks is a hidden exit and a tunnel leading to a second, secret, cellar.

Dervish cuts through the maze of wine racks, angling for the exit, but we're not even halfway when the door above gives and the werewolves roar down the stairs. We won't make it. And even if we get to the rack ahead of them, the panels won't close in time. They'll be able to surge into the tunnel after us. Not much room for fighting in there.

"You go," I pant, laying aside my axe and turning to face the werewolves.

"Are you mad?" Meera shouts.

"Go!" I yell, grabbing two bottles from a rack. "I'll follow."

Meera starts to argue but Dervish grabs her and shoves her ahead of him. He nods at me to wish me luck, then flees.

I face the onrushing werewolves. I have a plan. Sort of. Not a very good one, but if it works, it'll buy us some time. If it doesn't, the werewolves will soon be tucking into Bec burgers.

The wine racks form narrow corridors. Wide enough for one person, but two's tight and three's a squeeze. When the werewolves see me alone, they go wild and rush forward, getting entangled with each other in the inadequate space. When the dominant male bucks off the others, I toss the bottles at him, then turn and run. I make a left at the end of the corridor, leading the werewolves away from Dervish and Meera — and the only way out.

→Running through the cellar. I've managed to keep ahead of the werewolves. If they were human, with full control of their senses, it would be a simple matter for them to ensnare me. A pair could simply circle around and wait for me at the end of any of the narrow corridors. The third could chase me towards the others in about half a minute. Game over.

But these beasts work by instinct. They can't think far ahead. When they have the scent of prey, they can only focus on the chase. So they plough along behind me, slipping and sliding in their haste. I grab bottles of wine as I run, lobbing them at the werewolves. They don't do much damage but every bit helps.

I run into a dead end. I'd been expecting it. Part of the plan. I stop half a metre from the wall, turn and wait. The werewolves gibber with delight when they see I'm trapped. They inch forward, clawed fingers flexing, drool dripping from their fangs.

I've been working on the spell since I started running. There's not much more magic here than upstairs, but hopefully the thin traces will be enough. I wait until the lead werewolf is a metre away, then unleash the spell at the bottles of wine in the racks around me. "*Fly!*" I scream.

The bottles shake in their holders. The werewolves pause warily. The cork of one bottle pops out. Wine sprays from the neck, showering the female. She cringes, then laughs hoarsely, sucks wine from the hairs on her arms and licks her lips.

A few more corks pop. The werewolves are being showered with first-rate wine. They wipe it from their faces, scowling but unharmed, and nudge forward again. I start to think my plan has failed, then...

Dozens of bottles shoot off the racks and slam into the werewolves. The monsters howl with pain and fall to the floor in protective huddles. Glass shatters over and around them, pounding their shoulders, backs and heads. Cuts open and bones break. One bottle smashes most of the fangs in the lesser male's mouth.

I make my move, not waiting for the shower of glass to cease. I scurry up the wine rack to my left, using it as a makeshift ladder. I crouch on top, set my hands against the ceiling and strain with my feet, trying to topple the rack. If it was full of bottles, I couldn't budge it. But it's mostly empty and it rocks nicely beneath me. I sway it backwards and forwards a couple of times, then send it toppling over the werewolves, further confusing, enraging and delaying them.

I leap to the neighbouring rack as the first goes over, then hop to the next and the next, like a frog. There's not much space between the tops of the racks and the ceiling. An adult couldn't manoeuvre up here, but there's just enough room for a wee bec of a girl like me.

The screams of the werewolves are almost deafening in the confines of the cellar. But to my ears, hopping ever further away from them, it's like music. The bottles and rack won't stall the werewolves for long, but I don't need much time.

Seconds later I come to the exit. It's normally hidden behind what looks like an ordinary wine rack. Dervish has opened it and the two halves of the rack gape wide. I can see the secret corridor and Meera lurking within it. Leaping off the rack, I make a neat landing and snap to my feet like a gymnast finishing a complicated routine.

"Cute," Dervish grunts, then smiles and waves me through. I push past and he hurries after me. The mechanical rack slides shut behind us, cutting out the cries of the werewolves and sheltering us from the bloodthirsty beasts. We share a grin of relief, then hurry down the corridor to the safety of the second cellar.

A minute later we arrive at a large, dark door. It has a gold ring handle. Dervish tugs it open and we slip through. It's dark inside.

"Give me a moment," Dervish says, moving ahead of us, leaving the door open for illumination. "There are candles and I have matches. This will be the brightest room in the universe in a matter of–"

The door slams shut. A werewolf howls. Meera and I are knocked apart by something hard and hairy. Dervish cries out in alarm. There's the sound of a table being knocked over. Scuffling noises. The werewolf's teeth snap. Meera is yelling Dervish's name. I hear her scrabbling around, searching for the mace which she must have dropped when we were knocked apart.

I'm calm. There's magic in the air here. Old-time magic. Not exactly like it was when I first walked the Earth, but similar. I fill with power. The fingers on my left hand flex, then those on my right. Standing, I draw in more energy and ask for — no, *demand* light.

A ball of bright flame bursts into life overhead. The werewolf screeches and covers its face with a hairy arm. Its eyes are more sensitive than ours — perfect for seeing in the dark. But that strength is now its weakness.

As Dervish huffs and puffs, trying to wriggle out from beneath the werewolf, I wave a contemptuous hand at the beast. It flies clear of him and crashes into the wall. The werewolf whines and tries to rise. I start to unleash a word of magic designed to rip it into a hundred pieces. Then I recall what I learnt in the hall of portraits. Instead of killing it, I send the beast to sleep, drawing the shades of slumber across its eyes as simply as I'd draw curtains across a window. As it falls, I flick a wrist at it and the werewolf slides sideways and out through an open door, the one it must have entered through before we arrived.

Dervish sits up and looks at the door. "We have to

shut it," he groans, staggering to his feet. "Block it off before…"

At a gesture from me, the door closes smoothly. Blue fire runs around the rim, sealing it shut. I do the same with the rim of the door we came through. "Sorted," I grunt. "Balor himself couldn't get through those now."

Dervish and Meera gawp at me and I smile self-consciously. "Well, I *was* a priestess."

Dervish starts to chuckle. Meera giggles. Within seconds we're laughing like clowns. I've seen this many times before. Near-death experiences often leave a person crying or laughing hysterically.

"I wish I could have seen you go to work on those werewolves," Meera crows. "We could hear it, but we couldn't see."

"It's just a pity you couldn't do it some other way," Dervish sighs. "Some of my finest bottles were stored back there."

"You can't be serious!" Meera shouts.

"A Disciple can always be replaced," Dervish mutters, "but a few of those bottles were the last of their vintage."

My smile starts to fade, but then Dervish winks at me. "Only kidding. You were great." He wipes sweat and blood from his forehead, then coughs. "I'm beat. Meera was right — I'm getting old and slow. I need to sit down. I feel…"

Dervish's face blanches. His lips go tight and his eyes bulge. He staggers back a step, gasps for air, then collapses. Meera screams his name and rushes to his side.

"What is it?" I cry, whirling around, testing the air for traces of a spell being cast against us.

"Dervish?" Meera asks, holding his arms steady as he thrashes weakly on the floor.

"Who's doing this?" I bellow. "I can't sense anybody. I don't know what sort of a spell they're using."

"Quiet," Meera says. She tugs her cardigan off and slides it under Dervish's head. His face has turned as grey as his beard. His eyelids are closed. His chest is rising and falling roughly.

"But the spell! I must—"

"There isn't any spell," Meera says softly, stroking the tufts of hair at the sides of Dervish's head. She's studying him with warm sadness, like a mother nursing a seriously ill baby.

"Then what is it?" I stumble towards her, stopping short of Dervish's twitching feet. "What's wrong with him?"

Meera looks up. There's fear in her eyes, but it isn't fear of demons, werewolves or magic. "He's had a heart attack," she says.

WAITING FOR THE CAVALRY

→Heart attacks were rare in my time. People didn't smoke (tobacco wouldn't be introduced to our part of the world for nearly another thousand years) or eat unhealthy food. Most of us didn't live long enough to suffer the modern curse of middle-age. A few of my clan died of weak hearts, but they were exceptions.

Nevertheless, I'm a healer. Once Meera has explained Dervish's condition to me and we've laid him in a comfortable position, I set to work. Without touching him, I feed magic to his heart, softly warming it, keeping the valves open. Some colour seeps into his face and he breathes more easily, but he doesn't regain consciousness.

"Will he live?" Meera asks quietly.

"I don't know." I study his face for signs of improvement but find none.

The werewolves are hammering at the door behind us. People are attacking the other door with axes. I direct magic into the wood and walls to keep out the intruders. I also mute the sounds, so we can focus on Dervish and monitor his breathing.

"Can you look after him by yourself for a while?" Meera asks.

"Yes."

She moves away, digs out her mobile phone and presses buttons. "Hellfire! I don't have a signal."

I consider the problem, then mutter a short spell. "Try now."

Meera smiles her thanks, then makes several calls. She doesn't bother with the police. This is a job for beings of magic — the Disciples.

Meera's on the phone for half an hour. I keep a close watch on Dervish. He looks terrible, much older than he did an hour ago. I'll be surprised if he makes it through the next few days.

Meera finally puts her phone away and returns to my side. "How is he?"

"Alive. For now."

"Can you use magic to keep him healthy?"

"I can help. There's more power here than in the house, but it's still limited. If he has another attack…" I shake my head.

"Do your best," Meera says, giving my arm a squeeze. "Disciples are on their way. They'll be here within twenty-four hours. We can transfer him to a hospital then."

"In his state, that will be a long time," I tell her. "You should prepare for the worst."

She chuckles weakly. "I'm a Disciple, Bec. We always expect the worst."

We settle back and watch in silence as Dervish quietly duels with death.

→After a few hours the sounds of the werewolves and their companions fade. Have they left or are they lurking nearby, trying to tempt us out? No way of telling. Best not to venture forth and chance it. Safer to sit tight and wait for help.

We have to deal with a few practicalities. There's no water or food. We can go without food for a day, but we need water for Dervish. I try finding a spring in the ground below us. There isn't one but I sense a pipe running overhead, carrying water to the house. Extending my magic, I pierce a hole in the pipe and draw a jet of water through the ceiling. We fill vases and a few of the larger, ornately designed candlestick holders. Then I plug the hole with dirt and a shield of small pebbles. It should hold for a few days. It's a plumber's problem after that.

We can't improvise a drip, so I use magic to ease water down Dervish's throat. Meera feeds it to him from a vase and I make sure he doesn't choke or swallow the wrong way.

"I always hate it when a young person has a heart attack," Meera says. I don't think of Dervish as young, but I guess in this world he isn't old. "It seems so unfair, especially if they're in good shape and have taken care of themselves. Dervish never had the healthiest diet, but he exercised regularly. This shouldn't have happened."

She looks almost as drawn and tired as Dervish. This is hurting her. She still loves him. I know from her memories that nobody ever touched her heart the way Dervish did, even if he was unaware of it.

"Who did you call?" I ask, to distract her.

"Shark and Sharmila," she says. "I tried a few others but they were the only pair who could come."

"Will two be enough?"

"They're two of the best. Do you know them?"

"Sort of. Bill-E met them in a dream once."

She stares at me oddly, so I explain about the movie set of Slawter and a dream Bill-E, Grubbs and Dervish shared when they thought they were on a mission with Shark and Sharmila. It's a complicated story. Meera knows bits of it, but not all the details. I fill her in, glad to have something to discuss, not wanting to think about Dervish and what he's going through.

A thought grows while I'm talking, and when I finish explaining about Slawter, I make a suggestion to Meera. "I can open a window to the Demonata's universe. We can take Dervish through and find Beranabus. I'll be stronger there. I can do more to help. Beranabus could help too."

"From what I know of Beranabus, he's not the helping kind," Meera mutters, considering the plan. "Could you find him immediately? Take us straight to him?"

"No. We'd have to go through a couple of realms, maybe more."

She shakes her head. "We should stay. Dervish can't fight and we don't know what we'd find. There could be demons waiting for us there."

"I doubt it."

"There might be," she insists. "We don't know who was behind this attack. Maybe it was Lord Loss."

"I don't think so. I touched one of the werewolves. I... I have a gift. I can learn things about people when I touch them."

"What sort of things?" Meera frowns.

"I read their minds. Access their secrets. Absorb their memories. I've been able to do it since I came back to life."

"Have you read *my* mind?" she asks sharply and I nod shamefully. "How much did you learn?"

"A lot. But I'd never reveal what I know. I wouldn't even have taken it, except I've no choice. Every time I touch someone, I steal from them. I can't stop it."

"Why didn't you tell me?" Meera asks, looking more confused than angry.

"I would have eventually, but there was so much else to deal with…" I shrug it off. "Anyway, I touched one of the werewolves and saw into its mind. It was a jumble, shards of memory all mixed up. I couldn't make sense of most of what I saw. But I learnt his name, who he was before he changed and who he was passed on to."

"Well, come on," Meera says when I hesitate.

"His name was Caspar," I tell her. "He was a Grady. He turned into a werewolf when he was fourteen. His parents did what many of their kin do, and turned him over to the family executioners — the Lambs." I know about the Lambs from the memories of Bill-E and Beranabus.

"But the Lambs didn't execute him," Meera says, her expression fierce.

"No. I'm assuming the other werewolves were family members scheduled for execution too. But all of them wound up here."

"The guys with the guns…"

"They were probably working for the Lambs."

We stare at each other, then at Dervish lying unconscious by our feet. And the temperature of the room seems to drop ten degrees.

→Meera doesn't understand why the Lambs would do this. They sometimes keep werewolves alive, to experiment on them in an attempt to unlock their genetic codes and discover a cure. But only with the parents' permission.

"I can picture them keeping the beasts alive on the quiet," she says. "Very few parents care to commit their children to a lifetime of laboratory misery, even if they've turned into werewolves. It's no surprise if the Lambs told them their kids had been executed, then kept them alive to study.

"But why bring them here to attack us? And how did they organise them? They were working as a team, as if they'd been trained. I didn't think you could do that with werewolves. Even if you could, why send them against *us*?"

That's the key question. According to Meera, Dervish never had much love for the Lambs. They originally formed to execute children who'd turned, but over the decades they acquired more power and branched out into more experimental areas. Dervish didn't approve of that, especially since he didn't think science could find a cure for a magically determined disease.

"The Lambs never liked Dervish either," Meera says. "They thought if he explained more about demons, it might help them with their studies. But they'd no reason to attack him. At least none that I'm aware of."

"Maybe it's me," I mumble. "Grubbs turned into a werewolf – temporarily – and because of his magical powers, the Lambs couldn't stop him. Maybe they're afraid I'll turn too and become a menace."

"But they don't know you're one of the family," Meera says. "Dervish told them nothing about you. There's something we're missing…"

We spend hours debating the mystery. We get no closer to the truth, but at least it helps to pass the time. During the discussions, I think of another reason why the Lambs might have targeted me. But I say nothing of it to Meera, deciding to wait until the other Disciples arrive, so I don't have to repeat myself.

→Someone knocks on the door leading to the yard. Meera and I were both half-dozing. We jolt awake at the sound and I strengthen the magical fields around the doors and walls. Then a man shouts, "Little pigs, little pigs, let us come in!"

"Idiot," Meera grunts, but she's smiling. "It's Shark."

"I know. I remember his voice from Bill-E's dream."

I remove the spells and the battered door swings open. A tall, burly man in an army uniform enters, followed by an elderly Indian woman who walks with a limp.

"Sorry we're late," Shark says, hugging Meera and lifting her off the floor.

"How is he?" Sharmila asks, hobbling directly to Dervish.

"He's been like that since the attack," I tell her. "No change."

She stares at me suspiciously. "You must be Bec. I have heard about you."

"The dead girl who came back to life," Shark says. He's looking at me oddly. "I thought you'd be more like a boy, considering…"

"…I stole Bill-E's body?"

"Yeah."

"There's nothing of Bill-E left," I tell them. "Except his memories. That's how I know you and Sharmila."

Shark frowns. "I never met him."

"I did," Sharmila says, "but many years ago, when he was very young."

"I know. But he met both of you." I grin weakly at their confusion.

"Bec can tell you about that later," Meera snaps. "What's happening outside?"

"Nothing," Shark says. "All quiet. Your birds have flown the coop."

"You're positive? It isn't a trap, to lure us out of hiding?" Shark shakes his head. "Then let's get Dervish straight to a hospital. We can talk about the attack on the way. But I'll tell you this much — they weren't birds. They were *Lambs*."

→Shark and Meera carry Dervish up the steps out of

the cellar as gently as they can. Shark grumbles about what he's going to do to the Lambs when he catches up with them. He drove here in a van. There's a hospital trolley in the rear. We strap Dervish down and Sharmila produces a drip and heart monitor. She hooks Dervish up. I watch with interest — it's the first time I've seen such apparatus.

When Dervish is as secure as we can make him, I ask Shark if he's absolutely certain we're not going to be attacked.

"Nothing in life's an absolute," he replies, squinting at the trees, the mansion, the sky. "But if this was a trap, the time to attack would have been when we were moving Dervish up from the cellar. That's when we were most vulnerable. I'm confident we've nothing to fear for the time being."

"Then I've a favour to ask." I feel strange being so forward but this is no time to be shy. "I can open a window to the Demonata's universe from the cellar. I'd like you to go through and find Beranabus."

Shark blinks slowly. Sharmila is frowning.

"Have you ever been to that universe?" Sharmila asks.

"No."

"Then you do not know what you are asking. It is a place of chaos and peril. We have never been there without Beranabus to guide us."

"I know how dangerous it is," I mutter, flashing on

some of Beranabus's many memories of the hellish universe. "But I'll try to open the window to one of the less savage zones. Did Beranabus teach you a spell to find him once you're there?"

"No," Shark grunts. "But Dervish did."

"We have never tested it," Sharmila notes. "What if the window closes and we cannot find him? We will be stranded."

"Dervish might be dying," Meera hisses.

"I have sympathy for Dervish," Sharmila says coolly. "That is why I came when you summoned me. But can Beranabus heal him? And even if he can, why should we risk our lives for his?"

"It's not about helping Dervish," I say quickly before an argument develops. "We don't know who the Lambs were after. Their target might have been Dervish or Meera, but it was probably *me*."

"What if it was?" Shark asks.

"I'm important," I mutter, feeling embarrassed. "I can't explain — there isn't time — but I'm part of a powerful force which might mean the difference between winning and losing the war with the Demonata."

Sharmila's eyes narrow. "The Kah-Gash?"

"You know about it?" I sigh with relief.

"We helped Beranabus search for a piece once," Shark says. "It wasn't our most successful mission."

"I am not convinced of that," Sharmila says. "I always suspected… *Kernel?*" She raises an eyebrow.

My smile broadens. "Yes. He was a piece. Grubbs is another. So am I."

"What are you talking about?" Shark frowns.

Sharmila waves his question away. "Does Beranabus know?"

"Yes."

"Then why are you not with him?"

"He didn't want to keep us together until he found out more about how the weapon works. He thought I'd be safe here. Nobody else knew. At least we didn't think so. But if the attack was directed at me, maybe my secret's out. If that's the case…"

"…Beranabus must be informed." Sharmila nods. "I understand now."

"Care to explain it to the rest of us?" Shark asks, bemused.

"Later." She thinks about it for a few seconds. "I would go but I am old and slow, even when pumped full of magic. Besides, I know a lot about healing, so I might be of more help here. Meera?"

"I'm not as strong as you," Meera says.

"But you are younger and faster. In this instance that is important."

"I don't like that other universe," Meera mutters.

"Neither do I. Believe me, I would not send you there lightly."

"You really think this is necessary?"

Sharmila nods slowly. Meera sighs and agrees reluctantly.

"Shark?" Sharmila asks.

"You want me to place my life on the line without knowing the reason why?" he scowls.

"Yes."

His scowl disappears and he shrugs. "Fair enough."

"You understand how time works in that other universe?" Sharmila asks me. "It can pass quicker or slower than it does here. They might find him in a matter of minutes as we experience time or it could be several months."

"I know. But we don't have a choice. I'd go myself, except if it's a trap…"

"…demons might be lying in ambush for you. Very well. Let us not waste any more time. I will stay with Dervish. Shark and Meera will accompany you to the cellar." She smiles tightly at Shark. "You have been to hell in a bucket before, my old friend. Now it is time to go there without the bucket."

→In the cellar. I'm working on a spell to create a window to the demon universe. It's an area Beranabus goes to frequently — his father took his mother there when he abducted her. Because Beranabus has opened a window to that realm many times, it's a relatively quick and easy procedure, though it still takes me an hour.

As I complete it, a thin lilac window forms in the cellar. I get a shiver down my spine. I never saw a window like this in my own time, but Beranabus has been through thousands of them. He acts like it's no big thing, but he loathes these demonic passageways. He always expects to die when he steps through, having no real way of knowing what's lurking on the other side.

"Will you be all right staying here with Sharmila?" Meera asks.

"Yes."

"We should come with you and enter the demon universe later," Shark says. "If the Lambs attack you on the way to hospital..."

"I might not be able to open a window there," I explain. "It's easier if I'm in an area of magic."

"Even if Beranabus doesn't come with us, we'll return," Meera says.

"He'll come," I smile confidently.

"Because you're part of the Kah-Gash?"

"Yes. But also because we're old friends."

"I didn't think Beranabus had any friends," Shark grunts.

"Maybe not now. But he was a boy called Bran once and I was his friend then. He'd do anything for me."

"You're sure of that?" Meera asks.

I think about the night I sat with Beranabus and absorbed his memories. He always wears a flower in a buttonhole, in memory of me. "I'm certain."

"Right," Shark says, rubbing his hands together. "Keep a light burning — we'll be back in time for supper."

Shark steps through the window. Meera smiles wryly, then moves to hug me. I take a step backwards.

"I'd rather not touch. I don't want to steal any more memories from you."

"Don't be silly," Meera says, wrapping her arms around me. "If things go badly over there, you can remember my life for me."

We grin shakily at each other, then Meera slips through the window after Shark. I wait a couple of minutes in case they run into trouble and need to make a quick retreat. Then, as the window breaks apart, I douse the lights and climb the steps to help Sharmila escort Dervish to hospital.

PART TWO
WARD DUTY

snapshots of beranabus ii

After the death of the Minotaur, the years of wandering began. Beranabus had no difficulty finding his way out of the Labyrinth. He had explored every last alley of the maze. It had been home to him and he knew it intimately.

Sunlight disturbed the boy. Having grown up in darkness, the world of light seemed unbearably bright. He tried to brave the glare, but the pain was too great. Weeping, he retreated. Not knowing about the outside world, he assumed it would always be this bright, the way the Labyrinth had always been dark.

When the sun dropped and the sky darkened, Beranabus cautiously crept out again. It was still a lot lighter than he liked, but he was able to adjust to the shades of the night world. He looked back once at the Labyrinth, feeling sad and alone, remembering the good times, riding high on the Minotaur's shoulders, feeding on the fresh blood and meat of the beast's kills. Then, reluctantly, he turned his back on his childhood home and set off to explore this new, peculiar world.

Beranabus was a simple child. He couldn't speak. He could understand some of what other people said, but not everything. Most of the world was a mystery to him, filled with beings who made a huge amount of noise and fought lots of battles for no reason that he could see.

He shouldn't have lasted long in such a hostile environment.

But Beranabus had a remarkable gift, which saved him when he first entered the world — he could tame the wildest of creatures and find friendship in the most unlikely places. Wherever he went, he was accepted. People took him into their homes, gave him passage on carriages and boats, fed and clothed him, treated him with kindness and love.

Many took pity on the boy and sought to keep him and raise him as their own. But Beranabus liked to wander. After the confines of the Labyrinth, the open space of the world intrigued him and he wanted to see more of it. So, without any real design or purpose, he always moved on, slipping away from those who yearned to root him, feeling nothing more for them than he did for the dirt beneath his feet or the air whispering through his hair.

One day, when the boy was on the brink of his teenage years (although he'd been alive for more than two centuries), he witnessed a demon on the rampage. The monster had crossed near a small village and was busy killing as many humans as it could before it had to return through the window of light to its own universe.

The demon reminded Beranabus of the Minotaur. He had come a long way from Crete and seen much of the world and its people, but this was the first demon he'd encountered. The savage beast amused him. It was shaped like an octopus, but with several heads of various animals and birds. He liked the sounds the humans made when the demon killed them, and the patterns their blood created as it arced through the air in streaks and spurts.

He watched the massacre for a few minutes as if enjoying a show. The demon saw him, but didn't attack, mesmerised by the boy's strange aura, as all other dangerous creatures had been.

Murder meant nothing to Beranabus. He didn't understand concepts of right and wrong, good and evil. His mind was a muddled grey zone. Many had tried to teach him, but all had failed. The only difference in his head between a living person and a corpse was that the former was more entertaining.

When the demon retreated, Beranabus was curious to see what the beast would do next, who it would kill, what sort of mischief it would get up to. So he stepped through the window after the demon, out of his mother's universe, into the much darker and spectacularly violent playpen of the Demonata.

Beranabus had a whale of a time in the universe of his father. The demons were far more bloodthirsty than humans. They could kill each other in ways men had never dreamt of. Death didn't have to be swift either. A demon master could torment a lesser demon for decades... hundreds of years... millennia if it wished.

Beranabus drifted with delight from one crazy realm to another. He didn't need to sleep much, or eat and drink. And he aged at an even slower rate than on Earth. He was part of a universe of marvels and it seemed he could go on enjoying it for as long as he liked.

He had to be careful of course. He could tame most demons, but some resisted his charms and tried to capture him. Beranabus was uneducated, but he wasn't stupid. He knew what pain and suffering were, and while he loved to observe the torment of others, he had no wish to become one of the tortured.

That was when he discovered his gift of speed. He could run faster than any demon that chased him. So, on the occasions where he could not tame a demonic beast, he fled, laughing gleefully as he ran, safe in the knowledge that the demon would soon lose interest in him and abandon the chase for easier pickings. In the Demonata's universe there was always something else to kill.

Windows were plentiful. Although demons could only cross to the human world with the aid of a malevolent magician or mage, many could travel from one zone to another in their own foul realm. Their universe was an endless parade of blood-drenched worlds and galaxies. Some of the stronger demons could even create infinite, self-contained zones of their own, which somehow nestled within the larger, unified demon universe.

Whenever Beranabus tired of a realm, he searched for a window and usually found one quickly. He never worried about what he would encounter on the other side. Uncertainty and potential peril were all part of the delight of his life.

Eventually, inevitably, he stepped through a window to the human world. He knew he'd crossed universes as soon as he sniffed the air — it was less charged with magic. Instinct urged him to retreat, but curiosity tempted him on. A long time had passed — he could tell from the buildings around him — and he wanted to see what the people were like, how they varied from those he'd known, if they died any differently.

In the demon universe, windows could remain open indefinitely. He assumed that was the case here as well, but he was wrong. He spent only a handful of minutes in the town — just enough to realise that demons were far more interesting than humans — but when he returned to the spot where the window had stood, it was gone. He was stranded, a captive of the world where he had first begun.

When Beranabus discovered to his dismay that windows of magic were incredibly rare on this world, he travelled with fiery intent, hitching lifts with armies and traders, riding and sailing to the furthest reaches of civilisation. He was desperate to return to the universe of the fantastical demons.

This was the first time Beranabus's brain stirred actively. Until then he had wandered neutrally, observing whatever he chanced across. But now he went in search of something specific and moved with a purpose, carefully choosing those he travelled with, deliberately setting out to explore fresh locations full of promise.

As his brain took its first developmental staggers forward, he unconsciously learnt a few words and mimicked the speech of those he hitched rides with, although most of the time he only uttered gibberish. His mind was still a confused, chaotic country, full of storms and whirlpools. But he had taken the

*first steps towards understanding and intent, and the world —
the universes — would never be the same for him again.*

Some years later the boy found himself on an island, set at the
westernmost limit of the known world. Demons had broken
through and established a permanent tunnel. Thousands of
monsters had flooded the land. They were terrorising the locals,
laying siege to the villages and towns, slaughtering all in their path.

Beranabus eagerly trudged around the country in search of
the tunnel, admiring the torments perpetuated by the Dèmonata.
But as he moved from one village to another, a dim sense of
unease grew within him. He felt nothing substantial for the dead
humans he saw every day, or the terrified living who would soon
be butchered by the demons. But something about their plight
troubled him. He had changed inside, and although the change
was slight, it had altered his view of slaughter.

Human suffering was different to what he'd seen in the
demon universe. On this world, those who survived mourned
for the dead. Demons laughed at death, but people here cared
about their families and friends. Beranabus found it hard to
wring pleasure from their pain. It was too... human.

His unease made him more determined than ever to find the
tunnel and leave this world. In the Demonata's universe he
could revert to his old ways and simply revel in the merciless
mayhem. He didn't like the way he was changing. The world
was more fun if you could enjoy it with complete abandonment,
untouched by the misery of others.

As he instinctively learnt and practised new words, Beranabus sometimes tried to mutter his name aloud. He could remember what his mother called him, but he couldn't pronounce it. The closest he could get was "Bran". Those who heard him took it to be his name. Having a name was a new experience and Beranabus found it oddly comforting. He started to mutter "Bran" every time he met someone new, so they would know what to call him, but his mind was still a jumbled mess and he occasionally forgot.

After a time, as he was resting in a village on a tiny island at the centre of a lake, Bran came in contact with a druid called Drust. Bran sensed that Drust was also on a mission to find the tunnel. So, instead of moving on, he remained in the village and even let Drust send him to find others to assist him on his quest. Bran didn't know that the druid planned to close the tunnel, and he wouldn't have cared if he did. As long as he could race through before it shut, back to the universe of the demons, he would be content.

Finding people to help Drust wasn't easy. The druid was very precise in his request, demanding not just warriors, but a being of magic. Ideally he needed a fellow druid or priestess, but failing that, he'd settle for someone who had a healthy magical talent, even if it was undeveloped.

Bran didn't understand all that, but Drust meddled with the boy's mind, magically implanting his requirements. Bran had the power to counter the druid's influence, to break the spell Drust had woven around him. But he needed Drust to find the tunnel, so he accepted the druid's orders.

He tried in his befuddled way to recruit a band for Drust at several villages without success. At most there were no people of sufficient magic, and at two where there were, the people dismissed him as a mad child.

Finally, late one evening, he came to a ringed fort. He could sense a person of magic within — a young woman — but had no great hope of attracting her to his cause. Squatting outside the village wall, he waited for the curious warriors to come and examine him, as they had everywhere else. But when the door opened, the magician accompanied the warriors, and for Bran everything altered.

The woman — little more than a girl — looked no prettier than any other her age. Her power was unremarkable. The land was littered with hundreds like her. In his time Bran had sniffed with disinterest at beautiful princesses and powerful priestesses.

But something about this girl struck him hard. He showed no outward sign of it, and couldn't even express his feelings clearly to himself. But the moment he saw the girl — Bec — he fell madly and completely in love. It was love he had not known since his early years with the Minotaur, love he would never know again until she returned to him after many centuries of captivity. And although he couldn't voice his feelings, he knew on some deep level that he would do anything for this girl, kill if needed, give his own life for hers if he must.

So it was that Beranabus at last, without intention or knowledge of what it would mean, put his demonic interests behind him and became a real human.

A MAN'S GOTTA DO

→Dervish is hooked up to all manner of machines. He's wealthy, so he gets his own room and the best possible care and attention. The machines are incredible, so intricately designed, capable of detecting tiny flaws that Banba and I never could have, no matter how strong our magic. When the doctors and nurses aren't busy, I ask about the various consoles and monitors, memorising their answers. If I was ever granted the freedom to pursue a normal career, I'd work day and night to master these machines and become a modern-day healer.

It's been four days since Dervish's heart attack, three since we brought him to hospital. The doctor who first examined him was furious that we waited so long to admit him. But she was soon replaced by a surgeon who knew of the Disciples and Sharmila was able to explain the reasons for our delay.

Dervish's room is on the fifth floor, two floors down from the top of the hospital. It's close to an elevator shaft. There are armed guards stationed outside, but they keep their weapons hidden discreetly. Sharmila arranged for them to be here. The Disciples have many useful contacts.

Most of the guards are cold and distant, focused on their watch. But a couple chat with me during the quieter moments and one – Kealan – is outright friendly. Kealan's one of two trained medics who alternate shifts. They're more closely involved with us than the other guards — if we have to move Dervish in an emergency, Kealan or the other medic will handle any medical complications.

Sharmila or I have been with Dervish the whole time, except when his doctors are examining him. A cot has been set up in a corner of the room and we take turns sleeping there.

Dervish has flickered into consciousness a couple of times, but never for long, and he hasn't said anything or showed signs of recognition. His doctors aren't sure what state his brain is in. They don't think he suffered serious mental damage, but they can't say for certain until he recovers. *If* he recovers.

Sharmila has discussed the situation with her fellow Disciples. She considered going straight after the Lambs, but we're still not absolutely certain they were behind the attack. And even if they are directly involved, we don't know who they're working with or what we might walk into if we go after them. Better to wait for Beranabus.

I don't mind waiting. This is the calm before the storm. I'm sure the peace won't last. We'll soon have all the action we could wish for, and more. I'm enjoying the lull. In my previous life I was eager to leave the confines of my village and explore the world. If I could do it all again, having seen the terrors of the wide blue yonder, I'd probably stay at home and keep my head down. Not the most heroic of responses, but I never wanted to be a hero. I'd much rather lead an ordinary life. Normal people don't know how lucky – how blessed – they are.

→Sharmila is talking to Dervish, chatting away as if he's listening to her every word. You're supposed to do that with people who are comatose. Doctors say it can help, and even if it doesn't, it can't do any harm.

I've tried speaking to Dervish, but what can I say? I don't want to tell him about Bill-E – that period of our relationship is over – but we don't have much else in common. I've shared some of my previous life, described the rath where I lived, my people, our customs. But I don't know how interested Dervish is in ancient history. I worry, if he can hear, that I'm boring him.

Sharmila's reminding Dervish of their adventures in the demon universe when they were younger. She recalls their encounter with Lord Loss, Kernel surprising them all with his knack of opening windows, the loss of Nadia Moore — who would later resurface as the treacherous Juni Swan. I've heard most of it before and I'm feeling restless.

"Do you mind if I stretch my legs?" I interrupt.

"Not at all," Sharmila says. "I will call if I need you." She gave me a walkie-talkie a couple of days ago, so we could keep in touch. Mobile phones aren't allowed inside the hospital.

Kealan is on duty with three other guards outside the room. They don't ever seem to get bored, even though they just stand and stare at the corridor all the time. Kealan asks how Dervish is, then if I want to play a game of cards.

"Maybe later," I smile, "if you're still here."

"Where else would I be?" he chuckles wryly. Kealan's the only guard who looks unsuited to his job. I'm not sure why he got into this military business. I think he'd be much happier just being a medic. Maybe the army trained him and he has to serve a number of years with them before moving on.

I stroll through the various levels and wards of the hospital. I know the building well by this stage and many of the doctors and nurses have got to know me. They give me treats and make small talk if they're not busy. It's been quiet here since I came and some of the staff consider me a good luck omen. I'm even allowed into areas which would normally be off-limits, like the maternity ward on the second floor. It's my favourite part of the hospital. I love watching cute, wrinkled babies, gazing into their innocent eyes, most the colour of a clear blue sky.

But I head in a different direction on this foray, winding my way up to the roof. I've been stuck inside all day. I need fresh air. I'm also hoping to see a helicopter. It's exciting when one lands. I'd love to go up in one, but I suspect even good luck omens don't get to hitch rides in hospital helicopters.

It's evening. An overcast, patchy sky. I spend a long time watching the sun vanish and reappear from behind drifting clouds. My old teacher, Banba, thought you could read signs of the future in the movements of clouds, but I've never been able to predict anything from them. Still, when I've nothing else to do, I like to try.

"Where are you, Beranabus?" I whisper, hoping the clouds will answer. "How long will it take you to come?"

I'm not sure what we'll do if he doesn't find us soon. We can't wait forever. Where will we go when Dervish recovers or dies? Back to Carcery Vale? To stay at Sharmila's home or with other members of the Disciples? Into the universe of the Demonata to search for Beranabus?

I feel guilty when I think about Shark and Meera, and the mission I sent them on. It was necessary to summon

Beranabus. If the attack happened because I'm part of the Kah-Gash, he needs to know. But how likely is that? Maybe I secretly sent them to get him because I was missing my old friend.

A breeze blows in from behind me, tickling the hairs on the back of my neck. I shiver with delight and snuggle into the wind as if it was a giant cushion. Then I pause. This is a warm breeze, not like the cold blasts which whipped across the roof the other times I've been up here. And it's coming from a different direction. It feels unnatural.

I focus, senses locking on the currents of air, mentally tracing the breeze back to its origins. I wasn't good at this in the past, but my talent has blossomed since I died. My mind bounds off the roof like a magical hound and hurtles towards the ground. As it draws level with the first floor, it veers through a broken window, one that's been shattered from the inside out.

It comes to a halt in the centre of the room and my eyes snap open. There's a mage, a man of weak magic, but strong, evil intent. And in front of him stands a panel of light — a window into the universe of the Demonata. As I probe it with mental tendrils, I sense figures hurtling through. As much as I wish otherwise, it's not Beranabus or his Disciples. I'm a long way removed, but even from up here I'm able to tell that the creatures setting foot on our world aren't human. They're demons!

→I'm on the walkie-talkie before I take my first step. "Sharmila! Answer! It's an emergency! Over."

She replies as I'm taking my third step. "What is happening? Over."

"Demons. On the first floor. Move Dervish."

"Damn!"

Racing down the stairs, I feel the air fill with magic, flooding up through the building from the open window. That's good for me – more power to tap into – but it's also good for the Demonata. I try keeping track of the window, to get an idea of how many demons we'll have to deal with, but it's hard when I'm running. I'd have to stop and concentrate, but there's no time for that.

"Hey," a nurse shouts as I hit the fifth floor and race towards the elevator shaft, where I spot Sharmila, the four guards and Dervish. "No running!"

I don't stop. I reach Sharmila a few seconds later. The elevator has arrived. The guards are rolling Dervish in on a hospital trolley. I'm relieved Kealan was able to unhook Dervish from his banks of machines so quickly.

"Where are they?" Sharmila asks.

"I'm not sure. They entered on the first floor, but I don't know—"

"How many?"

"Give me a moment." I step into the elevator after the guards and Dervish. I focus as the doors close… my senses seep down through the building, searching for demonic targets…

With a gasp I jam a hand between the doors just before they close. The panels slide apart automatically.

"What are you doing?" Sharmila snaps.

"They're in the shaft," I hiss. "Three of them. Climbing the cables."

"Out!" Sharmila barks at the guards. As they roll Dervish back into the corridor, the nurse who shouted at me hits the scene.

"Where are you going with that patient? You can't move him without a doctor's orders. I'm calling the—"

Sharmila waves a hand at her. The nurse's eyes flicker, then she turns and walks away.

"The stairs?" Sharmila asks.

"More of them there. Eight or nine."

Her face pales. "Can we fight them?"

"If we have to. They're not strong. But there are so many of them…"

Balazs – the smallest of the guards – is on his walkie-talkie, talking softly but quickly. He finishes and clips it to his belt. "The roof," he says calmly. "A helicopter will be with us in five minutes."

"Bec?" Sharmila asks. "The elevator or stairs?"

I concentrate. The demons in the shaft are making fast progress. Those on the stairs are moving slower, pausing to pick off a few unfortunate nurses who get in their way.

"The stairs," I decide, hurrying ahead of the guards to open the door.

Gabor and Bence – the other two guards – push the trolley to the foot of the stairs, then each takes an end. They raise the wheels off the floor and start up the steps. Kealan moves alongside them, monitoring Dervish.

"You two go ahead," Balazs says to Sharmila and me, taking out a pair of pistols. "I'll hold off the demons."

"You cannot kill them with bullets," Sharmila says.

"I know," Balazs says softly. "But I can slow them down."

Sharmila starts to object, then nods curtly and flees up the stairs, no longer limping, using magic to move freely and swiftly.

"Do you want me to stay and help?" I ask Balazs.

"No," he says. "You'll serve more good if you stay with Dervish."

"You'll die," I note sadly.

"Dying's my job." He grins bleakly. "Now get the hell out of here and let me do what I'm trained for."

I stand on my toes and give him a quick hug. I get flashes of his mother's face. She was mauled by a demon. It took her several hours to die. A slow, painful death. Balazs is determined not to suffer as she did.

Releasing the doomed guard, I chase after the others, feeling the demons close on us from beneath.

* * *

→We've just passed the seventh floor, heading for the exit to the roof, when the gunfire starts. We pause, even the guards who are used to situations like this. Then we press on. By the time we crash through the doors at the top of the stairs, the hail of bullets has stopped.

Bence and Gabor check their watches. Their frantic eyes reveal how desperate the situation is. Unholstering their weapons, they silently head down the stairs.

"Where is the helicopter coming from?" Sharmila asks as Kealan wheels Dervish towards the landing pad.

"Nearby," Kealan says. "We'd have kept it here, but there wasn't space. The hospital helicopters took priority."

"Nobody said anything to me about that," Sharmila huffs.

"We make our own plans," Kealan says. "We don't discuss them with civilians, even Disciples. No offence meant."

"None taken."

Guns blare on the staircase.

"How much longer?" I shout.

Kealan checks his watch. "A minute. Maybe two."

I dart back towards the stairs. "Bec!" Sharmila screams.

"Don't worry," I pant. "I'm not going to fight them."

I didn't absorb any of Beranabus's magic when we touched, but I learnt a lot of his spells. There are many I can't use – there's more to magic than knowing the right words – but some I can. Reaching the doors at the top of the stairs, I draw upon the ancient magician's years of experience and prepare a holding spell.

Bullets are still being fired on the stairs. "Gabor! Bence!" I yell. "Come back!"

There's no response. A few seconds later the guns stop. There's the sound of scurrying footsteps — but not human feet. Grimacing, I unleash the spell and block the doorway with a shield of magical energy.

The first demon appears. It has a square, bloodstained head. Dozens of eyes. Three mouths. A tiny body. It leaps at me, wild with bloodlust, but crashes back off the shield. It snaps at the web of energy, trying to tear it apart with its teeth, but the barrier holds.

I back away from the doors, focusing my power. This is the first time I've tried this spell and the effort involved is greater than I thought. By tapping into the magic in the air, I can hold the shield in place, but I won't be able to maintain it for long, especially not with demons snapping and clawing at it. But I don't need much time, just a minute. It should be enough.

I'm halfway to the landing pad when I hear the whirring sound of helicopter blades and spot the craft humming towards us. I feel a sense of triumph like a hard ball in my gut. In their own universe, some demons are able to fly. But flight is difficult here. Strong demons might manage short bursts, but the beasts who crossed aren't especially powerful. Once we're in the air, we'll be safe.

I don't let thoughts of escape make me careless. I stay focused on the shield. I'm tiring fast — there's so little magic in this world. I can hold it for another couple of minutes maybe, but that should be all the time we...

Something powerful slips through the window on the first floor. Not a demon, but not human either. A beast far more dangerous than any of the others. It snaps questions at the mage who's been holding the window open, then howls at the top of its voice. The cry echoes up the stairs and corridors. The demons struggling with the shield pause to screech in response.

The new, mysterious monster throws itself through the shattered glass window of the room, digs its claws into the wall and scurries upwards, scaling the building like a jet-propelled spider. I start to yell a warning to Sharmila, but before the words have left my lips the creature hauls itself over the edge of the roof and leers at us maliciously.

The beast has the shape of a woman, but her skin is a mass of blisters and sores. Pus oozes from dozens of cracks and holes in her jellyish flesh. Her mouth is a ragged red slit, her eyes two green thimbles in a putrid, yellow mockery of a face. A few scraps of hair jut out of her head. She wears no clothes — the touch of any material would be agony on flesh so pustulent and tender.

The creature points at the helicopter, which has almost completed its descent, and barks a phrase of magic. The blades stutter, then stop. The helicopter shakes wildly, spins around a few times, then plummets several metres shy of the building. It makes a sharp, screaming sound as it drops. Then it hits the ground and there's an explosion, louder and more brutal than any movie bang ever prepared me for. Glass explodes in all the nearby windows. A giant ball of flame belches up into the sky, turning the evening red. Sharmila and Kealan are thrown to the floor and the unconscious Dervish slides off his trolley.

Only the woman and I remain standing, using magic to shelter ourselves from the force of the explosion. I sense the shield give way behind me and demons spill on to the roof. But I don't care about them now. I have a more dangerous foe to contend with.

The most frightening, bewildering thing is, I *know* her. It's impossible – I saw her die – but I'm sure I'm right. Her voice when she cast the spell was familiar and, misshapen as she is, if I squint hard, I can make out the lines of her original face. I saw and heard her in the cave the night when I returned to life. Even if I hadn't, I'd know her from Beranabus's memories. She was his assistant once — Nadia Moore. But now she serves a different master, our old foe Lord Loss. And she calls herself…

"Juni Swan," the semi-human monster gurgles, bowing with cynical politeness. Her lips move into a jagged line as she straightens — I think it's meant to be a smile. "Delighted to kill you."

She flicks a hand at me and the ground at my feet bellows upwards in a pillar of molten, burning tar.

UP ON THE ROOF

→Instead of trying to fight the black, scorching geyser, I ride it upwards, using the force of the blast to propel myself high off the roof and clear of the sizzling liquid. My lower legs are spattered and the tar burns through my flesh, but those are minor wounds. I can heal them easily once I've dealt with the more pressing dangers.

I land in a crouch, using magic to soften the blow. I don't take my eyes off the mutated Juni Swan. She's watching me with a wicked, twisted smirk. Her eyes blaze with a mad hatred. I don't know how she returned to life — it shouldn't be possible — but she hasn't come back cleanly. She's been reduced to a staggering, seeping carcass of cancerous cells. Her body looks like it's been eating away at itself for the past six months. The pain of holding it together and clinging to her frail grasp on life must be unendurable. I'm not surprised she's lost her grip on sanity.

"Little Bec," she sneers, her words coming thick and syrupy through the wasted vocal cords of her throat. "My master killed you once, but you cheated death, like me. I wonder if you'll come back again?"

"Who is she?" Sharmila screams, back on her feet, helping Kealan up.

"Juni Swan!" I shout.

"Juni…? You mean *Nadia*?" Sharmila gasps, staring with horror at this mockery of a human form.

"Not any more." Juni gives a sick chuckle, taking a few tottering steps towards us. Fleshy smears from her feet stick to the rooftop. She winces every time she moves. Her body is fragile, but her power is great. She's stronger than she was in the cave.

Kealan fires three times at Juni. The bullets stop mid-air, centimetres from her scarred, glutinous face. "Pretty little butterflies," she murmurs, turning two of the bullets into silvery, swollen insects — but these butterflies have oversized mouths and sharp teeth. She flicks a finger at them and they fly back to their source. I try to deflect them, but I'm too slow. They latch on to Kealan's eyes and dig in. He screams and collapses, blind within seconds. The butterflies continue chewing through to his brain.

I want to help Kealan, but I dare not turn my gaze away from Juni, even for an instant. She makes the third bullet rotate a few times, then sends it shooting at the middle of Sharmila's forehead. The old Indian lady redirects it with a short flick of her wrist and the bullet buries itself in the roof.

The demons from the staircase have split to surround Sharmila and me. There are six around me, five around Sharmila. The twelfth – the square-headed demon – bounds over to Kealan and finishes off the unfortunate guard.

"You should have stayed dead," Juni says, closing on me. The demons are keen to attack, but they're holding back, wary of Juni Swan. They must be under orders not to strike before she does.

"How's my broken-hearted boyfriend?" Juni asks, turning her head to study Dervish. She gasps with pain, a chunk of her neck ripping loose. Grimacing, she pushes the fleshy fillet back into place and uses magic to seal it. Part of me feels sorry for her. This is a terrible way for anyone to exist.

"Leave Dervish alone," Sharmila growls.

"Or what?" Juni jeers.

Sharmila tenses her legs, then leaps over the demons around her. She lands between Juni and Dervish, grabs the trolley, jerks off a side bar and hurls it at Juni, jagged end first. The tip strikes Juni's gooey face and drives through the rotting flesh and bone. She shrieks, her head snapping back.

Sharmila rips another bar loose to use against the demons who are scurrying after her. She thinks she killed Juni but she's wrong. As Sharmila turns, Juni yanks out the bar. Bits of yellowy-pink flesh trickle from the hole it leaves behind.

"You'll have to do better than that," Juni giggles, launching the bar at Sharmila. It hits her right shoulder, lifts her off her feet and sends her sailing across the roof. She smashes into one of the staircase doors. The bar thrusts through her flesh and deep into the wood, pinning her to the door. She screams in agony, blood pouring from her shoulder and mouth. She tries to wriggle free, but can't, pinned in place like a captured moth.

I'm truly scared now. It took a lot of power to throw a steel bar that hard. I don't have anywhere near that kind of strength, not in this world. In a one-on-one battle with Juni Swan, I won't stand a chance.

Juni fixes her insane, bloodshot eyes on me again. There's a tiny insect in the corner of one socket, chewing at the rotting flesh of her lower eyelid. "It's a pity," she mutters. "I hoped Grubbs would be here. I wanted to kill him at the same time as Dervish."

"He'll be here soon," I lie, trying to keep the tremble out of my voice. "Kernel too. And Beranabus." Her expression twitches when I mention the name of her old master. "You'd better get out of here before—"

"Billy Spleen was a bad liar," she cuts me off, "but you're worse. I wonder if you'll squeal like he did when I kill you?"

"Bill-E didn't squeal. I know. I was there."

"So you were. I forgot."

A crab-shaped demon with a cat's face jabbers something and shuffles towards me.

"Not yet," Juni snarls. "I want to torture her first."

The crab snaps at her and she scowls. "I don't care what he said. I…" A look of disgust crosses her face. "No. You're right. We'll kill them and get out of here. But not before we've had some sport." She waves at Sharmila. "The Disciple is yours, along with the humans below. Leave the girl and Dervish to me."

The demons peel away. Three of them – the fastest – converge on Sharmila and set to work on her legs, gobbling the flesh of her feet and shins, pausing only to dance diabolically to the rhythm of her tormented screams. The square-headed demon is still feasting on the remains of Kealan. The rest barrel down the stairs, back into the bowels of the hospital.

Juni smiles horribly. "Alone at last," she wheezes.

I say nothing, backing away slowly, trying to think of a way out of this. Down the wall and through the window on the first floor? But Lord Loss is probably waiting on the other side. I'm surprised he didn't cross with Juni. Maybe he wasn't sure who he'd find and didn't like the prospect of a run-in with Beranabus.

"I won't kill you immediately," Juni says, edging after me, leaving a trail of slime-like, bubbling flesh, blood and pus behind. "I'll keep you alive a while, like Sharmila." She points at the wailing woman. The monsters have stripped the flesh from her bones beneath the knees and are slowly moving up her thighs. Sharmila should have fainted by now. They must be keeping her conscious with magic.

"I'll kill you," I sob.

"I think not," she chuckles. "You're the one who'll perish tonight. But I'll kill Dervish first. I'll wake him and make sure he knows what's happening. Can't let him sleep through his death. I'll bring him round, no matter what shape his brain is in. Slaughter him nice and gruesomely. Then finish you off."

The square-headed demon gets through with Kealan and heads down the stairs to find more pickings below. I set my gaze on it, bark a quick spell and send it flying at Juni's head. She deflects it upwards. It squeals as it shoots into the air.

"You'll have to do better than that, little—"

I yank my walkie-talkie out and toss it at the demon. When it hits, I make it explode. The demon explodes too and its blood rains down on Juni. Before it splatters, I transform it into acid. It hits with a burning hiss. Juni shrieks and tries to brush away the acidic blood. A drop splashes over her left eye and it sizzles like an egg frying in a pan, washing the insect loose. She howls with rage, hate and pain.

I race towards the staircase. I'll grab Sharmila if I can and flee. A window between universes can't last more than a few minutes, even with a mage working to keep it open. If I can evade capture for that long, Juni and the demons will have to return to their own—

The door next to Sharmila tears free of its hinges and smashes into me, knocking me down. I saw it coming at the last second and erected a partial shield, otherwise I'd be dead. But it cracks a few ribs and bones, and almost punctures my lungs.

As I struggle to my feet, the door rises into the air, hovers a moment, then explodes in a hail of splinters. Again I manage to construct a weak barrier around me, which stops most of the splinters penetrating. But dozens hit home and pierce me, a few just missing my eyes, a long, thick shard almost staking me through the heart like a vampire.

"Look at the pitiful hedgehog," Juni gurgles as I writhe on the roof, trying to make the splinters pop out of my flesh. She's cleansed herself of the acidic blood, looking no worse than she did before. "All pink, bloody and spiky. I'm going to slice your stomach open and keep you alive while I fish your guts out. How do you like the thought of feeding on your own intestines before—"

A ball of crackling energy strikes Juni hard. She shrieks with shock as she's blown through the air, coming to a stunned stop a metre from the edge of the roof. As she staggers to her feet, she looks for her assailant. I look too and find him standing near the trolley, leaning on it for support, exhausted and the colour of death, but fired up for action — *Dervish!*

"Leave my girl alone, you crazy bitch," he growls, unleashing another bolt of energy. This one hits Juni in her distorted chest, blasts her off the top of the building, and she yowls like a cat on fire as she drops.

KIDS' STUFF

→Dervish takes out two of the demons feasting on Sharmila, using magic to pop their brains like grapes. They're dead before they hit the floor. The third glances up, sees that Dervish has beaten off Juni and disappears down the stairs.

Dervish limps across the roof. I'm closer and faster, so I get to Sharmila before he does. She's slumped unconscious. I leave her that way and pour magic into her legs to stop the worst of the pain and cauterise the open wounds. The demons have stripped her to scraps below her thighs. Most of the bones are intact, but I can't restore the flesh around them.

"Will she live?" Dervish barks, hobbling close to inspect the damage.

"Maybe. But I can't do much with the legs. She'll lose them."

He sighs, eyes drifting, then snaps back into focus. "Where are we? What's happening? Be quick."

"You had a heart attack. We're on the roof of a

hospital. You've been in a coma for four days. Demons are attacking. Juni Swan was leading them."

"I thought I killed her in the cave," he growls.

"You did. She came back."

"How?"

"I don't know." I gulp. "You didn't finish her off this time either. I can sense her. She's wounded but alive."

"Is she returning for more?" he asks eagerly, fingers twitching, for a moment looking half as crazy as Juni did.

"No," I answer, tracking her mentally as she slips through the window on the first floor. "You must have hurt her. She's gone back to the demon universe."

"Damn." He stares around, eyes going vague. He looks like he's about to collapse. I step forward to support him but he comes alert again and waves me away. "We're exposed. We have to get out of here."

"There are at least nine demons downstairs," I tell him. "We could create a barrier, block their route to the roof…"

"What if more cross and climb the walls?" he grunts. "No, we have to move." He takes hold of the bar pinning Sharmila to the door. "Can you make sure she doesn't feel this?"

"I'll do my best." Once I'm focused, I nod and he pulls sharply. The bar rips out of the wood and Sharmila's flesh. She moans softly, but I use magic to numb the pain and she falls silent again. Dervish slides around and takes Sharmila on his back, holding her arms crossed around his neck.

"Will you be able to carry her?" I ask. He's sweating and trembling.

"Only one way to find out," he mutters and staggers down the first of the stairs, back into the demon-infested building.

→We make our way down through the levels of the hospital. The air throbs with the screams and moans of people who were struck by glass shards when the windows shattered. We spot some of them as we descend. They're milling around helplessly, while nurses and doctors try to calm and help them.

I spy a demon on the fifth floor, chasing a man with a cast on his right leg. I look at Dervish, silently asking if we should help. He shakes his head. "We can't do anything," he wheezes. "I'm running out of strength. We need to save our energy — we might have to use it to break free."

"We weren't sure you were going to recover," I tell him as we stumble down the next set of steps.

"Maybe I wouldn't have. But they made the mistake of opening a window too close to me. The magic flooding through hit me like a wave and revived me."

"Magic brought you back to life?"

He nods. "And it's keeping me going. Which is fine. But when the window closes, I'm toast. That's why we have to get out of here. The demons will have to return to their own universe or perish when the window shuts, but there might be soldiers or werewolves waiting to move in."

We trudge on in silence, Dervish panting, struggling to support Sharmila. His legs are shaking badly. Even with all the magic in the air, he can't last very long. He might drop before we make the ground. If he does, I'll have to leave him. Sharmila too. I'm not a coward but it would be foolish to stay. In desperate times you have to act clinically. Dervish and Sharmila understand that and would only curse me if I let myself be slain for no good reason.

As we come to the second floor I spot a lizard-like demon slithering through the door from the stairs. I motion for Dervish to stop and we wait until the creature has passed. As we come abreast of the door, I glance through the circular window. There are two more demons with the lizard. One looks like an anteater, only it's bulkier and has several long snouts. The other is some sort of demonic insect with a heavy golden shell, the size of a large dog.

As I watch, they kill an elderly woman and a nurse, then claw open a door and slip into a ward out of sight. Dervish has moved on, but I remain where I am, a wretched feeling in my gut.

"Hurry," Dervish huffs. "We're nearly there."

"Dervish…" I say hesitantly.

"What?" he snaps.

"There are three demons."

"So?"

"They've gone into the maternity ward."

Dervish shuts his eyes and sighs. He looks more like a corpse than one of the living. I think he'd be happier if he was dead. I wait for him to say something, but he only stands silent and unresponsive.

"The babies," I whisper. "We can't let them slaughter babies."

"We should," Dervish croaks. "It's the first law of being a Disciple — if you don't stand a decent chance in a fight, *run*."

"I'm not a Disciple."

"I am." He pulls a weary face. "But to hell with it." He gently lays Sharmila down, stretches and groans, then steps up past me, pushes the door open and holds it like a doorman. "Ladies first."

→The ward rings with the sound of crying, but it's the natural noise of babies who have been abruptly awoken. I'm sure the mothers are terrified, but they're trying to control their fear so as not to alarm the little ones.

The half-dissolved bodies of two nurses line the corridor ahead of us. Fresh corpses. They must have tried to stop the demons. I pray we have more success.

Dervish is looking a bit better than he did on the upper floors. We're close to the window – the mage has managed to keep it open, curse him – so there's more magic in the air. He moves ahead of me, his legs no longer shaking quite so badly. His gown gapes at the back. I can see his bottom. That would make me smile any other time, but nothing strikes my funny bone at the moment.

We find the insect demon terrorising a young mother in a room on our left. She's no more than three or four years older than me. Another woman's with her. The pair are shielding the baby from the beast. It's snapping at them, relishing their fear, stretching out the terror.

"Hey, roach!" Dervish calls. The demon turns and Dervish fires an energy bolt at it. The demon shoots across the room and smashes into the wall. But it recovers quickly and propels itself at Dervish. He catches it and they roll to the floor, wrestling. "Go!" he shouts at me.

My instinct is to help him, but the other demons could slaughter several babies while we battle with this one. Better to advance. Even if I can't kill them, I can delay them and hope the window closes while we're fighting.

I let the women escape with the baby, then hurry down the corridor. I catch evidence of an attack in a room to my right — a small hand lying on the floor near the door, attached to nothing — but I don't stop to probe. Best not to look too closely at something like that.

The anteater demon staggers into the corridor ahead of me unexpectedly, erect on two legs, holding a squealing baby over its head. I see the child's mother frantically reaching for it through the doorway, but she's being held back by the other demon. She's too shocked to scream.

As one of the anteater's snouts attaches itself to the baby's face, I use magic to rip the infant away. It flies safely into my arms. A boy. I absorb his memories of birth as I set him down, then turn to face the demon.

The anteater's snarling. It barks a command and the lizard joins it. The mother rushes out of the room, darts past all three of us, snatches her baby and flees. I remain focused on the demons, waiting for them to make the first move.

The anteater rears back two of its snouts and spits twin tendrils of mucous at me. I deflect the missiles and they spatter the walls on either side, burning into them. One thing about demons — they love to spit acid.

The lizard scurries towards me, using its tail as a whip to accelerate. When it's a metre away, it gives an extra hard *thwack* with its tail and shoots up at me, jaws stretched wide to clamp around my throat.

I made my fingers hard while the lizard was advancing, transforming them into a makeshift blade, a trick I learnt from Beranabus. Now I duck and swipe at the lizard's stomach. But it realises my intention and sucks in. I open a shallow cut, but it's only a flesh wound.

The anteater is on me before I can react. It wraps two snouts around my chest, one around my neck, and lashes at my face with the others. The one around my neck is the worst. It digs in tight, cutting off my oxygen.

I drop to my knees, then spring into the air like a frog. I hammer hard into the ceiling, knocking chunks out of it and shaking up the anteater. Its snouts loosen and when we hit the floor again I jerk free and leap to my feet.

I create a small ball of fire and blow it up one of the anteater's snouts. When it hits the demon's head, an eye bursts. The anteater squeals and stumbles away. Before I can pursue it and finish it off, the lizard bites down on my hip and jabs its forked tongue deep into my flesh.

I shake the lizard off, but I feel poison in the wound. Deadly, fast-acting. If I don't deal with it immediately, I'll be dead within seconds.

I use magic to counteract the poison, expelling most of it from my system and sapping the sting from the rest. I'm successful but the healing spell is draining. There's not much fight left in me. The demons sense my weakness and move apart — the anteater's recovered from his nasal mishap — then advance, trapping me against a wall. I summon what's left of my power, but before I can unleash a spell against them...

A window of orange light opens a few metres away. The demons gawp at it. I prepare for the worst, expecting Lord Loss or Juni to emerge. This is the end. I'm going to die here, surrounded by demons and newborn babies. My only hope is that some of the young survive. If they do, I won't have entirely wasted my life.

A man steps through the window and my heart leaps.

"*Bran!*" I shout.

A grave-faced Beranabus winks at me, then glares at the quivering demons. "I bet you thought you'd make off with easy pickings," he growls. "You meant to harvest this crop of babies and gorge yourselves, aye?"

An anxious Grubbs steps through the window, followed by Kernel, who looks different somehow, and a cautious Shark and Meera.

"What do the pickings look like now?" Beranabus asks.

The demons turn and flee. Kernel, Shark and Meera set off after them.

"*Dervish?*" Grubbs snaps.

"Back there," I pant. "Hurry. He was fighting a demon. I don't know—"

Grubbs is gone before I finish.

Beranabus squats beside me. "Hello, little one," he says softly. Then he hugs me and I weep into his shoulder. I absorb more of his memories as I clutch him but I don't care about the theft. I'm just delighted that, despite all the odds, it looks like I'm going to end this evening of butchery alive.

THE SPLIT

→Back on the roof. The Disciples killed several demons and the mage who'd been helping them. A few of the beasts fled through the window before it closed. The rest died here, helpless without magic, choking to death on our clean, human air, then rotting like the disgusting, hellish globs that they are.

The patients and staff inside the hospital are safe, although not many remain. They're being evacuated. A huge operation, still under way. I watched it with Beranabus while we were waiting for the others to join us. I'm impressed by how swiftly the people of this time can move in an emergency, how selflessly they rise to the occasion and risk all to help.

Sharmila is lying close by, unconscious. Beranabus removed her thighbones and has been working on the tattered flesh, sealing off veins and arteries, mending nerve endings where he can, destroying others to lessen the pain that Sharmila will experience when she wakes.

Dervish is sitting nearby on the trolley, head bowed,

feebly stroking his beard, shivering from shock and the cold night air. His heart has held, but Beranabus had to help him climb the stairs, carrying him as Dervish had earlier carried Sharmila. Meera is sitting beside her dear friend, watching over him like a faithful hound.

Shark's by the staircase, ready to turn away anybody who ventures up this far. He enjoyed tackling the Demonata and ripping a few to pieces. He's delighted with his evening's work.

I'm bringing Beranabus, Grubbs and Kernel up to date, telling them about the werewolf attack, my gift of soaking up memories, what I sensed from the werewolf I touched, the assault at the hospital. Shark and Meera hadn't told them much — there wasn't time. It took them several weeks in the demon universe to find Beranabus. Thankfully they passed through zones where time moves faster than it does here.

"You're sure the Lambs masterminded the attack in Carcery Vale?" Grubbs asks. He's grown a few centimetres since I last saw him and towers above everybody. But he's lost some weight and doesn't look so healthy. His ginger hair has grown back – he was bald in the cave – but has been scorched bare in a few patches. There are dark bags under his eyes and an ugly yellowish sheen to his skin. He looks exhausted and distraught.

"I can't be certain," I admit. "We didn't see any

humans. Sharmila wanted to go after the Lambs once Dervish was safe, but we decided to wait until we'd discussed it with you. The werewolves *might* have been the work of some other group…"

"But they were definitely teenagers who'd been given to the Lambs?" Grubbs presses.

"Yes. At least the one I touched was. I don't know about the others."

"They must have been," he mutters. "I've never heard of anyone outside our family being inflicted with the wolfen curse. But why?" He glances at Dervish. "Have you been rubbing Prae Athim up the wrong way?"

"I haven't seen her since she paid us that visit before Slawter," Dervish answers. "I've got to say, I don't have much time for Prae, but this isn't her style. I could understand it if they were after something – you, for instance, to dissect you and try to find a cure for lycanthropy – but there was nothing in this for them. Those who set the werewolves loose wanted us dead. The Lambs don't go in for mindless, wholesale slaughter."

"But if not the Lambs, who?" Kernel asks. The bald, chocolate-skinned teenager was blind when I last saw him, his sockets picked clean by demonic maggots. He's restored his eyes in the Demonata universe, but his new globes don't look natural. They're the same blue colour as before, but brighter, sharper, with tiny, flickering shadows moving constantly across the surface.

"I think Lord Loss was behind the attacks," I answer Kernel's question. "Maybe he realised I was part of the Kah-Gash and wanted to eliminate the threat I pose, or perhaps he just wanted to kill Dervish and me for revenge. The attack tonight by Juni Swan makes me surer than ever that he sent the werewolves. It can't be coincidence."

"Juni Swan," Beranabus mutters guiltily. "I'd never have thought poor Nadia could turn into such a hideous creature. I don't know how she survived. Your spirit flourished after death, but you're part of the Kah-Gash. Juni isn't. Lord Loss must have separated her soul from her body some way, just before her death. That's why he took her corpse when he fled. But I don't understand how he did it."

He broods in silence, then curses. "It doesn't matter. We can worry about her later. You're right — Lord Loss sent the werewolves. I cast spells on Carcery Vale to prevent crossings, except for in the secret cellar, where any demon who did cross would be confined. Even if he found a way around those spells, he would have been afraid to risk a direct confrontation. If he opened a window, the air would have been saturated with magic. You and Dervish could have tapped into that. You were powerful in the cave, stronger than Lord Loss in some ways. He probably thought humans and werewolves stood a better chance of killing you. But that doesn't explain why the Lambs agreed to help him. Or, if they weren't Lambs, how they got their hands on the werewolves."

"Maybe he struck a deal with them," Dervish says. "Promised them the cure for lycanthropy if they helped him murder Bec and me."

"Would they agree to such a deal?" Beranabus asks.

"Possibly."

"Prae Athim's daughter turned into a werewolf," Grubbs says softly. "She's still alive. A person will go to all manner of crazy lengths when family's involved." He winks at Dervish.

"An intriguing mystery," Beranabus snorts. "But we can't waste any more time on it. We have more important matters to deal with, not least the good health of Dervish and Miss Mukherji — they'll both be dead soon if we don't take them to the demon universe. Open a window, Kernel."

Kernel starts moving his hands, manipulating patches of light which only he can see. That's his great gift — he can open a window in minutes instead of hours or days, to any section of the demon universe. In the past he couldn't work his magic on this world, but he seems to have developed since I last saw him.

"I'm not going," Dervish says.

"You can't stay here," Beranabus retorts.

"I have to. They attacked me… my home… my friends. I can't let that pass. I have to pursue them. Find out why. Extract revenge."

"Later."

"No," Dervish insists. "Now." He gets off the trolley and weaves to his feet. Meera steadies him. He smiles at her, then glares at Beranabus.

"It would help if we knew," Meera says in support of her friend. "The attack on Dervish and Bec might have been a trial run. The werewolves could be set loose on other Disciples."

"That's not my problem," Beranabus sniffs.

"There's been a huge increase in crossings," Meera says. "We've seen five or six times the usual activity in recent months. The Disciples are stretched thinly, struggling to cope. If several were picked off by werewolves and assassins, thousands of innocents would die."

"It might be related," Kernel says, pausing.

"Related to what?" I ask but Beranabus waves my query away. He's frowning.

"This could be part of the Shadow's plan," Kernel presses. "It could be trying to create scores of windows so that its army of demons can break through at once. We'll need the Disciples if that's the case — we can't be everywhere at the same time to stop them all."

"Maybe," Beranabus says grudgingly. "But that doesn't

alter the fact that Dervish will last about five minutes if we leave him here."

"I'll be fine," Dervish growls.

"No," Beranabus says. "Your heart is finished. You'll die within days. That's not a guess," he adds as Dervish starts to argue. "And you wouldn't be able to do much during that time, apart from wheeze and clutch your chest a lot."

Dervish stares at the magician, jaw trembling. "It's really that bad?"

Beranabus nods soberly. "In the universe of magic, you might survive. Here, you're a dead man walking."

"Then get him there quick," Grubbs says. "I'll stay."

"Not you too," Beranabus groans. "What did I do to deserve as stubborn and reckless a pair as you?"

"It makes sense," Grubbs says, ignoring the cutting comment. "If the attacks were Lord Loss trying to get even, they're irrelevant. But if they're related to the Shadow, we need to know. I can confront the Lambs, find out if they're mixed up with the demon master, stop them if they are."

"Is the Shadow the creature we saw in the cave?" I ask, recalling the dark beast who even Lord Loss seemed to be working for.

"Aye," Beranabus says. "We haven't learnt much about it, except that it's put together an army of demons and is working hard to launch them across to our world." He studies Grubbs, frowning as he considers the teenager's proposal. "You'd operate alone?"

"I'd need help," Grubbs says. "Shark and Meera."

"I want to stay with Dervish," Meera says.

"He'll be fine," Grubbs overrules her. "He has Beranabus and Bec to look after him. Unless you want to leave Bec with me?" He raises an eyebrow.

"No," Beranabus mumbles. "If you're staying, I'll take her to replace you."

"Then go," Grubbs says. "Chase the truth on your side. I'll do the same here. If I discover no link between Lord Loss and the Lambs, I'll return. If they *are* working for him, I'll cull the whole bloody lot."

Kernel grunts and a green window opens. "Time to decide," he tells Beranabus.

"Very well," the magician snaps. "But listen to Shark and Meera, heed their advice and contact me before you go running up against the likes of Lord Loss or the Shadow." He carefully picks up Sharmila and steps through the window with her. "Follow me, Bec."

I look around at the others, dazed by the speed with which things have been decided. Dervish is hugging Grubbs, squeezing him tightly, the way I wish he would have squeezed me all these long months.

"Are you OK with this?" Meera asks. "You don't want to stay?"

"I'll do what I must," I sigh.

"Take care of Dervish," Meera whispers.

"I will," I laugh, wishing I could remain with Meera instead of Dervish.

"Be wary," she croaks, dropping her voice even lower. "Beranabus has always been strongly driven, but he's almost insanely focused now. He says this Shadow he's been hunting is a massive threat to mankind and he's determined to defeat it at all costs. But he's old and fuzzy-headed. He makes mistakes. Don't let him lead you astray."

"I'll keep an eye on him," I promise.

Dervish and Grubbs complete their farewells and the elder Grady stumbles through the window, rubbing the flesh around his chest, fighting back tears.

"Sorry we couldn't have more of a chat," Grubbs says to me.

"Next time," I smile.

"Yeah," he grunts sceptically. I can tell he thinks there will never be a time for simple chat. We belong to the world of pitched battle and Grubbs believes we'll never escape it. I think he's right.

As Grubbs and Meera work their way across the roof to tell Shark about their new mission, I face Kernel Fleck. He's grinning at me sympathetically. "The world moves quickly when Beranabus is around," he says.

"What's it like through there?" I ask, nodding at the window.

"Bad." His grin slips. "The Shadow's promising the eradication of mankind and a new dawn of demon rule. Others have threatened that before, but it's convinced an army of demons — even powerful masters like Lord Loss — that it can make good on its vow. We could be looking at the end this time." Kernel puts one foot into the panel of green light bridging two universes and beckons half-heartedly. "Let's go."

I take one last look at the human world — the night is bright with fires from the crashed helicopter and police searchlights — then wearily follow Kernel into the den of all things demonic.

CHASING SHADOWS

→We're at an oasis in the middle of a desert. The trees are made out of bones, flaps of skin instead of leaves, and the well at the centre is filled with a dark, sulphurous liquid. The liquid's alive and can suck in and kill passers-by, but it only has a reach of two or three metres, so as long as we don't stray too close to it, we're safe.

The oasis was designed by a demon master a long time ago, based on something he'd seen on Earth. As much as demons hate humans and our world, they envy our forms and shapes. That's why many of them base their bodies on animals from our planet. They lack our imagination or the skills of Mother Nature.

We've been here for a week, although it's hard to judge the passage of time. There's one sun and moon above the oasis, like on Earth, but they never move. The sun shines for hours on end, holding its position in the sky, then abruptly dims to be replaced by the light of a three-quarters full moon.

I haven't had to eat or drink since I came, and I've

only slept twice, a couple of hours each time. The magic in the air is far thicker than it was on my world sixteen hundred years ago. I could perform amazing feats here, turn a mountain upside-down if I wanted. The trouble is, if I can do that much, so can the demons.

We haven't seen any of the Demonata yet. This is an abandoned region. Its master moved on or died, leaving only the skeletal trees and cannibalistic well. Individual demons wander through occasionally – some are picked off by the well – but incursions are rare. Beranabus has used it as a bolthole on several occasions.

Sharmila is still recovering, but we haven't been able to restore her lower legs. Magic works differently in each person. Kernel was able to replace his eyes when he lost them, but Sharmila can't grow new legs. You never know for sure what you can or can't do with your power until you test it.

Beranabus and I have used some of the bones and fleshy leaves from the trees to create artificial legs. We've attached them to Sharmila's thighs and she's spent the last couple of days adjusting, using magic to operate the limbs and keep her balance. She moves clumsily when she walks, and with great discomfort, but at least she's mobile. I don't know what will happen when she returns to the human world – the legs we've created won't work in a place without magic – but for now she's coping.

Dervish looks healthier too. I've taught him ways to direct magic into his heart, to strengthen and protect it. He should be fine as long as he stays here, but if he returns home the situation will rapidly change. His heart won't hold up long over there.

Dervish wove the material of his hospital dressing-gown in with scraps of flesh from the trees to create a costume. He's also given himself a full head of silver hair and stuck it up in six long, purple-tipped spikes. I was startled when I first saw it.

"I had spikes like this the last time I fought alongside Beranabus," he explained, blushing slightly. "I walked away alive then, so maybe they were good luck. We'll need all the luck we can muster when we fight again."

There's no doubt we'll have to fight, either the Shadow or its army. The first battles have already been waged. Before Meera and Shark tracked them down, Beranabus, Kernel and Grubbs were flitting from realm to realm, hunting demons and challenging them, trying to find out more about the mysterious Shadow.

We saw the Shadow the night Bill-E was killed. A huge, nebulous cloud of a monster, darker than any night, almost as black as the cave when I was sealed up there. Immensely powerful even by demonic standards.

Lord Loss said the creature would destroy humanity. The maudlin demon master craves human misery, feeding on it like a cat slurping milk. In my time he slyly helped me close a tunnel, to stop a demon invasion. He needs humans the way a fish needs water.

But he's afraid of the Shadow. He doesn't believe mankind can defeat this new threat. He sided with the creature, served as if he was an ordinary demon, not a powerful master. He did the Shadow's bidding, even though that might mean the end of the human suffering he cherishes.

Lord Loss's fear of the Shadow fills Beranabus with unease. He believes the war between humanity and the Demonata can't last forever. In the distant past, the powerful Old Creatures ruled the Earth and demons couldn't cross. By my time their power had waned. That led to the current war between humans and demons. Beranabus thinks we must find a way to block their passage between universes or they'll wipe us out completely.

The Kah-Gash has been Beranabus's only real hope. According to the ancient legends, the weapon can destroy a universe — ours or the Demonata's. He'd love to do that. It doesn't bother him that he'd be eradicating an entire life form. He sees this as a blood-drenched fight to the finish. The universes are colliding and only the victors will survive.

Beranabus has the Kah-Gash now — in the shape of Grubbs, Kernel and me — but he doesn't trust it. The weapon has a will of its own. It worked through us when the world was last threatened by a demon breakthrough but it's been silent since. We don't know what its plans or desires are.

Beranabus hoped to experiment, unlock the Kah-Gash's secrets, find out how to direct its great power. But so far he hasn't learnt anything new.

Unwilling to unleash the Kah-Gash, Beranabus instead hunted for the shadowy monster we'd glimpsed in the cave. Having no name for it, he dubbed it the Shadow. The more he chased it, the more apt that name became.

Beranabus has interrogated many demons who know about the Shadow, but not one knows its real name. It's rumoured to be more powerful than any other demon. They say it's been working in secrecy for hundreds of years. That it recently made itself known to a number of demon masters, recruiting them to help it achieve its ultimate aim — the removal of the human stain.

That's how demons see us, as a stain on the universes. They were here long before us and consider themselves superior. They hated the Old Creatures but respected them. They have nothing but contempt for our weak, mortal kind.

The Shadow has promised to kill every human and make the Demonata more powerful than ever. A few demons told Beranabus that it had even promised a return to the original state of the universes and the elimination of death, but we're not sure what that means. The demons weren't sure either.

Beranabus hasn't dared go after any of the masters. They're too powerful. He thinks the creature has made its base in Lord Loss's realm, but he dares not set foot there. And Kernel – who can usually find anything in either universe – isn't able to search for the beast since he doesn't know the thing's name and didn't see it in the cave, being blind at the time. Beranabus has tried to magically recreate a picture of the Shadow, but it always comes up blurred and indistinct.

We spent the first couple of days here arguing about what to do next. While I worked tirelessly on Sharmila's legs – and helped her adjust to the shock when she regained consciousness – Dervish pressed Beranabus to focus on the werewolf and demon attacks.

"You've been chasing this Shadow for months without result," he argued. "This is something concrete, a puzzle we can solve. Better to direct our energies at a problem we can crack than waste them on an enigma."

"But all else is irrelevant," Beranabus bellowed. "The Shadow is the greatest threat humanity has ever faced. We have to pursue it relentlessly, down as many blind alleys as it takes, until we find a demon who knows its name, where it comes from, how powerful it is. The knowledge is out there. We just have to find it. But we can't do that if we squander our time on a bunch of hairy Grady miscreants!"

Dervish countered by insisting the attacks were linked to the Shadow. We know Lord Loss is working for him, and that the revived Juni Swan works for Lord Loss.

"Maybe Lord Loss and Juni just want to kill us before the world is ruined," he said. "But they might be planning to use the werewolves to target the Disciples, kill as many as they can and clear the way for crossings."

Kernel supported Dervish. "We can't go after Lord Loss directly — he's too powerful," he said. "But we can target Juni. Lord Loss didn't show himself at the hospital but Juni was acting on his behalf. She might have been part of the group in Carcery Vale too. If more assaults on the Disciples are planned, she'll possibly act as the go-between again, conveying Lord Loss's orders to their allies. If we can trap her, we can find out what she knows about the Shadow."

Beranabus was swayed by that and told Kernel to devote himself to tracking her movements. I think he's keen to get his hands on Juni for personal reasons. She betrayed him. But it's not just revenge he's interested in. He also wants to know how she came back.

We don't understand how my soul remained trapped in the cave when I died, or how I returned to life. That's never happened before. Ghosts exist, but they're mere after-images of people. We don't know where a person's soul goes when they die, if there's a heavenly realm, if they get reborn or if they simply cease to exist. But they always move on. Never, in all of history, has a person's soul survived death and returned to life. Until me. And now Juni.

Beranabus believes I survived because I'm part of the Kah-Gash. The mystical weapon turned back time, so it could feasibly cheat death too. But Juni isn't a piece of the Kah-Gash. She shouldn't have been able to survive the destruction of her body. Her return troubles Beranabus deeply. He suspects it's linked to the rise of the Shadow. If the new demon leader has the power to restore life, maybe it shares other powers in common with the Kah-Gash. Beranabus wants — *needs* — to know.

So Kernel has been focusing on Juni and Lord Loss for the last few days. He's developed in many ways since the three of us worked in league as the Kah-Gash. He can do more than open windows now. He can search for several people at the same time, and track their movements — he knows when they switch from one realm or universe to the other.

Juni is currently in Lord Loss's kingdom, with her master. But as soon as she moves, Kernel will know and we'll blaze into action.

→I've spent a lot of time with Beranabus. He's changed

so much over the centuries, made himself hard and uncaring, believing he had to be like a demon in order to fight the Demonata. It helped that he is half-demon. There's a monster within him, always active, struggling to rise to the surface. Beranabus has to fight it constantly to maintain control, but through those battles he's learnt more about demons and their ways than he ever could have otherwise.

One of his greatest fears is that he'll go insane and the demon within him will take over. It would be the ultimate irony — the man who spent all his life battling to save humans from the Demonata turns into one of them and goes on a massive killing spree.

Beranabus can discuss such fears with me because I already know about them. I absorbed his secrets along with his memories, so he can't hide them from me. I know almost as much about the ancient magician as he does.

"Sometimes I wonder if my life's been worthwhile," he muttered last night when we were apart from the others. "I've gone without pleasure or company for most of my years. If we lose and the Demonata kill us all, there won't have been a point. Maybe I should have settled, married, had children, lived a normal life. It might not have made any difference in the end."

I tried to make him see that millions of people owe their lives to him, that the Demonata would have taken over our world many centuries before this if not for his stubborn resistance. But he's fallen into a dark state of mind. I think partly it's because of my return. I've made him aware of all that he's missed out on. If he'd allowed himself to be more human, he'd have had friends and family, and perhaps been much happier.

I'm sitting beneath the shade of a bony tree, trying to think of a way to ease Beranabus's troubled mind. Someone coughs close by, disturbing me. I open my eyes and find Dervish standing there. "Mind if I sit down?"

I nudge over. When he's sitting, he smiles awkwardly. We haven't said much to each other since he recovered. I think he's embarrassed — we'd had that big conversation prior to the attacks, but never had a chance to wrap it up.

"How are you getting on?" he asks.

"Not too bad."

"It's pretty boring here, huh?"

I shrug. "I'd rather this to the excitement of fighting demons."

He strokes one of his newly grown spikes. "What do you think of the hair?"

"Some of the warriors in my time styled their hair like that," I tell him.

"Yeah?" He looks proud.

"But they were all a lot younger than you."

He pulls a face. "I started going bald early, so I had no

choice other than adapt. But I never liked looking like the crown of an egg."

"Baldness suits old men."

"I'm not..." he starts to protest, then sighs. "No, you're right, I *am* old. It happened while I wasn't looking. Old, bald, dodgy heart, ignorant."

"Ignorant?" I echo.

"The way I treated you," he says softly. "I was an ignorant old man. If Billy or Grubbs had seen me acting that way, they'd have kicked me hard and told me to stop being an idiot."

"You were upset," I excuse him. "People do strange things when they lose a loved one."

"I should have known better," he grunts. "I would have been more sensitive a few years ago, but you don't see things so clearly when you let yourself become a grumpy old fogey. I used to criticise Ma and Pa Spleen – Billy's grandparents – for being cranky and small-minded. But I was turning into a carbon copy of them." He shudders.

"Bill-E loved his grandparents regardless of their flaws," I say. "He would have gone on loving and forgiving you too, no matter what."

"How about you?" Dervish asks.

I frown uncomfortably. I should say something diplomatic, but I was reared to speak my mind. "I don't love you. I hardly even know you."

"I didn't mean that," Dervish says quickly. "I meant, can you forgive me? Can we be friends? Or will I always be the ogre who made you tell him stories about a dead boy for months on end?"

"You'll always be an ogre," I say seriously, then laugh at his expression. "I'm joking. Of course we can be friends."

"We can start over?" he says eagerly. "Get to know each other properly?"

I nod and he sticks out a hand to shake on the deal.

"You know about my gift?" I say hesitantly.

"Yes. But I don't care. You don't hold things back from friends."

I smile, then shyly shake his cool, wrinkled, welcome hand.

→Kernel is off by himself, doggedly monitoring Juni's position. The rest of us are duelling, practising our skills, learning. It's difficult to define your magical limits. Magic is a mysterious, ever-shifting force. You can test yourself in certain ways on Earth, but you never know how far you can stretch until circumstances compel you to improvise.

Sharmila told me that when Kernel first came to this universe, Beranabus threw him at a flesh-eating tree to establish his magical potential. When his life came under threat, Kernel reacted and he fought free. If he'd been of lesser potential, he'd have perished. That's a cruel way to test a person, but there's no easy alternative. Magic is part of a harsh universe. Those who wish to channel its power must accept that.

Beranabus sends twin balls of fire shooting at Dervish and me. I turn the ball aimed at me into an icy mist, but Dervish isn't as swift. He disperses the flames, but not before they singe his beard and redden his cheeks and lips.

"You're slow," Beranabus grunts while Dervish repairs the damage.

"So are you!" Sharmila shouts, hitting Beranabus with a burst of energy from behind. He shoots forward, yelling with surprise, and smashes into a tree, sending bones flying in all directions.

"That hurt," Beranabus complains, staggering to his feet and rubbing the small of his back. He bends to pick some splinters out of his bare feet. We've all got rid of our shoes — they hinder the flow of magic.

"Be thankful I was not aiming to kill," Sharmila says coolly. "We are all slower and weaker than before. It is the penalty of old age. No one can avoid it."

"I've done better than most for a millennium and a half," Beranabus growls.

"But time catches up with us all eventually, even you."

Beranabus twists slowly left, then right, working the

pain out of his back. "I suppose you're right," he grumbles. "I've known for a long time I'm not as quick or powerful as I once was."

He waves a hand at Sharmila and her artificial legs snap apart. She collapses with a yelp of shock and pain.

"But there's life in the old dog yet," Beranabus shouts triumphantly, before guiltily hurrying to Sharmila's side to fix the damage.

→Kernel has kept himself distant, sitting in the open with his legs crossed, tinkering with the lights that only he can see, keeping tabs on Juni. Beranabus told me his bald assistant finds it hard to focus these days. Since he got his new eyes he's been seeing patches of light which were invisible to him before. He can't control the new patches and they distract him. He's been trying to ignore them, but I often spot him scowling and cursing, waving an irritated hand at the air around him.

In the middle of another dry, lifeless afternoon, as the others are resting while I leap from tree to tree testing my powers of flight, Kernel uncrosses his legs and stands.

"She's moving," he says.

We're by his side in seconds. His bright blue eyes are alive with flickering spots of light. He looks nervous.

"Where did she go?" Beranabus asks.

"Earth."

"And Lord Loss?"

"He stayed in his own realm."

"Can you tell where exactly she is?" Dervish asks.

"No." He frowns. "I should be able to, but I can't place it."

"Is she close to Grubbs?" Dervish presses.

Kernel concentrates, then shakes his head.

"Well?" Sharmila asks Beranabus.

"Kernel and I will investigate. The rest of you stay here."

"Nuts to that," Dervish huffs.

"Don't forget about your heart," Beranabus says. "Or Sharmila's legs. You're a pair of wrecks on that world. Let us check the situation and report back. We won't engage her if we can avoid it."

"What about me?" I ask. "I can survive there."

"Aye, but I'm asking you to wait. Please. Until we know more about what we're walking into."

I don't like it, but I know Beranabus worries about me. Better to go along with his wishes, so he can operate free of any distractions.

Kernel opens a window within minutes. It's a white panel of light. I think I can smell the real world through it, but that's just my nose playing tricks. Without saying anything, Kernel steps through, Beranabus half a step behind him.

"We'll give them five minutes," Dervish rumbles. "If they're not back by then, we—"

Beranabus sticks his head through the window, catching us by surprise. "It's an area of magic," he says. "Sharmila and Dervish will be fine there. Come on."

He disappears again. We glance at each other uneasily, then file through one by one, back to the human universe, in search of the semi-human Juni Swan and a host of shadowy answers.

PART THREE
ALL ABOARD

snapshots of beranabus iii

Beranabus thought his world had ended when I died. He'd been developing while we were together, the disjointed fragments of his mind linking up, learning to think and reason as other humans did. My magic helped. Unknown to me, I smoothed out many of the creases inside his brain, opening channels which were blocked. Perhaps, deep down, I loved him as he loved me. I was certainly fond of the strange boy.

When the rocks closed, trapping me in the cave with Lord Loss and his familiars, Beranabus went wild with grief. He tried to carve through the wall, using small stones and his bare fingers. When that failed, he kept vigil for several months, drinking from the waterfall inside the cave, abandoning his post only to catch the occasional rabbit or fox.

He held long, garbled conversations with himself in the darkness. Time got confused inside his head and sometimes he thought he was in the Labyrinth and the Minotaur was hiding behind a stalagmite. He'd repeat my name over and over, along with his own — he managed to say "Beranabus" for the first time in the cave. He wept and howled, and sometimes tried to bash his head open on the rocks. Normally he stopped before damaging himself, but a few times he knocked himself unconscious, only to awake hours later, scalp bruised and bloody, his ears ringing.

He knew I was dead, the rock wouldn't open, that I'd never step out and throw my arms around him. But for a long time he clung to the belief that a miracle would return me to the world. Then, one day, without warning, he kissed the rock, climbed to the surface and staggered away, with no intention of ever coming back.

Beranabus retraced our steps, following the route we'd covered from the shoreline to the cave. He hoped, by doing so, to recall any small memories of me that he might have forgotten. His vague plan was to march west to the shore, then back inland to the crannog where I'd first met Drust, finishing up at my village. After that... he didn't know. Thinking ahead was a new experience for him and he found it hard to look very far into the future.

When he reached the shore and gazed down over the cliff where we'd sheltered, to the ever-angry sea below, his plan changed. Grief exploded within him and he saw only one way to escape it. He'd had enough of demons and humans, slaughter and love. He didn't know much about death, but the many corpses he'd seen over the centuries had all looked peaceful and unthinking. Maybe he wouldn't feel this terrible sense of loss if he put life and its complicated emotions behind him.

Beranabus smiled as he stepped off the cliff and fell. His thoughts were of me and the Minotaur. He knew nothing of the possibility of a life after death, so he had no hope of seeing us again. His only wish was that our faces were the last images in his thoughts when he died.

The water was colder than he expected and he shouted with alarm when he hit. But as he sank into the new subterranean world, he relaxed. The cold wasn't so bad after a while, and though he didn't like the way the salt water washed down his throat, he'd experienced more unpleasant sensations in the universe of the Demonata.

That should have been the end of him, an anonymous, pointless death as Theseus had predicted so many centuries before. But beings of ancient, mysterious magic dwelt nearby and they were watching. Known to humans as the Old Creatures, they'd once controlled the world. Now they were dying, or had moved on, and only a few were left.

Some of those lived in a cave beneath the cliff which Beranabus jumped off — they were the reason Drust had gone there in the first place. They sensed the boy's peculiar brand of magic and curiously probed the corridors of his mind. The Old Creatures took an interest in the drowning boy and instead of letting him drift out to sea and a welcome death, they drew him to the cave against his will. He washed up on the floor, where he reluctantly spat out water and instinctively gasped for air, even though he would rather have suffocated.

When Beranabus could speak, he roared at the pillars of light (the Old Creatures had no physical bodies). He knew they'd saved him and he hated them for it. He cursed gibberishly, trying to make them explain why they hadn't let him die.

"We Have Need Of You," the Old Creatures answered, the words forming inside the boy's brain. "You May Be Able To Help Us."

Beranabus roared at them again, and although he couldn't

express his feelings verbally, the Old Creatures knew what he wanted to say.

"Yes, She Is Dead, But Her Soul Has Not Departed This World. She Can Return To You." Beranabus squinted at the shifting lights. "If You Remain With Us, Let Us Teach And Direct You, And Serve As We Wish, You Will Meet Your Bec Again."

The promise captivated Beranabus and filled his heart with warmth and hope. It didn't cross his mind that the Old Creatures could be lying, and he never wondered what they might ask of him. They'd said he'd see his young love again — that was all that mattered. Putting dark thoughts and longings for death behind him, he presented himself to the formless Old Creatures and awaited their bidding, leaving them free to mould and do with him as they wished.

Beranabus could never remember much of his time with the Old Creatures, even though he spent more than a century in the cavern. They taught him to speak and reason, completing his evolution from confused child to intelligent young adult.

As his intellect developed, he came to believe that the Old Creatures had lied about my return. He didn't blame them — he knew it was the only way they could have calmed and controlled him. He accepted my death and moved on. He was older and wiser, tougher than he'd been as a child, and although he still loved and mourned me, he had other issues to focus on. He had demons to kill.

Beranabus hated the Demonata — they'd slaughtered his

beloved — and the Old Creatures encouraged this hatred. They showed him how to open windows to the demon universe and explained how he could channel magic to kill the beasts. They sent him on his first missions, directing him to specific spots, targeting vulnerable demons.

Beranabus never questioned their motives. He assumed that everyone on this world hated the demons as much as he did, even though the Old Creatures were not of the human realm and seemed to be under no threat. They were more powerful — in this universe at least — than the Demonata, so they had nothing to fear from them.

As he developed a taste for killing, Beranabus spent more and more time in the demon universe, using the cave of the Old Creatures as a base which he visited rarely, when he needed to sleep, treat his wounds and recover.

One night, after an especially long spell butchering demons, he returned to the cave and the Old Creatures were gone. He would have known it even if he was blind. The magic had faded from the air and it now felt like a cold, dead place.

In a panic, Beranabus scaled the cliff which he'd hurled himself off many decades before and searched frantically for the Old Creatures. He found traces of them in a place called Newgrange. Druids had claimed the celestial dome and worshipped and studied the stars from there. But it had been built by the Old Creatures, who used it as a navigational point when travelling between worlds.

One of the Old Creatures was waiting in the gloom of the dome for Beranabus. It took the form of a small ball of swirling light, less grand than any of the pillars had been in the cave. "It Is Time For Us To Go," the Old Creature said. "We Must Leave This Planet."

Beranabus went cold. Without the protective magic of the Old Creatures, the world would be at the mercy of the Demonata.

"You're abandoning us!" Beranabus cried angrily.

"We Are Leaving," the Old Creature agreed, "But We Have Left You In Our Place. You Must Guard This World Now."

"I can't protect humanity by myself," Beranabus exploded. "I can't be everywhere at once, stop every crossing or kill every demon who makes it through."

"No," the Old Creature said calmly, "But You Can Try."

"Why?" Beranabus groaned. "Why desert us now, when we need you most?"

"Our Time Has Passed," the Old Creature said. "You People Must Fend For Yourselves Or Perish. We Cannot Protect You Forever." As Beranabus started to argue, the Old Creature hushed him. "We Have One Last Thing To Tell You, One Final Mission To Send You On."

"I won't be your servant any longer," Beranabus snarled, tears of rage hot in his eyes.

"There Was A Force Once, A Weapon Of Sorts," the Old Creature said, ignoring his protest. "The Kah-Gash. It Shattered Into A Number Of Pieces Which Have Been Lost

Ever Since. You Must Search For Those Fragments And Reunite Them."

"I don't understand," Beranabus said, intrigued despite his bitter fury.

"The Kah-Gash Can Be Used To Destroy An Entire Universe. If The Demonata Find The Pieces And Assemble Them, They Can Annihilate This Universe And Remove Every Last Trace Of Mankind. But If You Find Them. . ."

". . . I can destroy their universe!" Beranabus exclaimed.

"Perhaps," the Old Creature said. And then it was gone, the ball of light shooting through the hole in the roof, streaking towards the stars, not even bidding Beranabus farewell.

Beranabus had a hundred questions he wanted answered, but there was no one to ask. He could feel the loss of the Old Creatures in the air. They'd left artefacts behind — lodestones charged with powerful Old magic — but their influence would fade with time, opening the way for more demon attacks.

He had to act quickly. The Old Creature hadn't said as much, but Beranabus assumed there were demons looking for the Kah-Gash and he would have to race against them to find the missing pieces. It occurred to him that the demons might have been searching for millions of years, but that didn't deter him. He was arrogant. He believed he would succeed where the Demonata had failed, find the weapon and deliver the ultimate blow.

Setting off through the countryside, he steeled himself for what was to come. He sensed it wouldn't be easy, that it might take centuries — or longer — to locate all the pieces. But he would triumph eventually. Nothing could stand in his way. In his youthful arrogance he believed this was his destiny and that if he needed more time to complete his mission, he could even defy death if he had to.

KIRILLI

→I step through the window and find myself on a highly polished wooden floor. There are no walls or ceiling, only a clear blue sky and glaring sun far overhead. I squint and cover my eyes with a hand. When my pupils adjust, I slowly lower my hand and stare around with awe.

We're surrounded by water — we must be on a boat. Everywhere I look, an ocean stretches ahead of me, small waves lazily rippling by. I've only seen the sea once before and that was from the safety of land. Finding myself stranded in the middle of it makes me feel sick. Even though the floor is steady, my legs seem to wobble beneath me and I have to fight to calm my stomach.

"Easy, Little One," Beranabus murmurs, touching my arm and smiling.

"It's so vast," I whisper, eyes round.

"Aye, but it's only the sea. You've nothing to fear."

"But the monsters…" I catch myself. In my time we thought the sea was home to an array of terrors. Now I know that isn't so. I remind myself that I'm not living in the fifth century any longer. Frowning at myself for overreacting, I order my legs to steady and my stomach to stop churning.

Breathing more calmly, I pivot slowly and study the vessel on which we've landed. We're on the deck of a massive ship, a luxury cruise liner, but its grandeurs have been spoilt by a recent, vicious attack. Deckchairs are strewn everywhere. We're close to a swimming pool — the water is red and there are bodies floating in it. A man lies spreadeagled on a diving board, blood dripping from his throat into the water. More corpses dot the deck and some are draped over deckchairs.

There are carcasses everywhere. Freshly dead, with blood oozing from them. Men, women and children. Some are in crew uniforms, others in swimwear or casual clothes. Apart from the soft dripping noises of the blood, there's no sound, not even the chug of an engine. The boat is as dead as the butchered passengers and staff.

As I gaze with horror at the carnage, the more experienced Sharmila checks a few of the bodies to ensure they're beyond help. "Juni could not have killed all these people by herself," she says quietly.

"She could," Beranabus grunts, "but I don't think she did. You can see different marks if you look closely. A group of demons had a party here."

"Where are they now?" Dervish asks, fingers flexing angrily.

"That's what I'd like to know." Beranabus walks to the diving board, steps on to it and pushes the body off into the water as if it was a rubbish bag — he can be as detached as a demon when he needs to be. The splash disturbs the silence. We wait edgily, but nothing reacts to the noise.

"Are you sure Dervish and Sharmila are safe here?" I ask Kernel, trying to find something other than the corpses to focus on. "There's magic in the air, but I'm not sure it will hold."

"It's secure," he assures me. "We wouldn't have brought them over if we had any doubts. We're surrounded by a bubble of magical energy. The entire ship's been encased."

"Like the town of Slawter," Dervish notes, then tugs anxiously at his beard. "This bubble — it's pretty impenetrable?"

"Yes," Kernel says.

"So if the window to the oasis blinks out of existence, we're trapped."

Kernel smiles. "Don't worry. I'll keep it open. That's what I excel at."

Beranabus returns from the diving board. "They must have a lodestone on board. No demon could maintain a shield like this without a lodestone."

Lodestones are stones of ancient – Old – power. Demons can use them to seal off an area and fill it with magic. That lets them operate as if they were in their own universe. They can use them to open tunnels as well, if the stone is especially powerful. But they need human help. They can't do it alone.

Lodestones are rare. When the Old Creatures inhabited the Earth, they used the stones to help keep back the Demonata. But in their absence the demons learnt to turn the magic of the stones against the humans they were originally intended to protect. Beranabus scoured the world for lodestones centuries ago and destroyed as many as he could find, or sealed them off like the one in Carcery Vale. But some evaded him and remain hidden in various corners of the world. Every so often a mage or demon tracks one down and trouble ensues.

"Is Juni still here?" Dervish asks Kernel.

"Yes," I answer first. "I sense her near the bottom of the ship."

"This feels like a trap," Sharmila mutters.

"Aye," Beranabus says. "But you learn to live with traps when you're chasing demons." He looks around. "Are there any others, Bec?"

I let my senses drift through the areas below deck. "There's one demon with Juni. Not very powerful. If there are others, they're masking themselves."

"There's a window open down there," Kernel says.

"Fairly ordinary. Only weaker demons can cross through it."

"Could there be armed humans?" Dervish asks.

"Perhaps," I mutter. "Humans are harder to sense than mages or demons."

"We can handle a few soldiers," Beranabus barks. "I'll turn their guns into eels — see how much damage they can do with them then!"

"We should go back," Sharmila says. "Juni has set this up to ensnare us."

"Why would she be expecting us?" Dervish argues.

"Lord Loss may have reasoned that we would target Juni. Perhaps everything – the attacks on Dervish, Juni revealing herself on the roof of the hospital – was designed to lure Beranabus here. The demon master might be poised to cross and finish us off personally."

"Not through that window," Kernel insists.

"Then through another," she counters. "We have never been able to explain why Lord Loss can cross when other masters cannot, or how he goes about it."

Beranabus considers that, then sighs. "You could be right, but we might never get a better shot at Juni. If she's not expecting us, it's the perfect time to strike. If she is and this is a trap, at least we can anticipate the worst. The magic in the air means she'll be dangerous, but it serves us as much as her. If Lord Loss doesn't turn up, we can match her. If he does cross, we'll make a swift getaway."

"Are you sure of that?" Sharmila scowls. "If we have to open a new window…"

"We won't," Beranabus says. "Kernel will stay here and guard our escape route. You'll know if any other windows open, won't you?"

"Yes," Kernel says.

"Then keep this one alive and watch for signs of further activity. If you sense anything, summon us and we'll withdraw. Is everyone satisfied with that?"

He looks pointedly at Sharmila. She frowns then shrugs. Taking the lead, Beranabus picks his way across the bloody, corpse-strewn deck and the rest of us cautiously, nervously follow.

→My feet are soon sticky with blood, but I ignore my queasy feelings. This isn't the way the world should be, having to creep through pools of blood, past dozens of slaughtered humans. But when you find yourself in the middle of a living nightmare you have two choices. You can cower in a corner, eyes shut, praying for it to be over. Or you can get on with things and do your best to deal with the job in hand. I don't think I'm particularly brave, but I like to think I've always been practical.

We undertake a circuit of the upper deck before venturing into the depths of the ship, making sure there aren't any surprises waiting for us up here if we have to make a quick getaway. We don't find any demons or soldiers in league with the Demonata. Just one corpse after another, slowly frying beneath the merciless sun.

We're passing a row of lifeboats when I feel a twitch at the back of my eyes. It's the subtlest of sensations. I'd ignore it any other time. But I'm trying to be alert to the least hint of anything amiss, so I stop and focus. The twitch draws me to the third boat ahead of us. It hangs from hooks high above the deck.

"What is it?" Beranabus whispers. I feel magic build within him. He's converting the energy in the air into a force he can use.

"Somebody's there." I point to the lifeboat. "A man. Hiding from us. He's using a masking spell."

"Get ready," Beranabus says to the others. He points a finger at the hooks. They snap and the boat drops abruptly, landing hard on the deck. The man inside it yelps and tumbles out as the boat keels over.

Sharmila and Dervish step ahead of Beranabus, fingers crackling with pent-up magic. The man shrieks and wildly raises his hands, shouting, "I surrender!"

"Wait!" Sharmila snaps, grabbing Dervish's arm. "I know him."

The man pauses when he hears Sharmila's voice. He stares at her shakily as if he doesn't believe his ears or eyes.

"Kirilli Kovacs," Sharmila says.

"I… I recognise you… I think," he croaks.

"We met several years ago. You were with Zahava Lever. She was your mentor. My name is Sharmila—"

"—Mukherji," the man says, breaking into a big smile. "Of course. Zavi spoke very highly of you. She said you were a great Disciple, one of the finest. I should have recognised you immediately. My apologies. It's been a hard few…" He frowns. "I was going to say days, but it's only been hours."

"This is one of your lot?" Beranabus sniffs. We're all a bit mystified. The man is wearing a dark suit, but there are silver and gold stars stitched into the shoulders and down the sides. He sports a thin moustache and is wearing mascara. He looks like a stage magician, not a Disciple.

"This is my cover," he explains sheepishly. "I ran into fiscal complications…" He clears his throat. "Actually I gambled away my cash and my credit card was taken from me by a woman in… but that's another story. I had to get on the ship. I could have used magic but it was easier to get a job. So I did, as Kirilli the Konjuror. I've used this disguise before. It's always been effective. I can put on a first-rate stage show when I have to."

"Your standards are slipping," Beranabus says to Sharmila. "I might have to review the recruiting policy of the Disciples."

"I'm of a first-rate pedigree, sir," Kirilli snaps. "Even

the best of us can fall prey to the occasional vice." He tugs the arms of his jacket straight and glares.

"Zahava said Kirilli was an excellent spy," Sharmila says. "He is very adept at trailing people and hiding from them. The fact that he survived the massacre here is proof of that. The Disciples need spies as much as they need warriors."

"Precisely," Kirilli huffs. "There's a man for every job, as my dear departed father used to say."

"I bet he worked in sewerage," Dervish says drily.

Kirilli flushes, but ignores the jibe. "By the way," he says stiffly, "I didn't catch *your* names."

Beranabus shrugs. "This is Dervish Grady. That's Bec. I'm Beranabus."

Kirilli's jaw drops and he loses his composure completely.

Beranabus winks at me. "I have that effect on a lot of my idolising Disciples."

"Only until we get to know you," Sharmila mutters, then addresses Kirilli again. "Can you tell us what happened? Swiftly, please — we do not have much time."

"That's really Beranabus?" Kirilli says, wide-eyed. "I thought he'd look more like Merlin or Gandalf."

"He'll turn you into a hobbit if you don't start talking," Dervish growls.

Kirilli blanches, then scowls. "I was tracking a pair of

rogue mages," he says, adjusting his bow-tie — I spot a playing card up his sleeve. "They were planning to open a window."

"Why didn't you stop them?" Dervish asks.

"They were working for somebody else, taking orders from a superior. I wanted to expose their partner. I felt that was more important than stopping the crossing, although I hoped to do that as well."

"No prizes for guessing who their boss was," Dervish grimaces. "Ugly cow, disfigured, covered in pus and blood?"

Kirilli nods and shivers. "They were in regular contact, but I couldn't get a fix on who they were talking to. From what I overheard, it sounded like there were no imminent plans to open the window. They made it sound like they'd be on the boat for months, waiting for an order to act.

"They either knew I was eavesdropping and said that to fool me, or there was a change of plan. Either way, they opened the window earlier today. About twenty demons spat through and set to work on the crew and guests. I managed to shield myself. That's all I could do. There was no point fighting them — I wouldn't have stood a chance." He looks at us appealingly.

"You did all you could," Sharmila says kindly. "You are a spy, not a warrior. Besides, Disciples never fight when the odds are stacked against them. You have no reason to feel guilty."

Gratitude sweeps across Kirilli's face. "I expected the window to close after a few minutes but it stayed open and there was more magic in the air than I've ever experienced. The demons went on torturing and slaughtering. They took most of the people below deck. Maybe the sun bothered them and they wanted to do their work in the shade."

"No," Beranabus grunts. "Lodestones need blood. They were feeding it."

"What's a lodestone?" Kirilli asks but Beranabus waves at him to continue. "Balint and Zsolt – the mages – remained up top. They did their share of killing but nothing to compare with the demons. Not long before you lot arrived that woman… that *thing* crawled up from below." He shudders. "I wasn't sure if she was human or Demonata. I'm still not certain."

"I doubt if she knows herself any more," Beranabus says softly.

"She barked orders at the demons and they killed the last few survivors," Kirilli goes on. "Then they retreated through the window and the woman said a spell to close it. Balint and Zsolt were grinning, mightily pleased with themselves, but she turned on them. Melted them into twin pools of bloody goo. Laughed as they screamed for mercy. Told them they were fools to trust the word of a monster. She lay down and wallowed in their juices when they were dead, then went below deck. That's when I climbed into the lifeboat."

"Interesting," Beranabus murmurs. Then he winks at Sharmila. "This definitely stinks of a trap."

"So we will leave?" Sharmila asks eagerly.

Beranabus chuckles. "I've walked into more traps over the centuries than I can remember. The Demonata and their familiars think they're masters of cunning but they haven't got the better of me yet. Let Juni and Lord Loss spring their surprise. I'll blast a hole in it so big, you could sail this ship through."

"Are you sure?" Dervish asks uneasily. "Juni was your apprentice. She knows all about you. Maybe you have a weak spot which she plans to exploit."

Beranabus shrugs. "I love a challenge."

"I really do not think we should—" Sharmilla begins.

"We've no choice," Beranabus snaps. "She's our only link to the Shadow. It's a gamble, but this is a time for gambling. I don't think you understand the stakes. This is the end game. We don't have the luxury of caution. If we don't risk all and find out who the Shadow is and what its plans are, the world will fall." He waves at the corpses around us. "A world of *this*, Sharmila. Is that what you want?"

"Of course not," she mutters.

"Then trust me. We're precariously balanced and I might be testing one trap too many, but we can't play safe. It's all or nothing now."

"You truly believe matters are that advanced?" Sharmila asks.

"Aye." Beranabus's eyes glitter. "The Disciples have exercised caution over the years because there have always been other battles to fight. But this could be the final battle. Ever. Better to risk all on a desperate gamble than play it safe and hand victory to the Shadow. Aye?"

Sharmila hesitates, then smiles shakily. "*Aye*. If we fail, at least I will have the pleasure of saying, 'I told you so'."

"That's the spirit," Beranabus booms and heads for the nearest door. Without any sign of fear he leads us down into the bowels of the ship in search of the vile viper, Juni Swan.

HER MASTER'S VOICE

→We progress in single file, Beranabus leading, Sharmila second, then me and Kirilli, with Dervish bringing up the rear. As we start down the first set of steps, Kirilli whispers, "Care to let me know what's going on? I caught some of it but I'm in the dark on a lot of issues."

"There's a powerful new demon called the Shadow," I explain. "We need to find out more about it. Juni — the mutant you saw — possesses information."

"And all that talk of a trap…?"

"We think Juni or Lord Loss may have lured us here, that they might be trying to trap us. This could all be a set-up."

"The plot thickens," Kirilli says, trying to sound lighthearted, but failing to hide the squeak in his voice. "Any idea what the odds are? I'm a gambling man, so I knew where Beranabus was coming from when I heard him talking about the need to take risks. But I like to have an idea of the odds before I place a bet."

"We honestly don't know," I tell him.

He makes a humming noise. "Let's say two-to-one. Those are fair odds. I've bet on a lot worse in my time."

He's trembling. This is a new level for him. The wholesale slaughter on the deck shook him up and now he's being asked to disregard Disciple protocol – run when the odds are against you – and fight to a very probable death.

"You don't need to come with us," I murmur. "We left someone up top to keep our escape route open. You could wait with him."

Kirilli smiles nervously. "I'd love to, but I've always dreamt of standing beside the legendary Beranabus in battle. I was never this scared in my dreams, but if I back out now I won't be able to forgive myself."

We start down a long corridor. There are bodies lying in tattered, bloodied bundles at regular intervals. I wonder how many people a ship this size holds. Three thousand? Four? I've never heard the death screams of thousands of people. The noise must have been horrible.

"Have you fought before?" I ask Kirilli, to distract myself.

"Not really," he says. "As Sharmila said, I'm a spy. Excellent at sniffing out intrigue and foiling the well-laid plans of villainous rogues like Zsolt and Balint. But when it comes to the dirty business of killing, I'm more a stabber in the back than a face-to-face man. Never saw anything wrong with striking an opponent from behind if they're a nasty piece of work."

"I doubt if Juni will turn her back on you. The best thing is to trust in your magic and try not to think too much. If you're attacked, use your instincts. You'll find yourself doing things you never thought possible."

"And if my instincts come up short?" Kirilli asks.

Dervish snorts behind us. "That'll be a good time to panic."

Kirilli frowns over his shoulder at Dervish. "It's rude to eavesdrop."

"I'm a rude kind of guy," Dervish retorts. "Don't worry, you'll be fine. Hang back when we get there, fire off the occasional bolt of energy – at our opponents, not us – and try not to get in anyone's way."

"I can tell you're a true leader of men," Kirilli says sarcastically.

"Quiet," Beranabus snarls. "I'm trying to concentrate."

"Sorry, boss," Dervish says, then sticks his right hand under his left armpit and makes a farting noise. We all giggle, even Beranabus. It's not unnatural to laugh in the face of death. It's not an act of bravery either. You do it because you might never have the chance to laugh again.

→We descend slowly, exploring each level, wary of booby traps. But there are no secret windows, no army of demons, no humans packing weapons.

We pass a mound of bodies, mostly uniformed crew. They armed themselves with axes, knives, flares — whatever they could find — and tried to block off the corridor with bulky pieces of furniture. The demons ripped through them. They never stood a chance.

The lights suddenly snap off. Kirilli gasps and grabs my hand. I get images of his previous, limited encounters with demons, his stage act, the tricks he performs. He wanted to be a famous magician when he was young. Practised hard, but didn't have the style. Good enough for clubs and cruisers, but he never had a real crack at the big time. He was pleased when he joined the Disciples, proud of his talent. But he'd have much rather succeeded in showbiz, where the worst he'd have ever had to face was being booed off stage.

Emergency lights flicker on. There's a harsh metallic ripping sound somewhere far below. It echoes through the ship. The floor shudders, then steadies.

"Turbulence?" Beranabus asks.

"You only get that on planes," Dervish says. "It could be the roll of the sea but I doubt it. Have you noticed the lack of movement? We haven't tilted since we came aboard. The ship's been steady, held in place by magic."

"I knew there was something strange," Kirilli growls. "I get terrible seasickness. I have to take pills to keep my food down. But I've been feeling fine for the last few hours. I thought I'd found my sea legs at last."

The ripping noise comes again, louder than before. It reminds me of a noise Bill-E heard in a film about the *Titanic*, when the iceberg sliced through the hull and split it open.

"Any idea what's going on down there?" Dervish asks.

Beranabus shrugs. "We'll soon find out."

We press on.

→Eventually we hit the bottom of the ship. Except there isn't much left of it. When we step into the cavernous hold, we instantly see what the noises were. The lowest layer has been peeled away. A huge hole has been gouged out of the hull, twenty-five or thirty metres wide, stretching far ahead of us, through the middle of the hold and up the walls at the sides. Water surrounds the gap, held back by a field of magic. If that field was to suddenly collapse, the sea would flood through and the ship would sink swiftly.

There are bodies all over the place, but a huge pile is stacked in the centre of the floorless hold, resting in a heap on the invisible barrier. It looks like they're floating on air.

The tip of a large stone juts through the covering of corpses. Red streaks of blood line the cracks and indentations of the ancient stone. The bodies around it are pale and shrivelled. The stone has drunk from them. I recall the stone in the cave where I was imprisoned, when I sacrificed Drust, how it sucked his blood. These stones of magic are alive in some way. The Old Creatures filled them with a power we no longer understand.

A demon stands to attention behind the stone. He has a squat, leathery body and a green head, part human, part canine. A large, surly mouth. Four hairy arms and two long legs. Floppy ears. His white eyes are filled with fear and he holds himself rigidly, as if standing still against his will.

There's a grey window of light a few metres from the stone and demon. In front of it, grinning lopsidedly in her warped, pus- and blood-drenched new form, is the monstrous Juni Swan.

"You took your time getting here," she snarls.

"We stopped for a bite to eat," Dervish quips. Sharmila is studying the demon. Beranabus is looking at Juni with a mixture of sadness and disgust. Kirilli is just gawping.

"What happened to you?" Beranabus asks quietly.

"Don't you like my new body?" Juni croons, posing obscenely. "I preferred my old frame, but this is what I'm stuck with. The price of cheating death."

"How *did* you survive?" Beranabus presses, the pity in his voice vanishing in an instant. "Dervish killed you. I felt your soul leave. Did Lord Loss have the Board with him? Is that how he pulled off this trick?"

Juni shakes her head smugly. "That's for me to know and you to guess, old man." She looks at the rest of us, sneering spitefully. "I told them you'd come. My master said you wouldn't be so foolish, but I knew you would. You're arrogant. You never let the threat of a trap put you off. I always knew your ridiculous self-belief would prove your undoing — and so it has."

Beranabus stares at his ex-assistant, shaken by her hideous appearance and the mad hatred in her expression. "How did it come to this?" he croaks. "Life with me can't have been worse than what you're going through now."

"You don't know what you're talking about," Juni says. "You were far worse than Lord Loss. I serve him willingly, by my own choice, but I was a slave to you, with no say over what happened to me."

"But—" Beranabus starts.

"No!" Juni barks. "You're not worth arguing with." She glares at the rest of us. "You can choose too. You don't have to serve this fool or perish with him. Join me now and live. Stay loyal to him and die."

Dervish laughs. "You've lost your marbles. Nadia Moore would have known that wasn't an option. Even Juni Swan could have seen that it's a no-brainer. But you've become something warped and inhuman. Do you honestly believe any of us would throw in our lot with a thing as twisted and insane as you?"

Juni's lips tremble and the skin around her cheeks cracks in a series of tiny channels. "How dare you speak to me like that!"

"You were my love," Dervish says. "I'll speak to you any way I like."

She starts to curse him, then restrains herself and giggles. "We'll be lovers again, darling Dervish. I'll keep you alive in a body even more wretched than this. I'll lavish you with torment and pain. You'll beg me to kill you, every single day for the rest of time, but I won't."

"Sounds nasty," Dervish yawns.

"Um, I don't know how these things normally work," Kirilli speaks up, "but shouldn't we be ripping her into a million pieces instead of trading insults?"

"Don't knock the insults," Dervish growls. "This is the best part of a fight. If you don't get the digs in at the beginning, there'll be no time later."

"Who is this charlatan?" Juni huffs, glaring at Kirilli.

"A Disciple," Beranabus says. "A friend and assistant, as you once were."

"Assistant only," Juni corrects him. "Never a friend."

"You were Kernel's friend," Sharmila says softly. "You saved his life, even after you had turned traitor. Do you hate him too? Will you kill him along with the rest of us if you get the chance?"

"Without blinking," Juni says coldly. "I warned him not to get in my way again. I might not kill him today

– if he has any sense, he'll slip away when the rest of you are dead – but I'll catch up with him soon. It's the end of mankind's reign. Within a year we'll cleanse Earth of its human fungus and take the world forward into a new demonic era. Your precious billions are living on borrowed time, Beranabus, but you reckless fools don't even have that. Which is where Cadaver comes in…" She nods at the demon behind the lodestone.

"*Cadaver?*" Beranabus frowns.

"He stole the demon which was masquerading as Kernel's brother," Sharmila reminds him.

Cadaver whines and strains his neck. He's not a willing participant in this. He's a prisoner. When he opens his mouth and speaks, we learn who his captor is.

"Greetings, my brave, doomed friends."

Cadaver's lips are moving, but the words and accent aren't the demon's — they belong to the sentinel of sorrow, Lord Loss.

"A cheap trick," Beranabus grunts. "Too afraid to face us in person? Reduced to speaking through a puppet?"

"Why not use Cadaver's mouth?" Lord Loss counters, speaking from his realm in the Demonata's universe. "I gave it to him. I could have made use of any of my familiars, but I thought this one most fitting. Such a pity Kernel isn't here. I'm sure Cadaver's appearance would have revived many fond memories."

"I have had enough of this," Sharmila growls. She takes a step forward and raises her hand, taking aim at Cadaver.

"Wait," Beranabus stops her. "He's close to the lodestone. If we kill him, his blood will drench it."

"Will that make a difference?" Sharmila asks.

Beranabus grimaces. "I doubt he's there for show."

"Astute as always," Lord Loss murmurs through the unfortunate Cadaver. "You would have made a fine demon, Beranabus. You have wasted your talent on a far inferior species. But it's not too late to change. Join us. Live forever as one of the rulers of the universes."

"*Live forever?*" Beranabus laughs. "Nonsense! All things die. That's the nature of existence."

"Nature is about to be reversed," Lord Loss says.

"By who?" Beranabus asks. "Your shadowy master? What's his name? I can't serve him if I don't even know his name."

Lord Loss tuts. "No names, not unless you join us."

"Well, that's not going to happen," Beranabus sniffs. "And I don't think you really expected me to switch sides. So why are we here? Do you want to gloat before your master kills us?"

"No," Lord Loss says. Cadaver's head swivels and his eyes fix on me. "We want Bec."

Beranabus, Dervish and Sharmila shuffle towards me, forming a protective barrier. I'm touched by their show of support.

"What do you want with me?" I ask in a small, trembling voice.

"Your piece of the Kah-Gash, of course," Lord Loss says.

Beranabus puts a hand on the nape of my neck. His fingers are shaking. By reading his thoughts, I understand why. Though I'm afraid, I place my hand over his and squeeze, giving my assent.

"You can't have her," Beranabus croaks. "I won't let a piece of the Kah-Gash fall into your foul hands. I'll kill her first."

"But you love her," Lord Loss gasps with mock shock.

"Aye," Beranabus says. "But I'll kill her anyway."

Kirilli is gawping at us, confused and dismayed. Dervish and Sharmila look distraught but resigned.

"Then kill her," Lord Loss purrs and I catch a glimpse of his wicked leer in Cadaver's terror-stricken eyes. "It makes no difference. If she dies, the piece will be set free and faithful Juni will capture and deliver it to our new master. Death isn't an obstacle to us, not any longer."

Beranabus squints at Cadaver, not sure if this is a bluff.

"The piece was originally mine," Lord Loss says petulantly. "It lay dormant within me for hundreds of thousands of years. But when I shared my magic with Bec, back when I wished to preserve humanity, it slipped from my body into hers." Cadaver shakes a hairy finger at me.

"It can move from one being to another?" Beranabus frowns and his thoughts move quickly. He uses a spell to communicate directly with me. *Give it to me*, he whispers silently. *Pass it on*.

I can't, I reply. *I don't know how*.

"Master," Juni interrupts. "This window will close soon. If I am to return to your side, we must act now."

"Of course," Lord Loss says. "Wait a few moments more, my dear. Then you can come home."

Cadaver bends forward over the lodestone, but his eyes remain rooted on us. "I must say farewell, old friends," Lord Loss murmurs. "I don't think any of you will survive the coming battle. You have caused me much displeasure over the years, but I shall miss you."

His eyes settle on Dervish and he smiles. "Don't worry about how Grubitsch will cope without you. He walked into a trap, just as you did. He will be dead soon if he isn't already."

Dervish hisses and starts to respond, but Lord Loss is looking at Sharmila now. "There will be much chaos before the end," he tells her. "Humanity will be given time to scream before we cleanse the universe of its miserable stain. I will track down those you love and execute them personally. I will lavish extra attention on the children and babies."

Sharmila is close to tears, but she holds them back and curses Lord Loss foully. He chuckles and his gaze flickers to Kirilli. The stage magician braces himself. "Go on," he snarls manfully. "I can take any threat you dish out."

"I don't know who you are and I have no interest in you," Lord Loss says dismissively, and Kirilli deflates.

"Bec," the demon master hums, staring at me directly. "It has been such a long time since our paths—"

"Let's get out of here," I snap, backing away from the lodestone and the mound of dead bodies, having no desire to listen to more of his rhetoric.

"Aye," Beranabus says, retreating beside me. He thrusts a hand in Juni's direction, but she darts through the window before he can strike. A crazy, lingering cackle is her only parting shot at us.

"Very well," Lord Loss sighs. "Let the slaughter commence."

Cadaver's head explodes and the demon's blood soaks the lodestone. It glows beneath the stack of corpses, sucking the blood as it pumps from Cadaver's neck. A bolt of light shoots from the base of the stone, down through the watery layers of the sea, disappearing a second later into the murky depths below.

We should run. It's crazy to linger. But we're held, captivated, curious to see what will happen. This is new even to Beranabus, who's seen virtually everything in his time.

For a few seconds — nothing. Then a ball of light rises from the darkness of the ocean floor. It's larger than the ball which shot downwards, and expands the closer it comes. There's a dark glob at the centre, almost like a pupil in an eye. It's a long way off, but I'm certain it's the Shadow. A strange, tingling energy washes into the ship, saturating the air around us. I've never felt any magic quite like it.

"Enough!" Beranabus shouts. "Let's get out before it tears through the hold and rips us apart."

We surge towards the door, a terrified Kirilli leading the way, Sharmila behind him, then me. Dervish and Beranabus bring up the rear, preparing themselves to fight off the Shadow.

Just before we get to the door, something moves nearby. It's one of the humans. A woman. Her arms are twitching and her head is rising slowly. The demons must have mistakenly left her for dead.

"Wait!" I yell, breaking left. "There's a survivor." I bend over the woman, grab her arms and haul her to her feet. "Come on. We have to get out. I'll help…"

I come to a sickening halt. The woman's face is missing from the nose down. Scraps of her brain trickle down her chest as she gets to her feet, through the gap where her jaw should be. She can't be alive, yet she's looking at me. But not with warmth or gratitude — only with *hunger*.

My mind whirrs and I realise what's happening. But before I can yell a warning, dozens of corpses around us thrash, slither, then rise like dreadful ghouls. *The dead are coming back to life!*

SHIP OF THE LIVING DEAD

→Bill-E loved zombie films. He thought there was nothing cooler than corpses coming back to life and eating the brains of the living. But I don't think he'd have been thrilled if it happened to him in real life, like it's happening to us now.

The revived dead throw themselves at us slavishly, mindlessly, silently. They move as fluidly as in life, not in the shambling manner of movie zombies. Some are hampered by the loss of limbs and stumble sluggishly. But most are as quick on their feet as any living person.

They look more like living people too. They're not rotting, misshapen monsters. It's easy to rip the head off an inhuman beast from another dimension, but doing that to someone who looks human feels like murder. It's horrible.

The woman I picked off the floor tries to claw my throat open. I shove her away and turn to kick a man in the head before he bites my thigh. Ahead of me, a girl throws herself down the stairs and knocks Kirilli over. She snaps at his left hand and chews off his two smallest fingers. He screams, then sets her aflame, instinct lending him the magical fighting impulse which he previously lacked.

"Zombies!" Dervish snorts with disgust, scattering a handful with a ball of energy. "First werewolves, then demons, now zombies. What will they throw at us next?"

"There might not be a *next*," Sharmila says, helping Kirilli to his feet and shooting a bolt of fire up the stairs. There are shrieks from the zombies above us and the stench of burning flesh and hair fills the air. Sharmila grimaces, but sends another burst of flames after the first.

"You're not worried about this lot, are you?" Dervish says, sending more of the living corpses flying across the hold. "We can handle them. We've faced a hell of a lot stronger in our time."

"You miss the point," Sharmila replies with forced calm. "The dead are meant only to delay us. There is our true foe." She points to the centre of the hold. The ball of light is almost level with the ship. As we watch, it breaks around the hull and disintegrates. A black, hissing ball of nightmares explodes through the shield of energy and gathers around the lodestone.

We only got a glimpse of the Shadow that night in the cave. Here, in the lights of the hull, it's revealed in all its furious glory. The creature is the general shape of a giant octopus, about fifteen metres broad, ten metres tall, covered in a mass of long, countless, writhing tendrils, which whip around the lodestone, tightening and loosening as the creature saps strength from the ancient stone. A few of the living dead wander too close to the lodestone and are beheaded by some of the knife-like tentacles — the Shadow doesn't suffer fools gladly. The beast doesn't seem to have a face, but I'm sure it sees us and is focused upon us.

As I gaze with horror at the massive, pulsing creature of shadows, a fat man trailing guts hurls himself at me, gnashing his teeth. I flick him away with the wave of a hand and shuffle closer to Beranabus. He's eyeing the Shadow warily.

"It doesn't feel like a demon," I note.

"I know," he mutters.

"Can we outrun it?"

"We can try."

"The stairs are free," Sharmila calls. "But more of the dead are coming. If we are to flee, we must do so now."

"What are we waiting for?" Kirilli yells. He hasn't managed to cauterise his wound. Blood spurts from the jagged stumps where his fingers used to be.

"You think we can fight it?" Dervish asks, stepping up beside Beranabus.

"I don't know."

The window Juni escaped through blinks out of existence. That seems to decide Beranabus. "Let's test it," he grunts, moving away from the door, back towards the lodestone. "Maybe it's not as powerful as it thinks."

He unleashes a ball of bright blue magic at the Shadow. The ball strikes the creature directly and crackles around it. Its tendrils thrash wildly, then return to their almost tender caressing of the lodestone. Its body continues to throb. A high piercing sound fills the hold — I think the Shadow's laughing at us.

Sharmila bends, touches the invisible barrier where the floor should be and creates a pillar of fire. It streaks towards the lodestone, slicing through several zombies on the way. When it reaches the Shadow, Sharmila barks a command and it billows upwards, forming a curtain of flames. The Shadow's consumed, its tendrils retracting like a spider's legs shrivelling up. But when the flames die away, it emerges unharmed, oozes over the lodestone and slides towards us.

Dervish leaps through the air and chops at a thick tendril. He cuts clean through it, severing the tip. The amputated piece dissolves before it hits the floor, crumbling away to ash.

The Shadow catches Dervish with another tentacle, roughly shakes him, then flings him across the hold. Beranabus halts Dervish's flight and the spiky-haired mage drops to the floor a few metres in front of the magician, gasping with pain, his skin burnt a bright pink where the tendril touched him.

"Stuff this!" Kirilli pants, and darts up the stairs. I let him run. No point trying to make him fight if he doesn't want to. Besides, I doubt he could make much of a difference.

About a dozen walking corpses converge on me. I work a quick blinding spell, then plough through them as they mill around. I squat by Dervish as Beranabus and Sharmila engage the Shadow, and swiftly cool his burnt flesh.

"Are you OK?" I ask as he sits up, dazed.

"Three," he mutters. When I frown, he smiles sheepishly. "Sorry. I thought you asked how many fingers you were holding up."

I help him to his feet. He gulps when he looks at the Shadow, but advances to try again.

"What can I do?" I shout at Beranabus.

"Get out," he roars. "You're the one it's after."

"But I can't–"

"*Go!*"

Cursing, I turn and run. Before I'm even halfway to the door, I feel a whoosh of hot air on my back. Glancing over my shoulder, I see the Shadow directly behind me. It's swept past Beranabus and his Disciples, barrelling them aside. They lie sprawled on the invisible floor. They're picking themselves up, turning to help me — but too late.

The Shadow seizes me with several tentacles and lifts

me high into the air. I scream, pain filling all parts of my body at once. It's like being on fire, except the agony cuts deeper than any natural flame, burning through flesh and bone, turning my blood to vapour.

I somehow hold myself together. It takes every last bit of magic that I possess, but I fight the terrible, fiery clutch of the Shadow and wildly restore blood, bones and flesh as it grips me tighter and tries to fry me again. I'm absorbing memories from the beast, mostly garbled, but what I comprehend is more terrifying than I would have considered possible.

The Shadow's surprised I'm still alive. It meant to slaughter me and absorb the freed piece of the Kah-Gash. But it's not dismayed by my resistance. The beast is much stronger than me and knows it simply has to keep applying pressure. I can last a matter of seconds, no more. Then...

Beranabus is suddenly beside me, bellowing like a madman. He slashes at the tentacles, slicing through them as easily as Dervish did. The Shadow is more of a menace than any demon I've ever faced, but it's insubstantial. It's not by nature a physical creature. It can easily and quickly replace what we destroy, but it can't harden itself against our blows.

I fall free and Beranabus drags me away. Sharmila and Dervish dart into the gap we've left and attack the Shadow with bolts of energy and fire. It makes a squealing noise and lashes at them with its tentacles. They duck and dodge the blows, punching and kicking at the tendrils.

"Go!" Beranabus gasps and tries to throw me ahead of him.

"Wait," I cry, holding on. "I know what it is."

"Tell me later," he roars. "There's no time now."

He's right. I won't have the chance to explain, not with words. But I have to let him know. He thinks he can defeat this beast, that if they keep working on the tendrils, they'll eventually chop their way through to the body. He believes they can kill it, like any other demon.

He's wrong.

I clutch his small, clean hands and use the same spell he used earlier to bypass the need for words. He gasps as I force-feed him the information. Then his eyes widen and a look of shocked desperation crosses his face.

"*How?*" he croaks.

"I don't know," I sob.

Sharmila screams. The Shadow has ripped one of her legs loose. It rains to the floor in a shower of bones and flesh. A few of the zombies fall on the remains with vicious delight.

Beranabus is thinking hard and fast, trying to turn this in our favour. He's always been able to outwit demons who were certain they'd got the better of him.

Even in recent years, ancient, battered, befuddled, his cunning gave him a crucial advantage. He can't believe it will fail him now, but he's never had to deal with anything like the Shadow.

The lines of his face go smooth. He half-nods and his lips twitch at the corners. My heart leaps with hope. He's seen something. He has a plan!

"Tell Kernel," he wheezes, standing straight and scattering a horde of zombies as if swatting flies. "Tell him to find me."

"You want me to send Kernel down?" I frown. "But he's not a fighter. He—"

"Just tell him to find me," Beranabus sighs, then bends and kisses my forehead. "I loved you as a child, Bec, and I love you still. I always will."

Through the brief contact, I catch a glimpse of what he's planning. It's perilous. He probably won't make it out alive. But it's the only way. Our only hope.

"Don't watch," he says, and his voice is guttural, unnatural, as his vocal cords begin to thicken and change. "I don't want you to see me like this."

He whirls away and bellows at the Shadow, an inhuman challenge. Dervish and Sharmila glance back, astonished by the ferocity of the roar. Their faces crumple when they see what Beranabus is becoming.

I back away slowly, but I can't obey Beranabus's final command. I have to look. Besides, he thought my feelings would alter if I saw him in his other form, but they won't. If you truly love someone, you don't care what they look like.

Beranabus is transforming. He outgrows his suit, which falls away from him like a banana peel. His skin splits and unravels. Bones snap out of his head, then lengthen, fresh flesh forming around them. Muscles bulge on his arms and legs, like pustulent sores. They burst, then reform, even larger than before. Tough, dark skin replaces his natural covering. Only it's not really skin — more like scales.

A tail forces its way out through the small of Beranabus's back. It grows to two metres… three… four. Spikes poke out of it, as well as several mouths full of sharp teeth and forked tongues.

I catch sight of his face. Purplish, scaly skin. Dark grey eyes, round like a fly's, utterly demonic. His mouth is three times the size of my head, filled with fangs that look more like stalactites and stalagmites than teeth. Yellowish blood streams from his nose but he takes no notice. Raising his massive arms, he pushes through the undulating nest of tentacles and hammers a fist at the Shadow, driving it back.

"What the hell is that?" Dervish croaks, backing up beside me, helping the one-legged Sharmila along.

"Beranabus," I answer quietly. "The Bran we never saw. The demon side that he kept shackled. This is what he would have looked like if he'd let his father's genes run free, if he'd chosen the way of the Demonata."

Beranabus lashes the Shadow with his tail. The spikes rip through the shadowy wisps of its body, the teeth snapping at it, tearing open holes. The Shadow shrieks angrily but the holes quickly close and the beast fights without pause, smothering Beranabus with its tentacles.

Dervish, Sharmila and I are by the doorway. We should take advantage of the situation and race up the stairs. But we're mesmerised. We can't flee without knowing the outcome. Sharmila clears the stairs of zombies, to keep the route out of the hold open, but she doesn't take her eyes off the battling pair.

"Can he control himself like that?" she asks quietly as the behemoths wrestle.

"Not for long," I whisper. "This is the first time he's completely unchained his beastly half. If he maintains that shape and lets the monster run free too long, it will take over."

"How much time does he have?" Dervish asks.

"He doesn't know. He's not even sure he *can* turn back again. Maybe he's given it too much freedom. The Beranabus we knew could be gone forever. He might turn against us and work with the Shadow to destroy mankind."

Dervish and Sharmila stare at me as if I'm the one who's changed shape.

"Why would he take such a risk?" Sharmila gasps.

"He had to. I'll explain later. If we survive."

The beast that was Beranabus shrugs free of the Shadow's tentacles and staggers away. For an awful moment I think that he's about to attack us. But then he bellows at the Shadow and darts past it, making for the lodestone.

"Ah!" Sharmila exclaims with sudden hope. "If he breaks the stone..."

"...the Shadow will be sucked back to its own universe," I finish.

"We hope," Dervish adds gloomily.

Finding its path to me unexpectedly clear, the Shadow lunges forward, eager to finish me off. Then it pauses. It doesn't glance back — as I noted earlier, it doesn't have a face — but it's somehow analysing Beranabus. There's a brief moment of consideration — can it kill me and steal the power of the Kah-Gash before Beranabus breaks the stone?

The Shadow decides the odds are against it and reverses direction, launching itself at the transformed magician. It catches him just before he reaches the lodestone. The pair spin past. Beranabus roars with frustration as he shoots beyond his target. The Shadow whips him with its tentacles. Deep cuts open across his arms and legs, and many of the protective scales on his chest and back shatter under the force of the blows.

Just before they fly out of striking distance of the lodestone, Beranabus's tail twitches. The tip catches a notch in the stone and Beranabus jerks to a halt. The Shadow loses its grip and ends up in a heap. It's back on its tentacles within seconds but Beranabus has already jerked himself within reach of the lodestone.

He grabs the stone with his massive hands and exerts great pressure, trying to snap it in half. There's a cracking sound and a split forms in the uppermost tip of the rock. But then it holds and although Beranabus strains harder, it doesn't divide any further.

The Shadow hurls itself at Beranabus and lands on his back. Tendrils jab at him from all directions, destroying his scaly armour, penetrating the flesh beneath. One of his grey eyes pops. Several of his fangs are ripped from his jaw. Blood flies from him in jets and fountains.

Beranabus howls with agony, but otherwise ignores the assault and focuses on the lodestone. He's still trying to tear it in two. The stone is pulsing. The split at the top increases a few centimetres. The gap's just wide enough for Beranabus to jam his unnaturally large fingers into it. Snapping at the Shadow with the remains of his fangs, he transfers his grip to the crack, gets the tips of all his fingers inside and tugs.

There's a creaking sound, then a snapping noise, and the stone splits down the middle to about a third of the way from the top. Beranabus yells with triumph, wraps both arms around the severed chunk of rock and rips it free of the lodestone, tossing it to the floor as an oversized ball of waste.

The Shadow screeches and scuttles after the rock, perhaps hoping to reattach it. I quickly unleash my power and send the piece of stone shooting across the hold. It smashes into the side of the ship and explodes in a cascade of pebbly splinters.

Beranabus roars with ghastly, demonic laughter and bites into one of the Shadow's tentacles. As he rips it off, another tendril strikes the side of his head and slices through to his brain. The triumph that had blossomed within me vanishes instantly.

"*Bran!*" I scream and dart towards him. Dervish holds me back.

The Shadow strikes repeatedly at Beranabus in a tempestuous rage. It gouges great chunks of flesh from his chest and stomach. Scraps of lung, slivers of a heart and other internal organs splatter the broken lodestone. Then, in a childish sulk, the Shadow tosses him aside like an old doll it's finished playing with.

The demonic beast that Beranabus has become rolls over several times before coming to a rest near the side of the hull. Again I try to race to his aid, but Dervish has a firm hold and doesn't let go even when I bite him.

Beranabus raises his huge, transformed, scaly head. He glances at the Shadow and the lodestone with his one bulbous grey eye and grins. Then his head swivels and he looks for me. When he finds me struggling with Dervish, his grin softens and I see a trace of the Beranabus I knew in the expression. I also see the boy he once was — scatterbrained Bran. He smiles at me foolishly, the way Bran used to, and gurgles something. I think he's trying to say, "*Flower.*"

Then the grey light in his eye dims and extinguishes. The smile turns into a tired sneer. He coughs up yellow blood and tries to drag himself forward. But the strength drains from his arms. His body sags. A jagged breath dances from his lips and his head drops. By the time his forehead connects with the cold steel floor of the hold, the three thousand year old legend is part of this world no more.

GOING DOWN

→In desperation the Shadow clambers after me, but a funnel has formed in the water beneath the broken lodestone. It stretches far down and whirls violently, creating a magical vacuum which drags at the mass of shadows. The beast's rear tentacles are stiff behind it, drawn towards the vortex, and its body begins to lengthen and narrow. The creature strains against it, but the vacuum is too strong. There are laws which even the Shadow has to obey, at least for the time being.

In a rush, and with a hateful shriek, the Shadow's ripped away. It smashes through the lodestone, shattering the remains of the rock, and disappears down the funnel, howling all the way. Moments later the funnel collapses in on itself as swiftly as it formed.

I want to rush to Beranabus's corpse and bid him farewell. I'm weeping and all I want is to be by my dead friend's side. But that's not possible. Because now that the lodestone's magic has evaporated, the shield keeping the sea at bay has started to give way.

The fragments of the lodestone fall first, trickling

through cracks in the invisible barrier. Water seeps up through the cracks, spreading neatly across the surface of the shield. Then one of the living dead stumbles and drops out of sight as if crashing through a thin layer of ice.

"Let's get the hell out of here!" Dervish shouts, hauling me through the door.

"Beranabus!" I cry.

"We can't help him now," Dervish pants. As he says it, the shield flickers out of existence and water floods the hold.

The ship lurches. A wave of foaming water surges towards us, washing away the helpless bodies of the zombies. We should be washed away too, but Sharmila acts swiftly to avert catastrophe, establishing a barrier around us and the doorway. The wave breaks and seethes away, the sea temporarily cheated of its victims.

"Quick," Sharmila gasps, hopping up the stairs. "The magic is fading. The barrier will not hold."

She's right. I can feel the energy ebbing away at a frightening rate. I look one last time for the body of Beranabus, but the ocean has already claimed it. Wiping tears from my cheeks, I hurry after Dervish and Sharmila, knowing that if we don't climb sharply, we'll soon be joining Beranabus in his watery grave.

→We move a lot slower going up than we did coming down. It's not just the fact that we're climbing. We're tired and drained. We were fine when the air was thick with magic, but the unnatural energy is fading fast.

We're halfway up the second flight of stairs when I hear the sea gush up the corridors behind us. I've no idea how long we have. I imagine it would usually take a ship this size at least a couple of hours sink, but the hole in the hull was extremely large.

The zombies are still going strong. The strange magic of the Shadow which reanimated them is fading slower than the energy we were tapping into. While we're rapidly weakening, the zombies haven't been significantly affected.

We don't use bolts of magic any more, or arrogantly dismiss them with a wave of a hand. We're reduced to close-quarters fighting. We can still repel them with our charged fists and feet – the magic hasn't disappeared entirely – but there are thousands of zombies. If we're still here when the last of the energy fades, they'll swamp us. Unless the sea claims us first.

Sharmila's second leg fragments. She pumps magic into it to hold the bones and scraps of flesh together.

"Don't bother," Dervish grunts, lifting her. "Save your strength. Get on my back. I'll be your legs. You keep the zombies off."

"What about your heart?" Sharmila shouts.

"It'll hold for a while."

I can move much quicker than Dervish now that he's

burdened with Sharmila. I'm tempted to race ahead of them, up through the ship, away from the encroaching water. But they're my friends and they wouldn't desert me if I was in their position. If it becomes necessary to flee, I will. But as long as there's a chance we might all make it out alive, I'll stick with them.

I take the lead, knocking flailing, snarling zombies out of our way, pushing ahead, the undead humans crowding the staircase behind and in front. I should feel fear in the face of such warped, nightmarish foes, but my emotions are focused on Beranabus — there's only room within me for mourning.

I can't believe he's dead. It's hard to imagine a world without the ancient magician. He's been mankind's saviour for longer than anyone should have to serve. What will we do without him? I doubt the Disciples can repel the waves of Demonata attacks by themselves. Beranabus believed our universe created heroes in times of need. If that's true, perhaps someone will replace him. But it's hard to picture anybody taking the magician's place. He was one of a kind.

We hit another level. I'm about to lurch up the next set of stairs when I spot Kirilli Kovacs tussling with a gaggle of zombies. He's in bad shape, bitten and scratched all over. A dozen of the living dead surround him.

I should leave him. He doesn't really deserve to be

rescued and I can't afford to waste any of my dwindling power. But I can't turn my back on a man just because he's a coward. Kirilli didn't betray or undermine us — he simply gave in to fear, as many people would have.

Drawing on my reserves, I mutter a spell and gesture at the zombies packed around Kirilli. They fly apart and a path opens. "Run!" I yell. Kirilli doesn't need to be told twice. He stumbles clear of the zombies and is by my side moments later. Blood cakes his face, but his eyes are alert behind the red veil. He starts to say something.

"No time for talking," I snap. "Get up those stairs quick, and if you fall, I'll leave you."

Kirilli flinches, draws a breath, then darts ahead of me, taking pole position, staggering up the seemingly endless flights of steps towards the upper deck and its promise of escape.

→As we're forcing our way up another staircase clogged with zombies, Dervish gasps and collapses to his knees. One hand darts to his chest. I think it's the end of him, but Sharmila presses her hands over his and channels magic into his heart. She pulls a stricken face as she helps — the magic she's directing into his flesh means she has less to ward off the pain in her legs. But she has no real choice. Without Dervish to carry her, she's doomed.

Kirilli is struggling with the zombies. He's weak and

afraid. He lashes out at them wildly, not preserving his energy or channelling it wisely. I've tried warning him, but he either doesn't hear me or can't respond. He knows only one thing — he has to go up. That's tattooed on his brain, driving him on.

Thankfully the walking corpses are moving more like regular zombies now. Their magic is fading. The attacks are clumsier, less coordinated. But they're still on their feet, our scent thick in their nostrils, licking their lips at the thought of biting into our soft, juicy brains.

→As we hit the last step of another flight, Kirilli screams something unintelligible. I'm exhausted, but I push forward in reply to his cry, fearing the worst. But when I clear the step, I realise it was a yell of exhilaration, not dismay. We're back at the upper deck.

The ship is lurching at a worrying angle, and the deck is littered with hordes of zombies. But we get a fresh burst of hope when we breathe the fresh, salty air.

Dervish lays Sharmila down and squats beside her. "I need... a minute," he wheezes, face ashen, rubbing his chest.

"We can't stop," Kirilli shrieks, knocking over a zombie in uniform who's either the ship's captain or a highly placed mate.

"Shut up," I growl and crouch next to Dervish. "Let me help."

"No," he mutters. "Save your magic… for yourself."

"Don't be a fool." I shove his hands away and rest my left palm on his chest. I pump magic into him, enough to keep him ticking over.

"Do you know the way back to Kernel?" Sharmila asks, wincing from the pain in her thighs. They're bleeding at the stumps, the flesh we knotted together in the demon universe coming undone.

"Yes." I grin at her. "Perfect memory, remember?"

She returns the smile, but shakily. "Perhaps you should leave me here."

"We're not leaving anyone behind," I say firmly. "Except maybe Kirilli."

He stares at me with a wounded expression. "I hope you don't—" he starts.

"Not now," I stop him. My cheeks are dry. I must have stopped weeping at some point coming up the stairs. The ship is slipping further into the water. The angle of the deck to the sea is increasing steadily. Kernel's at the end of the ship which is rising. If we don't act quickly, we won't make it.

"Come on," I command. "One last push. We can rest once we slip through the window."

Dervish sighs wearily but staggers to his feet. He reaches for Sharmila. "Wait," I tell him and glance fiercely at Kirilli. "It's time you proved yourself worthy of rescue. Carry her."

"But I have a bad back," he protests. "I never lift anything heavier than—"

"Carry her," I repeat myself, "or I'll cut your legs off, glue them to Sharmila and let her walk out of here on *your* feet."

Kirilli gives a little cry of horror. He suspects I'm bluffing, but he's uncertain.

"I am not that heavy," Sharmilla chuckles. "Especially without my legs."

"We're nearly there," I tell the stage magician. "You won't have to carry her far."

"Very well," Kirilli snaps. "But if I throw my back out of joint, I'll sue." He flashes me a feeble grin and picks up Sharmila. I help settle her on his back, then push through the zombies converging on us, lashing out with both my small fists, praying for the strength to stay on my feet long enough to guide us all to safety.

→I'm almost fully drained. Only a sheer stubborn streak keeps me going. I refuse to fall this close to the end. It happened before, in the cave all those centuries ago. I almost made it out. I could see the exit as the rock ground shut around it. It was horrible to come up short with freedom in sight. I won't taste that defeat again.

Deckchairs and unbolted fixtures slide down the deck. Some of the zombies topple and slide too. Extra obstacles for us to dodge. The end of the ship continues to rise out of the water. A few more minutes and the angle will be too steep to climb. We'll slip backwards to perish with the zombies when the ship's dragged under.

We catch sight of the swimming pool. The window's still open and Kernel's in front of it. But he's struggling with a zombie. There are dozens around him and the window, separated from them by a circle of magic. But one has pierced his defences and is wrestling with him.

"Kernel!" I cry. "Hold on. We're almost with you. We—"

Kernel shouts something in response. He tries to tear himself away from the zombie, then reaches for its head to rip it loose — it's only attached by jagged strips of flesh to the neck. There's a flash of blinding light and we all cover our eyes, Kirilli dropping Sharmila out of necessity.

When I open my eyes a few seconds later, it's like looking at a bright light through several layers of plastic. I blink furiously to clear my vision. When I can see properly, I look for Kernel. The circle where he was is still in place. The zombies around it are all momentarily sightless, stumbling into each other, rubbing their eyes. But the window is gone. And where it stood – where Kernel and the zombie were battling – is an ugly swill of tattered flesh, clumps of guts, fragments of bones and several pints of wasted human blood.

THE ONLY WAY

→Stunned, I stare at the spot where Kernel and the window were. I'm not sure what happened. Where did the explosion of light come from? Are those the remains of Kernel and the zombie, or just one of them? Did Kernel slip through the window before it closed or did he perish here, the window blinking out of existence along with its creator?

"Is he dead?" Dervish roars, smashing the nose of a zombie which was about to sink its teeth into my skull.

"I don't know."

"Sharmila?"

She shakes her head uncertainly.

Dervish doesn't bother to ask Kirilli. He glances around, desperation lending a wild look to his already strained features. "The lifeboats," he mutters. "We have to get away from here or we'll be sucked under."

"But—" I begin.

"No time," he barks, staggering towards the nearest lifeboat. "Come on. Don't stand there gawping."

Kirilli moans and stumbles after Dervish, picking up

Sharmila without having to be told. She punches weakly at a couple of zombies, not much strength left. We're all firing on our final cylinders. Only the promise of escape keeps us going. But I've thought of something Dervish hasn't. Escape will be more complicated than he thinks.

→Dervish is working on a lifeboat when I reach him. He doesn't have the magic to release it, so he's having to manually lower it over the side. Kirilli is helping.

"We had a safety drill a few days ago," Kirilli boasts. "Leave it to me. I know what to do. If we pull this lever here…"

"That's where the oar goes," Dervish growls, pushing Kirilli aside.

The lifeboat slides towards the edge of the ship, but comes to a sudden halt just above the rails. "It's stuck," Dervish grunts, pushing at it, looking for something – anything – else to pull.

"No," I sigh, keeping an eye on several zombies heading our way. "It's the barrier. The ship's still encased in a bubble of magic."

"Nonsense," Dervish snorts. "That's gone. My heart wouldn't be hammering like a pneumatic drill if–"

"The barrier's still there," I stop him. "I don't know how, but it is." I point at the nearest zombie, a woman a long way ahead of the others. "Kirilli, grab her and throw her overboard."

"With pleasure," Kirilli says — the zombie is much smaller than him. He runs across, picks her up and chucks her over the rail. She bounces off an invisible wall and lands on top of Kirilli. As she chews his left forearm he squeals and wriggles free. He kicks her hard, then glares at me. "You knew that was going to happen!"

I ignore the irate conjuror and lock gazes with Dervish. The fight has sapped his strength. He looks like an old man ready for death.

"The barrier might crumble before the ship sinks," Sharmila suggests, more out of wretched hope than any real conviction.

"It's as strong as when we arrived," I disagree. "We could have maybe swum out through the hole in the bottom – the barrier must be breached there, since the water's coming in – but we can't get back to the hold to try."

"The zombies!" Dervish cries, coming alive again. "We can use them to punch a hole through the barrier. I did that in Slawter, exploded a demon against the wall of energy. It worked there — it can work here."

"I'm not sure," I mutter, but Dervish has already set his sights on a zombie. Finding extra power from somewhere, he sends the dead person flying against the invisible barrier and holds it there with magic.

"Sharmila," he grunts. "Blast it!"

The old Indian lady tries to focus, but she's too exhausted.

"Leave this to me," Kirilli says, preening himself like an action movie hero. He slides a playing card out from underneath his torn, chewed sleeve, takes careful aim and fires it at the zombie. When it strikes he shouts, "Abracadabra!" and the card and zombie explode.

"There," Kirilli smirks. "I'm not as useless as you thought, am I?"

"Nobody could be," Dervish murmurs, but the humour is forced. The explosion hasn't dented the barrier. It holds as firmly as before.

"They're not powerful enough," I note sadly, felling another zombie as it attacks. "The magic they're working off isn't the same as ours. They're puppets of the Shadow, not real creatures of magic. We could butcher a thousand against the barrier, but it won't work any better than exploding normal humans."

"That's why Juni sent the demons back to their own universe," Dervish groans. "So we couldn't use them if we got away from the Shadow."

"Lord Loss isn't a fool," I smile sadly. "He learns from his mistakes."

"We're finished," Dervish says miserably.

"Aye," I sigh, unconsciously mimicking Beranabus. "All that's left to determine is whether the zombies eat us or if we drown in the deep blue sea."

I stare at the ranks of living dead shuffling towards us. The Shadow's magic is dwindling. Many of the zombies have fallen and lie twitching or still, returned to the lifeless state from which the Shadow roused them. But a lot remain active, clambering up from the lower levels, massing and advancing, hunched over against the sharp, angled incline of the deck. If the ship doesn't sink within the next few minutes, they'll overwhelm us.

"I don't want to drown," Kirilli says softly. "I've always been afraid of that. I'd rather be eaten." He tugs at the tattered threads of his jacket, trying to make himself presentable. Facing the oncoming hordes, he takes a deep breath and starts towards them.

"Wait," Sharmila stops him. She's smiling faintly. "Disciples never quit. Zahava must have taught you that. We carry on even when all seems lost. When dealing with matters magical, there is always hope."

"She's right," I tell him. "If Kernel's alive, he might open another window and rescue us. Or I could be wrong about the barrier. Maybe it will vanish before the ship sinks and we can clamber overboard."

"What are the odds?" Kirilli asks.

"Slim," I admit. "But you don't want to surrender to the zombies, only to spot the rest of us slipping free at the last second, do you?"

Kirilli squints at me, struggling to decide.

"Actually I was not planning on a miracle," Sharmila says. "We have the power to save ourselves. We do not need to rely on divine intervention."

"What are you talking about?" Dervish frowns.

"There is a way out," Sharmila says. "We can blow a hole in the barrier."

"You've sensed a demon?" I cry, doing a quick sweep of the ship, but finding nothing except ourselves and the zombies.

"No," Sharmila says. "We do not need demons." She looks peaceful, much younger than her years. "*We* are beings of magic."

Dervish's expression goes flat. So does mine. We understand what she's saying. As one, our heads turn and we stare at Kirilli.

"What?" he growls suspiciously.

"No," Sharmila chuckles. "I was not thinking of poor Kirilli. I doubt he would volunteer and we are not, I hope, prepared to turn on one of our own and murder him like a pack of savages."

"We'll draw lots," Dervish says quickly. "Kirilli too, whether he likes it or not."

"Draw lots for *what?*" Kirilli shouts, still clueless.

"There will be no lottery," Sharmila says firmly. "Bec is too young and Kirilli is not willing."

"Fine," Dervish huffs. "That leaves me and you. Fifty-fifty."

"No," Sharmila says. "You must be a father to Bec. She has lost Beranabus. She cannot afford to lose you too."

"Wait a minute…" Dervish huffs.

"Please," Sharmila sighs. "I have no legs. I am the oldest. I have no dependants. And I am now too weak to be of any use — I do not think I could find the power to kill you even if you talked me into letting you take my place."

Dervish gulps and looks to me for help. He wants to persuade her not to do this, to let him be the one who goes out in a blaze of glory.

"Everything she says makes sense," I mumble, practical as always.

"Quickly," Sharmila snaps. "There is almost no magic left. It might be too late already. If you do not act now, it will fade entirely and we will all be lost."

"You're a stubborn old cow, aren't you?" Dervish scowls.

"When I have to be," she smiles.

Dervish checks with me and I nod sadly. We move side by side and link hands. Focusing, we unite our meagre scraps of magic. I wave a hand at Sharmila and she slides across the deck, coming to a stop next to the invisible barrier. She sits up and wipes blood from her cheeks. She smiles at us one last time, then serenely closes her eyes and places her hands together. Her lips move softly in prayer.

Dervish howls, partly to direct our magic, partly out of horror. I howl too. Blue light flashes from our fingertips and strikes Sharmila in the chest. The light drills into her head, snapping it back. For a moment her form holds and I fear our power won't be strong enough.

Then the light crackles and a split second later Sharmila explodes. Her bones, guts, flesh and blood splatter the barrier behind her, while the unleashed energy hammers through the shield, creating a porthole to freedom.

We're both shaken and crying, but we have to act swiftly or Sharmila will have died for nothing. We try nudging the lifeboat over to the hole in the barrier but the restraints won't let it be moved in that direction. Weary beyond belief, I yell for Kirilli to join us. When we link hands, I draw on his energy — he hasn't used as much as we have, so he has a fair supply in reserve. I snap the ropes and chains holding the lifeboat in place. Guided by us, it glides through the air, centimetres above the deck. We shuffle along after it.

When the boat is level with the gap, I edge forward, dragging the others with me, refusing to focus on the gory remains of Sharmila which decorate the rim of the hole. I glance over the rails. We're high up in the air. The water's a long way down. Two options. We can let the boat drop and try to scale down to it. Or...

"Climb in," I grunt.

"Will it fit?" Kirilli asks, studying the lifeboat, then

the hole, trying to make accurate measurements of both. Typical man!

"Just get in, you fool!" I shout. "That hole could snap shut in a second."

Kirilli scrambles in. When the contact breaks, the lifeboat drops and lands on the deck with a clang. I push Dervish ahead of me, then crawl in after him. The zombies are almost upon us, mewling with hunger.

I grab Kirilli's left hand and Dervish's right. Focusing the last vestiges of our pooled magic, I yell at the lifeboat and send it shooting ahead.

It catches in the hole, jolts forward a few centimetres under pressure from me, then stalls. It's too wide. We're stuck. Worse — it's plugged the hole, so we can't try jumping to safety. What a useless, stupid way to—

The lifeboat pops free with a sharp, creaking noise. We shoot clear of the hole, the barrier and the ship, gathering momentum. We sail through the air like some kind of crazily designed bird. We're whooping and cheering.

Then, before any of us realises the danger of our situation, we hit the sea hard. The boat flips over. I bang my head on the side. My mouth fills as I spill into the sea. I try to spit the water out, but I haven't the energy. As I sink slowly, I raise my eyes and steal one last look at the sky through the liquid layers above me. Then the world turns black.

ALL AT SEA

→Arms squeeze my stomach and I vomit. My eyes flutter open and I groan. My head's hanging over the edge of the lifeboat, bits of my last meal bobbing up and down in the water beneath me. I know from the memories flooding into me that Dervish is doing the squeezing.

"It's OK," I groan as he tenses his arms to try again. "I'm alive."

Dervish gently tugs me back over the side. There's water in the bottom. Kirilli is bailing it out with his hands. But we're afloat and the lifeboat doesn't look like it sustained any major damage.

"We thought we'd lost you," Dervish says, smiling with relief. "Kirilli fished you out, but you were motionless…" He clears his throat and brushes wet hair back from my eyes. The tenderness in his expression warms me more than the sun.

"Have I been unconscious long?" I ask.

"No."

"The ship…?"

"Still there."

Dervish helps me sit up and we gaze at the sinking vessel. It's listing sharply. It can't last much longer. We're quite far away from it, but if I squint I can make out the shapes of zombies throwing themselves through the hole in pursuit of us. They don't last long once they hit the water.

Kirilli stops bailing and studies the ship with us. We don't say a word. It's a weird sensation, watching something so huge and majestic sink out of sight. It's as if the ship is a living creature that's dying. I feel strangely sad for it.

"All those people," Dervish sighs as the last section slips beneath the waves in a froth of angry bubbles. "I wish we could have saved them."

"Beranabus," I whisper, fresh tears welling in my eyes. "Sharmila. Kernel."

"A costly day's work," Dervish says bitterly. "And we didn't even destroy the Shadow. It'll come after us again. We've lost our leader and two of the strongest Disciples. If Lord Loss was telling the truth, Grubbs is probably dead too. Hardly counts as a victory, does it?"

He doesn't know how true that is. I start to tell him what I learnt about the Shadow, but Kirilli interrupts.

"When I left you in the hold," he says shiftily, "I hope you didn't think I was running off. I just wanted to make sure the stairs and corridors were clear, so we could make a quick getaway together."

"Of course," Dervish murmurs. "It never crossed our thoughts that you might have lost your nerve and fled like a cowardly rat, leaving the rest of us in the lurch. You're a hero, Kirilli."

Dervish claps sarcastically and Kirilli looks aside miserably. I put my hands over Dervish's and stop him. "Don't," I croak. "He helped us in the end. We couldn't have escaped without him."

"I suppose," Dervish mutters.

Kirilli looks up hopefully. "You mean that?"

"We'd never have shifted this boat ourselves," I assure him. "We needed your magic. If you'd fought in the hold and used up your power, we'd have all died."

"Then it worked out for the best," Kirilli beams. "I did the right thing running. I thought so. When I was down there, sizing up the situation, I—"

"Don't push your luck," Dervish growls. Then he narrows his eyes and studies Kirilli closely. "Are those bite marks?"

"Yes," Kirilli says pitifully. He stares at the stumps where his fingers were bitten off. He must have unwittingly used magic to stop the bleeding, scab over the flesh and numb the pain. He'll be screeching like a banshee once the spell fades.

"Those beasts bit and clawed me all over," Kirilli says

sulkily, ripping a strip off a sleeve to wrap around the stumps. "I'm lucky they didn't puncture any vital veins or arteries. If I hadn't fought so valiantly, they'd have eaten me alive."

"Such a shame," Dervish purrs, shaking his head.

"What?" Kirilli frowns.

"You've seen a few zombie films in your time, haven't you?"

"One or two," Kirilli sniffs. "I don't like horror films. Why?"

"You must know, then, that their saliva is infectious. When a zombie bites one of the living, that person succumbs to the disease and turns—"

"No!" Kirilli cries, dropping the strip of shirt and lurching to his feet. "You're joking! You must be!"

Dervish shrugs. "I'm only telling you what I've seen in the movies. It might all be nonsense, but when you think about it logically…"

As Kirilli's face crumples, Dervish winks at me. I stifle a smile. This isn't nice, but Kirilli deserves it. Not for being a coward, but for trying to lie. A good scare will do him no harm at all.

→We drift for hours. The sun descends. Night claims the sky. After letting Kirilli fret for an hour, Dervish finally told him it was a wind-up. Kirilli cursed us foully and imaginatively. But he calmed down after a while and we've been silent since, bobbing about, absorbing the refreshing rays of the sun, thinking about the dead.

It all seems hopeless without Beranabus, especially knowing what I do about the Shadow. Mankind has reached breaking point and I can't see any way forward. I doubt if even Beranabus could have made a difference. There are some things you can't fight. Certain outcomes are inevitable.

Kirilli has spent the last few minutes examining the lifeboat, scouring it from bow to stern. He returns to his seat with a bottle of water and a small medical box. "Good news and bad," he says, opening the box and looking for ointment to use on his wounds. The healing spell must have passed because he's grimacing. "The good news — both oars are on board, there are six bottles of water and this medical box. The bad news — there's no radio equipment or food, and once we drink the water we can't replace it."

"Do you know if the crew of the ship sent a distress signal?" Dervish asks.

"No idea. Even if they did, would it have penetrated the magical barrier?"

"Probably not," Dervish sighs. "Can I have some water?"

Kirilli takes a swig, then passes it across. "Not too much," he warns. "That has to last."

Dervish chuckles drily. "It'll probably last longer than me. My heart could pop any minute."

"Let me check." I place my hand on his chest and concentrate. I can sense the erratic beat of his heart. He's in very poor condition. He needs hospitalisation or magic. If we could cross to the universe of the Demonata, we'd be fine.

I try absorbing power from the air, to open a window, but there's virtually nothing to tap into and I'm in a sorry state. The moon will lend me strength when it rises, but it won't be enough.

"Were you trying to open a window?" Dervish asks softly.

"Yes."

"No joy?"

"I'll be able to later, when I'm stronger," I lie. But Dervish sees through me.

"No tears," he croaks as I start to cry. "Don't waste the moisture."

"It's OK," Kirilli says, trying to cheer me up. "Even if there was no distress signal, the ship's absence will be noted. The seas are monitored by computers and satellites. Most passengers had mobile phones and were in regular contact with family and work colleagues. They'll be missed. I bet there'll be an army of planes, helicopters and ships out here by dawn."

"What if we've drifted so far they can't find us?" Dervish asks.

"We can do without the pessimism, thank you," Kirilli protests.

Dervish laughs, then his expression mellows. "Listen," he says earnestly, "if I do croak and help doesn't come, I want you to use my remains. Understand?"

"I'm not sure I do," I frown.

"There's not much meat on these bones, but it'll keep you going for—"

"No!" I shout. "Don't be obscene."

"I'm being practical," he says. "I'm letting you know I won't object if—"

"There'll be no cannibalism on this boat," I growl. "Right, Kirilli?"

"He has a point," Kirilli mutters. "He wouldn't just be a food source — humans are seventy per cent water. And we could use his skin for shelter. His bones might come in handy too, if we have to fight off sharks or—"

"Nobody's eating anybody!" I yell, then burst into tears.

"OK," Dervish soothes me. "I was only trying to help. Don't worry. If you don't want to eat me, I won't force you." He pulls a crooked expression. "Does that sound as crazy as I think?"

I laugh through my tears. "You idiot! Besides," I add, wiping my cheeks clean, "it doesn't matter whether we live or die. It might even be better if we perish on this boat. I'm not sure I want to go back."

"What are you talking about?" Dervish frowns.

I take a deep breath and finally reveal what I learned on the ship. "I touched the Shadow and absorbed some of its memories. I told Beranabus. That's why he gambled so recklessly and sacrificed himself. He knew the Shadow couldn't be defeated, that we couldn't kill it. Sending it back to the Demonata universe for a while was the best we could hope for."

"I don't believe that," Dervish snorts. "I don't care how powerful it is. Everything can be killed."

"Not the Shadow," I disagree.

I lie back in the boat and stare at the darkening sky, listening to the waves lap against the sides of the boat. It's peaceful. I wouldn't mind if I fell asleep now and never awoke.

"The Shadow's not a demon," I explain quietly, and Dervish and Kirilli have to lean in close to hear. "It's a force that somehow acquired consciousness. I don't know how, but it has."

"A force?" Dervish scowls.

"Like gravity," I explain. "Imagine if gravity developed a mind, created a body and became an actual entity — Gravity with a capital G, intelligent like us, able to think and plan."

"That's impossible," Dervish says. "Gravity's like the wind or sunlight. It can't develop consciousness."

"But imagine it could," I push. "You've seen the true

nature of the universes. You know magic exists, that just about anything is possible. *Imagine*."

Dervish takes a moment to adjust his thinking. "OK," he says heavily. "It's a struggle, but I'm running with it. Gravity has a mind. It's given itself a body. And it's coming after humanity. Is that what you're telling me?"

"Almost," I smile weakly. "But it's not gravity. It's an altogether different force. More sinister. Inescapable. Every living being's final companion."

"Don't tease us with riddles," Dervish snaps. "Just spit it out."

"I think I already know," Kirilli says softly. "The greatest stage magician ever was Harry Houdini. He was a master escapologist. He could cheat any trap known to man. But there was one thing he couldn't escape, no matter how hard he tried, and it caught him eventually — the Grim Reaper."

"Aye."

I sigh as Dervish stares at me with growing understanding and horror, then close my eyes and cross my hands over my chest. I think about Beranabus, Sharmila, Kernel. Dervish's weak heart. The trap Lord Loss set for Grubbs. What will happen to Kirilli and me if help doesn't arrive in time.

Dead ends everywhere. The dead coming back to life on the ship. Juni and me returning to life from beyond the grave. The Shadow's promise to the Demonata, that they'll live forever once the war with humanity is over.

"The Shadow is ancient beyond understanding," I whisper. "It's as old as life. It doesn't have an actual name. It never needed one. But we've given it a title. The demons have too. It's the darkness when a light is quenched, the silence when a sound fades. It takes the final breath from the smallest insect and the mightiest king. It knows us all, stalks us all, and in the end claims us all.

"The Shadow is *Death*."

WOLF ISLAND

WOLF ISLAND

SHADOW PLAY

→A five-headed demon with the body of a giant earwig bears down on me. I leap high into the air and unleash a paralysing spell. The demon stiffens, quivers wildly, then collapses. Its brittle legs shatter beneath the weight of its oversized body. Beranabus and Kernel move in on the helpless bug. I follow halfheartedly, stifling a yawn. Just another dull day at the office.

One of the demon's heads looks like a crow, another a vulture, while the rest look like nothing on Earth. It opens its bird-like beak and squirts a thick, green liquid. Beranabus ducks swiftly, but the spit catches Kernel's right arm. His flesh bubbles away to the bone. Cursing with more irritation than pain, he uses magic to cleanse his flesh and repair the damage.

"We could do with a bit of help here," Kernel growls as I stroll after them.

"I doubt it," I grunt, but break into a jog, just in case the demon's tougher than we anticipated. Wouldn't want to let the team down.

The earwig unleashes another ball of spit at Beranabus. The elderly magician flicks a hand at the liquid, which rebounds over the demon's heads. It screams with shock and then agony. Kernel, back to full health, freezes the acidic spit before it fries the creature's brains. We want this ugly baby alive.

I leap on to the demon's back. Its shell is slimy beneath my bare feet. Stinks worse than a thousand sweaty armpits. But in this universe that doesn't even begin to approach the boundaries of disgusting. I confronted a demon made of vomit a few months ago. The only way to subdue it was to suck on the strands of puke and sap it of its strength. Yum!

This wasn't a career move. I didn't read a prospectus and go, "Hmm, drinking demon puke… I could do that!" Life just led me here. I'm a magician, and if you're born with a power like mine, you tend to get drawn into the war with the Demonata hordes. I fought my destiny for a long time, but now I grudgingly accept it and get on with the job at hand.

The earwig shudders, overcoming my paralysing spell. It tries to buck me off, but I dig my toes in and drive a fist through the shell. I let magical warmth flood from my fingers. An electric shock crackles through the demon. It squeals, then collapses limply beneath me.

Beranabus and Kernel face the demon's vulture-like head and interrogate it. I stay perched on its back, hand immersed in its gooey flesh, green blood staining my forearm, nose crinkled against the stench.

"What is it?" Beranabus shouts, punching the twisted head, then grabbing the beak. "What's its real name? Where's it from? How powerful is it? What are its plans?" He releases his hold and waits for an answer.

The demon only moans in response. There are thousands of demon languages. I can't speak any, but there are spells you can cast to understand them. I generally don't bother. I'm sure this demon knows no more about the mysterious Shadow than any of the hundreds we've tormented over the last however many months that we've been on this wild goose chase.

The Shadow is the name we've given to a demon of immense power. It's a massive, pitch-black beast, seemingly stitched together out of patches of shadow, with hundreds of snake-like tentacles. Beranabus thinks it's the greatest threat we've ever faced. Lord Loss – an old foe of mine – said the Shadow was going to destroy the world. When a demon master makes a prediction like that, only a fool doesn't take note.

We've been searching for the monster ever since we first encountered it in a cave, on a night when I lost my brother, but saved the world. We've been trying to find out more about it by torturing creatures like this giant earwig. We know the Shadow has assembled an army of demons, promising them the destruction of mankind and even the end of death itself. But we don't know who it is, where it comes from, exactly how powerful it is.

"This is your last chance," Beranabus growls, taking a step back from the earwig. "Tell us what you know or we'll kill you."

The demon makes a series of spluttering noises. Beranabus and Kernel listen attentively while I scratch my neck and yawn again.

"The same old rubbish," Kernel murmurs when the demon finishes.

"Unless it's lying," Beranabus says without any real hope.

The earwig babbles rapidly, panicked.

"Spare you?" Beranabus muses, as if it's a novel idea. "Why should we?"

More squeaks and splutters.

"Very well," Beranabus says after a short pause. "But if you discover something and don't tell us…" There's no need for him to finish. The magician is feared in this universe of horrors. The earwig knows the many kinds of hell we could put it through.

I withdraw my hand from the hole in the earwig's shell and jump to the ground. We're in a gloomy realm, no sun in the dark purple sky. The land around us is like a desert. I make my hand hard and jab it into the dry earth, over and over, cleaning the green blood from my skin. Kernel opens a window while I'm doing that. When I'm ready, we step through into the next zone, in search of more demons to pump for information about the elusive, ominous Shadow.

INNER SILENCE

→Six demons later, we rest for a while on a deserted asteroid in the blackest depths of demonic space, each of us sheltered by a magical force field which provides oxygen and warmth. Beranabus creates a few balls of light, directing the rays down, shielding us from any passers-by. In this universe you're never safe, even in areas usually devoid of life.

You don't have to sleep, eat or drink much here, but it helps to rest every so often and recharge your batteries. I haven't been to this spot before, so I go on a stroll in case there's anything worth seeing. We've cut a wild, meandering route through demon territories since I linked up with Beranabus. He's worried that Lord Loss or others of the Shadow's forces are tracking us, so we've kept on the move, hopefully several steps ahead of any pursuers.

The asteroid's as uninteresting as I thought it would be, just pitted rock, not even any unusual formations. I thought this universe was amazing when I first came.

The physical laws vary from zone to zone. I've seen mountains floating overhead. A world made of glass. I've been inside the bowels of giant demons. Squashed miniature worlds, killing billions of bacterial demons with a well-placed foot.

I'm not so easily impressed now. It wears you down, the constant weirdness, torturing, killing. Days and demons blur. You can't stop and marvel at wonders all the time. You start to take them for granted. I see a demon the size of a city, with the face of the Mona Lisa. Big deal. All I care about is how to kill it.

I'm not scared any more either. I was, the first few demons we fought. The old Grubbs Grady yellow streak shone through and I had to battle hard to stand my ground and not flee like a spineless loser. But fear fades over time. I no longer worry about dying. It's going to happen sooner rather than later — I've accepted that. I don't even give thanks any more when we scrape through a fierce battle.

But close fights are rare. Most of the demons we target are weak and craven. We don't tackle the stronger beasts, focusing instead on the dregs of the universe. I could defeat most of them single-handed. We always work as a unit, but don't often need to. I've fought thousands of demons, but I could count the number of times my life has been in danger on the fingers of one hand.

Fighting demons and saving the world might sound awesome, but in fact it's a bore. I used to have more excitement on a Friday night at home, watching a juicy horror flick with Bill-E or wrestling with my friend Loch.

→Kernel's playing with invisible lights when I return. His eyes were stabbed out in Carcery Vale. I thought he'd be blind for life, but you can work all sorts of miracles in this universe. Using magic, he eventually pieced together a new pair. They look a lot like his original set, only the blue's a shade brighter and tiny flickers of different colours play across them all the time.

The flickers are shadows of hidden patches of light. Apparently, the universes are full of them. When a mage or demon opens a window between realms, the mysterious lights cluster together to create the fissure. But only Kernel can see the patches. He can also manipulate them with his hands, allowing him to open windows faster than any other human or demon.

Beranabus was worried that Kernel might not be able to see the lights when he rebuilt his eyes, but actually his vision has improved. He can see patches he never saw before, small, shimmering lights which constantly change shape. He can't control the newly revealed patches. He's spent a lot of time fiddling with them, without any success.

I sit and watch Kernel's hands making shapes in the air. His eyes are focused, his expression intense, like he's under hypnosis. There are goose bumps on his chocolate-coloured skin. Beads of sweat roll down his bald head, but turn to steam as they trickle close to his eyes. He freaks me out when he's like this. He doesn't look human.

Of course he's *not* entirely human. Nor am I. We're hosts to an ancient weapon known as the Kah-Gash, which sets us apart from others of our species. Together with Bec – a girl from the past, but returned to life in the present – we have the power to reverse time and, if the legends are to be believed, destroy an entire universe. Coolio!

I'm constantly aware of the Kah-Gash within me. It's a separate part of myself, forever swirling beneath the surface of my skin and thoughts. It used to speak to me but it hasn't said anything since that night in the cave. I often try to question it, to find out more about the weapon's powers and intentions. But the Kah-Gash is keeping quiet. No matter what I say, it doesn't respond.

Maybe if Kernel, Bec and I experimented as a team, we could unearth its secrets. But Beranabus is wary of uniting us. We couldn't control the Kah-Gash when we first got together. It took a direction of its own. It worked in our favour on that occasion, but he's afraid it might just as easily work against us next time. The old magician has spent more than a thousand years searching for the scattered pieces of the Kah-Gash, but now that he's reassembled them, he's afraid to test the all-destructive weapon.

I miss the voice of the Kah-Gash. I was never truly alone when it was there, and loneliness is something I'm feeling a lot of now. I miss my half-brother, Bill-E, taken from me forever that night in the cave. I miss school, my friends, Loch's sister Reni. I miss the world, the life I knew, TV, music — even the weather!

But most of all I miss Dervish. My uncle was like a father to me since my real dad died. In an odd way I love him more than I loved my parents. I took them for granted and assumed they'd always be around. I knew they'd die at some point, but I thought it would be years ahead, when they were old. Having learnt my lesson the hard way, I made the most of every day with Dervish, going to bed thankful every night that he was still alive and with me.

I could tell Dervish about the demons, the dullness, the loneliness. He'd listen politely, then make some dry, cutting comment that would make it all seem fine. Time wouldn't drag if I had Dervish to chat with between battles.

I wonder what he's doing, how he's coping without me, how much time has passed in my world. Time operates differently in this universe. Depending on where you are, it can pass slower or quicker than on Earth. Kernel told me that when he first came here with Beranabus, he thought he'd only spent a few weeks, but he returned home to find that seven years had passed.

We've been trying to stick to zones where time passes at the same rate as on Earth, so that we can respond swiftly if there's a large-scale assault or if Bec gets into trouble. But Beranabus is elderly and fuzzy-headed. If not for the emergence of the Shadow, I think he'd have shuffled off after the fight in the cave to see out his last few years in peace and quiet. Kernel has absolute faith in him but I wouldn't be shocked if we returned to Earth only to find that a hundred years have passed and everyone we knew is pushing up daisies.

As if reacting to my thoughts, Beranabus groans and rolls on to his back. He blinks at the darkness, then lets his eyelids flutter shut, drifting into sleep. His long, shaggy hair is almost fully grey. His old suit is torn in many places, stained with different shades of demon blood. The flower in the top buttonhole of his jacket, which he wears in memory of Bec, is drooping and has shed most of its petals. His skin is wrinkled and splotchy, caked with filth. His toenails are like dirty, jagged claws. Only his hands are clean and carefully kept, as always.

Kernel mutters a frustrated curse.

"No joy?" I ask.

"I can't get near them," he snaps. "They dart away from my touch. I wish I knew what they were. They're bugging the hell out of me."

"Maybe they're illusions," I suggest. "Imaginary blobs of light. The result of a misconnection between your new eyes and your brain."

"No," Kernel growls. "They're real, I'm sure of it. I just don't know what…"

He starts fiddling again. He needs to lighten up. It can't be healthy, wasting his time on a load of lights that might not even be real. Not that I've done a lot more than him in my quieter moments. I wish I had a computer, a TV, a CD player. Hell, I'd even read a book — that's how low I've sunk!

I'm thinking of asking Kernel to open a window back to Earth, so I can nip through and pick up something to distract me, when Beranabus stirs again.

"Was I asleep for long?" he asks.

"A few minutes," I tell him.

He scowls. "I thought I'd been out for hours. That's the trouble with this damn universe — you can't get any decent sleep."

Beranabus stands and stretches. He looks around with his small, blue-grey eyes and yawns. This is about the only time you can see his mouth properly. Mostly it's hidden behind a thick, bushy beard. All our hair was burnt away when we travelled through time, but it's grown back. I think he looked better without the beard, but he likes it. I grew my ginger hair the same way as before too. I guess you always go with what you're used to.

"I suppose we'd better—" Beranabus begins.

"Quiet!" Kernel hisses, cocking his head. This is a new tic of his. Several times recently he's shushed us. He says he can hear muted whispers, hints of sounds which seem to come from the patches of light.

A few minutes pass. Kernel listens intently while Beranabus and I keep our peace. Finally he relaxes and shakes his head.

"Could you make out anything?" Beranabus asks.

"No," Kernel sighs. "I'm not even sure it's speech. Maybe it's just white noise."

"Or maybe you're going crazy," I throw in.

"Maybe," Kernel agrees.

"I was joking," I tell him.

"I wasn't," he replies.

"Well, whatever it is, it can wait," Beranabus says. "We've had enough rest. Open another window and we'll go find a few more demons."

Kernel sighs, then concentrates. Roll on the next round of inquisitions and torture.

TO THE RESCUE

→We're chasing a flock of terrified sheep demons. Each one is covered with hundreds of small, woolly heads. No eyes or ears, just big mouths full of sharp demon teeth. All the better to eat you with, my dear.

Beranabus thinks the sheep might know something about the Shadow. Stronger demons prey on these weak creatures. He's hoping they might have heard something useful if any of the Shadow's army struck their flock recently. It's a long shot, but Beranabus has devoted his life to long shots.

As we close in on the frantic demons, Kernel stops and stares at a spot close by.

"Come on!" Beranabus shouts. "Don't stop now. We—"

"A window's opening," Kernel says, and Beranabus instantly loses interest in everything else.

"Start opening one of your own," the magician barks, moving ahead of Kernel to protect him from whatever might come through. I step up beside the ancient magician, heart pounding hard for the first time in ages.

"Wait," Kernel says as Beranabus drains magic from the air. "It's not a demon." He studies the invisible lights, then smiles. "We have company."

A few seconds later, a window of dull orange light forms and the Disciple known as Shark emerges, quickly followed by Dervish's old friend, Meera Flame.

"Shark!" Kernel shouts happily.

"Meera!" I yell, even happier than Kernel.

Beranabus glares suspiciously at the pair.

Meera wraps her arms around me and I whirl her off her feet. We're both laughing. She kisses my cheeks. "You've grown," she hoots. "You must be two and a half metres tall by now!"

"Not quite," I chuckle, setting her down and beaming. Meera used to stay with us a lot and helped me look after Dervish when he was incapacitated a few years back. I had a big crush on Meera when I was younger. Hell, looking at her in her tight leather trousers and jacket, I realise I still do. She's a bit on the old side but doesn't show it. If only she had a thing for younger guys!

Kernel and Shark are shaking hands, both talking at the same time. I've never seen Kernel this animated. Shark's wearing army fatigues, looking much the same as ever.

"Hi, Shark," I greet the ex-soldier.

He frowns at me. "Do I know you?"

"Grubbs Grady. We…" I stop. I've met Shark twice before, but the first time was in a dream, and the second was in a future which we diverted. As far as he's concerned, I'm a stranger. It's simpler not to explain our previous encounters, especially as I saw him ripped to bits by demons the second time.

"Dervish told me about you," I lie. "I'm Grubbs, his nephew."

Shark nods. "I can see a bit of him in you. But you've got more hair. You're a lot taller too — what's Beranabus been feeding you?"

"Enough of the prattle," Beranabus snaps. "What's wrong?"

As soon as he says that, the mood switches. Shark and Meera's grins disappear.

"We were attacked," Meera says. "I was at Dervish's. We—"

"Was it Lord Loss?" Beranabus barks. "Is Bec all right?"

"She's fine," Shark says.

"But Dervish…" Meera adds, shooting me a worried glance.

My heart freezes. Not Dervish! Losing my parents, Gret and Bill-E was horrific. Dervish is all I have left. If he's gone too, I don't know if I can continue.

"He was alive when we left," Shark says.

"But in bad shape," Meera sighs. "He had a heart attack."

"We have to go back," I gasp, turning for the window.

Shark puts out a hand to stop me. My eyes flash on the letters S H A R K tattooed across his knuckles, and the picture of a shark's head set between his thumb and index finger. "Hold on," he says. "We didn't come here directly. That leads to another demon world."

"Besides," Kernel adds, "if the demons are still at the house…"

"We weren't attacked by demons," Meera says. "They were…" She locks gazes with me and frowns uncertainly. "*Werewolves*."

We gawp at her. Then, without discussing it, Kernel turns away and his hands become a blur as he sets about opening a window back to the human universe.

→Beranabus crosses first. I'm not far behind. I find myself in a hospital corridor. It looks like the ward where they keep newborn babies. Bec is on the floor close to us. There are two demons. One has the features of an anteater, but sports several snouts. The other is some sort of lizard. Beranabus is addressing them with savage politeness — he's ultra protective of his little Bec.

"What do the pickings look like now?" he asks as Kernel, Shark and Meera step through after us. In response, the demons bolt for safety. Kernel and the Disciples race after them.

"*Dervish?*" I snap at Bec, not giving a damn about demons, babies or anything else except my uncle.

"Back there," Bec pants, pointing back down the corridor. "Hurry. He was fighting a demon. I don't know—"

I run as fast as I can, long strides, readying myself for the worst. I glance into each room that I pass. Signs of struggle and death in some of them, but no Dervish. I pause at the door of what looks to be an empty room. I'm about to push on when something grunts.

Entering, I spot Dervish to my left, half-obscured by an overturned bed. There's a demon on top of him, shaped like a giant insect with a golden shell. It's snapping at Dervish's face, mandibles grinding open and shut. I'm on it in an instant. I make a fist and smash through its protective shell. It shrieks and turns to deal with me, but I fill its guts with fire and it dies screaming. When I'm sure it's dead, I toss it aside and bend over my startled, bleary-eyed uncle. He slaps at me feebly. Doesn't recognise me. He's finding it hard to focus.

"Hey, baldy," I chuckle. "Things must be bad when you can't squish a damn cockroach."

Dervish relaxes and his eyes settle on me. The smile which lights his face is almost enough to bring me to tears.

"Grubbs!" he cries, throwing his arms around me.

"Don't go all blubbery on me," I mutter into his shoulder, fighting back sobs.

Dervish pushes himself away, touches my face with wonder, then says in that wry tone I recall so well, "You could have sent me a card while you were away."

"No post offices," I grunt, and we beam at each other.

→Waiting while the Disciples cleanse the hospital of demons. I should help them, but this will probably be the only private time I get with Dervish. Things have a habit of moving swiftly when Beranabus gets involved. Once they finish off the last demon, talk will turn to the werewolf attack and there might not be any time to sit with my uncle and chat. I've devoted a huge chunk of my life to Beranabus's cause. I'm due a few minutes of down time.

"I told you healthy eating wasn't worthwhile," I say, nudging Dervish in the ribs (but gently — he looks like blood mixed in with lumpy porridge). "You told me I should watch my diet. But who had a heart attack first?"

"As illogical as ever," Dervish scowls. "I thought you might have matured while you were away, but obviously you haven't."

"Seriously, how have you been?" I ask.

"Apart from the heart attack?"

"Yeah."

He shrugs, looking older than I'd have thought possible. "I'm about ready to follow Billy into the wide blue yonder."

My face stiffens. "Don't say that, not even joking."

"No joke," he sighs. "I was given a single task by Beranabus — guard the entrance to the cave — and I screwed it up. I told Billy's mum I'd look after him — some job I did of that. I took you in and promised you'd be safe with me, then…"

"I *was* safe with you."

"Yeah, I really protected you. Lord Loss and his familiars didn't get anywhere near you on my watch, did they?"

"That wasn't your fault," I tell him heavily. "You did the best you could. For me *and* Bill-E."

"Then why is he dead and why are you lost to me?" Dervish moans.

"Because we live in a world under siege," I say. "Life sucks for mages and magicians — *you* taught me that. Bad things happen to those of us who get involved, but if we didn't fight, we'd be in an even worse state. None of it's your fault, any more than it's the fault of the moon or the stars."

Dervish nods slowly, then arches an eyebrow. "*The moon or the stars?*"

"I always get poetical when I'm dealing with self-pitying simpletons."

We laugh. This is what I love best about my relationship with Dervish — the more we insult each other, the happier we are. I'm trying to think of something disgusting and hair-curling to say when Beranabus appears. He's using baby-wipes to clean his hands.

"Still alive?" he asks Dervish.

"Just about."

"We're finished here. Time to go."

It's not fair. We've only had a few minutes together. I want to ask Dervish about Bec and how they're coping. How he explained Bill-E's disappearance to our neighbours. What's happening with my friends. I want to complain about my life with Beranabus and boast about all the action I've seen.

But those are childish, selfish wishes. We're in the middle of a maternity ward. I've seen several dead and dismembered bodies already — nurses, mothers, babies. There are probably dozens more scattered throughout the hospital. I'd be the shallowest person in the universe if, in the face of all that tragedy, I moaned of not having enough time to spend with my uncle.

"Where are we going?" I ask.

"The roof," Beranabus says. "We need to discuss the situation before moving on. It's more complicated than we thought. Bec says the demons who struck were led by Juni Swan." I stare at him incredulously, then start to shout questions. "Not now!" Beranabus stops me. "We'll talk about it on the roof."

"I don't think I can make it that far," Dervish says.

Beranabus mutters something beneath his breath – it sounds like, "I hate the damn Gradys!" – then picks up Dervish.

"I can carry him," I say quickly.

"No," Beranabus grunts. "Keep watch for any demons we might have missed."

Settling Dervish on his back, the magician heads for the stairs. I follow a metre behind, eyes peeled for monsters all the way up the blood-drenched steps to the roof.

NEW MISSION

→The voice of the Kah-Gash whispers to me as we're climbing the stairs, stunning me by abruptly breaking its months-long silence. *You can join with the others.*

I pause, startled by its sudden and unexpected reappearance. Then, not wanting to let Beranabus know – he might toss Dervish aside in his eagerness to make enquiries of the Kah-Gash – I carry on as normal, addressing it internally. "What do you mean?"

Can't you feel the magic inside Bec and Kernel calling to you?

I have been feeling a strange tickling sensation since I stepped through the window. I put it down to chemical irritants in the air — one thing you can't say about the demon universe is that it's polluted. I've become accustomed to fume-free atmospheres. But now that the Kah-Gash has clued me in, I realise the tickling is the force within myself straining to unite with Bec and Kernel.

"What would happen if we joined?" I ask.

Wonders.

"Care to be a bit more specific?"

No, it answers smugly. I'm not sure if the Kah-Gash is a parasite feeding off me, or if it's woven into my flesh, a part of me like my heart or brain. But its voice bears echoes of mine. I've used that smart-alec tone more times than I can remember.

I'm worried about letting my piece of the Kah-Gash link with the other parts again. What would it do if I gave it free rein? Could we trust it?

You are the control mechanism, the voice says, the first time it's ever told me anything about the nature of itself. *With my help, you can unify the pieces and unleash your full power.*

"But could we control it," I press, "and make the weapon do our bidding?"

To an extent, the voice answers cagily.

"What does that mean?" I grumble, but there's no reply. "Hello? Are you still there?"

Unite us, it says impatiently. *Unleash me. Become the Kah-Gash.*

"Without knowing what I'm letting myself in for? No bloody way!" I snort.

Coward, the Kah-Gash sneers, then falls silent. I feel the tickling sensation fade. I continue up the stairs, brooding on what the voice said and wondering what would have happened if I'd given in to it.

* * *

→On the roof. Another Disciple, Sharmila Mukherji, was seriously wounded by Juni. Her legs are missing from the thighs down. Beranabus is working on the stumps, using magic to stop the bleeding and patch her up. She's unconscious. It doesn't look to me like she'll ever recover.

Dervish is resting on a hospital trolley. Meera's sitting beside him. Shark's guarding the door to the roof, to turn back any curious humans. The rest of us are gathered around Bec, listening to her story.

She tells us about Juni Swan, who's somehow come back to life in a cancerous mockery of a body. Bec says Juni is insane, but more powerful than before. Dervish blasted her from the roof, catching her by surprise when he recovered from the coma he'd been in since his heart attack. I want to go after her, to finish her off, but Bec is adept at sensing where people and demons are, and she says Juni has already fled. Revenge will have to wait for another night.

I thought it would be awkward being around Bec, that she'd remind me of Bill-E, that I'd feel resentful. When he died, she took over his corpse, came back to life, then remoulded the flesh in her original image. In effect, she stole his body. But there's nothing of my half-brother apart from the occasional word or gesture. I have no trouble thinking of her as a separate person with the same right to exist as any other.

Bec speaks quickly, detailing how werewolves attacked our home in Carcery Vale, backed up by humans with guns. She tells us she can absorb people's memories when she touches them. When grappling with a werewolf, she learnt it was a Grady boy who'd been handed to the Lambs to be executed. But the Lambs – executioners set up to dispose of teens with the lycanthropic family curse – didn't kill him. Instead they kept him alive, and found a way to use him and other werewolves as trained killers.

"You're sure the Lambs masterminded the attack in Carcery Vale?" I ask.

"I can't be certain," Bec says. "We didn't see any humans. Sharmila wanted to go after the Lambs once Dervish was safe, but we decided to wait until we'd discussed it with you. The werewolves *might* have been the work of some other group…"

"But they were definitely teenagers who'd been given to the Lambs?" I press. If she's right about this, we have a known enemy to target. If she's wrong, I don't want to waste time chasing an irritating but harmless gang of humans.

"Yes," Bec says. "At least the one I touched was. I don't know about the others."

"They must have been," I mutter. "I've never heard of anyone outside our family being inflicted with the wolfen curse. But why?" I glance at Dervish. "Have you been rubbing Prae Athim up the wrong way?" She's the head honcho of the Lambs. Her and Dervish don't see eye to eye on a number of issues.

"I haven't seen her since she paid us that visit before Slawter," Dervish answers, looking bewildered. "I've got to say, I don't have much time for Prae, but this isn't her style. I could understand it if they were after something – you, for instance, to dissect you and try to find a cure for lycanthropy – but there was nothing in this for them. Those who set the werewolves loose wanted us dead. The Lambs don't go in for mindless, wholesale slaughter."

"But if not the Lambs, who?" Kernel asks.

"I think Lord Loss was behind the attacks," Bec says. "Maybe he realised I was part of the Kah-Gash and wanted to eliminate the threat I pose, or perhaps he just wanted to kill Dervish and me for revenge. The attack tonight by Juni Swan makes me surer than ever that he sent the werewolves. It can't be coincidence."

"Juni Swan," Beranabus echoes, with the guilty look that crosses his face whenever talk turns to his ex-assistant. "I'd never have thought poor Nadia could turn into such a hideous creature. I don't know how she survived." He looks at Bec. "Your spirit flourished after death, but you're part of the Kah-Gash. Juni isn't. Lord Loss must have separated her soul from her body some way, just before her death. That's why he took her corpse when he fled. But I don't understand how he did it."

He mulls it over, then curses. "It doesn't matter. We can worry about her later. You're right — Lord Loss sent the werewolves. I cast spells on Carcery Vale to prevent crossings, except for in the secret cellar, where any demon who did cross would be confined. Even if he found a way around those spells, he would have been afraid to risk a direct confrontation. If he opened a window, the air would have been saturated with magic. You and Dervish could have tapped into that. You were powerful in the cave, stronger than Lord Loss in some ways. He probably thought humans and werewolves stood a better chance of killing you. But that doesn't explain why the Lambs agreed to help him. Or, if they weren't Lambs, how they got their hands on the werewolves."

"Maybe he struck a deal with them," Dervish says. "Promised them the cure for lycanthropy if they helped him murder Bec and me."

"Would they agree to such a deal?" Beranabus asks.

"Possibly."

"Prae Athim's daughter turned into a werewolf," I say softly, recalling my previous meeting with the icy-eyed Lambs leader. "She's still alive. A person will go to all manner of crazy lengths when family's involved." I shoot Dervish a wink.

"An intriguing mystery," Beranabus snorts. "But we can't waste any more time on it. We have more important matters to deal with, not least the good health of Dervish and Miss Mukherji — they'll both be dead soon if we don't take them to the demon universe. Open a window, Kernel."

Kernel eagerly sets to work on a window. His eyes have held up so far, but they won't last indefinitely. The problem with building body parts in the demon universe is they don't work on this world. If he stays too long, Kernel will end up blind as a bat again, with a pair of gooey sockets instead of eyes.

"I'm not going," Dervish says.

"You can't stay here," Beranabus replies quickly, angrily.

"I have to. They attacked me... my home... my friends. I can't let that pass. I have to pursue them. Find out why. Extract revenge."

"Later," Beranabus sniffs.

"No," Dervish growls. "Now." He gets off the trolley and almost collapses. Meera grabs him and holds him up. He smiles at her, then glares at Beranabus. He might be within a whisker of death, but that hasn't affected my uncle's fighting spirit.

"It would help if we knew," Meera says quietly in defence of Dervish. "The attack on Dervish and Bec might have been a trial run. The werewolves could be set loose on other Disciples."

"That's not my problem," Beranabus says callously. He's never been overly bothered about his supporters, and always stresses the fact that they sought him out and chose to follow him — he didn't recruit them.

"There's been a huge increase in crossings," Meera says, which is troubling news to me. "We've seen five or six times the usual activity in recent months. The Disciples are stretched thinly, struggling to cope. If several were picked off by werewolves and assassins, thousands of innocents would die."

"It might be related," Kernel says, pausing and looking back.

"Related to what?" Bec asks, but Beranabus waves her question away. He's frowning, waiting for Kernel to continue.

"This could be part of the Shadow's plan," Kernel elaborates. "It could be trying to create scores of windows so that its army of demons can break through at once. We'll need the Disciples if that's the case — we can't be everywhere at the same time to stop them all."

"Maybe," Beranabus hums. "But that doesn't alter the fact that Dervish will last about five minutes if we leave him here."

"I'll be fine," Dervish snarls.

"No," Beranabus says. "Your heart is finished. You'll die within days. That's not a guess," he adds when Dervish starts to argue. "And you wouldn't be able to do much during that time, apart from wheeze and clutch your chest a lot."

Dervish stares at the magician, badly shaken. I'm appalled too. "It's really that bad?" Dervish croaks.

Beranabus nods, and I can see that he's enjoying bringing Dervish down a peg. He doesn't like people who challenge his authority. "In the universe of magic, you might survive. Here, you're a dead man walking."

"Then get him there quick," I say instantly. "I'll stay."

"Not you too," Beranabus groans. "What did I do to deserve as stubborn and reckless a pair as you?"

"It makes sense," I insist calmly. "If the attacks were Lord Loss trying to get even, they're irrelevant. But if they're related to the Shadow, we need to know. I can confront the Lambs, find out if they're mixed up with the demon master, stop them if they are."

"Is the Shadow the creature we saw in the cave?" Bec asks.

"Aye," Beranabus says. "We haven't learnt much about it, except that it's put together an army of demons and is working hard to launch them across to our world." He stares at me, frowning. He doesn't want to admit that I might have a valid point, but I can tell by his scowl that he knows I do.

"You'd operate alone?" he asks sceptically.

"I'd need help." I glance around. Shark's an obvious choice. I can channel a lot of magic here, but there are times when it pays to have a thickly built thug on your side. But I'll need someone sharp too — I don't have the biggest of brainboxes. "Shark and Meera," I say, with what I hope sounds like authority. Shark can't hear me, but to my surprise Meera responds negatively.

"I want to stay with Dervish," she says.

"He'll be fine," I tell her, trying to sound confident, not wanting them to know how nervous I feel — I've never taken on a mission like this before. "He has Beranabus and Bec to look after him. Unless you want to leave Bec with me?" I ask the magician.

"No," he mumbles, as I guessed he would. "If you're staying, I'll take her to replace you."

"Then go," I say. "Chase the truth on your side. I'll do the same here. If I discover no link between Lord Loss and the Lambs, I'll return. If they *are* working for him, I'll cull the whole bloody lot."

Kernel grunts and a green window opens. "Time to decide," he tells Beranabus. I look from the magician to Meera. She's not happy, but she doesn't raise any further objections.

"Very well," Beranabus snaps. "But listen to Shark and Meera, heed their advice and contact me before you go running up against the likes of Lord Loss or the Shadow." He picks up the unconscious Sharmila. "Follow me, Bec," he says curtly and steps through the window.

Bec stares at us, confused. I flash her a quick grin of

support, which she misses. Meera steps up to her and asks if she's OK. Before I can hear her reply, Dervish is hugging me, squeezing me tight.

"I don't want to leave you," he says, and I can tell he's struggling not to cry. I have a lump in my throat too.

"You have to go," I tell him. "You'll die if you stay here."

"Maybe that would be the easiest thing," he sighs.

I squeeze his ribs until he gasps. "Don't you dare give up," I snarl. "Mum and Dad... Gret and Bill-E... they'd give anything to be where you are now — alive. It doesn't matter how much pain you're in or how sorry you feel for yourself. Alive is better than dead. Always."

"When did you become the sensible one?" Dervish scowls.

"When you became a pathetic mess," I tell him lightly.

"Oh," he grins. "Thanks for clearing that up." He clasps the back of my neck and glares into my eyes. "Be careful, Grubbs. If you die before me, I'll be mad as hell."

"Don't worry," I laugh. "I'll outlive you by decades. I'll be dancing on your grave fifty years from now, just wait and see."

Dervish smiles shakily, then releases me and staggers through the window, massaging his chest with one hand, just about managing not to weep. I hate watching him go. I wish he could stay or that I could leave with him. But wishes don't mean a damn when you've been selected by the universe to spend your life fighting demons.

"Sorry we couldn't have more of a chat," I say to Bec, and I genuinely mean it. I'd like to sit down with her and listen to her full story, learn what life was like sixteen hundred years ago, what she makes of the world now, if *Riverdance* is anything like the real deal.

"Next time," she smiles.

"Yeah," I grunt, not believing for a second that our paths will cross again. In this game you soon learn not to take anything good for granted. The chances are that Bec or I – probably both – will perish at the hands of demons long before the universes can throw us back together.

I think about bidding Kernel farewell, but he doesn't look interested in saying goodbye, so I simply wave at him. He half-waves back, already focusing on Bec. She's his companion now. I mean nothing to him if I'm not by his side, so he won't waste time worrying about me. I know how he feels because I feel the same way about him.

"Come on," I say to a slightly befuddled-looking Meera. "Let's go and break the news to Shark. Do you think he'll mind us volunteering him for a life or death mission?"

"No," Meera sighs as we cross the roof to the doorway. "That dumb goon would be offended if we left him out."

GETTING STARTED

→It's chaos downstairs. Juni Swan forced down a helicopter during the duel on the roof. The flames are still flickering, though the teams of firefighters who were quick on the scene have the worst of the blaze under control. Shattered glass from the hospital windows lines the surrounding streets like crystal confetti. The dead and wounded are everywhere, covered in blankets or being nursed by bloodied, shaken medics. Police buzz around like angry bees.

Shark has no problem talking his way through. A few words with the commanding officer and we're being escorted past the teams of baying news reporters to a spot in the city where we're free to go our own way. The Disciples have contacts in some pretty high places.

First things first — we're exhausted and need to sleep. We find the nearest hotel and book three connecting rooms. The receptionist regards us warily and almost refuses us entry, but when Shark produces a platinum credit card and says he'll pay up front, and that he wants their best rooms, the man behind the desk undergoes a swift transformation.

I'd like to talk through events with Shark and Meera, but both disappear to their beds as soon as we've tipped the bellboy and shut the doors, so I've no choice but to follow their lead.

The room's large, but it feels cramped after a year spent sleeping wild – if not often – beneath vast demonic skies. I open the windows and stick my head out, breathing in fresh air as I replay the scenes from the hospital. Why the hell did I volunteer to stay behind? I could be with Dervish now, catching up, taking care of him. Instead I've promised to track down Prae Athim and put a stop to whatever's going on between Lord Loss and the Lambs. Just *how* I'm going to do that is a mystery. I spoke before I thought, like an over-eager hero. I've been hanging around Beranabus too long!

Withdrawing, I decide the plans can wait. I go to the toilet, then undress and slide beneath the soft bedcovers. I'm worried I won't be able to sleep, that I'll lie awake all night. But within a minute my eyelids go heavy and seconds later it's lights out.

→Breakfast in bed is heavenly. I eat like a ravenous savage, bolting down sausages, bacon, eggs, mushrooms. And toast! How can a few burnt bits of bread smeared with churned-up cow's milk taste so delicious?

There's a knock on one of the connecting doors while I'm mopping up the juice from my baked beans. "C'm' in," I grunt.

Meera appears like an angel, in an ivory-white nightdress. Washed, manicured, the works. You'd never guess that twelve hours earlier she'd been elbow-deep in demon blood.

"Wow!" I exclaim, dropping the toast and clapping.

She beams and gives me a twirl, then perches on the edge of my bed and picks up the toast. "Do you mind?"

"Not at all," I grin, though I'd have bitten the hand off anybody else who tried to take my last piece.

"I've been up for hours," she says.

"You should have woken me."

"Why? Did you want a manicure too?"

"Very funny. But I could have done with a haircut."

"That's for sure," she sniffs. "I ordered some clothes for you. I can't wait to see you in them. I love dressing up boys, especially fashion-challenged teens."

"Me? Fashion-challenged? I never used to be."

"Well, you are now." She takes my tray and tugs at the bedsheets. "Come on. Chop-chop!"

"Whoah!" I yelp, only just managing to grab on to the sheets in time. "I'm naked under here!"

"That's OK," she says. "You sleepwalked into my room last night and did a dance on my rug. I saw it all then."

I stare at her, more horrified than I've been in the face of any demon. Then she winks wickedly and races out of the room before I batter her to death with a pillow.

→Shark's the last to rise. We hold a conference in his room while he tucks into lunch, wearing a robe which just about covers his privates.

"So," he mumbles through a half full mouth. "What's the plan?"

I scratch my head and smile sheepishly. "I kind of hoped you guys would have one..."

Shark and Meera share a wry glance.

"I thought you were our leader," Meera says.

"You set the ball rolling," Shark agrees. "We just came along for the ride."

"I don't know what to do," I grumble. "It was easy in the demon universe. We cornered demons, beat them up and sometimes killed them. It's different here. I don't know where to start. How will we find Prae Athim? It seemed like the simplest thing in the world last night, but now..."

"Not such a big shot in the cold light of day, is he?" Shark jeers.

"Don't tease him," Meera tuts. "It was brave of him to volunteer."

"But stupid." Shark points a thick finger at me. "What

use are you to us? Why shouldn't we leave you here and pick you up when it's all over?"

Stung, I focus on the bed. The mattress quivers and comes alive. It throws off the startled Shark, then bucks from the bed and lands on his back, driving him down. He lashes out, bellowing with alarm, but the mattress smashes him flat and pounds at him relentlessly.

"Enough," Meera says softly, laying a hand on my shoulder.

I scowl at her, then ease up. I'm sweating slightly.

A bruised Shark gets to his feet, smooths his robe and studies me calmly. "OK, I'm impressed. You're a magician?"

"Yes."

"How powerful are you?"

I shrug. "I never really tested myself on this world. That trick with the mattress tired me, but I could do a lot more."

"How much more?" Shark presses.

"No idea," I answer honestly. "But in the absence of any windows between universes, I'm stronger than any mage we'll face."

"I suppose we might as well bring him along," Shark says grudgingly to Meera.

"Where do we start?" Meera asks. "Do you know where Prae Athim's based?"

"I never even heard of her before last night," Shark

says. "I knew about the Grady werewolves and the Lambs, but they were never my problem. Still, this won't be the first time I've gone looking for someone. We'll find her."

"We could do with some help," Meera notes. "They have armed troops, as we saw in Carcery Vale."

"The Disciples?" Shark asks.

"The Disciples," Meera agrees.

The pair produce mobile phones and start dialling.

→The mages aren't interested in our mission. This is a bad time for humanity. Demons are attempting to cross faster, and in greater numbers, than ever before. The Disciples are rushed off their feet, dashing from one crisis to another. There have been six successful crossings this year and more than a dozen foiled attempts. And those are only the recorded attacks — more probably went unnoticed. Over five hundred people that we know of have died, not including those at the hospital last night. That's an average decade's worth of action.

The Disciples that Shark and Meera chat with over the course of the day don't care about werewolves or the Lambs. They don't even respond when told that Beranabus is involved. Most times, the mere mention of his name is enough to whip them into action. But not now. We can fight our own battles as far as they're concerned.

Shark and Meera turn to their other allies when the Disciples fall through. They have a network of contacts — soldiers, politicians, police officers, doctors, etc. They call on them for support when demons cross and create merry hell. The operatives move in to clear up the mess, bury the dead, comfort the survivors, kill the story before it spreads.

Meera's contacts are mostly media types and corporate directors. She rings around, asking about the Lambs, but the Grady executioners keep a low profile. She learns that they have several worldwide bases, but Prae Athim could be at any of them.

Shark takes a different approach. He phones a guy called Timas Brauss and tells him to come as swiftly as possible. He then contacts people in armies or who were once soldiers. He sets about assembling a small unit of men and women with a variety of skills — explosives experts, mechanics, pilots, scuba divers and more. He won't need them all, but he puts in place a large force to draw from. They're more cooperative than the Disciples. Shark seems to command a lot of respect in military circles.

The calls continue into the night. It's the most frustrating day I've spent in a long time. There's nothing I can do except sit, listen and run errands for Shark or Meera, fetching them food and drink.

I try to watch TV, but I can't get comfortable. I'm

worried that Shark and Meera will think I'm slacking. Eventually I crawl into bed, tired and grumpy, thinking I should have stayed in the demon universe. At least I served some bloody good over there!

THE FILTHY TWELVE

→My phone rings unexpectedly. Jolted awake, I check the time on the bedside clock — 07.49. Picking up the phone, I yawn, "Yes?"

"It's me," someone says in a strange accent.

"Who?"

A pause. "You're not Shark."

"No, I'm Grubbs. Shark's in the next room. Do you want me to—"

"It doesn't matter," he interrupts. "I'm Timas Brauss. Tell the receptionist to let me up."

A couple of minutes later there's a knock on my door. I open it to find an incredibly tall, thin man in the corridor. He must be seven or eight centimetres taller than me. Skinny as a stick insect, with long, bony fingers. Floppy red hair, an even darker shade than mine. A startled pair of blue eyes, as if he's in a constant state of shock.

He pushes past me without a word. Looks around the room and up at the ceiling. He's carrying a couple of laptops and a briefcase. He sets them down, then drags the desk by the wall out into the middle of the floor and lays his gear on top of it. Fires up the laptops, takes a few plug-ins out of the briefcase and connects them up.

"Wi-Fi is a blessing from the gods," he mutters as I stare at him. "It was hell on Earth when I had to hook these up to ordinary phone lines. Who are we looking for?"

"A woman called…" I hesitate. "Do you want me to wake Shark?"

Timas shakes his head. "I can work without him. Who are you after?"

"Prae Athim."

"Spell it."

When I've done that, I tell him she works for an organisation called the Lambs. I start to describe the attacks and why we want to find her, but he holds up a hand. "That is enough information for me to be getting on with," he says curtly and bends over his laptops like a pianist. He's soon tapping away at a fierce speed, oblivious to all else, working on both computers at the same time.

→Meera wakes before Shark. She's surprised to find the odd-looking stranger in my room, but says nothing once I've told her in whispers of his approach to business. We eat breakfast, then return to watch Timas Brauss. At one stage I ask if he'd like anything to eat or drink. He shushes me without looking up.

Shark finally rises close to midday. When he steps in to find Timas hard at work, he doesn't look surprised. Stretching, he nods at Meera and me, then grunts at the man hunched over the laptops. "What do you have?"

Timas spins neatly to face Shark, letting his fingers rest on his knees. He looks like an overgrown schoolboy. "I have a full profile of the woman, Prae Argietta Athim. Do you want to know her background?"

"Couldn't care less," Shark sniffs. "Where is she?"

Timas clicks his tongue. "I would need more time to answer definitively. But I can tell you where she should be if she's adhering to her regular schedule."

"That'll do," Shark says.

Timas reads out a long address, down to the postal code, finishing off with her floor and office number.

"It's a regular building?" Shark asks.

"Yes. The Lambs own the complex. A mix of offices, laboratories and miscellaneous divisions. I've downloaded a schematic plan of the structure and environs."

"Let's see." Shark pushes Timas aside and studies the right-hand screen. Meera and I edge over to look at it with him. The blueprints mean nothing to me – my eyes go blurry from looking at all the lines – but Shark nods happily as he scrolls down. "Should be easy enough to crack. Security systems?"

"Downloading," Timas says, tapping the other laptop.

"How much longer?"

"Maybe an hour. They are very cleverly protected. An invigorating challenge."

Shark stretches again. He looks pleased. "Unless they've packed the corridors with troops, this should be a piece of cake. We'll put a small team together, waltz in, grab Prae Athim, shake her up… be home in time for supper."

"You really think it'll be that easy?" Meera asks sceptically.

"Like hell," Shark grins. "But you know me — ever the optimist."

→ While Timas continues to play his keyboards, Shark gets back on the phone to those on his shortlist. Meera also makes a few calls, in case any of her contacts have discovered anything about the Lambs. I sit around as impatiently as the day before, twiddling my thumbs.

The first of Shark's team arrives at five, a chunky woman called Pip LeMat, an explosives expert. She's followed by three men over the course of the evening — James Farrier, Leo DeSalle and Spenser Holm. They're all soldiers but I don't learn much more about them. They retire with Pip and Shark to his room shortly after they arrive, making it clear they don't want to be disturbed. Apart from the clinking of bottles and glasses, and the occasional cheer or bellow, we don't hear from them for the rest of the night.

Shortly before eleven, Timas steps away from his laptops, takes a blue satin handkerchief from a pocket and dabs at his forehead, then folds it neatly and puts it away again. "Could I have some milk and a selection of whatever pastries the hotel has in stock?" he asks.

"Pastries?" Meera frowns. "This late?"

"Yes please," Timas says calmly. "I would like an ice pack also, for my frontal cranium, and could you please make up a cot for me beside the desk?"

"I'm sure we can find a room for you," Meera says.

"No thank you," Timas replies. "I would prefer a cot."

"I'll see what I can rustle up," Meera says, then whispers to me. "I'm going back to my room when I'm finished. This guy gives me the creeps."

I hide a smile, wait until she's gone, then ask Timas how he knows Shark.

"He killed my father," Timas says in a neutral tone, studying the back of the TV and frowning with disapproval.

Timas's English is excellent, but it's clearly not his first language. I think he must have made a mistake. "Do you mean he worked with your father?" I ask.

"No. He killed him. My father was trying to summon a demon. He meant to sacrifice me and my sister as part of the ritual. Shark saved me."

"And your sister?"

"He was not in time to help her." Timas walks around the rest of the room, making a survey of the remote controls, light fixtures, telephones… everything electronic.

"Shark felt he was to blame for my sister's death," Timas says. "He should have saved her. He didn't react quickly enough. Guilt-ridden, he developed an interest in my future. I was already heavily involved with computers, so he put me in touch with people who knew more than I did. I worked with them for a time, then with some others. When Shark realised I was the best in my field and could be of use to him, he re-established contact.

"I relished the challenge I was set and indicated my desire to work with him on subsequent projects. He summons me every so often. I drop everything to assist him. The people I work for understand. They know how important Shark's work is. Do you work for Shark too?"

"Not exactly. We're… associates." The word doesn't sound right, but I don't want Timas thinking I'm Shark's lackey.

Timas thinks about that for a moment, then sighs. "I hope they have *pain au chocolat*. That's my favourite." Then he falls silent and stares at his laptops, not moving a muscle, barely even blinking.

→Four more soldiers arrive the next morning, three men and one woman. Shark introduces them only by their first names — Terry, Liam, Stephen and Marian. They don't show any interest in Meera or me, so we don't bother with them either. Probably better that way. If we have to fight, some of us might die, and it's easier to cope with the death of someone you're not friendly with.

"Has it clicked yet?" Shark asks as we gather in my room around Timas, who's beavering away at his laptops after a short night's sleep.

"Huh?" I frown.

"Do a head count. Twelve of us. *The Dirty Dozen*. I love that film."

"I hope that's not your only reason for deciding on that number," I growl.

"It's as good a reason as any," he chuckles. "But that wasn't the key factor. I have access to a helicopter and it holds twelve. I could have commissioned a larger craft but I'm familiar with this model. I can fly it if I have to, though James will be doing most of the flying — he's the best pilot I know. Handy with a rifle too. If we need a sniper, James Farrier's our man."

"What's Timas like with a gun?" I ask.

"Not bad," Shark says. "But it needs to be a high-tech weapon with some kind of computer chip. He doesn't like ordinary guns, but if you hand him something complicated that he can play with, he's in his element."

"Timas isn't altogether there, is he?" I mutter.

Shark smiles. "You think he's a loon. Most people do. But he's passed every test he's ever been set. He's been probed by experts and they've all come away saying he's weird, but nothing more. In theory, he's as sane as you and me."

Shark moves into the middle of the room, takes up position beside Timas and claps loudly. We cluster round him in a semi-circle. Timas looks up, but keeps an eye on his laptops.

"No long speeches," Shark says. "You know I don't call for help unless things are bad. We need to find a woman. She might be mixed up with some seriously dangerous demons. If not, it'll be a walk in the park.

"But if we've guessed right, it'll get nasty. We're talking direct contact with powerful members of the Demonata. We don't want to fight. We only want to establish a link between the woman and the demons. But things could swing out of control and we might find ourselves in over our heads. If we do, you're all dead. You should know that now, before we begin, so you have the chance to back out."

Shark waits. Nobody says anything.

"Figured as much," he barks. "Timas — you got everything we need?" Timas removes USB sticks from both laptops, slips them into his shirt pocket and nods. "Then let's go," Shark says, and the hunt begins.

MEERA'S WAY

→We take a commercial flight. One of Shark's contacts meets us at the airport before we fly out, with tickets and fake passports for those who need them. The photo of me is a few years old. I don't recognise it.

"Where'd you get this?" I ask.

"I found it on the web," Timas answers. "You were photographed when committed to an institute for the mentally unbalanced. After your parents were killed?" he adds, as if I might have forgotten.

"No wonder I look like a zombie," I mutter, running my thumb over the face in the passport, remembering those dark days of madness. I used to think life couldn't possibly get any worse. How little I knew.

We sit in pairs on the plane, splitting up so as not to attract attention. I'm with Timas. I'd rather have sat with Meera, but James moved quickly to snag the seat next to her. He's chatting her up. I try keeping an eye on them, but as soon as the engines start, my stomach clenches and I grip the armrests tight, flashing back on my most recent experience in a plane.

"Do you want to know the statistics for global aeronautical accidents for the last decade?" Timas asks as we taxi out on to the runway.

"No," I growl.

"I only ask because you look uneasy. Many aeroplanes crash every year, but they are usually personal craft. Statistically we are safer in the air than on the ground. I thought familiarity with the facts might help."

"The last time I was on a plane, demons attacked, slaughtered everyone aboard and forced it down," I snarl.

"Oh." Timas looks thoughtful. "To the best of my knowledge, there are no statistics on demon-related accidents in the air. I must investigate this further when time permits. There are blanks to be filled in."

He leans back and stares up at the reading light, lips pursed. After a minute he switches the light on, then off again. On. Off. On. Off. The engines roar. We hurtle down the runway and up into the sky. Timas's eyes close after a while and he snores softly. But his finger continues to operate the light switch, turning it on and off every five seconds, irritating the hell out of me.

→Another of Shark's crew is waiting for us when we touch down. We drive in a van to a nearby hangar and park outside, close to a large, silver helicopter. Shark's soldiers are laughing and joking with each other, excited by the prospect of adventure. They tumble out of the van and circle the helicopter. James pats it and purrs. "This is my baby now. The Farrier Harrier. Bring it on!"

"Statistically, helicopters are not as reliable as aeroplanes," Timas remarks, but I pretend I didn't hear that.

We take our seats. James invites Meera to sit up front with him, but to my delight she sniffs airily and gives him the cold shoulder.

"You can sit beside me," I tell her, and with a warm smile she accepts my offer. James glares at me and I smirk back.

Timas takes the seat beside James. He's fascinated by the banks of control panels. He asks a couple of questions, then observes silently as James fires up the propellors. I can see Timas's reflection in the glass. He switches between frowns and smiles as he watches the pilot at work.

"I've saved the best for last," Shark roars as we rise smoothly. There are headsets with microphones but nobody's bothered to put them on. Shark stands, bending to avoid hitting his head on the ceiling, and jerks his seat up to reveal a hidden compartment crammed with guns.

The cabin fills with excited "Ooohs!" and "Aaahs!", audible even over the noise of the blades. Shark passes the weapons round to the eager soldiers. I shake my head when he offers me one. I've no experience of guns and I don't want to learn. Magic's cleaner and more effective. Meera doesn't bother with a gun either.

"What about rifles?" Pip shouts, having loaded her gun and jammed it into her waistband.

"And grenades?" Stephen yells.

"Stacks of them," Shark grins. "We'll break them out during the journey. It'll help pass the time."

Meera and I roll our eyes at one another and turn our attention to the scenery beneath. We watch the ground roll away behind us, airport hangars giving way to open countryside dotted with farms and the occasional house. After a while the houses multiply, becoming small villages and towns, feeding into the suburbs of the city where we're headed for our showdown with Prae Athim and her werewolf-armed Lambs.

→With Timas navigating, we soon locate the building. It looks like any other, lots of glass and steel, nothing special. Luckily it has a flat roof, and although it's not intended for helicopter landings, Timas assures us that it's structurally sound and will support our weight.

"Headsets!" Shark bellows. When we're all hooked up, he outlines the plan. "James stays with the helicopter — he'll hover nearby after dropping us off. Once we're on the roof, we'll force our way down the staircase to the eleventh floor. Terry and Spenser will stay on the staircase to keep it clear. Leo will take out the elevator. There's another staircase — Marian and Liam will head for that. The rest of us will hit Prae Athim's office."

"What if she's not there?" Meera asks.

"Then we'll find out where she is."

"Don't you think that's a rather heavy-handed approach?" Meera challenges him. "If she's elsewhere and gets wind of our attack, we'll lose the element of surprise."

"You have another idea?"

"Yes," Meera says calmly. "We ask them to let us in."

Shark laughs, then scowls. "You're serious?"

"Absolutely. Politeness often succeeds where brute force fails."

"Brute force has always worked pretty well for me," Shark disagrees.

Meera flashes him her sweetest smile. "Let's try it my way. If it doesn't work, we can hit them hard, but at least we have options. If we do it your way, there's no plan B."

"It's always good to have a plan B,"Terry chips in.

"It can't hurt to try her approach," James says from the front of the helicopter. I'm sure he's only saying it to score points with Meera.

"OK," Shark shrugs. "Take us in, Farrier. Meera, it's your show — for now."

As Meera talks us through her simple plan, we drift

in over the building, hover closer to the roof, then set down. James kills the blades and as silence settles over us, we sit in place and wait.

Security guards soon spill on to the roof. Thirty or more. They're all armed, but only with handguns.

"A few are ex-military," Leo murmurs, studying the guards as they fan out. "But most look to have been privately trained. We could take them with our eyes shut."

"Leave the *taking* for a while," Meera says and slides out of the helicopter. She nods for Shark and me to accompany her. As Shark moves forward, she tuts and looks pointedly at his weapons — a couple of revolvers and a small rifle strung across his back.

"Do I have to?" Shark pouts. Meera raises an eyebrow. Sighing, he drops his weapons and clambers out in a foul mood.

We take several steps away from the helicopter, then wait, hands in plain sight. One of the guards – an officer – speaks into a microphone attached to his shirt, waits for orders, then comes to meet us. His troops train their guns on us but keep them slightly lowered, so if one of them fires by accident he won't draw blood.

The officer stops a metre in front of us. He's wearing a ring with a large gold L set in the centre. Prae Athim wore a similar ring when I met her.

"Can I help you folks?" the officer asks with forced politeness.

"We have an appointment," Meera replies smoothly.

The officer seemed prepared for any answer except that one. He blinks stupidly. "An appointment," he echoes.

"With Prae Athim. Could you tell her Meera Flame and co are here?"

"We're not expecting any visitors," the guard says, his voice taking on a slightly threatening tone.

"*You* might not be," Meera smiles, "but Prae is. Let her know we're here and I'm sure she'll authorise our entry."

The guard looks troubled. He tells us to stay where we are. Moving out of earshot, he speaks into his microphone again. After a short conversation he calls to us. "Somebody's coming up. Please maintain your positions."

The guard returns to the ranks and waits with the others. As he passes orders along, the guards lower their weapons another fraction. I start to relax. Looks like they don't mean to turn this into a shooting match. At least not yet.

A couple of minutes later, as Shark fidgets, the door to the roof opens and a tall, handsome, tanned man emerges. He's wearing a suit, but no tie. His hair looks like a film star's, thick and carefully waxed into shape. He smiles smoothly and his teeth are a perfect pearly white. Meera's right hand shoots to her hair and she tries to pat it into place, suddenly irritated by the sharp wind whipping over the rooftop, making her job impossible.

"Good afternoon," the man says, stopping half a metre closer to us than the guard did. He has a smooth voice. "My name's Antoine Horwitzer. How may I be of service?"

"We're looking for Prae Athim," Shark says as Meera gazes open-mouthed at the man. He nudges her in the ribs and she recovers swiftly.

"Yes," she snaps, a red flush of embarrassment spreading from the centre of her cheeks. "We have an appointment. Is she here?"

"One would expect her to be present if one had an appointment and had flown in by helicopter to keep it," Antoine chuckles. "But I don't believe you really arranged a meeting, did you, Miss...?"

"Flame," Meera says with a nervy laugh. "Meera Flame."

"She already gave her name to the guard," Shark growls, eyes narrowing.

"Indeed," Antoine says with a little nod. "I was being disingenuous. I wanted to see if she would give the same name again."

"Why shouldn't she? It's her real name."

"And you are...?" Antoine asks.

"Shark."

"No surname?"

"No."

Antoine's smile flickers. Shark can be intense. He's staring at the man in the suit as if pondering whether or not to cut his heart out and eat it.

"If Prae's here, she'll vouch for us," Meera says. "You're correct — we don't have a scheduled meeting. But she'll want to see us."

"What about the rest of your group?" Anotine asks, smile back in place. He waves at the soldiers in the Farrier Harrier. "I'm no expert, but those guns don't look like toys. Will Miss Athim welcome armed thugs as well?"

"They're our travelling companions," Meera says. "They mean no harm."

"What if I asked them to dispose of their weapons and leave the helicopter?"

"No," Shark barks before Meera can answer.

Antoine's brow furrows, giving the impression that he's thinking this over, but I believe he knew exactly what he was going to say before he set foot on the roof. He doesn't look like a man who leaves much to chance.

"I can't admit you unless I know why you've come," Antoine says eventually.

"We can discuss that with Prae if you tell her we're here," Meera replies.

"You're fishing," Antoine chuckles. "You want me to

reveal whether or not she's in the building. But I'm not prepared to tell you unless you answer my questions first."

"It's not your place to make a call like that," Meera says icily. "Prae Athim is the CEO. I don't know what your position is, but if you—"

"Actually, there's been a recent managerial shift," Antoine interrupts. "I am the current chief executive. If you wish to proceed, you'll have to deal with me. Otherwise..." He shrugs.

"You've replaced Prae Athim?" Meera asks, startled.

"Not in so many words," Antoine answers evasively.

Meera shares a glance with Shark. He's frowning uncertainly. She doesn't look sure of herself either. I decide it's time for me to step in. I've been standing idly on the sidelines long enough.

"We're here to talk about werewolves," I mutter, drawing my shoulders back to create as much of an impression as I can.

Antoine blinks, his smile crumbling. "And you are...?"

"Grubbs," I tell him, then correct myself. "Grubitsch Grady."

"Ah. I've heard of you. Dervish Grady is your uncle."

"Yes."

Antoine doesn't scratch his head – I doubt he'd ever resort to such a common gesture – but his fingers twitch and I think that's what he'd like to do.

"Werewolves attacked Dervish," I say softly. "At his home. In a team. Backed by people with guns." I stare pointedly at the guards.

"This is an interesting development," Antoine says after a short pause. He looks down at his highly polished shoes and this time I get the impression he really is thinking about what to say next.

When he looks up, his eyes are clear. "I think I'd better invite you down to my office. Will you accompany me, please?" He stands to one side and extends a hand towards the door.

"What about the others?" Shark asks, jerking his head at those in the helicopter.

"They're not necessary."

"I want them there," Shark growls. "Weapons and all."

Antoine prods at his lower lip with his tongue. Then, with a shrug, he says, "Why not? I'd hate to be mistaken for a discourteous host."

Shark's surprised. This means we either have nothing to fear, or else Antoine Horwitzer has another team within the building and is confident they can handle ten armed and experienced soldiers.

I think Shark would like to pull out, but we've nowhere else to turn. If we flee now, our investigation will be blown before it's properly begun. Grumbling to himself, he summons the others, leaving only James inside the Harrier.

"He's going to start the engine," Shark tells Antoine.

"To be ready for a quick getaway," Antoine murmurs wryly. "I'd do the same thing in your position." He winks at me and I find myself smiling. I distrust this man – he's too smooth – but at the same time I like him.

"Shall we?" Antoine asks as the members of Shark's team eye up the guards, who look a lot more nervous now that they have a good view of Shark's Dirty Dozen.

"I'd like you to answer one of our questions first," Meera says. "Is Prae Athim here or not?"

"Not." Antoine lets his smile fade. "Miss Athim has been missing for some time. And our core specimens – what Master Grady referred to as werewolves – have vanished too."

On that baffling, disturbing note, he leads the way into the building. They might be called Lambs, but as we pass out of the sunlight and into the gloom of the staircase, I think of them more as Lions — and we're entering their den.

ALL THE KING'S WOLVES

→We walk down a flight of steps, then squeeze into an elevator, just us and Antoine Horwitzer. If he's nervous about sealing himself in with nine soldiers, he doesn't show it. Presses the button for the eleventh floor and smiles pleasantly as we descend.

No one speaks until the doors open. As Pip and Terry nudge out, Antoine says, "A moment, please." He's tapping the control panel of the elevator. "Could you tell me some more about the attack you mentioned?"

"I thought we were going to do that in your office," Shark growls suspiciously.

"That was my intention," Antoine replies. "But upon reconsideration I think there might be a better place for our discussion. There's no need to go into the full story here, but if you could provide me with just a few details…"

Shark looks at Meera. She shrugs, then quickly runs through the attack at Carcery Vale. Antoine listens silently. His smile never slips, but it starts to strain at the edges. When Meera finishes, he nods soberly and presses a button low on the panel. There's a buzzing noise. Everyone tenses.

"Nothing to worry about," Antoine says calmly, pushing a series of buttons. "I'm taking us to the lower levels. That requires a security code."

"How low does this thing go?" Shark asks.

"There are ten floors beneath the ground," Antoine says. "I thought we'd check out the lower fourth and fifth." He pauses, his finger hovering over the number 2. "This is the final digit. Once I press this, the doors will shut and we'll drop. If you have any objections, this is the time to raise them."

Shark thinks about it, then sniffs as if he hasn't a care in the world. Antoine presses the button. The buzzer stops. The doors slide shut. We slip further into the bowels of the building.

→We step out of the elevator and find ourselves in a corridor much like any other. But when we follow Antoine through an ordinary-looking door, we discover something completely unexpected.

We're in a huge, open room, dotted with cages, banks of machines and steel cabinets. The cages all seem to be several metres square and three or four metres high. Some show evidence of having been inhabited recently – faeces and scraps of food litter the floors – but most look like they've never been used.

"This is a holding area," Antoine says, taking us on a tour. "As you can see, we try not to cram too many specimens into one place. Despite this limit, if you'd come here a couple of months ago, you'd have had to wear ear plugs — the din they create is unbelievable."

Timas stops by one of the machines and studies it with interest.

"That locks and unlocks the cage doors," Antoine explains. "There are other devices linked to it — overhead cameras, lights, air conditioner, water hoses, implant initiators."

"Implants?" I ask.

"Most of the specimens are implanted with control chips. In the event of a mass escape, we could disable them within seconds. We take as few risks as possible when dealing with creatures as swift, powerful and savage as these."

"You don't need such bulky equipment," Timas says disapprovingly.

"It's psychological," Antoine counters. "Staff feel safer if they have a big, obvious machine to turn to in case of an emergency."

"Ah," Timas smiles. "The human factor. What silly beings we are."

Antoine looks at Timas oddly, then leads us out of the room, into a smaller laboratory. There are several people at work, some in white coats, others in normal clothes. Glass cases line the walls. I go cold when I see what's in them — hands, heads, feet, ears, bits of flesh and bone, all taken from deformed humans... from *werewolves*.

"What is this?" I croak.

"Unsettling, aren't they?" Antoine remarks, studying a pair of oversized eyes floating in a jar of clear liquid. "I'm not convinced it's necessary for them to be displayed in so lurid a fashion, but our technical geniuses insist—"

"What the hell *is* this?" I shout, losing my temper.

Antoine blinks at me, surprised by my anger. Then his expression clears. "How thoughtless of me. These remains come from relatives of yours. I must apologise for my insensitivity. I never meant to cause offence."

"Don't worry about that," Shark says, squeezing my shoulder to calm me. "But Grubbs is right — what is this place? It looks like Frankenstein's lab."

"To an extent it is." Antoine sighs. "This is where we experiment upon many of our unfortunate specimens. As you know, we've been trying to find the genetic source of the Grady disease for decades, searching for a cure. Our experts need a place to dissect and reassemble, to study and collate. It's an unpleasant business, but no worse, I assure you, than any institute devoted to animal experiments."

"These aren't animals," I snarl. "They're human."

"They were once," Antoine corrects me. "Now..." He

pulls a face. "As you said, your uncle was attacked by werewolves. You didn't qualify that because you don't think of them as humans with a defect. When the genes mutate, the specimens become something inhuman — although, if we ever crack the rogue genes, perhaps we can restore their humanity."

Timas has wandered over to a computer console. "I assume all of your results and data are backed up here."

"They're stored on a mainframe," Antoine says, "but they're accessible through most of the computers in the building if you have clearance."

"You still use mainframes?" Timas tuts. "How primitive." He runs a finger over the keys. "I'd like to study your records. I know nothing of lycanthropy. I find myself intrigued."

"Sorry," Antoine says stiffly. "Our database is off-limits to all but the most strictly authorised personnel. As I'm sure you'll agree, this is a sensitive matter. We wouldn't want just anybody to have access to such incendiary material."

"This is all very interesting," Meera butts in, "but it doesn't explain about Prae Athim or what you said on the roof regarding the missing *specimens*."

"I'm coming to that," Antoine says patiently. "Trust me, this will be simpler if we proceed step by step." He walks ahead of us and turns, gesturing around the room. "As I was saying, we've been extremely busy, cutting specimens up, running tests on live subjects, introducing various chemical substances into the veins of random guinea pigs in the hopes of stumbling upon a cure."

"Any luck?" Shark asks.

"No," Antoine says. "We've ploughed untold millions into this project – and others around the globe – with zero success. If not for the continued support of wealthy Gradys, and our dabbling in parallel medical fields, we would have faced bankruptcy long ago."

"'Parallel medical fields'?" Meera echoes.

"We might not have unravelled the mysteries of the Grady genes, but our research has led to breakthroughs in other areas. As a result, we have become a worldwide pharmaceutical giant. Steroids are our speciality, though we're by no means limited to so finite a field."

Antoine looks like he's about to give us a breakdown of the Lambs' success stories. But then, remembering why we're here, he returns to the relevant facts.

"As you can imagine, specimens are difficult to come by. Very few parents wish to hand their children over for medical experimentation, even if they're no longer recognisably human. Many children have been placed in the care of the Lambs in the past, but only to be... decommissioned."

"You mean executed," I growl.

Antoine nods slowly. "In most circumstances, the parents never enquire after the child once we take it into custody. The less they know about the grisly details, the better. A few ask for ashes to be returned, but almost nobody requests a body for burial. And since ashes are easy to fake…"

"You don't kill them!" I'm furious. This could have happened to Gret or Bill-E. The thought of them winding up here, caged, experimented on, humiliated, treated like lab rats… It makes me want to hit somebody. My hands clench into fists and I glare at Antoine. It takes all my self-control not to attack.

"It sounds inhumane," Antoine says quietly. "I admit it's a betrayal of trust. But it's necessary. We do this for the good of the family. I've seen the grief and anguish in the eyes of parents who've watched their children turn into nightmarish beasts. If we have to lie to prevent that from happening to others, so be it."

"It's wrong," I disagree. "They wouldn't have given their children to you if they knew what you planned to do with them."

"True," Antoine says. "But we can't search for a cure without specimens to work on. Isn't it better to experiment than execute? To seek a remedy rather than accept defeat?"

"Not without permission," I mutter obstinately.

"I wish you could see it our way," Antoine sighs. "But I understand your point of view. This is a delicate matter." He looks decidedly miserable now. "But if you can't find any positives in what I've shown you so far, please be warned — you're absolutely going to hate what I reveal next."

Before I can ask what he means, he turns and pushes ahead, leading us to an exit, then down a set of stairs to the next level and the most horrific revelation yet.

→A cavernous room, even larger than the holding area above. Hundreds of cages, many obscured by panels which have been set between them, dividing the room into semi-private segments. The stink is nauseating. Antoine offers us masks, but nobody takes one. As we progress further into the room, I feel sorry that I didn't accept.

Some of the cages look like they've never been used, but many show signs of long-term occupancy, caked with ground-in filth. There are old blood and urine stains, scraps of hair everywhere. I spot the occasional fingernail or tooth. There are people at work in several cages, trying to clean them out. It's a job I wouldn't accept for the highest of wages.

"This smells almost as bad as that world of guts we visited," Shark mutters to Meera. She looks at him blankly. "Oh, right. You weren't there. It was Sharmila."

"Nice to know you can't tell the difference between me and an Indian woman twice my age," Meera snaps. Shark winces — he's made the sort of error a woman never forgets or forgives.

"This is another holding pen," Antoine says. "But it's more than just a place to hold specimens. It's where we breed our own varieties, to increase our stock."

For a moment I don't catch his meaning. Then I stop dead. "You've been *breeding* werewolves?" I roar.

"The reproductive organs alter during transformation," Antoine explains, "but most specimens remain fertile. We always knew it was possible for them to breed, but we didn't follow up on that for many years. It's a delicate process. The pair have to be united at precisely the right moment, otherwise they rip each other apart. We tried artificial insemination, but the mothers refused to accept the young, killing them as they emerged from the womb. We could sedate and restrain them during the birthing process, of course, but it's much easier to—"

Losing my head completely, I take a swing at Antoine Horwitzer, intent on squeezing his brains out through his nose and ears, then stomping them into mincemeat.

Shark catches my fist. The suited leader of the Lambs ducks and recoils from me with a startled cry, while Shark restrains my trembling hand, staring at me coldly.

"Let go," I cry, angry tears trickling from my eyes.

"This isn't the time," he says quietly.

"I don't care. It's barbaric. I'm going to—"

"Kill him?" Shark hisses. "What will that achieve? He's just a pretty face in a suit. They'd replace him in an instant."

"But—"

"Remember our mission. Think about what's at stake. This guy's an ant. We can come after him later — and the rest of his foul kind. Right now we have bigger fish to fry. Don't lose track of the rabbit, Grubbs."

I struggle to break free. Then my brain kicks in and I relax. Shark releases me, but watches warily in case I make another break for Antoine, who's squinting at me nervously.

"You know your problem?" I snap at Shark. "You use too many metaphors. Ants, fish and rabbits, all in the same breath. That's an abuse of the language."

Shark smiles. "I never was much good at school. Too busy reading about guns." He steps away, clearing the area between me and Antoine.

"Why?" I snarl. "Did you breed them to sell to circuses? To test your products on? Just to prove that you could?"

"We did it to experiment and learn," Antoine says. "The intake of regular specimens wasn't sufficient. We needed more. Also, by studying their growth from birth, we were able to find out more about them. We hoped the young might differ physically from their parents, that we could use their genes to develop a cure. There were many reasons, all of them honest and pure."

"No," I tell him. "Nothing about this is honest or pure. It's warped. If there's a hell, you've won yourself a one-way pass, you and all the rest of your bloody Lambs."

Antoine stifles a mocking yawn. I almost go for him again. Meera intervenes before things get out of hand.

"You didn't need to show us these pens," she says. "So I thank you for your open hospitality. It's hard for us to take in, but you knew we'd have difficulties. I imagine you struggled to adjust to the moral grey areas yourself at first."

"Absolutely," Antoine beams. "We're not monsters. We do these things to make the world a better place. I wasn't sure about the breeding programme to begin with. I still harbour doubts. But we've learnt so much, and the promise of learning more is tantalising. Do we have the right to play God? Maybe not. But are we justified in trying to help people, to do all in our power to repay the faith of those who invest money and hope in our cause? With all my heart, I believe so."

Antoine smiles at me, trying to get me back on side. I don't return the gesture, but I don't glower at him either. Shark's right — this isn't the time to get into an argument. Antoine Horwitzer is our only link to Prae Athim. We have to keep him sweet or he might shut us out completely.

"Where are they?" I ask, nodding at the empty cages. "You said they vanished. What did you mean?"

Antoine nods, happy to be moving on to a less

sensitive subject. "Prae was head of this unit for twenty-six years. She's been general director of the Lambs for nineteen of those. She worked on a number of private projects during her time in charge, commandeering staff and funds to conduct various experiments. She had a free rein for the past decade and a half.

"Under her guidance, the breeding programme was accelerated. Bred specimens develop much faster than those which were once human — a newborn becomes an adult in three or four years, with an expected lifespan of ten to twelve years. We'd always bred in small numbers, but Prae increased the birth rate. Some people wondered why, but nobody challenged her. Prae was an exemplary director. We were sure she had good reasons for implementing the changes.

"A few months ago, she began making startling requests. She wanted to close down the programmes and terminate all specimens."

"You mean kill all the werewolves?" Shark frowns.

"Yes. She said a new strain of the disease had developed and spread. We couldn't tell which were infected. If left to mutate and evolve, the strain might be passed to ordinary humans. She wanted to remove them to a secure area of her choosing, where they'd be safely disposed of.

"Nobody believed her." Antoine's face is grave. "There were too many holes in her story, no facts to support her theory. She argued fiercely, threatened to resign, called in every favour. But we weren't convinced. We insisted on more time to conduct our own experiments. Prae was allowed to continue in her post, but I was assigned to monitor her and approve her decisions.

"Just over six weeks ago, Prae Athim disappeared. She left work on a Thursday and nobody has seen her since. That night, operatives acting on her behalf subdued regular staff, tranquillised the specimens, removed them from their cells and made off with them. We've no idea where they went. We've devoted all of our resources to tracking them down but so far... nothing."

Antoine smiles shakily. "I hoped she'd followed through on her plan to destroy the specimens. That would have been a tragic loss, but at least it would have meant we didn't have to worry about them. Now it seems my fears – that she had an ulterior motive – have been borne out. If some of them were sent to attack Dervish Grady, we're dealing with a far greater problem. We have to find the missing specimens as swiftly as possible. The consequences if we don't are staggering."

"I'm not that worried about the werewolves," Shark sniffs. "They're secondary to finding Prae Athim. I mean, how many are we talking about? A few dozen?"

Antoine laughs sharply. "You don't understand. I told

you earlier — Prae Athim has worked in this unit for twenty-six years. But this is just one unit of many. We have bases on every continent and have been running similar programmes in each. Prae didn't just take the specimens from this complex. She took them from *everywhere*. There's not one left."

Shark's expression darkens. "How many?" he croaks.

"I don't have an exact number to hand," Antoine says. "Some of the projects were under Prae's personal supervision, and records have been deleted from our system. It's impossible to be accurate."

"Roughly," Shark growls.

Antoine gulps, then says quietly, so that we have to strain to hear, "Somewhere between six and seven hundred, give or take a few." And his smile, this time, is a pale ghost of a grin.

TIMAS ON THE JOB

→Six or seven hundred werewolves on the loose, in the hands of a maniac most likely in league with Lord Loss. Nice! Demons rarely have time to kill many people because they can only stay on this world for a few minutes, while the window they crossed through remains open. But hundreds of werewolves, divided into groups of ten or twelve, set free in dozens of cities around the globe…

If each only killed five people, I make that three and a half thousand fatalities. But it's more likely they'd kill ten times that number, maybe more.

We're in Antoine's office on the eleventh floor. It used to be Prae Athim's. It's a large room, but with twelve of us it's a tight fit. Nobody's said anything since we came in. We've been looking through photos of the *specimens* which Antoine gave us, studying the data that he has on file.

I know from my own brush with lycanthropy that werewolves are strong and fast. I felt like an Olympic athlete when it was my time of turning. But I'm still seriously freaked by what I'm reading. I never knew they were *this* advanced.

I shouldn't let it matter. The Shadow must remain the priority. If it succeeds in uniting the demon masses and breaking through, the world will fall. The damage a pack of escaped werewolves might cause is nothing in comparison.

But how can I ignore the possibility of tens of thousands of deaths? Beranabus could. He's half-demon and has spent hundreds of years subduing his human impulses. We're statistics to him. He'd take the line that a few thousand lives don't make much difference in the grand scheme of things, that we have to focus on the millions and billions — *real* numbers.

I can't do that. Even if we find out that the attack in Carcery Vale has nothing to do with the demon assault at the hospital, that Prae Athim isn't working with Lord Loss, I have to try and stop her. I won't let thousands of people die if I can prevent it. Especially not when the killers are relatives of mine.

Perhaps crazily, I still think of the werewolves as kin, even those bred in cages. They're part of the Grady clan. That makes it personal.

"We have to find them," I blurt out, without meaning to. All heads in the office bob up and everybody stares at me. I'm sitting by one of the large windows, the city spread out behind me. Any of the people on the streets, eleven floors down, could fall victim to the werewolves if Prae Athim unleashes them.

"We have to stop this." I get to my feet, discarding the photos I'd been mutely studying.

"Maybe there's nothing to stop," Meera says unconvincingly. "Maybe Prae was telling the truth about a new disease and took them to dispose of safely. Perhaps the few who were sent to attack Dervish were simply being used to settle an old score, and were then executed along with the rest."

"Bull!" Shark snorts. "If she'd wanted to kill them, she'd have slaughtered them in their cages. It would have been a lot simpler than smuggling them out."

"Probably," Meera sighs. "I was just saying *maybe*…"

"What will she do with them?" Marian asks.

"I guess she'll drop them off in a city somewhere," Shark replies. "Let them run wild. Maybe collect them at the end and take them on somewhere else."

"But why?" Marian frowns. "Why not build bombs, poison a city's water supply or develop chemical weapons? Hijacking hundreds of werewolves to use as crazed assassins… it's like something out of a *Batman* comic!"

"Crazy people don't think the way we do," Meera says glumly. "They have all sorts of warped ideas and plans, and if they gain enough power, they get to inflict their mad schemes on others."

"Like Davida Haym in Slawter," I note.

"There's another possibility," Terry says. "She might have done this for humane reasons. Maybe she suffered a moral crisis. Decided they'd been mistreating these creatures. Took them somewhere isolated, to set them free."

"Unlikely," Antoine says with a cynical smile. "Her people killed seventeen of our staff during the breakouts. Many more were seriously injured. Hardly the work of a good samaritan."

"I've seen fanatics who think animals are nobler than humans," Terry says. "They'd happily kill a human to save a dog or cat from abuse."

"Prae Athim isn't an animal rights activist," Antoine says firmly. "I refuse to entertain the notion that she did this to free the specimens, that she stood waving them off as they returned to the wilds, happy tears in her eyes."

"He's right," Shark says. "We have to assume this was done with the intent of creating maximum havoc."

"So let's track her down and stop her," I snarl. "We can't just sit here and talk about it. We have to… to…" I throw my hands up, frustrated.

"We all know how you feel," Meera says sympathetically. "But until she makes a move, there's nothing we can do. The world's a big place. You could hide seven hundred werewolves just about anywhere. We can't—"

"I could find them," Timas interrupts. "If I had access to your mainframe," he adds, smiling at Antoine.

"I told you — the records have been wiped," Antoine scowls.

"It's virtually impossible to wipe a mainframe completely clean," Timas says. "That's one of the reasons I was surprised you still used one. I can perform at the very least a partial restore."

"We've had experts working on it for the last six weeks," Antoine says sharply.

"I'm sure you've employed some of the best people in the business," Timas says earnestly. "But I'm the *very* best."

"Even assuming you could restore it," Shark rumbles, "how would that help us? She's unlikely to have outlined her secret plans on a work computer."

"You can't move that many bodies around without leaving a trail," Timas says. "If I find out more about the creatures, I can use that information to fish for clues on the web."

"What do you mean?" Shark asks.

"They didn't take the cages," Timas notes. "That means they transported them in cages of their own. Once I know what the cages are made from, I can search for companies who specialise in this type of construction and find out if they've filled any large orders recently. If they have, I'll learn where they delivered the cages to.

"If I can determine how the werewolves were tranquillised, I can track the drugs back to where they were manufactured, then trace them through delivery records.

"How did they transport the creatures — aeroplanes, articulated trucks, trains, boats? I'm assuming they moved at least some of them across international borders. There will be a trail of red tape, no matter how surreptitiously they went about it. I've followed such trails before and enjoyed a large measure of success.

"Do you want me to continue explaining or shall I get started?" Timas addresses this question to Antoine Horwitzer.

Antoine's torn. "Is he really that good?" he asks Shark.

"Yes."

"If he can do what he says… he will have access to confidential information. He'll have to sign a privacy clause. We need absolute affirmation that he'd never reveal—"

"You present the forms, he'll sign them," Shark cuts in.

Antoine struggles with the idea for a couple of seconds, then sighs. "Very well. I'll log you in and provide you with the relevant security codes."

"No need," Timas says, sliding on to Antoine's plush leather chair. "I can crack them. The exercise will serve as a useful warm-up."

"How long will it take?" Shark asks as Timas's fingers dance across the keyboard.

"A few days, I imagine," Timas replies absently. "Quicker if we get a lucky break. Longer if she's hidden her trail artfully. I'll need complete privacy. And my equipment from the helicopter."

"I'll have it sent down," Shark says and ushers us out.

"Perhaps I should stay and keep an eye on him," Antoine says nervously.

"No chance," Shark responds firmly and pushes out the suave chief executive, ignoring his spluttering protests.

→Some of the rooms on the uppermost floor have beds, or couches which pull out into sleeping cots. Members of the higher echelon move around a lot between buildings owned by the Lambs. Given the secretive nature of their business, they often prefer to stay onsite rather than check into hotels.

I'm sharing a room with Spenser and James. They don't speak to me much. They know I'm part of Beranabus's world of magic and demons, but they've had little first-hand experience of that. They find it hard to think of me as anything other than an especially large but otherwise unremarkable teenager. I'm not too bothered. I find most of their conversation pretty boring — weapons, planes, helicopters, war, battle tactics. I'm happy to be excluded.

I spend my spare time experimenting, testing my powers. I don't know how much I'm capable of doing on this world, in the absence of magical energy. I want to find out what my limits are, so as not to exceed them and leave myself exposed.

I'm pretty good at moving objects. Size doesn't seem to matter — I can slide a heavy oak wardrobe across the floor as easily as a telephone. I spend a couple of hours moving things around. I'm pretty beat by the end, and not back to full fitness until the next morning. It's reassuring that I can recharge, but worrying that it takes so long once I've been drained.

Other manoeuvres are more demanding. I can heighten my senses – to eavesdrop on a conversation, or view a scene from a few kilometres away – but that takes a lot of effort and quickly eats into my resources. I can't change shape, but I can make myself partially invisible for a very short time. I can create fire and freeze objects, but again those demand a lot of me. I can shoot off several bolts of magical energy, but I'm good for nothing for hours afterwards.

There are all sorts of compensating spells which I could make use of if I knew them. But I refused to dabble in magic when I lived with Dervish and I didn't need spells in the Demonata universe — if a spell was required there, Beranabus took care of it. He wasn't interested in training Kernel or me, just in using us to bully and kill demons.

I wish I'd demanded more of Beranabus and Dervish. Mages can do a lot with a few subtle spells. As a magician I could do even more. I get Meera to teach me some simple incantations, but we don't have time to cover much ground.

I worry about my uncle constantly. What's he doing? Where is he? Time moves differently in the other universe, usually faster or slower than here. Years might have passed for him, or only minutes. Is he alive or dead? I've no way of knowing. Beranabus taught me how to open windows, so I could go and find them. But I couldn't guarantee how long that would take.

I have to remain here until our mission's over. I'm the reason the others are involved, the one who vowed to track down Prae Athim and uncover the truth. I can't cut out early. That would be the selfish act of a child, which I'm not. I'm a Disciple. We see things through to the end. No matter how scared and alone we feel.

→Four days pass. Everyone's impatient for news, but Timas refuses to provide us with partial updates. On the few occasions that Shark barges into Antoine's office and demands answers, the reply is always the same. "I'll summon you promptly when I've concluded my investigations."

Timas finally reaches that conclusion shortly before dawn of the fifth day. Shark hammers on our door, waking us all, then sticks his head in and shouts, "The office! Now!"

Five minutes later we're all huddled around Timas and his computers. We're bleary-eyed, hair all over the place, typical early morning messes. Except Timas. As far as I know, he's worked almost non-stop since I last saw him, sleeping only two or three hours a night. But he looks as perky as an actor in a TV advert.

"I've found them," he says without any preliminaries. "They're on an island. It has no official name, but the Lambs nicknamed it Wolf Island. Prae Athim purchased it through a fifth-generation contact several years ago."

"What's a fifth-generation contact?" I ask.

"A contact of a contact of a contact of a contact of a contact," Timas intones. "She conducts most of her business that way, making it almost impossible to trace anything back to her personally. *Almost*," he repeats with a justifiably smug smile.

"Where's the island?" Shark grunts.

Timas passes him a stapled printout of about twenty pages, then hands copies around to the rest of us. The small sheaf is crammed with all sorts of info about the island, its history, dimensions, wildlife, plant life, natural formations. There are several maps, most of the island, but also of the surrounding waters, noting currents, depth, temperatures, sea life.

"They've built a base," Timas points out. "Page nine.

They constructed it on the island's largest crag, so they need only face an assault from one direction if the werewolves get out of control. That extra measure wasn't a necessity — the fortifications are sound, with more than six separate security systems in place, powered by a variety of independent generators. The werewolves might have the run of the island, but the people inside the compound are quite–"

"The beasts are running free?" Shark interrupts.

"Yes. That's on page four. They were set loose once delivered to the island, though they can be recaptured, singly or in small groups, using a variety of equipment provided for such a purpose."

"Maybe Terry was right," Meera says dubiously. "Perhaps Prae took them there to let them live naturally."

"I think not," Timas purrs, "and would refer you to page fourteen, appendix Bii, in support of my opinion."

Antoine and a few of the others flick forward. Shark tosses his copy of the report aside and snaps, "Don't play games. Just tell us."

"No games," Timas says mildly. "The appendix outlines everything concisely. But if you would prefer an oral report…"

"I would," Shark snarls.

"No!" Antoine gasps, turning a shade paler beneath his tan. He must be a speed-reader because he's already flicking from page fourteen to fifteen, eyes scanning the lines super-fast. "This can't be right. I would have known."

"The figures are accurate," Timas says. "Nothing is speculative." He faces Shark. "A third have been genetically, surgically and electronically modified by Prae Athim and her team. She found a way to corrupt their metabolisms. This allowed her to do two things. First, using steroids, implants and a variety of drugs, she created faster, stronger animals. Second, by operating on their brains and using other implants, she was able to train them."

"They can't survive at those levels," Antoine says, glancing up from his report. "Their bodies can't hold, not subjected to such degrees of abuse."

"Their long-term prospects are grim," Timas agrees. "But they can last a few years, or so the scientists believe."

"What have they been trained to do?" Shark asks.

"Nothing too complex," Timas says. "They can hunt in small groups, in pursuit of predefined targets — like hounds, they can be given a person's scent. They're not as reliable as hounds. In a crowded environment they might be distracted and chase others instead. And they'll turn on their handlers afterwards unless subdued. But that's a huge step forward."

"I'd no idea she'd advanced to such a stage," Antoine whispers. "We've been trying to install control mechanisms for decades. We could have done so much good if we'd known about this. We still could."

"The Lambs are finished," Shark says, "at least as far as werewolves are concerned. Do you really think people will trust you with their young once word of this gets out? And it will — have no doubt about that."

"You're right," Antoine sighs. "But those on the island are still alive. If we can bring them back under our authority and follow up on these incredible breakthroughs…"

"You're assuming we'll leave any of them alive," Shark laughs brutally. Before Antoine can react to that, he says to Timas, "What's the best way to hit them? Do we need more troops?"

Timas purses his lips. "If the original implants had been left intact, we could have electronically disabled them from the air. But they were all secretly removed or rendered inactive prior to the abduction. The safest way would be to blanket-bomb the island."

"No!" I cry. "You can't just kill them. They were human once."

"They're not any more," Shark shrugs.

"I won't let you," I growl.

"You can't stop me," he says blankly.

"Actually, I can." I raise a hand and let little forks of blue lightning crackle between my fingertips. Shark squints at me, taking my measure.

"He'd whup you," Meera says to Shark. "He's a magician. You wouldn't stand a chance."

"Probably not." Shark grimaces. "Besides, I don't

trust fly-boys and their damn guided missiles. They could level the compound by accident, and we need Prae alive. Options, Timas?"

"Go as we are." He holds up his copy of the report, flicks to near the end and taps the page. "There are very few guards. It's mostly scientists and medics. If we just hit the compound, we can drop in and make a neat job of it."

"You're sure?" Shark asks.

"Absolutely," Timas says. "I can provide you with a complete breakdown of the odds if you wish."

"No need," Shark smiles. "Twelve it is."

"Thirteen," Antoine corrects him.

Shark laughs. "You're not serious."

"Never more so. I'm coming."

"You're not," Shark says, his smile disappearing. "This is a job for soldiers and Disciples."

"I won't pretend to be an action hero," Antoine says with quiet dignity. "I'm not your equal in matters such as these. But I'm coming regardless. I run this operation now. I'm not sure what you want with Prae, but if you don't kill her, I plan to bring her to justice. And there's the matter of the specimens. They have to be returned. Or perhaps we can continue our work on the island. I need to undertake a study before I make a proposal to the board."

"You can do that later," Meera says. "Let us go in, shut down Prae's operation and take control of the situation.

You can fly in after we're finished and—"

"You don't understand!" Antoine shouts, losing his temper for the first time. His jaw trembles as he glares at us. "This happened on *my* watch. I was supposed to control her. There have already been calls for my head. I'm hanging on to this job by my fingernails. If the board of governors finds out about this island and that I let you waltz in unrestricted and unmonitored…"

Antoine looks appealingly at Shark. "I need to come with you. And it won't be a one-way favour. I can help. I know Prae, her people, the specimens. I can advise and caution if necessary."

"It'd be dangerous," Shark says. "If you come, you're on your own. Nobody will risk their life to save yours."

"In this business, you never expect anyone to be helpful," Antoine smirks, in command of his temper again. "Do I have time to pack a few things?"

"No," Shark snorts and marches out of the office. The rest of us follow him up the stairs to where the helicopter is waiting and off we set for Wolf Island. *Aroooooo!*

PREY

→We manage to squeeze into the Farrier Harrier, even though it isn't meant to hold more than twelve. We fly all day, Shark and James taking turns to pilot. We set down a couple of times to refuel, eat and stretch our legs. Stop at dusk for dinner at an army base, then continue through the night. I catch a few hours of sleep, using a sleeping spell to drop off.

We make our final stop shortly after nine in the morning. Breakfast, a walk, exercise. Then Shark talks us through our plans. We scour maps of the compound, Shark highlighting our route and alternatives in case we run into problems. It's pretty simple — break in, grab Prae Athim, secure the area around her office and interrogate her there, or else abduct her and make a quick getaway.

Meera doesn't suggest a polite approach this time. Prae Athim is way out of control. Subtlety won't work on Wolf Island.

Shark finishes by asking for any last-minute comments or enquiries. Antoine sheepishly raises a hand. "Will you try not to cause unnecessary damage? Some of the equipment is very expensive. If we can recycle it later, we can recoup some of the costs of this debacle."

Shark glares at Antoine. "If we come through this and I receive an invoice for wreckages, I'll find you, string you upside down and make you eat your own brains before I kill you. Understand?"

Antoine flushes. "I was only—"

"Be quiet," Meera snaps.

Antoine pouts, but shuts up. Shark casts an eye around. "Last chance to back out. Anyone?" Seven of the nine soldiers promptly raise their hands. "You should be in a sitcom," Shark jeers, then claps his hands together loudly and stands. "Let's go!"

Back on the helicopter. Within minutes we're over open water. No retreating now. We're in this to the bitter, bloody end.

→The island is one of many in the area, all deserted, most uninhabitable. This is one of the largest. A lot of grass, wild flowers, trees. We spot the werewolves as we skim the treetops. Spread across the island in small groups, most relaxing, some eating (I don't think much of the natural wildlife exists there any more), a few fighting. Mutated, vicious, hairy monstrosities, all fangs, claws and muscles. Some howl at us as we pass overhead, though we can't hear them over the roar of the blades.

The wolf within me tries to force its way to the surface, howling silently in reply to its warped brethren. I'm one of the cursed Gradys. I should have turned into a werewolf. I only survived because I'm a magician. My magic self wrestled with my wolfen side and triumphed. But I've never rid myself of the wolf, only driven it down deep inside.

I don't have any difficulty keeping my wolfish instincts in check, but I'm surprised to find that a part of me doesn't want to remain in control. I'm excited by the creatures running free beneath us. Life would be much simpler if I abandoned my humanity and ran wild with them, gave myself over to animalistic pleasures, free of the burdens of duty and responsibility.

I'm envious of my twisted relatives, but sad for them too. Because I know their freedom is temporary. If it all goes wrong and Prae Athim turns the tables on us, she'll use these *specimens* for her own sick ends. But life won't be much better for them if we succeed. Antoine Horwitzer will take over, pick the werewolves off one by one, slice them open and carry out all manner of unpleasant experiments.

I'm so glad Gret and Bill-E aren't down there. In a weird way I'm glad they're dead, rather than captive on this island. Better to be out of life entirely than struggle through it as a tormented, hopeless, inhuman victim.

The others are studying the werewolves with a mixture of curiosity and loathing. They have no ties to these unfortunate mutants. They view them simply as enemies. If our plan works, we should have no dealings with the werewolves. But if complications set in, the soliders might find themselves up against the killer beasts, and in that case they'll have to be ruthless.

Antoine is the only one not awed by the spectacle. He stole a quick glance at the werewolves when we hit the island's edge, then closed his eyes, dug rosary beads out of a pocket and began to pray. I hadn't pegged him as a religious type, but when I think about it, it makes sense. After all, the Lambs named themselves after a biblical quote.

My stomach clenches and I almost throw up. It's the werewolf, fighting to free itself. I stop staring at Antoine and focus on driving the wolf back inside. It retreats reluctantly and I feel sorry for it. If I could let it loose for a while, somewhere it couldn't cause damage, I would, just to give it a taste of freedom.

The compound walls come into sight. I was expecting a fence, but there isn't one, only a long wall of high, thick, metal panels. Lots of werewolves are gathered by the wall, hurling themselves at it, clawing its smooth grey surface, howling at those inside, the stench of human flesh thick in their nostrils. (The stench is also thick in mine.

My lips tremble and I am careful not to drool.)

As we approach the wall I catch my first glimpse of the compound. It's built on the extended tip of the island, surrounded on three sides by cliffs and water. The werewolves have only one route of attack. Even if they could swim (Antoine told us they can't), they'd struggle to climb the sheer cliffs, despite their claws.

The compound's nothing special. A series of grey, drab buildings with flat, aluminium roofs. There are lots of grooves in the ground, which Timas points out, speaking through the microphone on his headset.

"They use the grooves to slot the walls into place," he explains. "An ingenious system. Just lay the grooves, then slide the panels around and click them together. Makes it easy to shuffle the rooms and alter the layout."

"Those walls can't be sturdy," Shark grunts.

"They are," Timas insists. "Designed to withstand anything nature can throw at them. The architects couldn't take chances, not with hundreds of werewolves lying in wait on the other side."

There's a landing pad inside the main wall, to the left. A single helicopter stands idle. There are several motorboats stored under tarpaulins at either side of the crag, rope ladders stacked beside them. In the event of an evacuation, that's how the staff would leave, lowering the boats and climbing down into them.

Guards spill out of the nearest building as we touch down, cocking rifles and pistols. One roars through a megaphone, commanding us to come out unarmed.

"This is it!" Shark yells, brandishing his handguns. "Don't kill if you can help it, but don't show too much mercy either. These guys knew what they were signing up for. They've already murdered seventeen people. They'll rip us to shreds if we give them the chance."

He rolls out and across the ground, leaps to his feet and opens fire, supported instantly by his team, even Timas, wielding a high-tech weapon that provides him with all sorts of fascinating feedback.

Meera and I share a worried glance, then slide out after the others on to the bullet-riddled tarmac, leaving James and Marian to guard the helicopter. Antoine stumbles out after us, still praying, crouched low, sweat staining the collar of his otherwise spotless shirt.

The air is ablaze with gunfire. A number of guards are already lying wounded or dead. Others are firing wildly. It's a simple matter for the well-trained members of Shark's squad to pick them off.

The last few, realising the futility of their position, discard their weapons and thrust their hands into the air. The gunfire ceases. Leo darts forward and makes them lie down, then handcuffs their wrists and ankles. While he's doing that, the other soldiers advance to the open door and surround it. When Leo joins them, Shark holds up three fingers and counts down. Liam and Terry burst through, laying down a spray of advance fire. In pairs, the rest of the team follow them in. Meera and I bring up the rear, Antoine and Pip ahead of us. The bloodshed sickens me. I don't mind slaughtering demons, but these are *people*. It's not right. I know we have no choice, that these guys are murderers, but still…

Cool inside. Air-conditioned. Brightly lit. Liam and Terry are already at the end of the room and halfway through the door to the next room or corridor. No sign of anybody else. These are living quarters. Bunks, cabinets, racks for clothes, photos of models and relatives pinned to the walls. Those we hit outside must have been relaxing. They wouldn't have been expecting an attack. I wish they hadn't reacted so swiftly. If we'd caught them in here, we wouldn't have had to kill so many.

"You OK?" Meera asks as we wait for the call to advance.

"Not really," I groan.

"I know it's hard," she says quietly. "Try not to think of them as humans but as demonic assistants."

"But they probably know nothing about the Demonata," I protest.

"They knew about the seventeen Lambs they killed," Meera snaps. "These aren't innocents."

"But they're still people. I don't feel comfortable killing like this."

Meera smiles wanly. "That's a good thing. Try and hold on to that attitude. The world's packed with too many trigger-happy goons."

"Like Shark?" I grin shakily.

Meera's face puckers into something between a scowl and a smirk. Before she can answer, one of the soldiers – I think it's Spenser – shouts affirmatively and we're moving forward again, further into the heart of the compound.

→We don't encounter much resistance. The occasional guard or two. We're able to overpower most of them and leave them handcuffed, alive. We only face one real obstacle, when several guards block a long corridor and fill it with furniture. They have a great vantage point. If we try to rush them, we'll be cut down before we get halfway. But Shark isn't fazed. He calls Pip forward. She studies the piled-up furniture, makes a few calculations, then takes off her rucksack and roots through it. Produces a small round object. It looks like a thick CD.

"Who's good with Frisbees?" Pip asks.

"Here," Liam says. He takes the disc, aims, then glances at Pip. "Do I need to press anything?"

"No. But if you don't throw it quickly, you'll lose an arm."

Liam yelps, then sends the disc skimming down the corridor. It hits the mound of furniture near the base and explodes on contact. The desks, chairs and cabinets fly backwards, obliterating the guards behind them. We're on the scene seconds later, Shark's troops handcuffing any survivors. Stephen bends over a seriously wounded man. Starts to cuff him, then pauses, studies his injuries, sets him down and presses the barrel of his gun to the man's head. I look away but I can't drown out the retort of the muffled shot.

We push on, the air thick with the stench of scorched wood, blood and whatever was in Pip's bomb. Antoine's still praying. I almost feel like joining in.

The corridors and rooms all look the same to me, but the soldiers know exactly where they're going. A couple of minutes later, we're at the door of Prae Athim's office. There are no markings to confirm that, but Timas is certain. He steps ahead of us and raps softly. "Knock, knock," he calls. "Anybody home?"

He pushes the door open and we spill in.

A large room. Grey walls. Harsh fluorescent lights. A single bed. A black, high-backed leather chair in the centre of the floor. Someone's sitting in it, facing away from us. I can only see the person's lower legs, but I'm sure it's Prae Athim.

"Hey!" Shark barks. No answer. He looks at us. Nods at Pip to advance and check for explosives. She creeps forward, skirting the chair, pistol trained on the person in it. As she angles to the front, she pauses, face crinkling. Shaking her head, she stoops, checks the chair for wires and devices, then puts her hand on one of the arms and swivels it around.

I was right. It's Prae Athim. But, to my bewilderment, she's strapped down, a strip of tape across her mouth, incapable of movement or sound.

We gawp at the sight. Prae Athim glares at us. Shark gulps, then strides forward and grabs hold of one end of the tape over her mouth. Before he can tear it free, somebody shouts a weird word. Whipping round, I spot Antoine Horwitzer, arms wide, grinning crazily. He yells a couple more words and the air shimmers behind him. Too late, I realise the nature of the trap we've walked into. I start to roar a warning, but the window opens before I can.

It's an enormous dark window. As I stare at it, horrified, a deformed, miserable-looking creature slithers through. It has the general shape of a woman, but her flesh is bubbling with sores and boils. Pus and blood seep from wounds all over her body. There's a rancid stink. The eyes are swimming bowls of madness in a ruined face. The mouth is a jagged gash. I know who this abomination is from Dervish's description, but I would have recognised her anyway.

"Hello, Grubbs," the thing that was once Juni Swan gurgles. "Have you missed me?"

There's no time to answer. Right behind Juni, dozens

of guards file in three abreast, weapons cradled to their chests. Spreading out, they take aim. Before a stunned Shark and his team can react, an officer bellows a command and the air around us is ripped apart by a lethal hail of bullets.

OPEN SEASON

→Without magic we'd have perished instantly. But magical energy streams through the window, as it always does when a passageway between universes is opened. Tapping into that instinctively, I throw up a barrier between us and the guards. The bullets mushroom against it and drop harmlessly to the floor. As more troops flood into the room, I strengthen the barrier and start thinking about ways to make it a one-way shield, so that we can fire at them.

Before I can do that, Juni barks a short command. The window pulses, then snaps out of existence. The flow of magic stops, and though a strong residue is left in the air, I now have to work off a dwindling supply. Altering the shield would take a lot out of me. Too much.

"How long can you hold that?" Shark yells.

"A couple of minutes," I guess.

"Pip!" he roars.

"On it," she mutters, darting to the rear of the wall to my right. There's a corridor on the other side which bypasses the section of the building we came through. Shark was keeping it in reserve in case we needed an escape route.

As Meera frees Prae Athim, the guards on the other side of the shield part to allow Juni Swan and a smirking Antoine Horwitzer to advance. They come to within a couple of centimetres of the barrier. Juni smiles crookedly at the shield, then at me.

"Nice work, Grubbs," she gurgles, her voice a hoarse mockery of what it once was. "But what more can you do in the absence of demonic energy?"

"As much as you," I snarl.

"Possibly," she chuckles. "But I don't have to do anything. Not with so many finely armed humans to depend on."

"Did you pay them much?" Shark sneers.

"Antoine recruited them on my behalf," she says.

"Most humans have a price," Antoine chuckles. "I've always been adept at calculating such sums."

"I'll have your head for this, Horwitzer!" Prae Athim screams, ripping the tape from her mouth and thrusting a finger at Antoine. "You're finished!"

"Don't be silly," he coos. "You can't do anything to me. Your reign has come to its natural end. I run the Lambs now."

"Why this way?" she snarls. "You were always power-hungry, but you'd have squeezed me out eventually.

Why betray us to monstrous fiends like this?"

"Careful," Juni growls. "You don't want to hurt my feelings."

"It's the dawn of a new age," smiles Antoine. "Our associates can provide us with the cure for lycanthropy, but that's only the tip of the iceberg. I was never much interested in that side of the business. While you were wasting money on werewolves, I was busy making it in other fields. We're already a major force, but when we move into areas of supernatural energy, we'll be in a class of our own."

"I'm ready," Pip calls.

"Give us a minute," Shark says, then squares up to Juni. "I never liked you. When you were Beranabus's assistant, all you ever did was complain. You're weak and petty, a disgrace to the Disciples."

Juni stares impassively at Shark. "Insult me all you like. You'll be dead soon. We'll see who's laughing then." She looks around and spots Meera. Her smile blossoms again. "You had a lucky escape in Carcery Vale. You won't get away this time."

"You were in the Vale?" Meera frowns.

"Of course," Juni says. "I was outside. I was sorely tempted to break into the cellar. I could smell the three of you and I knew Dervish was incapacitated. But my master warned me to be wary of Bec... of the Kah-Gash."

"So that's what this is about," I snarl, our suspicions – that the attacks were the work of Lord Loss and the Shadow – confirmed. "You want the Kah-Gash."

"Obviously," Juni sniffs. "Did you think my master would stand by and let you wield the most powerful weapon ever known? That he'd wait for you to learn how to use it, so you could destroy our universe?"

"But why try to kill us?" I frown. "The werewolves could have ripped Bec to pieces. Surely you need her – and me – alive."

"Not at all," Juni sneers. "Our new master deals in death. I'm proof of that — he released my soul and let me walk among the living again. I'm here to harvest your spirit, just as I would have harvested Bec's if she'd been killed. It's simpler to let others do our dirty work, then steal your parts of the Kah-Gash as you perish. We weren't sure how powerful you might be, so—" She gasps, clutches her chest and bends over. Takes several breaths, then stands again.

"You don't look too healthy," I laugh wickedly.

"This body won't last long," she says. "A shell for my soul to inhabit. I'll return to death soon, and return gladly. But rest assured, your uncle's in far worse shape. I saw him just before I came here."

I stiffen fearfully. "You're lying."

"No," she says. "He was on a pleasure cruiser, although he didn't seem to be getting much pleasure out of it. My new master decided to deal with Bec personally, and since Dervish and Beranabus were with her, they're dead now, or will be soon. Just like you when your barrier crumbles."

I start to press her for more information, but Shark grips my arm. "We've learnt all we need to know. Time to get out of here."

"But Dervish—" I cry.

"—will have to look after himself," Shark finishes. He yells at Pip, "Now!"

There's a small explosion. As the dust clears, Pip slips through a hole in the wall and the others push after her. I glance at Juni. She's smiling.

"My team will catch up with you outside," she says. "And I've another surprise lined up. I'll wait here. I don't need to be too close when you die."

"Any last words for the board, Prae?" Antoine asks. She hits him with some of the foulest insults I've ever heard, but he doesn't even blink. He's loving this. It would be easy to blame myself for not seeing through him before, but he conned us all. Besides, there's no time for self-blame. If we reach the helicopter before Juni's soldiers, we might get out of here. We're not finished yet — if we're fast.

"Later!" I snap at Juni, locking gazes with her, letting her see how serious I am. I mean to kill her the next time we meet, as slowly and painfully as possible.

Juni only laughs with mad delight at the threat, then waves mockingly. "Run, run as fast as you can, but I'll catch you, little ginger-haired man."

"Grubbs!" Shark shouts. He's standing by the hole in the wall. Everyone's gone through except him and Meera.

I hold Juni's gaze one last second, then turn my back on the mutant and her troops, and dive for safety. As I squeeze through the hole, I hear the sounds of dozens of feet scuffling out of the room as the soldiers set off to intercept us.

The race is on.

→ Running as fast as we can, Timas in the lead. He's playing with the tiny console on his gun as he runs. He looks the least worried of us all.

"I can't believe you trusted that charlatan," Prae Athim pants, glancing over her shoulder at me.

"He told us you stole the werewolves," I growl. "Based on your previous threat to kidnap Bill-E and me, why wouldn't we believe him?"

"Anyway, he worked for *you*," Meera chips in. "Why didn't you see this coming?"

"Enough!" Shark huffs as Prae bristles. "If they catch us before we make it outside, it doesn't matter who's to blame — we'll all be crapping bullets."

We push on in silence. I'm finding it difficult to keep

up. Although I'm fit, I'm used to operating on magic. It's been a long time since I worked up a sweat. I'm out of practice.

I can hear Juni's guards, their cries to one another. They're keeping pace with us but can't break through. We have a slight advantage, but it's *very* slight. And if they make it to the yard before us, or if there are more out there already...

The corridor feels much longer than it appeared on the map. I start to think we're in a maze, doomed to wander in circles until we run into Juni's troops and are mown down. I consider using magic to guide us out. But that would be a waste of energy. I have to hold it back. Use it only when the situation is truly desperate. Which probably won't be long.

Timas bursts through a door and sunlight streams in. Finding an extra burst of speed, we hurry through, out into the yard where we fought with the first group of guards. It's deserted except for James and Marian in the Farrier Harrier. As soon as they see us, James fires the engines up to full, readying the helicopter for a swift getaway.

We race for the chopper. I picture myself clambering to safety along with everybody else. We lift off, zip out over the water, laughing at our narrow escape, leaving Juni behind to curse and rant. But in my heart I know it won't be that easy. And sure enough, before we've taken six strides, Juni's troops hit the scene and the gunfire starts.

Pip LeMat is ahead of everyone, having overtaken Timas, so she should have been the safest. But she's the first to catch a spray of bullets. She hits the ground hard and doesn't move, blood already seeping from beneath her still form.

Shark and the others spin 180 degrees, even as Pip is falling, and open up with their own weapons. "Run!" Shark yells at Meera and me. "Get out of here. We'll cover you."

I start to protest, but Meera pushes me forward. "Don't argue!" she shouts.

"We can't just leave them," I cry as half of Terry's head disappears. He remains standing a moment, then slumps forward. Leo takes a hit to the shoulder. He roars with pain, but continues to return fire. Prae Athim grabs Terry's gun and pitches in with the others, screaming manically.

"You heard what Juni said," Meera snarls. "You're the only one who matters. If she gets her hands on you, we're done for."

"Like we're not already!" I shriek.

"All the rest of us have to worry about is death," Meera says. "From what Juni said, that's only the start for you. If the Shadow gets your piece of the Kah-Gash..."

I stare at her helplessly. I know she's right, but these

soldiers have become our friends. We can't simply abandon them.

"A barrier," I wheeze. "We can construct a shield and—"

Meera slaps me hard. "Get in that helicopter or they'll have died for nothing."

I stare at her numbly, then lurch forward. Bullets rip up the ground close by my feet, but I don't flinch. My eyes are filling with tears. I don't want to escape if the cost is losing Shark and his team, but Meera's right. We have no choice. The Kah-Gash mustn't fall into the Shadow's hands.

I'm about halfway to the Farrier Harrier when a klaxon blares, overriding the noise of the helicopter and guns. I shouldn't stop, but I can't help myself. Pausing, I glance back and see Juni's men retreating into the building. At least a dozen have been killed or are lying wounded. But everyone else is ducking out of sight.

Shark was crouched low, but now he stands and stares after the departing troops. He's as confused as I am. Then, as the squeal of the klaxon dies away, we hear something else. A grinding noise coming from the outer wall of the compound.

We whirl as one, just in time to see the wall split in several places. We should have seen this coming. Timas told us, when he was explaining about the grooves in the ground. Everything here is built out of metal panels which can be swiftly slid together — or just as easily slid apart.

As we watch with a sickening sense of helplessness, panels roll back, leaving gaping holes in the wall. Seconds later I spot the first werewolf sniffing at the gap. Then it catches our scent and bounds ahead, followed by dozens more. They converge on us like giant locusts, screeching, howling, free at last to attack and kill.

RUNNING THE GAUNTLET

→"The helicopter!" Shark roars, leading the break for our only hope of survival. We pound after him, but I see within seconds that we haven't a snowman in hell's chance. The werewolves are closer to the helicopter than we are and they can run faster.

Alert to the danger, James starts to take his Farrier Harrier up, out of the reach of the onrushing werewolves. But he's not quick enough. One of the larger beasts takes a running leap and grabs hold of the skid on the pilot's side. Marian levels her gun at it, but the weight of the werewolf causes the helicopter to lurch and she's jolted off target. The werewolf hauls itself up on to the skid and drives its fists and head through the pilot's window. It locks its jaws on James's terror-stricken face and savages him.

James battles hopelessly against the werewolf, tries to thrash free, fails, then goes limp. The helicopter spins out of control, swishes left then right, then banks and smashes into the compound wall. The rotors snap off with an ear-splitting squeal. The blood-spattered glass shatters and the body of the helicopter buckles inwards. But it doesn't explode like I expect it to.

I spot a shaken, bloodied Marian struggling from the remains of the wreckage. Three werewolves jump her while she's half out of the helicopter. They drive her back inside and finish her off, fighting over the scraps.

The first werewolf is on us before we can feel any pity for James and Marian. Shark takes careful aim and fires a bullet through the centre of its head. Then he changes direction and darts for the helicopter which was already here when we arrived. He bellows at us to follow.

Werewolves quickly fill the area around us. Shark and his remaining soldiers fire at them freely, wounding, maiming, killing. I can't work up any sympathy for my unfortunate relatives. It's them or us now.

Timas stoops over Pip's body as we pass, swiftly loosens her rucksack and burrows through it as he runs, whistling casually. He picks out a device, smiles, shakes his head and carefully replaces it. Never drops his pace, keeping up with the rest of us even though he's not concentrating.

Some of the werewolves are distracted by the stranded, wounded survivors of Juni's forces — easy pickings. The ground between us and the helicopter partially clears. Shark and his team focus their fire on those who remain in our way, opening a path. Hope flares within me. The despair I felt seconds ago evaporates. We're going to make it!

We reach the helicopter. More and more werewolves are closing on us, but it doesn't matter. Liam, Stephen and the injured Leo cut down those closest to the helicopter and stand guard outside, keeping the area clear while the rest of us clamber in.

Shark and Timas bundle into the cockpit. Shark whoops and tries to start the engine. There's no response. He frowns, ducks, looks beneath the control panel. Comes up pale-faced. "They removed…" He curses, then stares at Timas with wild hope. "Any way you could…?"

Timas takes his nose out of Pip's rucksack long enough to peer down. "No," he says. "This is going nowhere." He continues rummaging through the rucksack.

"The boats," Meera gasps. "Werewolves can't swim."

"It would take at least two minutes to lower a boat," Prae says miserably. "We could cut one free and drop it, but we'd still have to climb down the ladders. They'd clamber after us or hurl themselves off the cliff on top of us. We'd never make it."

"I could put a shield in place at the top of the ladder," I pant.

"You'd need a bigger shield than that," Timas murmurs. "Didn't you notice the slits in the cliffside walls of the compound when you were studying the maps? They're so the guards can fire at anything attacking from the seaward direction. They can pick us off if we try to descend."

"Could you cover us from gunfire and werewolves all the way to the bottom?" Shark asks.

"I don't know," I groan. "I can try."

"I don't like it," he growls. "We'd be too exposed. Any other suggestions?"

"Can you get us inside the compound again?" Meera asks Prae.

"No. I don't know the security codes."

"Timas?"

"I could figure them out," he says calmly, "but it would take several minutes."

There's a scream. Leo goes down, tackled by a pair of small werewolves. Liam and Stephen fire into them, but it's too late. When they fall away, Leo's eyes are wide and lifeless, a shredded mesh where his throat should be.

"Out of time," Shark sighs. "Let's try for the boats and just hope for—"

"Caves!" I shout, flashing on an image of a map of the island. I grab Prae's right arm. "Are there caves near here?"

"I don't know," she scowls. "I wasn't involved with this project. I haven't—"

"There are a few within reach," Timas cuts in. He

looks at me curiously. "What sort of cave are you interested in?"

"One with a single entrance, so we can block it off and seal ourselves in."

"What will that achieve?" Shark frowns.

"If I have a few hours, I can open a window to the Demonata universe."

Shark stares at me, then the boats, then the breached perimeter wall and the hordes of werewolves flooding through. He calculates the odds.

"If we don't make it to the cave, we can break for the sea and jump off one of the cliffs," Timas says thoughtfully.

"So we'd have a plan B," Shark nods. "OK. The cave. Go for it!"

Spilling out of the helicopter, we face the oncoming ranks of werewolves and press stubbornly – suicidally – forward into the thick of them.

→Barbaric madness. Blasting our way through the wild, fast, powerful, stinking, howling creatures. Shark, Timas, Liam, Stephen, Spenser and Prae gather in a tight circle around Meera and me. They stand three on either side, backs pressed in against us. We move like a crab, edging forward awkwardly. The soldiers and Prae shower the werewolves with bullets, but it won't be long before one breaks through, then another, then all.

"This is crazy!" I yell, changing my mind. "We'll never make it. Let's try the boats."

"No," Timas responds. "If we reach the wall, we'll be over the worst. Notice how the flow of werewolves has lessened? Most of the beasts within quick reach of the compound are already here."

"So?" Shark shouts, never taking his eyes off the beasts, firing every few seconds, measuring his bullets carefully, not wasting any.

"I have a plan," Timas says. "It should buy us some time."

"What sort of a plan?" I ask suspiciously.

Timas jiggles Pip's rucksack at me. "The sort that goes *boom*!"

One of the larger, incredibly muscular werewolves leaps through the air. Bullets from more than one gun lace his body, but he lands on top of Spenser and yanks him away from us. The werewolf tumbles after the soldier and drops dead a second later. But the damage is done. Spenser's cut off. Before he can rejoin the group, half a dozen wolfen savages are covering him. He dies screaming a woman's name.

We push on, no time to mourn our fallen friend. I'm itching to use magic, but I have to save myself. No point wasting my energy on getting to the cave if I can't open a window to safety once we're there.

We creep closer to the wall, the werewolves dogging

our every step, snapping and clawing at us, trying to press through the rain of bullets. I notice that most of the larger beasts are hanging back behind the smaller specimens. They must be some of the enhanced creatures, those who were physically and mentally altered, trained to hunt in packs. They're letting the weaker creatures hurl themselves at us, to tire us, so they can move in when we're more vulnerable.

According to Timas, the Lambs created more than two hundred of these newer, deadlier werewolves. I can't count more than fifty around us. That means the rest must be spread across the island — or waiting for us outside the wall.

I think about sharing this potentially fatal piece of news with the rest of the team, but see no point in freaking them out. If a hundred-plus of the stronger, smarter savages are lying in ambush, we're finished. No point worrying the others. If that's our fate, let their last few minutes be filled with hope instead of dread.

→We make the wall without any more casualties. Shark and the soldiers look completely drained. But they never slow or waver. True professionals, driving themselves on past the point of exhaustion.

We move into one of the gaps in the wall and pause at a shout from Timas. He, Shark and Liam train their weapons on the mass of werewolves on the compound side of the wall. Stephen and Prae cover the rear, picking off the stray werewolves who haven't invaded yet or are just arriving.

"Give me a few seconds," Timas says once we've established our precarious position. He slips out of his place, passing Meera his gun.

"I don't know how to use this," she screeches.

"Point it at a target and pull the trigger," Timas says. "I've set it to its simplest mode." He nudges her forward with an elbow, then digs into Pip's rucksack and produces several small devices. He hands a few to me.

"Do I just throw them?" I ask.

"I'd rather you simply held them for me," he says, fiddling with those in his own hands. "If they're not lobbed accurately, they might explode in the wrong direction. That would be bad for us."

"Timas!" Shark shouts. "We can't hold much longer. They're crowding in."

"My plan wouldn't work if they didn't," Timas says, then gently tosses one of his devices forward. It lands a metre ahead of us, less than two metres from the rabid wave of werewolves. "Close your eyes," he purrs, lobbing another bomb after the first, then covering his face with an arm.

The first device explodes as I snap my eyes shut. The second explosion follows almost instantly. Screams replace howls. I chance a look. It's like a bulldozer has ploughed through the werewolves ahead of us. Dozens are on the ground, dead or bleeding, whimpering and confused. Those to the sides are barking with anger and fear, backing away from the carnage. Before they can recover their wits, Timas lobs three more devices, one left, one right, one straight ahead.

"These are a bit more destructive than the first two," he warns. "You might want to cover your ears also."

His warning comes just in time. I've only barely jammed my hands over my ears when the devices explode. The vibrations shake my brain around inside my skull. When I look again, the devastation is unbelievable, like a field of dead in a war movie. Those not caught by the blasts are scrambling backwards, yowling with pain, ears and noses bleeding. Werewolves have much sharper senses than humans. This must be sheer agony for those not killed.

Timas turns neatly and takes another device from me. Looking back, I see that the creatures on the other side of the wall have come to an uncertain halt. Several are rubbing at their ears and whining. Nowhere near as disorganised as those who bore the brunt of the explosions, but shaken all the same.

When Timas lobs the bomb at them and it explodes, the surviving werewolves bolt like a pack of panic-stricken dogs. Timas tips an imaginary hat to them, twirls like a ballerina, grabs another device from me and throws it at those on the compound side. The werewolves might not be the brightest creatures in the world, but they've seen enough to know that when the tall, red-headed guy throws something, it means trouble. Roaring abominably, they break and flee, even the enhanced beasts.

We don't waste time congratulating Timas, just bolt for the freedom of the island beyond the wall, determined to take full advantage of the lull, certain it won't last long. Timas is the only one who doesn't run immediately. He remains behind, setting more devices in the ground between the gap in the wall.

Moments later he catches up with us and retrieves the bombs which I've been holding. His rucksack looks pretty flat now, but he doesn't seem worried. He grins at me as he pockets a couple of the explosives. "That was the first practical experience I've had of controlled detonations," he says.

I gawp at him. "You'd never used a bomb before?"

"No. I'd read about them, but this was the first chance I had to put my knowledge to the test." He looks back and frowns at the hole in the wall, the cloud of dust in the air, the dismembered bodies of the butchered werewolves. "What do you think? Eight out of ten, or am I being too generous?"

"Shut up, you genius of an idiot," I laugh. "And run!"

***

→We race to the top of a small incline, Timas leading the way. We pause to catch our breath and gather our wits. I can already see a few werewolves sniffing around the gap in the wall. As they creep through, one steps on a landmine and sets it off. The others scatter at top speed.

I feel like cheering, but I don't want to tempt fate. Besides, it won't take them long to try one of the other, unmined gaps. Once they discover a safe way out of the compound, they'll pursue us again, only this time they'll be even more determined to hunt us down, to make us pay.

Timas sets another couple of devices at the top of the little hill, covering them with loose earth, like someone planting seeds.

"What else do you have in there?" Shark asks, nodding at the rucksack.

"Not much," Timas sighs. "I have a few mines in my pockets and some grenades in case we run into resistance. As for the rest… enough to bring down the cave entrance. There won't be much left over."

"Did anybody else notice the larger breeds?" Prae pants. "At the rear?"

"Yes," I answer softly, but I'm the only one.

"Horwitzer's work," she growls. "They're even deadlier than the others. They hung back where it was safe, waiting for the ideal moment to strike. If there are more of those, or if they catch up with us before we make it to the cave…" She shakes her head.

"If Timas is right, there's a couple of hundred of them in total," I tell her.

Prae's face goes ashen.

"None of that," Shark snarls, clicking his scorched fingers in front of her eyes. "We won't have pessimism. By any account we should be dead already. But we're not. Having come through that, we can survive anything. If you disagree, keep it to yourself."

Prae chuckles weakly, then pushes to her feet and looks over the island. I stand and stare too. We can't see anything except grassland, which gives way to bushes and trees. But I can hear the howls of werewolves. They're getting closer.

"Shark," I say nervously.

"I know." He stretches, then groans. "My back's killing me. Never had trouble before. I might have to think about retiring after this one."

We all laugh. It's the free and edgy laughter of people who've come through hell and lived to tell the tale, but have to face the journey at least one more time.

Shark clicks his tongue and everyone rises. Liam and Stephen are covered in blood, filth and scraps of hairy flesh. Meera hasn't returned Timas's gun, but is cradling it like a baby. Prae's trembling, but holding herself together. Only Timas looks unconcerned, as if we're on a leisurely stroll. The rest of us are beaten and worn.

But we're alive. And that gives me hope. We might make it off this island yet, damn the odds. If we do, it'll rank as one of the greatest escapes ever, up there with Beranabus's finest death-defying shimmies. I almost want to survive just to prove to the magician that he's not the only cat with nine lives.

If he's still alive. Thinking about him reminds me of Juni's taunt, that Dervish, Bec and Beranabus have been set upon by the Shadow. Are they in an even worse spot than us? Has Beranabus been catapulted into the afterlife ahead of me, along with Bec and my uncle?

Before I can dwell on that grim possibility, Shark barks a command. As we sprint down the opposite side of the incline, all other fears and thoughts are forgotten. Running… werewolves… the cave. There's no room inside my head for anything else.

CAVEMEN

→The howls intensify as we run, coming from all
directions, a cacophony of wolfen roars tightening
around us like a net. But we don't spot another
werewolf until, cutting our way through a small copse,
one leaps from a tree without warning and drags Shark
to the ground. The pair roll away from us, and though
the soldiers in our group swiftly train their weapons on
the beast, I'm sure they're too late. I resign myself to the
loss of our leader.

But Shark isn't ready for the grave just yet.
Staggering to his feet, he shoulders the howling
werewolf away. The others can't shoot because he's in
their way, and Shark lost his gun in the attack.

"Down!" Stephen yells, desperate to put a bullet
through the werewolf's head.

Shark has other ideas. Jerking a knife from his belt,
he leaps on the savage beast and drives the blade into
its stomach, chewing on its left ear for extra impact.
The werewolf screams and claws at Shark's back,

ripping his shirt and much of his flesh to shreds. But Shark jabs at it a second time and a third, and its hands drop away. Moments later he shrugs it off and hobbles free.

"Are you OK?" Meera asks as he rejoins us, casting a worried look at his injuries.

"I've cut myself worse shaving," Shark grunts. He retrieves his rifle and pushes up beside Timas, ignoring the blood pooling around the waistband of his trousers.

As we clear the copse, we spot an army of werewolves surging towards us from our far left. The beasts at the front look like they're part of the enhanced breed. We can also hear crashing and snapping sounds in the trees behind us — the pack from the compound has almost caught up.

"There!" Timas shouts, swivelling right. I can't see anything except a lot of rocks jutting out of the ground, but he seems sure of himself. As we hurl ourselves after Timas, I pray desperately that his map-reading skills were as accurate as he led us to believe.

I don't look back as we run, but I hear the werewolves closing in. The creatures who've been chasing us from the compound have merged with those arriving fresh on the scene to create a chorus of howls and screeches that could drown out the sound of a nuclear detonation. I feel hot breath on the back of my neck. I hope it's just my imagination.

Timas reaches a rock, grabs it with his left hand and pivots, lobbing a bomb over our heads as he swings out of sight. The explosion and screams of the werewolves are music to my ears. But as I come in line with the rock and duck around it, I catch sight of the beasts, no more than several metres behind, and my glee shrivels up like the petals of a flower at the heart of a furnace.

There's no sign of Timas. For a horrified second I think he's been snatched by a werewolf. But then I see his bony arm and narrow fingers jerk out of a hole, beckoning us on.

Shark is next to make it. He dives in and Timas's arm disappears. The rest of us come abreast of what looks like just a hole in the rock, less than a metre high. But as I look closer I see that the floor is lower than the ground out here, so you can stand inside. It's more of a tunnel than an actual cave, but I'm not going to complain about that.

Shark pops up like a jack-in-the-box. He aims over our heads and fires at the werewolves. There's a grunt three or four centimetres behind my ear and I realise they're even closer than I feared.

Screaming madly, I wrap an arm around Meera's waist and hurl her into the hole, like a basketball player making a slam dunk. She smashes against one of the walls inside the entrance and cries out with pain. But at least she's out of the reach of the werewolves.

Prae ducks in after Meera and scurries forward. I almost collide with Stephen as we both try to push in at the same time. We pause and I flash on a ridiculous image of us standing here, politely muttering, "No, after *you*," until we're carved up and consumed. But then Stephen slaps my back and I gratefully dive in ahead of him.

Meera and Prae have shuffled deeper into the cave. Timas is hooking up a series of devices to the walls around the entrance. For once he isn't grinning. By his expression, you might even think he was slightly perturbed.

Shark is still standing half out of the cave, roaring as he empties his cartridge into the hordes of werewolves. Stephen falls into the cave backwards, firing as he topples. He takes out a werewolf which was just about to snap Shark's head off.

"Back!" Timas yells.

Shark immediately withdraws. Liam, who was covering the rest of us from outside, dives into the hole after him. But he comes to a stop mid-air, arms outstretched, legs caught. He screams. Shark curses and grabs for Liam's hands. He catches them and tugs hard. Liam screams again.

"Hold on!" Stephen shouts, wriggling forward, firing around Shark and Liam.

Liam jerks forward a few centimetres. It looks like Shark has him, but then he's wrenched out of the cave.

For a brief moment I'm dazzled by sunlight. Then the hole fills with the heads and upper torsos of dozens of werewolves. They snap and lash at each other, fighting to be first in.

Before the werewolves can sort themselves out and slither into the cave, Timas yells, "Everybody down!" I catch sight of him pushing a button on a tiny detonator as I leap for safety. Then there's the mother of all explosions and the roof around the entrance comes crashing down, muting the howls of the werewolves, plunging us into darkness, entombing us beneath the ground.

→Nobody says anything for several minutes. We can't — the air's clogged with dust and bits of debris. We crawl away from the rubble in search of cleaner air, heads low, covering our faces with jackets and T-shirts, breathing shallowly. The roof slopes downwards and after a while we have to bend. When that becomes uncomfortable, we sit and wait for the air to clear. I'm exhausted. I could happily fall asleep where I'm sitting.

Shark breaks the silence. He coughs, spits out something, then says, "Who's still alive?"

"Me," Timas answers brightly.

"Me," Prae Athim gasps.

"Me," Stephen says morosely — I think he was good friends with Liam.

"Me," I mutter through the fabric of my T-shirt, not ready to chance the air yet.

"Me," Meera groans, "though I feel like half my ribs are broken. What the hell did you throw me in for, Grubbs?"

"I was trying to save you," I growl.

"I could have saved myself," she snaps.

"Ungrateful cow!"

"Chauvinist pig!"

We laugh at the same time.

"Cute," Shark huffs. "Now somebody tell me they brought a torch." Nobody says anything. "Brilliant. So we're stuck here in the—"

Something glows. I tug my T-shirt down and squint at the dim light. It's coming from Timas's gun, from the small control panel I noticed earlier. Humming, Timas makes a few adjustments and the glow increases, just enough to illuminate the area around us. He looks up. His grin is firmly back in place, though it looks a bit eerie in the weak green light.

"Remind me to kiss you when this is over," Shark says, struggling not to smile.

"Me too," Meera adds. "Seriously."

Timas shrugs as if it's no big thing, then raises his rifle so we can see more. We're in a tight, cramped cave (or spacious tunnel, depending on how you look at it). The roof is much lower than it was at the entrance and dips even more further back. The rocks are jagged and jab into me. The floor is sandy and littered with sharp stones. It's humid and dusty from the explosion. But I'm too grateful to be alive and in a werewolf-free zone to feel anything but utter delight – love, almost – for our surroundings.

"How far back does this run?" Shark asks.

"That information wasn't on the charts," Timas says, then sets his rifle down. "Wait here." He crawls away from us. We wait, breathing softly, nobody needing to be told that air might be precious. Timas is gone for what feels like two minutes… three… four.

I see him returning before I hear him. He can move in almost perfect silence when he wishes. He returns to his rifle, picks it up and sets it on his lap. "The news is both positive and negative," he says. "The cave is approximately thirty metres long, but it doesn't finish with a wall. There's a small gap between roof and floor. Air is blowing through from the other side. So we needn't fear suffocation."

"That sounds good to me," Shark says. "What's the bad news?"

"The floor isn't solid." Timas scrapes a nail through the layers of sand, grit and small stones beneath us.

"So?" Shark growls.

"This area is riddled with small caves and tunnels. I've no idea how large the opening on the other side of the hole is – it wasn't on any of the maps – but if it's large enough to permit entry, or if it can be enlarged, and the werewolves catch our scent, they'll be able to burrow through."

Shark frowns. "If the hole's small, we could block it."

"Yes," Timas says, "but that won't hold them. As I said, the floor isn't solid. With their claws, it wouldn't take them long to dig through. We could shoot the one in front and use its body to jam the entrance. But the soil here is extremely poor. Others would be able to dig under or around it.

"But, hey," he adds with a shrug. "It might never happen."

"Let's assume it will," Shark sniffs, then peers around for me. "What about that window you promised?"

"I'll get to work on it." I lean against the wall and rotate the creaks out of my neck. I'd kill for paracetamol.

"Do you need us to be silent, get out of your way or anything?" Shark asks.

"No." I close my eyes, reaching down to the magic within me. As the others start discussing the situation, I drown out their voices. There are all sorts of ways to open windows, depending on the mage or magician. Some need to sacrifice a human or even themselves. Most just use spells. A powerful mage can open a window in half a day, no matter where they are, while others need several days.

I've only opened windows twice before, once in the cave where Beranabus was based before he started searching for the Shadow. The other was in an area within the demon universe. Both times there was plenty of magic to tap into, and I managed to complete the window within a couple of hours. It will be hard and slow this time. I told Shark I could do it in a few hours but it might take me –

Between seven and eight hours, says the voice of the Kah-Gash, startling me.

"Where were you when I needed you?" I growl silently.

It won't be enough time, the Kah-Gash says, ignoring my criticism.

"What do you mean?"

The werewolves will work their way through within the next hour. They have your scent and a few of the smarter creatures are already searching for another way in. They'll find it.

I curse, then ask the Kah-Gash if it can help us.

You can help yourself, it replies with typical vagueness. *First, get out of here. I'll explain the rest when I have to. You must trust me and act quickly when I give the order. There won't be much time.*

"Then why not tell me now?" I grumble, but it's gone silent again.

Sighing, I open my eyes and debate whether I should try to build a window regardless. Beranabus is wary of the Kah-Gash. He's not sure if we can use it or if it might attempt to use us instead. Maybe it's trying to trick me. Perhaps it wants me to die here, so that Juni can harvest my soul and present it to her new master.

As I'm mulling over my decision, I listen to the conversation around me. Prae is outlining her fall from grace, how Antoine Horwitzer outfoxed her.

"I knew about some of the experiments," she says, "but I didn't know he'd taken things this far. I sensed something foul when I found out he was training packs to hunt. That served no curative purpose. I delved deeper, exposed more of the rot and revealed my misgivings to the board."

"Let me guess," Meera says drily. "They betrayed you?"

"I don't think they were all involved," Prae scowls, "but most of the members were on Horwitzer's side. Next thing I knew, I was being packaged up and posted here, where I've been stewing for the last month or however long it's been."

"Dervish thought the Lambs were rotten at the core," Meera says bitterly. "That's why he had so little to do with them. But he never guessed they might be in league with the Demonata."

"I knew nothing about that," Prae protests. "Dervish never told me anything about demons, even though I pleaded with him to share his information. If he'd been more forthcoming, perhaps–"

"Don't you dare," Meera growls. "This isn't Dervish's

fault. And even if you weren't dancing to Antoine's tune, you certainly played along when it suited. You already confessed to knowing about some of the experiments. I bet you knew about the breeding programme, right?"

"Not that they'd been bred in vast numbers or to such an altered state," Prae says quietly.

"But you knew the basics. You approved the general aims of the project. Yes?"

"We needed more specimens," Prae sighs. "Where else could we get them?"

"I bet you didn't let your daughter breed," Meera sneers.

Prae stiffens. "What do you know about Perula?"

"Nothing," Meera says. "But she wasn't one of those picked to be experimented on, was she? You wouldn't do that to your own daughter. It wasn't a case of progress at any price. You spared your own."

Prae looks at Meera miserably and, to my surprise, I feel sorry for the deposed Lamb. I sense guilt stirring within her. Prae believed she was following the path of righteous experimentation. Now she's seen the flipside. Antoine Horwitzer could never have made his move if Prae hadn't done so much of the groundwork. She's responsible for a lot of this, and awareness of that must hurt like hell.

But that doesn't matter. If the werewolves dig through, the innocent will perish just as gruesomely as the guilty. I have to decide whether I can trust the voice of the Kah-Gash. Since I don't have any real alternative, I choose to heed its advice.

"I can't build a window."

The others look round at me, startled.

"What's wrong?" Meera gasps. "Has Juni cast a spell against you?"

"No. There isn't time. The werewolves will find the other entrance. They'll be on us inside an hour."

"That's an interesting prediction," Timas says. "What are you basing it on?"

"Magic." I lock gazes with Shark. "We have an hour. I can't open a window that quickly."

"Try," he snarls.

I shake my head. "I'd just waste my power. We need to find another way."

"There isn't any," he says icily. "You were our only hope once we chose this cave over the other options."

"I don't think many werewolves are going to gather at the other side," I tell him. "Only the smartest ones have thought of looking for another entrance. I doubt if they'll share their find with the rest — they'll want us for themselves. If we can get through those few..."

"What?" Shark laughs cruelly. "Fly out of here? Find another cave?"

"There isn't one nearby," Timas says.

"See?" Shark spits.

"But we're close to water," Timas adds. "Maybe a

three- or four-minute run. The cliff is much lower there than around the compound. We could jump and probably survive the fall. From this point we're out of sight of those in the compound, so we could swim to another island."

"Where I could open a window!" I cry, excited.

"I don't like it," Shark says stubbornly. "We should stay here and stick to our original plan. You can't know for sure that they'll find…"

A vibrating howl stops him. It drifts to us from the narrowest point of the cave. Seconds later we hear the echoes of soft scrabbling sounds, distant, but not distant enough for comfort.

"An hour," I repeat glumly.

Shark sighs and raises a weary eyebrow at Timas. "You held back some of the explosives?"

"A few, for an emergency," Timas confirms.

"Good." Shark cracks his knuckles. "I think we're going to need them."

THE FINAL PUSH

→We wait for them to dig through to us. It's horrible, sitting here helplessly, the sounds of the tunnelling werewolves growing louder, coming closer. We can hear them snuffling and whining softly, hungrily. The only positive thing is that there don't seem to be many of them. It looks like I was right about the smarter few opting to keep us for themselves.

The downside is that the smarter beasts are also the stronger, faster, deadlier creatures. But we'll happily take the fiercer few over the weaker masses. Shark did an ammunition tally earlier. They're all down to one rifle each, none of them full, no spare clips. They have handguns which won't last long. They won't be able to keep the werewolves back with sustained fire like before. If we have more than a few dozen beasts to deal with between here and the sea, we'll run dry in no time and it'll be hand-to-hand combat after that.

While we're waiting, the glow from Timas's gun fades, then dies, leaving us in complete darkness.

Luckily Timas has already set his explosives, so it doesn't affect our plans, just our nerves.

The werewolf within me is excited by the closeness of its twisted kin. It wants to dig from this side of the hole and link up with its soulmates. I'm tempted, in a sick way, to unleash it and let it loose on Shark, Meera and the others. It's a bit like the feeling I get when I'm standing on a cliff or high building, looking down at a suicidal drop. I start thinking about what would happen if I stepped off, the rush of the fall, the shattering collision, the quiet emptiness of death. Part of me wants to experience the thrill of complete surrender...

But I've always ignored that niggling voice and I ignore it now. Hold tight. Stay focused. Wait.

→We can smell them now and hear their laboured panting. We've moved down the cave, as close to the lowest point as we can crawl. I thought it would have made more sense to stay back from the blast, but Timas insists he knows what he's doing. "Time is of the essence," he says. "We have to risk getting singed."

The werewolves sound like they're no more than a metre away. Maybe the first one is already sticking its head through, sliding into our cave. Impossible to tell in the darkness. I want Timas to detonate the bombs immediately, before it's too late, but he only hums and whistles, waiting... waiting...

Finally, when I think my nerves are going to snap, Timas whispers, "Shut your eyes, cover your ears and keep your fingers crossed." A second or two later the rocks explode outwards. I'm struck by a few chips and stony splinters, but they're only scratches. Light floods the cave. I open my eyes, but can't see very far through the dust cloud.

"Go!" Timas coughs and we crawl on our knees until we can stand and run crouched over.

Scraps of flesh, bones, guts and hair line the floor. Blood's everywhere, making it slippery underfoot. My stomach rumbles. It's been a long time since breakfast. The wolfen part of me would happily tuck in and make short work of the offal.

We stumble out of the tunnel, Stephen and Shark in the lead, Meera and me in the middle, Timas and Prae bringing up the rear. The sunlight is glorious after the darkness of the cave, but there's no time to lap it up. A couple of werewolves are staggering around, bloodstained, shaking their heads, dazed. No sign of any others. We've come through on the far side of the rocky outcrop, out of sight of the multitudes.

"Come on," Shark hisses. "Let's—"

A growling sound from my left. I whirl and catch sight of a werewolf leaping through the air. It was hiding behind a rock. Three others emerge from behind similarly sized rocks. The cunning beasts have set an ambush!

The first werewolf lands on Shark and knocks away his rifle. Shark snarls as the werewolf growls. He grabs its head and jerks it left then right, trying to snap the beast's neck before it chews his face off.

Stephen makes the crucial mistake of aiming at the werewolf attacking Shark instead of the other three behind it. Two of them tackle him as he squeezes off his first shot. He yelps, then he's gone, covered by the werewolves, their claws and fangs glinting in the sunlight as they tear into him. He doesn't even have time to scream.

The final werewolf bounds towards Meera, Prae and me. Meera raises her rifle and the beast stops and glares at us — it clearly knows what a gun is, the damage it can cause. It looks around. Stephen's bullet struck the first werewolf just above its heart, wounding but not killing. It's still struggling with Shark and has driven him back into the tunnel. He's managed to free his knife and is slicing at the beast's throat.

The werewolf who was coming after us chooses the easier option. It changes direction and dives after Shark, driving him further back. Meera fires at it. Misses. Starts after it, to help Shark.

"Get the hell out of here!" Shark bellows, smashing the first werewolf's face with an elbow, ducking to grab the second by its waist. He whirls it round and hurls it away. "Go!" he screams at us furiously as the werewolf regains its feet and leaps at him again.

"Come on," Timas says, tapping my shoulder.

"But—" Meera and I start to protest at the same time.

"Stay and die," Timas says calmly, "or run and live. Your choice." He sets off, Prae Athim just behind him.

Two of the werewolves are still snacking on Stephen. The other two are forcing Shark further back. There are no more in sight, apart from the befuddled few we first spotted. But it's surely a matter of seconds rather than minutes before others come running to investigate the explosion and howls.

I find myself moving before I consciously make the decision, my feet one step ahead of my brain. Shark's our leader. He gave us an order to run. We'd be fools if we ignored him, and Shark never tolerated fools gladly.

My last glimpse of the burly ex-soldier is of him wrestling with one werewolf, while keeping the other at bay with his knife, backing up into the shadows of the tunnel, conceding ground reluctantly, stubbornly. Then the dust from the explosion enfolds and obscures him and the werewolves, swallowing them whole.

With a cry of hate and fear, I turn, grab Meera and flee after Timas and Prae. It seems hopeless without Shark. I was sure he'd be the last of us to fall. Without him all is surely lost. But he went down fighting and the rest of us owe it to him to give it our best shot. If we fail, we should at least die valiantly — like Shark.

→The scent of the sea thickens in my nostrils as we run, drawing me towards it. There are howls behind us. The werewolves have found our trail again. But we've worked up a solid lead. We have half a chance.

"This is it," Timas pants as we struggle up a steep rise. "When we get to the top... it's a sixty metre run... to the edge... give or take a few... metres." He sneaks a quick look back. His brow creases and his large eyes narrow. "We won't make it. They'll catch us."

"We have to... try," I cry, lungs bursting, legs aching.

"Someone has to lay down... covering fire," he says. "I'll stop at the... top and make my last... stand."

"No!" Meera shouts. "We've lost too many already."

"We'll all die if I don't," Timas says simply.

"I'll do it," Prae gasps. She's lagging a few paces behind the rest of us. "I'm the slowest. Besides, they're *my* werewolves."

"I'm a better shot," Timas says. "This is my job. It makes more sense... for me... to stay."

"What the hell," Prae wheezes. "Let's both do it... and die together."

"As you wish." We're almost at the top. Timas slaps my back. "One last push and... you're there. Don't slow or look back. Run, jump, swim. Meera..." She looks around. "I'm sorry I won't... be able to claim... that kiss you promised."

"Don't worry," Meera says. "I lied. I wouldn't have

kissed you anyway." The tall man's face drops and Meera groans. "I'm joking!"

Timas's smile lights up his face again. With a cheerful wave he stops, turns, swings his rifle round and opens fire. Glancing over my shoulder, I see Prae halt, drop to her knees, take aim. The werewolves are damn close, dozens of them, the larger, enhanced members to the front, leading the pack.

I mount the crest of the rise after Meera. The clifftop lies enticingly ahead of us, the sixty-odd metres away that Timas calculated. My heart leaps in my chest. I catch up with Meera. We're going to make it! I don't care if we perish when we dive, if the tide's out, or if we're driven under by vicious currents. At least we won't die here on this cursed, savage island of…

Werewolves. Streaming towards the edge of the cliff from our left and right. They've split into two groups and flanked us. The smarter beasts must have guessed our plan. Rather than waste themselves on Timas and Prae, they branched around. As we watch in horror, they dart ahead of us and form a barrier across the top of the cliff, two or three bodies deep. Some remain to the sides, to ensure we don't veer off.

We come to a stop. Meera points her gun at the creatures ahead of us, then does a quick headcount and lets it drop. She looks at me and shrugs. We share a bitter smile. I'd like to hug her, but I haven't the energy. With incredible weariness we half-crouch and cross our arms on our knees. We're panting like thirsty dogs, surrounded, trapped, waiting for the werewolves to close in and brutally finish us off.

THE BEAST WITHIN

→One of the werewolves howls commandingly. A couple to his left and right return the cry, along with a few on the flanks and behind us. But when those howls die away, there's silence, which is more unsettling than the noise. I've got used to the violent baying of these beasts. Silence seems creepier.

Scrabbling noises behind us. I cock my head and look back. Timas and Prae scramble over the rise, guns raised but not firing. They stop when they spot us and the ranks of werewolves beyond. Prae looks confused. She turns slowly in a circle, studying the ring of twisted creatures, then shuffles towards us. Timas advances beside her, walking backwards, rifle still aimed. Werewolves from the other side follow them as far as the top of the incline, then stop at a howl from the one near the cliff.

"This is amazing," Prae says, joining Meera and me. "They have a group leader. Even those which haven't been modified are obedient. There are other dominant members too." She points out a few of the larger werewolves. She's excited by the discovery, momentarily forgetting her fear. "I never would have believed it if I hadn't seen it. I doubt even Antoine knows about this. His experiments succeeded far beyond his aims. They've become a true pack." There are tears of happiness in her eyes.

"What happens if we kill the leader?" I ask. "Will the rest split?"

"Of course not," she snorts. "One of the other dominant members would replace him. Or her — maybe the females are superior." She sighs. "I wish I had time to conduct a thorough study."

At a howl from the group leader – one of the largest werewolves, with dark grey hair – the pack starts to close around us. A couple of the smaller werewolves dart forward, but are immediately dragged to the ground and beaten or killed by the dominant members. The rest obediently hold the line.

"We'll hit those at the centre and try to squeeze through," Timas says. He still hasn't turned. "Concentrated fire. If we can make them part a few metres, we stand a chance."

"I'm game," Meera says, straightening and picking up her discarded weapon.

"It's hopeless," Prae mutters, but aims her gun too.

Tell them to stop, the Kah-Gash says abruptly.

"Stop!" I gasp. As they look at me questioningly, I

hold up a hand for silence and concentrate on my mysterious inner voice.

If they fire now, there will be chaos and you'll all die. These beasts have become an organised pack. You must use that against them.

"How?" I ask aloud.

Fight them on their own terms.

"I don't know what you mean."

The voice sighs contemptuously. *Do I have to do everything for you?* Before I can answer, it says curtly, *Unleash the wolf.*

"Which one?" I frown.

The one inside you, fool!

"I don't—"

We haven't time to argue. I said you'd need to obey me without question. They're closing in. Unleash the wolf. Give it free rein. Trust me.

I hesitate. The werewolf within my skin is something I fear completely. I've gone to great efforts to keep it imprisoned. In my nightmares it has often burst free and caused havoc, killing all around me. I'm determined not to let those dark dreams become reality. The Kah-Gash understands that. It helped me push the werewolf down deep when I didn't know how to do it myself. So why is it telling me to release the beast now? Is this part of the Shadow's plan? Will I play into the hands of the Demonata if I—

Last chance, the Kah-Gash warns as the werewolves creep to within six or seven metres of us.

Cursing silently, I reach inside with magic and tear at all the barriers which I've put in place over the last year, ripping them to shreds, pulling down the wall of safeguards which has protected me from my more beastly, bloodthirsty half. The wolf at my core is startled, suspecting a trap. Then, as I encourage it forward, it realises this is real and leaps to the surface, howling with delight.

My temperature shoots up, my skin tightens, my bones seem to crack, snapping away from each other, thrusting upwards and outwards.

I fall to the ground, crying out with pain. Vaguely aware of Meera shouting, trying to help, and Timas roaring, asking for orders to fire. I shake my head. My eyes are hardening. There's blood in my mouth. I raise a trembling hand and stare at it. The nails lengthen while I watch, fingers curling inward, hairs sprouting from my knuckles. Then my sight flickers and blurs.

My gums split, my teeth grow, my lips extend. I cough, lungs altering, heart pounding faster than it ever did before. Muscles rip and strain, then knot again. White noise fills my ears, threatens to deafen me, then fades, leaving me with a better sense of hearing than ever.

"He's turning into one of them!" Timas cries, open panic in his voice. I sense him levelling his gun at me.

"No!" Meera shouts, grabbing the barrel of his rifle, jerking it sideways.

Sight returns. Colours are different, not as keenly defined, but my field of vision has expanded and I can see more sharply, as if viewing the world through a magnifying glass. I spot Timas and Meera struggling. Prae Athim is gawping at me. The werewolves have stopped and are staring. Some paw the ground, eager to sink their fangs into us, but held in place out of fear of the dominant pack.

Something howls, a cry of jubilation, triumph and violence. As the muscles in my throat constrict, I realise the howling comes from *me*. As that understanding sinks in, I get to my feet, arms flexing, and gaze down at my new body.

My clothes are ripped and falling off my limbs. I'm naked, but I'm not bothered. What need have animals of clothes?

I howl again with savage exultation. Then I look for the group leader. Finding him, I chuckle throatily and step forward. With a challenging grunt, I beckon him on.

The werewolf snarls. I can smell his uncertainty. He's not sure if I'm human or wolfen. I howl again, clearing matters up. His eyes narrow and, with a howl of his own, he charges. He's huge, arms like trunks, but only slightly bigger than me. I plant my feet, twist and drive my shoulder into the werewolf's chest.

He's knocked to the floor. Around him, the creatures wail and screech. As he rises, furious, I kick him hard in the side of his head. He falls again. I'm on him before he can rise a second time. Setting my teeth on his throat, I bite. Blood fills my mouth and I drink greedily. This is what the werewolf within me has been waiting for all its life. I could squat here and sup until the sun sets.

But the other dominant werewolves have different ideas. Seeing its chance for glory, one darts forward and latches on to my arm. Sinks its fangs deep into my flesh. I break free of the dead werewolf with a muffled cry of pain, then wrench my arm away and head-butt the challenger. Its skull cracks and it drops.

Another attacks, gibbering madly. I grab it by its crotch and throat, lift it up, hold it over my head, then toss it into the pack. Those it lands on go wild and tear it to pieces.

A fourth werewolf steps forward, the largest yet, with the widest shoulders and longest fangs. A female. She looks edgy. If she was a true leader, she would have led from the beginning. I think she's the strongest creature on the island, but she lacks courage. She's only challenging me now because she thinks she has to, that I'll work my way through the dominant members of the pack, one by one, to ensure complete command.

I leap at the werewolf. She lashes out. I let her fist connect with the side of my head, then laugh. I throw a few punches, gnarled hands flying faster than they did when I was human. The challenger stumbles away from me, dazed. I grab her head, jerk it back, fasten my teeth on her throat… then growl.

The werewolf whimpers. I growl again and the whimpering stops. I release her and shove her away — alive. The beast stands, head lowered, subjugated. I glare at the others in the dominant pack, then sweep my gaze over those they command. I roar a question, but not a single one answers.

Returning to the body of the original leader, I lower my head and chew at his throat, leaving myself open to attack. When the werewolves hold their ground, I know there will be no more challenges. Standing again, I look around victoriously, taking it all in… the cowed werewolves, those I've killed, the shocked faces of the three humans. I fill with a sense of power and joy. Raising my head to the sky, I howl long and loud, and all around me the werewolves howl back in obedient, respectful response.

They're *my* pack now.

THE TURNED WORM

→"Grubbs?" one of the women gasps, eyes filled with horror. "Is that you?"

I crook my neck and stare at her. There's no Grubbs here. Werewolves don't need names. Tags like that are a human weakness. I think about killing her for daring to address me that way.

"Grubbs?" she says again, taking a hesitant step towards me.

A werewolf howls, warning her off. I roar at it angrily — I can protect myself. It lowers its head and whines. I fix my eyes on the woman. My stomach rumbles. The blood of the previous leader is like honey on my lips. But how much sweeter would the blood of a soft human be?

"Meera!" the other woman snaps. "Don't get too close. He might—"

"Grubbs won't hurt me," the one called Meera says confidently.

I snarl at her arrogance and raise a claw to rip off her

face. No one has the right to make decisions for me. This woman's made her last mistake. If I let her get away with it, the others will think they have leeway too. I have to kill her, for the good of the pack, to maintain order.

"Don't be silly," Meera says, smiling weakly at my upraised hand. "You won't hurt me. What would Dervish say if you did? You remember Dervish, don't you?"

I growl uncertainly, hand held above me like a hammer. *Dervish*. The one who guarded me when I needed guarding. Even the wildest beasts have respect for those who rear them. But Dervish isn't here. He's in trouble. He needs help. He's...

"Put down your guns," Meera says, dropping hers and crossing her arms.

"Are you sure about this?" the tall man asks.

"What have we got to lose?"

He shrugs and carefully lays down his weapon. The other woman gulps, but follows suit. All three stand shivering, unarmed, at my mercy. I feel the eyes of the pack on me. They have the scent of humans in their nostrils. Their mouths are wet with lust, as is mine. If I deny them their feed, my hold over them will crumble. A leader must do what's right. Part of me wants to spare this trio, but mercy is a luxury I can't afford. It's time to block out the memories of my human past and...

Don't be an idiot, a voice says. My eyes flick around with fury, looking for the one who dares speak to me in such a manner. But then I realise the voice is coming from within. *You're a mix of human and werewolf, cemented by magic. You can make new rules.*

"But they're hungry," I reply silently. "I am too. We have to eat."

There's plenty of food elsewhere, the voice says slyly and sends an image of the compound flashing through my brain.

I grin wolfishly, then howl at the pack. They look dubious, so I howl again, fiercer than before, promising them the world, knowing they'll turn on me if I fail to deliver. This time they roar excitedly in response. Those at the rear set off for the compound. Seconds later almost every werewolf on the cliff is streaking inland, eager to be among the first to the feast. Only several of the more advanced beasts hold their place at a commanding cry from me. These, the largest and smartest, will be my personal retinue. They'll travel with me, to dispense my orders. In return, I'll see that they enjoy the lion's share of the spoils.

I face the confused humans and growl softly, trying to communicate. Their expressions are blank — they can't understand. Frowning, I remould the cords of my throat, allowing my face to melt back to something more like its original shape. My teeth retract and my lips soften. I have total control over this body. I realise now that I always did. I could have manipulated myself this way since birth if I hadn't been so afraid of what I might turn into. I'm more than flesh and bone. I'm a spirit, a force, a power. I'm not shackled to any single form.

"Grubbs?" Meera says, searching my eyes for traces of humanity.

"You came *this* close to being eaten," I mumble, eyeing her darkly.

Meera's face fills with relief. "You're *you*!" she cries, throwing her arms around my broader, taller, twisted, hairier body.

"What happened?" Prae asks, studying me with a mix of fascination and horror. "Did the werewolf explode within you?"

"I unleashed it," I explain shortly.

"Are you human or werewolf?" Timas enquires politely.

"Both." I take a step back from Meera. Her eyes flicker down to my lower body and she raises an eyebrow. I don't blush – werewolves know no shame – but I pick up my discarded trousers and tie them around my waist. "We don't have much time," I mutter. "We have to move fast."

"I take it we're not jumping off the cliff now," Meera comments wryly.

"No." I focus on Timas. "Can you get us back into the compound?"

"Yes," he says. "It will take a while, but—"

"Work quickly," I snap. "We're hungry." As the others stare at me, I turn from the sea and break into a trot, eager to feed.

→I feel more alive than ever. I'm sure I look awful, no better than any of the mutated werewolves I now command. But I don't care. Looks have never mattered to me less. After all the stress of recent years, the struggle between human, wolf and Kah-Gash, I've finally found a happy balance. This is who I'm meant to be, not man, werewolf or magician — but *this*. A mix of all three, uniquely disfigured and warped. For the first time in my life I feel complete.

Meera, Timas and Prae are nervous of me, and rightly so. If I turned on them, as I'm tempted to, they wouldn't stand a chance. But I choose not to attack. These are my allies, and while I don't feel like I need them any more – except Timas, to get into the compound – I honour our friendship. Besides, as the Kah-Gash pointed out, there are lots of others I can kill.

The humans struggle to keep up, but I don't make allowances. If they fall behind, they'll have to fend for themselves. I control the werewolves, but I know instinctively that my hold over them is fragile. If I don't maintain complete dominance, I'll lose them.

I can't wait to get my teeth on Juni Swan's throat.

Revenge is what I'm focused on. I barely spare a thought for Dervish and the danger he might be in. All I care about is killing the she-fiend who betrayed us. When I've ripped her flesh from her bones and wallowed in her blood… then I can turn to other matters. Maybe. Unless I decide to stay here and become ruler of Wolf Island.

→The compound. Timas is hard at work on a security access screen. I smell the fear of the soldiers inside. They know we're out here. Several of their finest technicians are united against Timas, playing cat and mouse games with him as if locking horns over a chess board. But he's stripping away their defences, one by one. He's better than they are. It's just a matter of time before he outfoxes them.

By concentrating on my senses of smell and hearing, I follow the movements of those nearest us. They're lining the tight corridors, checking weapons, preparing to blast wildly at anything that comes through. They're frustrated. If the designers had built slots into these walls, as they did in those at the sides, they could have mown us down. But an assault like this was never taken into account. The outer wall was meant to hold. The plan, if it fell, was to block off all other entrances to the compound, then escape by boats stored at the rear of the complex. After all, there was no way brainless werewolves could short-circuit the security systems.

The soldiers could flee before we invade, and make a break for freedom. But they've been ordered to stand and fight. Juni doesn't care about losses. It will probably amuse her to watch them die.

She's still there. She has a distinctive, rotting stench. She's waiting for us deep within the compound. I don't know why. Perhaps she thinks she can get the better of me. More fool her if she does.

A couple of werewolves howl and others take up the cry. They're growing impatient. They aren't ready to mutiny yet, but they're not far from it. Bending close to Timas, I growl, "A few more minutes. Then things get nasty."

"You can't rush a job like this," Timas replies calmly. "I'm going as fast as I can."

"Go faster," I snarl. "When they turn, I won't be able to hold them. I'll be the first they attack, but you won't be far behind."

"Then we'd better hope time is on our side," Timas chuckles, never looking up.

"Leave him alone," Meera snaps. "You're distracting him."

"No he isn't," Timas says. "I can multitask."

"Do you think they know we're here?" Prae asks, pressing an ear to the wall.

I frown at such a ludicrous question, then remember that she doesn't have the same sharp senses I do. "They know," I tell her. "They're waiting for us."

"Our forces will be cut down," she says quietly, studying the werewolves. "It will be a massacre."

"Many will die," I agree, "but not all. We'll overwhelm them."

"But at such a cost…" Prae sighs. "Is it worth it? Maybe we should just take the boats and get out of here."

"They'd call in fresh troops," Meera says. "They'd fire on the werewolves from the air and wipe them out — they couldn't afford to leave them alive now that we know about Wolf Island. At least this way the beasts have a fair chance."

"I hate this," Prae mutters. "It was never meant to end in a bloodbath. I wanted to save lives, not be responsible for wholesale slaughter."

"Then you shouldn't have become a Lamb," Meera says.

Before Prae can respond, Timas whistles softly. "No more time for bickering. The gates of hell are about to open for business."

He presses a button. Panels slide apart. Werewolves howl and surge forward. A mass of guns discharge at the same time and the air turns red with blood.

THE SHAPE OF THINGS TO COME

→Dozens are slaughtered within seconds, torn to ragged, fleshy shreds by the frenzied fire of Juni Swan's soldiers. But the stench of blood only drives the rest of us wilder. We push on without pause, leaping over the jerking bodies of the dead and dying, ignoring the peril, the bullets, the fallen. Not a single beast turns and runs.

I'm among the pack, unable to restrain myself, risking all just to be one of the first to claim a human heart. It's crazy. I should hold back and let them do my dirty work. But for a few mad moments I lose control. I press forward with the others, howling and bellowing, as much of a target as any other werewolf.

Then we're on the terrified soldiers, hacking at them, tearing guns from their hands, chowing down on their sweet, soft flesh and oh-so-chewable bones. Human screams are added to the cacophony of gunfire and howls. The line disintegrates beneath us. I'm past it before I know what's happening, staring at an empty corridor. I have to stop, swivel and dive back into the fray to claim my victims and be part of the barbaric, bloody feast.

I don't know how much time passes. It could be seconds or minutes. All I'm aware of is the killing and feasting. My world becomes an endless pool of thick, salty blood, springy flesh, brittle bones, juicy inner organs. I butcher heartlessly, wolfishly. I don't know how many. Bodies are tossed around and pulled apart like chicken wings at a party.

When the bloodlust finally passes – when I've had my fill – my senses return. I spit out a mouthful of soggy flesh. I'm drenched in blood, my ears and head ringing with noise. I stare at my red, twisted hands and wait to feel disgust and shame. But nothing hits me. I'm neither appalled nor shocked. In this new form I have no delusions. I'm a killer. Whether a killer of demons, werewolves or humans... no matter. I've butchered with magic in the Demonata universe. Now I've murdered with my hands and teeth here. I feel no more for the people I've slaughtered than the demons I fried. To a beast like me, there's no real difference.

I look around for Meera, Timas and Prae. I find them standing in a doorway, transfixed, faces pale, eyes awash with horror. Even the usually unflappable Timas Brauss looks disturbed. I sneer at their expressions, wipe a hand across my lips, then lick them clean.

"Sorry I didn't offer you anything to eat," I chuckle hoarsely.

"Grubbs… you… this…" Meera can't find words to express what she feels.

"I did what I had to," I grunt. "It was a fair fight."

"But you enjoyed it!" Meera gasps. "You laughed as you killed. The way you drank…"

"I was thirsty," I shrug.

Before Meera can say anything else, I call my private retinue of advanced werewolves to my side. Not all of the chosen come — some are dead. But most assemble, grinning ghoulishly, blood dripping from their chins.

"Let's go and find Juni," I tell them, and over the mounds of dead bodies we climb.

→Not all of the soldiers perished at the perimeter. Some dropped back when they realised their cause was lost. They're fleeing through the compound, pursued by ravenous werewolves. I don't know where they think they can hide. It's over. They'll be tracked down and slit from groin to skull. Running only adds sport to the slaughter.

It's hard not to give in to temptation and hunt with the pack. Juni's just one person (or whatever the hell it is that she's become). There are so many others to chase and murder. I have to focus to keep my feral nature in check. I tell myself Juni will be worth it, that the joy of killing her will be greater than a dozen human deaths.

But I'm not convinced. I think I might be happier if I surrendered to my desires and ran wild. I'd like to butcher freely while the butchering's good.

I'm aware of Meera, Timas and Prae arming themselves, picking guns from the corpses. I don't bother with weapons. I relied on magic and my wits before. Now I have something even better — claws and fangs.

Some of the werewolves sniff longingly at the humans, but the members of my personal guard warn them off with soft growls. Give it a few days and they might not be so obedient. But there's plenty for all to eat now, so they're willing to let these three snack-boxes on legs pass unmolested.

We press further into the building. The stench of Juni's sickly sweet sweat fills my nostrils. I hope she's sweating with fear, that she's trapped, nowhere to run, dreading our confrontation. If she's not afraid now, I'll show her fear before I kill her. I don't want her to die without knowing what it's like to tremble in the clutches of one more twisted and vicious than yourself.

As I'm closing on her location, I feel a sweep of something like air gushing through the compound. It's warm and tingling. It seeps into my pores, filling me with power.

Magic.

I should be grateful for the extra strength, but I'm not. The wash of magic through the building can only mean one thing — a window has been opened. I'm not afraid of what might come through — I'd fight any number of demons — but I don't want Juni skipping ahead of me to safety in the foul universe she's chosen to call home.

"Quick!" I roar, darting ahead of the others, shouldering a door aside, rushing down a corridor, homing in on the scent of Juni Swan.

"Grubbs!" shouts Meera. "Wait. Don't go in there alone."

But nothing can stop me. A couple of seconds later, wild at the thought that I might miss my chance for revenge, I break through another doorway and into the room where we discovered Prae Athim bound and gagged.

The window hovers near the back of the room, a jagged red panel of light. I dart towards it, meaning to follow Juni, even though I know it's suicide. Then a bolt of energy knocks me sideways. Searing pain eats into my flesh, forcing a scream from my lips.

I stagger and realise I've been tricked. Juni's still here. She was standing to the left of the door. Easy to spot if I'd been paying attention, but I lost my wits for a few vital seconds. Now she has the upper hand.

As I lurch towards her, she mutters a spell and the floor at my feet explodes. Splinters shoot into my stomach, chest and face. I instinctively jerk my head back.

Roaring, I raise a hand to protect my eyes. Ignoring the stinging pain of the splinters buried in my flesh, I set my sights on the pustulant, bloodstained, flesh-dripping Juni Swan. She's smiling insanely. Beyond her, in the doorway, I see Meera and the others, separated from us by an invisible barrier. The werewolves of my retinue are digging at the barrier with their claws, but it will take more than brute force to penetrate Juni's magic shield.

"Did you think I'd leave without saying goodbye?" Juni giggles.

"I'll kill you!" I roar. "I'll rip your head from your neck and—"

"Please don't finish," Juni interrupts. "I detest vulgarity." She waves a hand at me and the splinters expand and burrow deeper into my skin. I gasp and collapse to my knees. Another couple of seconds and they'll pierce my heart and brain.

If you'll allow me some leeway... the voice of the Kah-Gash murmurs. The splinters shoot out of my body and rain down on Juni. That catches her by surprise. With a shriek, she covers her eyes, protecting them as I did. For a moment she's defenceless.

Using the newly developed muscles in my legs, I spring across the room and bowl Juni over. I slam her to the floor and drive a claw into the putrid, oozing flesh of her stomach. She moans, eyes shooting wide, baring her teeth, trembling with agony. I make a fist, grab some of her inner organs and jerk hard. My hand shlups out, trailing guts. Blood splatters the floor. I gurgle with delight.

Juni screams, then covers the hole in her stomach with a hand. Magic flares and the flesh around the hole heals. I don't care. While she's repairing herself, I latch on to her head, jam my fangs into the bone behind her right ear, and start chewing my way through to her brain.

Juni's fresh screams fill me with delight. I almost pull away to enjoy her expression. But I know how dangerous she is. I can't give her any freedom. Best to chew quickly and disable her.

Heat flares in my fangs. I try desperately to bite down. I'm almost through the hard covering of the skull. So close to her brain. But the heat's too much to bear. With a cry of pain and rage, I break free.

Juni's at my throat with incredible speed. Newly grown fingernails dig into the flesh beneath my chin, while the fingers of her other hand tighten around my neck. I sense the fingers stretching, looping, meeting at the back and melting into each other, tightening into a noose. I try to roar but my vocal cords are squeezed shut.

I slam an elbow into Juni's ribs. Several crack. She grunts, but doesn't release me. She's cackling. Pokes her face up close to mine. Her left eye was punctured, but it grows back as she taunts me.

"Thought you could kill sweet Juni?" she screeches. "Thought a pup like you could overcome a full-grown mistress of dark magic?" Her fingers tighten another notch. "What do you think now, *Grubitsch*?"

I wheeze at her, then manage to get hold of the hand around my throat. Filling my fingers with magic, I sever through the flesh and bones of the noose, then yank myself clear. Panting, I make a fist and smash it into her face. Her nose shatters, splattering me with blood, pus and slimy snot.

"You look like hell," I snarl.

"You can talk," she sneers, running a scornful eye over my deformed features.

For a moment we grin at each other and get our breath back.

"It's not too late," Juni purrs. "Join us. I sensed you killing those pitiful humans. You've found your true self. Come with me. Put the last vestiges of your useless human morals behind you. With us, you can kill forever. There's a whole world of humans to torment and butcher. You can be a glorious, wolfen god."

"I bet I could have you too," I chuckle darkly.

"Maybe," she smiles. "Lord Loss is my master, but you could be my mate. I can change out of this grotesque form, be any woman you wish. In the new world, anything will be possible."

"There's just one problem," I sigh.

"What?" Juni frowns.

"I hate your guts," I hiss and spring on her.

I drive my fist towards the hole where Juni's nose used to be. My plan is to jam a few fingers in the gap, widen it, then claw out her brain, scoop by gloopy scoop. But Juni's faster. She ducks, then lashes at my stomach with a leg. I wasn't expecting a bloody kung fu move! I'm sent hurtling backwards and slam hard into the wall. My head cracks and my neck almost snaps.

She's on me before I hit the floor, hands a blur, jabbing incessantly. I try to roar, but all that comes out is a startled croak. I get a glimpse of her throat and lunge for it. Juni shimmies and rams a forearm into my mouth, gagging me. As I choke, she sends what feels like a million volts of magic sizzling through my body. I scream mutedly and go limp. Juni hits me with another burst of energy. Another.

Blood's pumping from my nose, mouth and ears. Even from my eyes. I'm seeing events through a red mist. I reach deep within myself, looking for the power to strike back, but I'm in disarray.

Forgetting about magic, I lash out at Juni. She laughs, removes the arm from my mouth and wraps it around me. Squeezes tight, like a boa constrictor.

"Poor Grubbs," she coos, wiping blood from my eyes. "You don't have the hang of magic, do you? You're strong, but experience is everything. My master told me to be wary, but I knew I had the beating of you. When the soldiers and werewolves failed, I decided to finish you off myself."

I spit blood at her. She stops it mid-air, letting the pearly drops float in front of my eyes. Then she leans forward, extends her tongue and delicately slurps the red pearls from the air, as though tasting an exquisite wine.

"Now it's time to die," she says. Her face is blank. The madness and hatred in her eyes have been replaced by a cold business-like look.

I struggle feebly. This can't be happening. I'm the pack leader, a magician, part of the Kah-Gash. I've fought and defeated stronger demons than this servant of Lord Loss. I should be dancing on her corpse, not fighting for breath, locked within her suffocating embrace.

"A kiss," Juni hums, pressing her face to mine. "I'll suck your last breath from your body along with your part of the Kah-Gash. I'll take everything and own you completely. You might think it's the end, but your agonies are just beginning. I have the power of death. I'll pluck at the strings of your soul until the end of time, and every strum will draw a thousand screams."

She covers my mouth and inhales, drawing the last of my oxygen from my lungs. I go limp, senses crumpling. It's like she's sucking me down a tunnel into herself. I can't fight. I'm helpless. I'm doomed.

Then, for no apparent reason, she breaks the contact and blinks, staring at me as if stabbed in the back. My heart leaps hopefully. Someone must have found a way past the barrier, snuck up behind her and struck while she was gloating over me. I glance over her shoulder in search of my saviour but I can't see anyone.

Juni releases me and takes a step back. Her expression clears and she smiles. Then she laughs, and the laughter strikes me harder than any of her blows. She screams with crazy delight, jumping up and down on the spot, bits of her diseased flesh dropping off like bloated ticks.

"Oh, Grubbs!" she cries. "You absolute darling. How delicious. How ironic. The saviour of the world... protector of mankind... *Hah*!"

I slump to the floor, take a painful, rasping breath and stare at Juni. Has she lost herself entirely to madness? Have I been saved by a mental breakdown?

"I just had a vision, darling Grubbs," Juni says, backing up to the window. "I had them all the time when I was Beranabus's assistant. I catch glimpses of the future. That's why he valued my services so highly. I served Lord Loss in the same way when I joined him. That's how we knew the cave in Carcery Vale was going to be reopened, why we acted when we did.

"But this vision was the most vivid ever. You were in it, the star of the show. It was the near future... *very* near.

You were at your most powerful, tapping into the sort of power that would allow you to crush me like a bug."

Juni sticks a hand through the window. It's pulsing at the edges. It will close soon, but not before she fires off her parting shot.

"I saw the world destroyed," she whispers. "It was blown to pieces. The seas bubbled away, lava erupted, the land split and crumbled. Everyone died, young and old, good and bad. Then a ball of fire burst from the heart of the planet, incinerated the globe and blasted the ashes off into space, before spreading to consume the universe — worlds, suns, galaxies, all.

"You were there," she sobs, crying with happiness. "But you weren't trying to stop it. You made no attempt to save the world. You couldn't... you didn't want to... because *you* were controlling the mayhem. The Demonata won't destroy your universe, Grubbs Grady — *you* will!"

With that she skips through the window, giggling girlishly. Moaning wildly, I drag myself after her, but before I'm even halfway the window disintegrates, and all I can do is lower my face to the cold, hard, blood-drenched floor and weep.

THE DEVIL'S IN THE DETAILS

→As magic drains from the air, the barrier blocking the doorway gives way. Meera, Prae and the werewolves stumble into the room. Timas enters via the hole which Pip blew in one of the side walls earlier. He must have circled round while I was fighting Juni. A dangerous manoeuvre – he could have been attacked by a rogue werewolf – but he got away with it. Not that it mattered. Juni had blocked that entrance too.

"Grubbs," Meera cries, rushing over. "Are you OK?"

I moan pitifully, reaching for a window which is no longer there, Juni's prediction echoing in my ears. It can't be true. She was mocking me. It's part of some horrible game.

But she had me at her mercy. I was helpless. It would have been a simple matter to finish me off. She spared me because she saw me destroy the world in the future. Nothing else makes sense. I'm more valuable to her alive than dead. I can do what she, Lord Loss and the Shadow can't.

"You're wounded," Meera says, fussing over me. "You have to heal yourself."

"Leave me alone," I cry, hammering the floor and cursing.

"The magic's fading," Meera hisses. "Use it to heal yourself or you'll die."

"Good," I mutter. Better if I die. I can't wreck the world if I'm dead.

"Grubbs!" she snaps. "Don't be an ass. Heal yourself. *Now*!"

I sigh miserably, then focus my power on the bleeding wounds, broken ribs and ruptured inner organs. It would be for the best if I perished, but I can't give up on life. I'm not that much of a hero.

"What happened?" Timas asks.

"Didn't you hear?" I wheeze, working on my chest and upper stomach.

"The sound faded out," Timas says. "It was like someone turning down the volume on a television set."

"It was the same for us," Meera says.

So Juni didn't want the others to hear her prediction, in case they decided to kill me for the good of mankind. I consider telling them. I'm pretty sure one of them — maybe all three — would put a bullet through my head if they knew of the threat I pose. But that would be another form of suicide, so I hold my tongue and shake my head.

"Just more of the same rubbish," I grumble. "She said she was sparing me for her master, that Lord Loss wanted to kill me himself."

"Strange," Timas notes. "She was happy to let the werewolves slaughter you."

"I guess she knew I'd survive. It was all a set-up. She never meant for me to die, only the rest of you, so that she could relish my pain."

Timas makes a sceptical humming noise, but says no more. I continue healing myself, Meera watching closely to make sure I don't miss anything. The power's fading fast, but I've dealt with most of the life-threatening injuries. I'll live.

The werewolves – there are five in the room with us – are sniffing the floor by one of the walls. They're growling. I bark at them to be quiet. Listening carefully, I hear scrabbling sounds. Someone's crawling away in a hurry.

"The maps you studied earlier," I say to Timas, rising painfully but standing steady on my feet once I'm up. "Did they show any tunnels or crawlways running off this room?"

"No," Timas says, edging up beside the werewolves.

"Then they weren't as complete as you thought," I sniff.

"You're right," he says, tapping the wall. "There's a hidden panel. I'm sure I can find the opening mechanism if you give me a few—"

I snap at the werewolves. The largest smashes a fist into the metal panel. Again. A third time. It crumples under his fourth blow, snapping loose at the upper and left edges. The werewolf gets a few fingers into the gap and wrenches off the panel, revealing a small passage.

The werewolf who removed the panel darts into the crawlway, but stops at a command from me. Shuffling forward, I stoop and stare into the gloominess. I can't see the person scuttling away from us, but I can smell him. It's a familiar, cultured scent. I smile viciously.

"After me," I say softly, then lower myself to my hands and knees. I edge forward, moving faster than the man ahead of me, steadily catching up, making heavy snarling noises, letting him know I'm coming, savouring the intoxicating smell of his mounting fear.

→The crawlway opens out into a large room at the rear of the compound. There are several boats stacked at the sides, but all the hulls have been shattered, holes punched through the shells, making them as seaworthy as sieves. I figure Juni wanted to give her soldiers an extra incentive to stand and fight. She made sure nobody shipped out early.

Antoine Horwitzer is struggling with one of the useless boats, hauling it towards an open section at the far side of the room. I can smell and hear the sea, the crash of the waves, the cries of the gulls. Antoine is sobbing, his jacket tossed to one side, shirt ripped, trousers dirty. He must know he can't get anywhere in the boat, but desperation drives him on.

As the others emerge behind me, I raise a hand, holding them in check. Antoine doesn't know we're here. He's totally focused, head bent, straining painfully, using muscles he probably hasn't tested in years. I'm amused by the sight of him dragging the wreck of a boat towards the edge. For a while I forget about Juni Swan and her terrible prophecy, and just enjoy the show.

Finally, when he has about a metre to go, I cough softly.

He freezes. Moans. Gives the boat an especially strong tug. Doesn't look up.

"Antoine," I laugh, stepping towards him.

He looks back, gauging how much further he has to go. His arms relax and his shoulders slump when he realises he can't make it. He turns his desolate gaze on me and his eyes widen as he takes in my monstrous form, my blood-soaked body and limbs, my fangs and wolfen face.

"What happened to you?" he gasps.

"Teenage angst," I chuckle. I whistle at the werewolves and they spread out. Meera, Timas and Prae are directly behind me.

Antoine shrieks when he spots the werewolves. Turns and races for the edge, to leap into the sea below. Drawing from the faint traces of magic in the air, I halt him, exerting an invisible hold over the fallen executive. He struggles wildly, then sees that it's hopeless. Giving up, he faces me.

"I'm going to kill you," I growl, advancing menacingly. "Juni got away, so I'm going to take out all my frustration on you. It will be slow and painful. Suitable payback for the lives you've ruined, the friends of mine you've killed."

"I didn't kill anyone!" he squeals.

"No, your kind never do," I sneer. "You leave it to others. You just set things up and give the orders."

"Please," Antoine sobs, throwing himself to his knees. "Don't do this. It serves no purpose. Put me on trial. Let the proper authorities deal with me. You're not a killer. There's no evil in your soul. Don't—"

"Look at me!" I roar. "Do you think you'll be the first I've killed today? I wasn't a murderer, but you changed me. I'm a monster now. And I'm hungry."

"Meera!" Antoine whines. "Prae! Please, I beg you. You're civilised people. Help me."

"We can't," Prae says coldly. "Even if we wanted to — and personally I have no problem with him gutting you — we couldn't. He's not ours to control. He's one of your *specimens*. You helped create him — now you have to deal with him."

Antoine stares at Prae in disbelief. I draw closer, growling softly in anticipation of the kill. Antoine's eyes harden. "Don't be so hasty, my hairy friend," he murmurs, sounding more like his old self. "There are others to consider."

"Like who?"

"Your uncle," he says smoothly, and I come to an abrupt halt.

Antoine rises, brushing dirt from his shirt and trousers. He frowns at his untidy condition, then runs a hand through his hair and shrugs. "I suppose this means an expensive trip to my tailor when I get back."

"You've got five seconds to tell me what you know about Dervish," I snarl.

"Oh, I have more time than that," Antoine grins. "Your uncle's in a perilous situation. There are forces moving against him even as we speak. It will take more than five seconds to—"

"Tell me!" I shout. "Now. Or I'll torture it out of you."

"I'm sure you could," Antoine says slickly, "but how long would it take? I'll hold out as long as I can, just to spite you. After all, you've already vowed to torment me. I don't know how long I can stand the pain, but minutes are precious. Do you dare waste them?"

I want to throttle him so badly it hurts. But he knows how important Dervish is to me. I don't want to cut a deal with this treacherous viper, but time's against me.

"What do you want?" I growl.

"My life," Antoine replies.

I think about it, then curse. "OK. I won't kill you. Now talk."

"Not so fast," Antoine says. "I want to add a few conditions before I divulge all that I know. Such as a boat without a hole in it, a compass and map, some—"

"Time's all you have to bargain with!" I snap. "If you don't tell me what you know immediately, I might as well torture you."

Antoine licks his lips nervously, then decides he has no choice but to play out the hand and hope for the best.

"A trap was laid for your uncle and some others," he says. "The girl called Bec was the one they wanted, but your uncle and Beranabus were important to them too. Juni didn't reveal all the details, but from what I gathered, the trap was partially successful. Beranabus was killed, but the—"

"No!" Meera cries, taking a step in front of me. "Beranabus can't be dead."

"According to Juni, he is," Antoine says calmly.

"But—" Meera starts to exclaim.

"Leave it," I cut in. "If Beranabus is dead, he's dead. Let this worm finish telling us what he knows about Dervish."

Meera doesn't like it, but she pulls back.

"Bec and your uncle escaped," Antoine continues. "The attack took place at sea, on a giant cruiser. They got off before it sank and are adrift in a lifeboat. Juni was furious. When she calmed down, she told me to send a crew to intercept the lifeboat and finish the job. They have instructions to kill Dervish and bring Bec back alive. Taking no chances, I roused three separate units and dispatched them from different locations. The first should be upon your uncle—" He checks his watch. "— in sixteen minutes."

"Call them off," I hiss.

"I can't from here," he smirks. "But if you would kindly accompany me to my temporary office…"

I tremble with rage and hatred. If only I could rip the tongue from his mouth and swallow it whole — that would wipe the smirk from his face. But he has the upper hand, at least until I know that Dervish is safe. I'll have to allow him his smugness for a while. I start to agree to take him to his office, but Timas speaks before me.

"There's no need to relocate. I can see a radio unit in one of the boats. There are telephones and computer terminals set in the walls. We can communicate with the outside world from here."

"No," Antoine snaps. "There are things in my office which I need."

"Such as?" Timas asks with a little smile.

Antoine glowers. I see in his features that he had a plan in mind. The office was an excuse. He thought he could trick us and escape some other way.

"Don't play games," I say softly. "Your only hope is to prove that Dervish is alive and that we need you to protect him. If I think you're trying to weasel out, all bets are off and all promises are revoked."

"Come with me," Timas says commandingly, taking Antoine by the elbow and leading him to one side. "We'll work on it together. Tell me everything you did and how to undo it. I'll see to the rest."

"But... my equipment..." Antoine says weakly.

"We have all the equipment we need," Timas says, taking a radio unit from a boat and fiddling with the dials.

With a bitter sigh, Antoine casts aside whatever plan he had in mind, sits beside Timas and talks.

→The minutes pass quickly. Part of me is sure we'll be too late. Antoine's Lambs will have caught a strong wind and picked up Bec sooner than anticipated. Gunned Dervish down and dumped him in the sea for the fishes to feast on. I'm prepared for the worst and ready to rip Antoine to pieces when he breaks the bad news. My wolfen half is looking forward to that. It doesn't care about Dervish or anything except slaughter and feeding.

Dimly aware of Timas and Antoine talking on the radio, Antoine issuing codes and commands. Meera and Prae are listening in, but I'm too agitated to follow it all. I have very little patience since I changed.

Thinking about Juni's prediction again. I want to dismiss it. Me? Destroy the world? Ridiculous!

Except… it isn't. I've known since that night in the cave outside Carcery Vale that I have the power to annihilate not just a world, but a universe. Beranabus believed the Kah-Gash could be used against the Demonata, but it's a demonic weapon. Why should it work for us against those who created it?

I wish the contrary old magician was here. I need advice and guidance. But according to Antoine he's dead, killed on a ship, lost at sea. I should be in shock. I never liked the old buzzard, but he's protected this world for more than a thousand years and he's been my mentor for the last several months. His death should have hit me hard. But I only feel annoyed — why did he let himself fall into a trap now, of all times, when he was most needed?

"There we go," Antoine says, turning away from the radio. He salutes me with a sneer.

"What's the story?" I bark at Timas.

"We converted the assassination squad into a rescue crew," Timas says. "I was going to send Disciples, but it was simpler to use those already close to the scene. They've taken the survivors on board and are flying back, but not to the city where Juni had arranged to meet them."

"Dervish?" I mutter, dreading the response.

"Alive," Timas says. "In bad shape — all three of them are — but breathing."

"Three?" Meera echoes.

"Dervish, Bec and a Disciple called Kirilli Kovacs. You know him?" Meera shakes her head. "Apparently he was on board when they went to the ship."

"What about Sharmila?" Meera asks.

"Dead," Timas says simply. "Along with Beranabus. Maybe Kernel too, but they weren't sure about that. A few thousand passengers and crew were murdered also."

"A good day's work," Meera snaps at Antoine.

"You can't blame me for what happened on the ship," he huffs. "I had nothing to do with that." He smiles thinly at me. "Those on board the helicopter have orders to release the hostages only in *my* presence. A little insurance policy."

I stare at Antoine without blinking. "Dervish is safe?" I ask Timas.

"Yes."

"Then we're finished here."

I still haven't blinked. Antoine's fidgeting now.

"You haven't forgotten your promise, have you?" he laughs, trying but failing to sound light-hearted.

I shake my head slowly. And grin wolfishly.

"I assume you're a man of your word?" Antoine says stiffly.

"I'm not a man," I answer quietly. "But yes," I add as

he turns an even paler shade of white beneath his tan. "I said I wouldn't kill you, and I won't."

Antoine breaks into a smile. All his confidence and arrogance come flooding back. He takes a step forward, eager to establish control of the situation. I raise a gnarled, semi-human hand to stop him.

"I said *I* wouldn't kill you," I repeat slowly. "But I said nothing about *them*." I gesture at the five werewolves.

Antoine laughs feebly. He thinks I'm joking. Then he looks deeper into my eyes and realises I'm as serious as death.

"No!" he croaks. "You can't. Your uncle — they'll kill him if I'm not there."

"I'll take that chance," I chuckle, then click my tongue. Five pairs of wolfen ears prick to attention and the room fills with growls of grisly delight.

"Please," Antoine sobs, backing up. "I did what you asked. I cooperated."

I turn my back on him and nod at Meera, Timas and Prae.

"Are you certain you want to do this?" Meera asks as the werewolves advance and Antoine whimpers and begs for mercy.

"Yes," I say flatly.

"It's a callous act," she warns. "This will stain your soul forever. You might regret it when—"

"When what?" I snap. "When I turn back into a

human? When we defeat the Demonata and skip off into the sunset, holding hands? That isn't going to happen. This is what I am. Get used to it."

I step out of the room, feeling nothing but a dim sense of pleasure that Dervish is alive. "I don't think I have a soul any longer, if I ever had to begin with," I tell Meera softly. "And my only regret is that there aren't more like Antoine to kill."

Then the air fills with Antoine's screams. I march ahead without looking back, smiling savagely as the scent of the traitor's blood reaches my nostrils. I lift my nose and breathe in deep. My eyes narrow. My mouth waters. My stomach growls.

Delicious.

LAST MAN STANDING

→I want to leave the island immediately, take a boat and sail for civilisation, to be reunited with Dervish. But there are details to sort out first. As anxious as I am to press on, I don't want to leave a job half-done.

First, with Timas leading the way, we sweep the compound in search of any survivors. I'm not sure if I'd take them captive or kill them, but there aren't any, so that's a question which ultimately doesn't require answering. Werewolves howl gratefully as I pass. Their previous leader never treated them to anything like this. They think it's going to be like this all the time, dozens of soldiers to feast on every day. I'm sorry that I'll have to disappoint them. Maybe I can round up more of Antoine's collaborators and send them over — home delivery, Grubbs Grady style!

Once we're sure the compound's clean, Prae asks if I can move the werewolves out, so that she can re-establish the perimeter.

"Everything's changed," she sighs, running a hand through her grey hair. "We can't take them back — I won't subject them to slavery and experimentation again, not after this — but we can't just leave them here. They'd starve."

"I'm taking some with me," I tell her and all three of them stare at me. "The attacks won't stop. Juni will send others against us. We'll have to fight again. And again. I'd rather do that with my pack than without them."

"But how will you control them?" Meera asks. "Off this island... in a city... you can't keep them like hounds."

"Yes, I can," I growl. "I'll have to treat them to a kill every so often, but that shouldn't be a problem, not with the sort of action I'm anticipating. I won't take them all, just the more advanced. Thirty, forty... no more than fifty."

"I don't think that's a good idea," Meera says.

"Too bad," I grunt. "Demons can't be killed by normal humans, but these have been tainted by the blood of the Demonata. They're creatures of magic. They can kill just about anything Lord Loss sends against us. So they're coming with me."

"What about the rest?" Prae asks before Meera can force an argument. "Will you move them out of the compound, so that I can restore the wall? I'll remain here and order supplies, do what I can to make their lives as pleasant as possible. This will be my new mission, putting right some of the many things I did wrong."

"You really think you can?" I frown. "Antoine wasn't working alone. The Lambs betrayed you. Are you sure you can make demands of them now?"

"I know most of those who sided with Antoine," Prae says, cheeks flushing with anger. "I'm sure I can expose the rest. I'll knock the Lambs back into shape. Remind everyone of our original mandate — to help those afflicted with the curse. We'll still search for a cure, but we won't breed or lie any more. We won't even need to execute. We can offer an alternative now — this island."

"A holiday resort for werewolves?" I chuckle.

Prae smiles. "It sounds crazy, but why not? We couldn't do it before — they'd have ripped each other to pieces. But they've been altered. The modified creatures can control the others. We'll do the rest, feed them, guard them from the outside world, introduce new members into the fold as we reap them over the years."

I like the idea of a werewolf sanctuary. "OK. I'll give the order to retreat. You get to work on the walls. But Prae," I stop her as she turns. "If you don't treat them right, I'll come back. Understand?"

"My daughter's one of *them*," Prae says tightly. "I'll treat them right." Then she leaves, Timas in close attendance to help her with the computers, while I howl and direct my pack towards the exits.

→As the werewolves depart, I scan them for the strongest and smartest. I grunt at those I like the look of and hold them back. They willingly group behind me. They don't know what I want, but they trust me and wait as patiently as they can.

I gather thirty-seven in total. Large, muscular, spectacularly ugly beasts. The weirdest personal army in history, but they won't let me down. We'll kill demons together, as many as Lord Loss and the Shadow pit against us. Bathe in their blood. Grow fat on their flesh. Sharpen our fangs on their bones.

My wolfen troops put Shark's dirty dozen to shame. I smile wryly when I think about the ex-soldier. He would have appreciated the final push, the slaughter and blood-drenched victory. He'd have understood why I had to kill Horwitzer. Antoine was a worm who had to be squashed. Meera thinks I'm a monster for ordering his death, but Shark would have done the same. So would Beranabus and Dervish.

A year ago... hell, even a few hours ago, I wouldn't have. I was a child, with a naive sense of honour. Not any more. We're fighting a war. The survival of the human race is at stake. Winning is all that matters. If we have to become kill-crazed beasts to defeat the demons, so be it.

We don't have the luxury of guilt. Those of us who protect the world must place ourselves outside the morals of those we fight for.

When the last sated member of my pack crawls past, dragging a half-chewed leg, I give Prae and Timas the signal. They throw the relevant switches and the panels of the wall rumble back into place, sealing us off from the open spaces of Wolf Island. As the panels clang shut, my heart aches slightly. I want to be outside with the jubilant werewolves, running free. But I have obligations. My place lies away from this island.

"Come on," I growl at Meera and Timas. "Let's lower the boats and get the hell out of here."

"If you need help sorting out the Lambs, give me a call," Meera tells Prae. "I'll do whatever I can."

"Thank you." Prae smiles weakly. "I think I'll be able to handle matters myself, but I'll bear your offer in mind. Good luck with whatever you're heading off to do. I suspect our problems are minor compared to yours. I hope—"

"Wait!" I snap, stopping near the edge of the cliff. A few of the boats were torn to pieces by the werewolves while we were waiting for Timas to open the doors of the compound, but most are intact and secured in place. One, however, has been lowered, and a rope ladder dangles next to where it stood. Creeping forward, I glance over the edge and spot a figure below, bobbing about in a boat. It's a man. He's lying on his back, as if soaking up the sun.

"No way!" I roar.

"Who is it?" Meera shouts, but I don't stop to answer. Grabbing hold of the rope ladder, I throw myself from rung to rung. I'm dimly aware of Timas and Meera scrabbling after me, but most of my thoughts are focused on the man in the boat.

As I draw close to the last few rungs, I turn to study the figure. A dark mood descends. I'm convinced I was mistaken, that I only saw what I wanted to see. Or if it's really him, that he's dead. But when he half-raises a hand to salute weakly, I know that he's real and alive.

"*Shark!*" I yell, jumping into the boat and grinning with open joy.

"You look… weird," Shark wheezes, running a dubious eye over me.

"How?" I gasp. "The cave… the werewolves…"

"What?" the ex-soldier scowls as Meera and Timas climb into the boat and stare at him like he's a ghost. "You don't think I can… take care of a few werewolves… by myself?"

"But…" Meera shakes her head, smiling slowly.

"I'd have been in trouble if… you hadn't swept the rest of the pack away," Shark mutters, sitting up, leaning forward and wincing. "But when I came out of the cave and found… the island deserted, it was simple to hobble over here and… lower a boat. I wanted to come and see what… was happening inside the compound, but that would've… been pushing my luck. Besides, I thought you might need to make… a quick getaway."

Shark's bleeding all over. His left ear has been bitten off. I can only barely see his right eye — it's a miracle he didn't lose it, as most of the flesh around it has been clawed away. He's missing the tops of all four fingers on his left hand, and the thumb and half his index finger on the right. As he leans further forward, I see a jagged hole in his lower back. Timas sees it too and bends over for a closer look.

"Some of your entrails are poking through," Timas says, reaching out to prod them back into place.

"Leave my guts alone," Shark growls, slapping the taller man's hand.

"You're a bloody wonder," I chuckle, then grab hold of the ladder. "Patch him up," I tell Meera and Timas. "I'll sort out extra boats for the werewolves."

"*Werewolves?*" Shark squints.

"We're taking some with us. I'm their leader now."

"I can't wait to hear about it," Shark says drily. "Just keep them well the hell… away from me."

"You're getting yellow in your old age," I grin, then shimmy up the ladder.

The last thing I hear, as I'm climbing out of earshot, is Shark asking Timas and Meera, "So, who's good with a needle and thread?"

TOODLE-PIPS

→I keep humming a tune to myself, one Dervish used to sing when he'd had a bit too much wine. "Speed, bonny boat, like a bird on the wing." But in my head I change it to, "Speed, bonny wolf."

I don't like boats. Too slow. We could have taken the helicopter that was on the island when we arrived – we'd have found the missing parts if we'd searched – but we couldn't have squeezed in all my werewolf buddies. Besides, I don't think Shark is in any fit state to play pilot. Timas and Meera patched up the worst of his wounds, but he looks dozy and keeps drifting in and out of consciousness, slumping over, then snapping awake when a wave hits the side of the boat.

Shark's with me and thirteen werewolves. He's covered in blood and smells like the juiciest steak in the world. I need to stay beside him to keep the werewolves in line or they'd fall on him and finish the job their brethren started.

Timas and Meera are in separate boats, a dozen werewolves to each. Meera's big-time edgy. Keeps checking over her shoulder to make sure the creatures aren't sneaking up. Timas, on the other hand, looks as content as any seafaring captain. He sings jaunty songs to his hairy, bemused passengers, and calls for them to join in the choruses. Apart from a few coincidental howls, he's not having much luck with that. I don't think there's going to be a choir of werewolves any time soon.

"I don't like the way they're looking... at me," Shark mutters, a minute or so after regaining consciousness from his latest blackout. "Like I'm lunch."

"Don't worry," I tell him. "They've already had lunch. Dinner too. You'll be fine until supper."

"Funny guy," Shark pants, then passes out again.

I check that Shark's OK, then focus on Timas in the boat ahead of me. He said he knows where he's going, that he's read lots of books about navigation. A while ago I might have been worried, but I trust the oddball now. If we were adrift in a snow storm in Alaska, I'd follow Timas Brauss before I followed an Eskimo.

→Timas guides us safely to dry land, and though we bump about a lot while docking, we come through unscathed. Unloading the werewolves, Timas looks pleased with himself, as he has every right to. An ambulance is waiting. We buckle Shark on to a trolley and roll him into the back of the vehicle. His eyelids flutter open as we're settling him in place. He looks around, scowls and tries to get up.

"Easy," I say, pushing him down and tightening the straps around his chest.

"I'm not going anywhere," he barks. "I'm coming with you to… help Dervish."

"You're in no condition to fight," I chuckle.

"I don't care. I'm coming whether you… like it or not."

"I thought you said you were going to retire when we got off Wolf Island," Meera reminds him.

"I said I was going to *think* about it," he growls.

"Well, think some more on the way to hospital," she snaps and slams the door shut. His curses turn the air blue until the driver switches the siren on and hits the accelerator.

"I'm glad I won't be there when they finish operating on him," I note.

"Me too," Meera says, smiling at me. "How do you feel?"

"Hungry," I reply, then wink at her alarmed expression.

"You really believe you can control them?" Meera asks as we herd the werewolves into the waiting trucks, which will take us to the nearest airport and a specially chartered plane.

"Child's play," I smirk.

Timas is waiting for us at the trucks. He says nothing as I usher in the werewolves, standing by in case I need him. When the last door has been locked, he clears his throat. "I should keep watch over Shark. He'll want to return to action as soon as he's fit — probably before — and he's going to need help. I can do more for him than you."

"That's fine." I smile warmly and shake his hand, but lightly, aware that I could crack his fingers like twigs if I squeezed too hard. "Thanks, Timas. We wouldn't have made it off the island without you."

"I know," he says, then turns to Meera. "Time to make good on that promise."

"What promise?" Meera squints.

Timas grabs her and bends her backwards, supporting her with one arm. "A kiss for your sweet prince," he murmurs, smooching up to her.

Meera pretends to struggle, but then grins and treats him to a kiss that's even hotter than Shark's curses. It's an old-style movie kiss, except with more slurping and tongue action.

"Break it up," I growl.

The pair come up for air, their faces red.

"That was nice," Timas gasps.

"Very," Meera agrees, and pecks his nose. "To be continued," she purrs, then turns from him with the natural grace of a model and sashays away.

"See you soon," I mutter.

"*Extremely* soon," Timas nods and hits the road, clicking his fingers like a hepcat.

→ Meera's on her mobile for most of the trip to the airport, deep in conversation with some of her fellow Disciples. Her face is creased with worry when she cuts the connection.

"Bad news?" I ask.

"There are reports of three potential crossings," she says. "All in major cities. The windows are due to open within the next forty-eight hours unless we can find the mages responsible and stop them."

"Three at the same time," I mutter. "Hardly coincidence."

"No," Meera snorts. "One's in the city where Dervish and Bec are."

"So Juni must already know that Antoine's troops failed."

"I hoped we'd have more time, but apparently not." Meera sighs. "I'll arrange to have them moved as soon as possible."

"No." My face is stone. "Let the demons come. I'll deal with them. It'll be a good opportunity to test my pack."

"Are you sure?" Meera frowns. "Juni and her masters want the pieces of the Kah-Gash. If you and Bec are in the same spot, they'll have a double shot at it. Maybe you should stay away from her until—"

"No," I growl. "No more running. They want a fight? I'll give them one they won't forget in a hurry."

"Juni beat you once," Meera reminds me.

"She won't again," I whisper. Not because I believe I can turn the tables on her, but because she doesn't want to. She needs me to destroy the universe.

"Grubbs?" Meera says softly. "Why didn't Juni finish you off?"

I don't answer. Thinking about what the mutant monster predicted. Wondering, not if it might be true, but rather how it will happen and when.

"Grubbs?" Meera says again.

I shake myself. "It doesn't matter. Are you coming?"

Meera sighs. "No. I want to, but I'm needed elsewhere. I can be of more use in the other cities, either help find the mages and kill them, or try to drive back the demons if they cross. I think we're all going to have to work very hard over the next few days to prevent a massacre that makes the losses on Wolf Island look like a drop in the ocean."

"I'll come when I can," I promise. "Tell the other Disciples that if they fail – if demons break through – I'll mop up. Once I've dealt with those coming to attack Dervish and Bec, I'll go wherever I'm needed and I'll bring my werewolves. We can fight them now. We don't need to be afraid."

"You idiot," Meera chuckles. "Of course we do." She hugs me tight, then stands on her toes, hauls my head down and kisses my coarse, hairy cheek, ignoring the bits of human flesh caught between my fangs and the stench of blood on my breath.

She releases me and I draw back to my full height. Part of me wants to plead with her to come with me. We can pick up Dervish and Bec, then fly to a deserted island like the one we just left. An apocalypse is coming. It would be easier to sit it out, enjoy what time we have left and face the end with a resigned laugh.

But I'm Grubbs Grady. Magician. Werewolf. Kah-Gash. I don't do retreat.

"Give my love to Dervish," Meera sniffs, then leaves me to make my own way to the plane. The last I see of her, she's climbing into the front of an army jeep, talking on her mobile, looking lovelier than ever as she prepares to go to war.

With a self-mocking smile, I offer up a quick prayer to whatever gods might be listening. "If reincarnation is real, and I die soon, let me come back as Timas Brauss's lips!"

Then I head off in search of my half-dead uncle, hoping he doesn't croak before I have a chance to bid him goodbye.

THIS IS THE END, BEAUTIFUL FRIEND

→Dervish refused to be admitted to a hospital. If demons attack him and Bec again, he doesn't want to be in a public building, where innocents might catch the crossfire. So the team set in place by the Disciples swiftly established a temporary medical base in a derelict building in a rundown part of the city where he, Bec and the other survivor were taken.

Antoine Horwitzer's soldiers are waiting for me when I arrive. They line the corridor, heavily armed, exchanging dark glances with several troops in different uniforms who are working for the Disciples. The air bristles with tension when I walk in. The commanding officer of the Lambs' group steps forward and runs a cold eye over me.

"Where's Horwitzer?" he growls.

"Dead," I say bluntly.

"You killed him?" the officer snarls.

"No." I whistle and the werewolves lurch into view. "They did."

The officer's face blanches. His men raise their weapons defensively. The other soldiers raise theirs too, even more alarmed than the Lambs.

"You have a choice," I say calmly. "Fight and die, or lower your arms and walk away. Horwitzer's reign is over. The Lambs are back under the thumb of Prae Athim. Surrender now and we'll call it evens."

The officer licks his lips. "I'd want safe passage for my men," he mutters. "And I'll have to confirm it with—"

"No time for confirmations," I bark. "Drop your weapons and run, or stand, fight and die."

The officer studies the slavering werewolves and comes to the smart conclusion. He lowers his gun and gives the order for his men to follow suit. I growl at the beasts behind me and they part, affording the humans safe passage. Once they've filed out of the building, I bring my werewolves in, line them up in the corridor and ask to be escorted to Dervish's room. The soldiers are uneasy – I can smell their fear – but they do as I request. One takes me, while the rest remain, eyeing the werewolves anxiously.

I find Dervish relaxing on a bed in a large room, clothed in a T-shirt and jeans, no shoes or socks, hooked up to a drip and monitors, staring reflectively at the ceiling. Bec's in a chair nearby, head lowered, snoozing. She's also hooked up to a drip. In a bed further over, another man, swathed in bandages, is sitting up and entertaining a gaggle of wide-eyed nurses. A couple of fingers on his left hand have been cut or bitten off, reminding me of Shark.

"—but I wasn't afraid of a few stinking zombies," the man – it must be Kirilli Kovacs – is saying dismissively. "I laid into them with magic and fried them where they stood. If there hadn't been so many, I'd have waltzed through unscathed, but there were thousands. They overwhelmed me, and the others too. It looked as if we were doomed but I didn't panic. I gathered Dervish and the girls and ploughed a way through."

"You saved their lives," a nurse gasps.

"Pretty much," the man says with a falsely modest smile.

I clear my throat. Dervish looks over and beams at me. Bec's head bobs up and she studies my twisted body with a frown. Kirilli Kovacs scowls at me for interrupting, casts a sheepish glance at Dervish, then lowers his voice and continues his story.

"Sorry I didn't bring any chocolates," I tell Dervish, walking over to the bed and taking my uncle's hands. He squeezes tight. I squeeze back gently, not wanting to hurt him. He squints as he studies me.

"There's something different about you," he says.

"I've started styling my hair differently," I laugh.

"Oh. I thought it was that you were a metre taller, a hell of a lot broader, look like a werewolf and are naked except for that bit of cloth around your waist. But you're right — it's the hair."

"There's something strange about yours too," I murmur, staring at the six punk-like, purple-tipped, silver spikes that have appeared on his head since I last saw him. "The tips are a nice touch. Very anarchic."

We grin at each other. Dervish looks like death and I guess I don't look much better. We must make some pair.

"How's the heart?" I ask, letting go and taking a step back.

"Fine," he says.

"It's not," Bec disagrees. She stands, taking care not to dislodge the drip. "We heard about your transformation. Meera said you'd be bringing others with you."

"They're waiting outside. What about his heart?"

"I need a transplant," Dervish says. "Care to volunteer?"

"He needs to return to the demon universe," Bec says, ignoring Dervish's quip. "The doctors have done what they can, but if he stays here…" She shakes her head.

"Can you open a window?" I ask.

"Not right now. I'm not operating at full strength."

I formulate a quick plan. "Juni knows you're here. A window's being opened somewhere in the city. Demons will pour through. The air will fill with magic. I want you to tap into it, open a window of your own and get him out of here."

"Don't I have any say in this?" Dervish asks.

"No."

My uncle chuckles, then lays back and smiles. "I won't go," he says.

"Take him somewhere safe," I tell Bec. "If I survive, I'll come—"

"You didn't hear me," Dervish interrupts. "I won't go."

"Of course you'll go," I snap. "You can't stay here. You'll die."

"So?"

"Don't," I snarl. "We haven't time for this self-sacrifice crap. You're hauling your rotten carcass out of here and that's that."

Dervish's smile doesn't dim. "I've been thinking about it since we were rescued. Do you know that Beranabus and Sharmila were killed?"

"Yeah," I mutter.

"We're not sure about Kernel," Dervish continues. "He disappeared. There was a lot of blood and scraps of flesh, but they mightn't have been his. Maybe he's dead, maybe not." Dervish shrugs, grimaces with pain, then relaxes again. "I want to choose my place and manner of death. Beranabus and Sharmila were lucky — they died quickly, on our own world. But they could just have easily suffered for centuries at the hands of the Demonata and been butchered in that other universe, far from home and all they loved."

"Those are the risks we take," I say stiffly.

"Not me," Dervish replies. "I'm through. I served as best I could, and if this body had a bit more life in it, I'd carry on. But I'm not good for anything now. I'm tired. Ready for death. I'll fight when the demons attack, but if we repel them, I want to find a peaceful spot and give up the ghost in my own, natural time."

"Don't be—" I start to yell.

"Grubbs," he interrupts gently. "I think I've earned the right to choose how I die. Don't you?"

I stare at him, close to breaking. Dervish is all I have left in the world. I think of him as a father. The thought of losing him…

"I reckon I'll last a few months if fate looks on me kindly," Dervish says. "But that's as much as I dare hope for. My body's had enough. Time's up. The way I've pushed myself, the demons I've faced, the battles I've endured… I was lucky to last this long."

"But I need you," I half sob.

"No," he smiles. "The thought that you might was the one thing that could have tempted me to return to the universe of magic and struggle on. But you don't need anyone any more. I saw it as soon as I looked at you. You've found your path, and it's a path you have to travel alone. Beranabus was the same. Kernel. Bec too."

He looks at Bec and winks. "Grubbs isn't the only one I'll be sorry to leave," he says, and the pale-faced, weary girl smiles at him warmly.

I think of things I could say to make him change his mind, but the horrible truth is, he's right. I can see death in his eyes. Every breath is an effort. He's not meant to continue. The afterlife is calling. It will be a relief for him when he goes.

Sighing, I sit on the bed and glare at the dying man. "If you think I'm going to start crying, and say things like 'I love you' — forget it!"

"Perish the thought," Dervish murmurs. "In your current state, I'll be pleased if you don't start eating me before I'm dead."

"I'd never eat you. I have better taste."

We laugh. Bec stares at us uncertainly, then joins in. She sounds a bit like Bill-E when she laughs, and for a few happy moments it's as if me, my brother and uncle are together again, relaxing in Dervish's study, sharing a joke, not a care in the world.

→We spend the rest of the time chatting. Dervish and Bec bring me up to date on all that's happened since I left them at the hospital, locating Juni on a ship full of corpses, finding a lodestone in the hold, the Shadow using it to cross, Beranabus destroying the stone and expelling the Shadow but losing his life in the battle.

"He went heroically, in the best way," Bec says with a mournful smile. "He wouldn't have wanted to go quietly."

Then Bec tells me the Shadow's true identity. It's death. Not a chess-playing, suave, sophisticated Death like in an old, subtitled movie Dervish made me watch once. Or the sexy, compassionate, humorous Death in Bill-E's *Sandman* comics. This is a malevolent force. It hates all the living creatures of our universe and wants to cut us out of existence.

"How do we fight Death?" I ask. "Can we kill it?"

"I don't think so," Bec says.

"But it has a physical shape. If we destroy its body of shadows, maybe its mind will unravel. You said it didn't always have a brain?"

"From what I absorbed, its consciousness is relatively new," Bec nods.

"So if we rip it to pieces, maybe it'll go back to being whatever it was before?"

"Maybe." She doesn't sound convinced.

"I can be the inside man," Dervish says, only half joking. "Once Death claims me, I can work behind the lines and try to pass info back to you."

"Perhaps you could," I mutter. "Do you think it preserves everyone's soul, that the spiritual remains of all the dead are contained within that cloud of shadows?"

"No," Bec answers. "It's using souls now, but from what I understand, it wasn't always that way. It was simply a force before, like the blade of a guillotine — it ended life. Finito."

I scratch my bulging, distorted head. "This is too deep for me. I don't think I'll ask any more questions. I'll settle for killing or dismembering it."

"You believe that you can?" Bec sounds dubious.

"Of course." I stare at her. "Don't you?"

She shrugs, but says nothing. I see defeat in her expression. She thinks we've lost. She's convinced our number's up.

"Hey," I huff. "Don't forget, we're the Kah-Gash. We can take on anything. If Death was all-powerful, it wouldn't need the help of Lord Loss and his stooges. We can beat it. I'm sure we can."

I look from Bec to Dervish, then back at Bec again. "Remember what Beranabus preached? He thought the universe created champions to battle the forces of evil, that we weren't freaks of nature, but carefully chosen warriors. I used to think he was loco, but not any more. Look at me."

I flex my bulging muscles and bare my fangs. "You can't tell me this is a fluke. I didn't turn into a werewolf by chance, when the chips were down. I was primed to transform. The universe gave me a power it knew we'd need. You probably have dormant powers too. We'll change if we have to. Adapt to deal with whatever we're up against. The Shadow doesn't stand a chance."

Bec looks at me sceptically. "What about Kernel? The universe didn't prepare him. He's dead."

"You don't know that," I contradict her. "Maybe he transformed like me and turned into a panel of light."

Bec giggles. I smile but it's forced. I feel like a hypocrite, offering her hope when Juni's prophecy is ringing in my head.

I start telling them about my experiences, Shark's dirty dozen, Timas Brauss, Antoine Horwitzer, the trip to the island. I'm about a third of the way through my story when Dervish's fingers twitch and he lifts his nose. A second later I catch the buzz of magic. A window has opened and the air's filling with magical energy.

"I'll tell you the rest later," I groan, getting to my feet and smiling lazily as magic seeps through my pores, charging me up.

"If there is a later," Dervish grunts, unhooking himself from the drip and the machines. He stands. A couple of the nurses with Kirilli Kovacs hurry over, scolding Dervish and demanding he get back into bed. "Peace!" he roars. "Demons are coming. Do you want me to lie here and let them slaughter you all?"

The nurses share a startled glance, then back off. Dervish wriggles his bare toes, checks that the tips of his spikes are stiff, then cocks an eyebrow at me. "Awaiting your orders, captain."

I prepare a cutting reply, then realise he's serious. He's looking to me to lead. That's a first. I've always followed, bouncing from my parents to Dervish to Beranabus to Shark. Now I'm being asked to make the decisions, issue the call to arms and lead others to their deaths. I should be unsure of myself, but I'm not. Dervish was right. I don't need a guardian any more. I'm ready for leadership. More than that — I *want* to lead.

"We'll hit them hard," I growl. "We'll take the werewolves and soldiers. We don't know what they're going to send against us — demons, armed guards, maybe the Shadow itself. So we'll go prepared for anything."

I start for the door. Dervish and Bec trail close behind. In the bed across from Dervish's, one of the nurses says brightly, "Good luck!" But she's not saying it to us. She's saying it to Kirilli Kovacs.

I pause and look back. Kovacs is lying with his sheets pulled up to his throat. He looks like he's about to be sick. I think he was hoping we'd sweep out without noticing him, so he could pretend he didn't know we'd gone.

"Well?" I grunt, amused. Dervish told me a bit about Kovacs and his less than avid love of fighting, but even if he hadn't, I could have seen with one look that this guy's chicken, Disciple or not.

"Aren't you going, Kirilli?" a nurse asks, frowning.

"Of course I am," he puffs. "I just thought… I mean, I'm still recovering…" He waves his injured hand at me, smiling shakily.

"I got up from my deathbed," Dervish murmurs. "Surely you aren't going to let a few missing fingers hold you back?"

"No!" Kovacs cries as the nurses glower accusingly. "I just meant…" His face darkens. He shoots me a look of pure spite, then recovers instantly. With a breezy smile, he turns to the nurses. "What I meant was, I have no desire to go to war in a dismal state of attire. I know my suit's a touch the worse for wear, but if you good ladies could fetch it for me, so that I might cut a dashing figure as I stride into battle to save the day…"

The nurses like that. They quickly bring Kovacs his suit, which turns out to be a natty, badly shredded stage magician's costume, with faded gold and silver stars stitched down the sides. But I must admit he wears the rags well. Pats dust away, tuts at the blood, then tips an imaginary hat to the nurses. "Later, ladies," he purrs. Then, to a murmur of approving coos, he slides ahead of me, flashes me a reassuring smile — as if I needed encouragement — and exits like a politician heading off to settle an important affair of state.

→I bark at the werewolves in the corridor, leaving Dervish to round up the human troops. With a few simple grunts, I let the beasts know we're going to fight. They howl happily in response.

I'm excited as we step out of the building. I don't care what the enemy sends against us. According to Juni, I'm the worst threat to mankind in any universe. I've only myself to be afraid of really.

Dervish, Bec and Kirilli edge up behind me, backed by about fifty soldiers. Kirilli's teeth are chattering, but he stands his ground and lets magic gather in his hands. I don't plan to rely on him, but he might prove useful.

Bec looks more resigned than afraid. She's trying hard to believe we can win, not just this fight but all those still to come. But it's hard. In her heart she feels we're doomed. She'll give it her best, but she doesn't think we can triumph, not in the end, not against Death.

Dervish is smiling. He figures he's going to be dead soon, one way or another, so what does he have to worry about? He's picked his spot and chosen his fight. If he dies, it'll be on home turf. That's all that matters to him now.

The soldiers are nervous, though some hide it better than others. They know a bit about demons, that they can't kill the monsters, only slow them down. They're not in control of this situation, and I know how frustrating that can be. But the Disciples have chosen well. This lot will stand, fight and die if they have to.

And they will.

I look around at my misshapen pack of werewolves and smile jaggedly. Of all those with me, these are the ones I'm counting on to cause the greatest upset. If our foes don't know about my lupine retinue, they're in for a nasty surprise. Demons are used to having it easy on this world. Most humans can't kill them, and they rarely have to face more than a couple of Disciples at a time. Thirty-seven savage werewolves are going to make for a very different experience!

I sniff the air. I hear horrified screams coming from several streets away. I'm eager to get stuck in, but I delay the moment of attack, thinking about Juni's awful prophecy. Then, wiping it from my thoughts, I roar and let the werewolves break loose. As they race to confront the demons, I pound along in the middle of them. Dervish, Bec, Kirilli and the soldiers lag behind. I'm grinning wolfishly, no longer worried about prophecies. Let the world end. Hell, let me be the one to end it! What does it matter? Nobody lives forever. If mankind's destined to bite the bullet, let's bite and be damned.

We turn a corner. I see hordes of demons running wild, humans fleeing the monstrous creatures. With an excited yelp, I lead my misshapen troops into action. As I zone in on the demonic army, I smile and think there's at least one guarantee I can make. If Juni's right, and it's my fate to destroy this planet, the poet got it wrong. The world won't end with a bang *or* a whimper. It'll end with the death screams of a thousand demons and a defiant, carefree, savage, wolfen howl.

Look out for

THE DEMONATA

Volumes 9 and 10

Taking you to hell
September 2011

THE SAGA OF LARTEN CREPSLEY: BOOK ONE

Birth of a Killer

Out now in paperback.

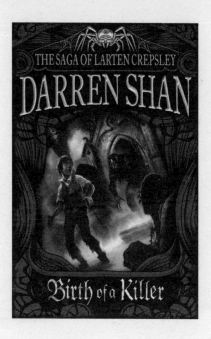

When terrible events force young Larten Crespley to flee his home he finds himself alone in the world. Then he meets the mysterious Seba Nile, who introduces him to the ways of the vampire clan. Travelling with Seba, Larten experiences the adventures he has always dreamed about. But will he turn his back on humanity and join a world from which there can be no return...?

THE SAGA OF DARREN SHAN